HEAD OVER HEELS

Lila laughed. "If I win, you write my term paper. And if *you* win, I write yours. How does that sound?"

Jessica swallowed. If she lost the bet, she'd have *two* term papers to write. And at this point she could barely imagine writing one!

But she wasn't about to let Lila see how worried she was. "You're on," Jessica said cheerfully.

"Fine," said Lila. "We'll make the carnival the cutoff point. Just think, if Bruce and Regina break up before then, you won't have to worry about your term paper!"

And if they don't, Jessica thought uneasily, *I might as well hang myself.* She looked across the cafeteria to where Bruce and Regina were sitting and shook her head. *This bet is too important to lose*, Jessica thought. *If Bruce and Regina don't break up on their own in a few days, I'm going to have to do my best to help them!*

Bantam Books in the Sweet Valley High Series
Ask your bookseller for the books you have missed

#1 DOUBLE LOVE
#2 SECRETS
#3 PLAYING WITH FIRE
#4 POWER PLAY
#5 ALL NIGHT LONG
#6 DANGEROUS LOVE
#7 DEAR SISTER
#8 HEARTBREAKER
#9 RACING HEARTS
#10 WRONG KIND OF GIRL
#11 TOO GOOD TO BE TRUE
#12 WHEN LOVE DIES
#13 KIDNAPPED!
#14 DECEPTIONS
#15 PROMISES
#16 RAGS TO RICHES
#17 LOVE LETTERS
#18 HEAD OVER HEELS

SWEET VALLEY HIGH

HEAD OVER HEELS

Written by
Kate William

Created by
FRANCINE PASCAL

BANTAM BOOKS
TORONTO · NEW YORK · LONDON · SYDNEY · AUCKLAND

RL 6, IL age 12 and up

HEAD OVER HEELS
A Bantam Book / April 1985

Sweet Valley High is a trademark of Francine Pascal

Conceived by Francine Pascal

Produced by Cloverdale Press Inc.,
133 Fifth Avenue, New York, N.Y. 10003

Cover art by James Mathewuse

ISBN 0-553-24825-1

Published simultaneously in the United States and Canada

Bantam Books are published by Bantam Books, Inc. Its
trademark, consisting of the words ''Bantam Books'' and the
portrayal of a rooster, is Registered in U.S. Patent and
Trademark Office and in other countries. Marca Registrada.
Bantam Books, Inc., 666 Fifth Avenue, New York, New York
10103.

PRINTED IN THE UNITED STATES OF AMERICA

O   0 9 8 7 6 5 4 3 2

HEAD OVER HEELS

One

"Jessica Wakefield," Elizabeth called, knocking firmly on the door of her twin sister's bedroom, "were you planning on waking up at some point this morning?"

Hearing her twin's groan, Elizabeth pushed open the door to Jessica's bedroom. "Come on, Jess," she urged, pulling up the blinds and letting light pour into the room. "Good Lord," she said, looking around her. "It looks like you've been dynamiting in here. How can you sleep in this mess?"

Jessica sat up in the rumpled sheets, stretching her slim arms over her tousled blond hair and yawning. "What time is it, Liz?" she asked crossly. "It feels like it's about four in the morning."

1

Elizabeth laughed. It was like Jessica not to have a clock in her room. She lived by what her parents sometimes referred to as Jessica Standard Time. Being on time was *not* one of her concerns.

Apart from a mole on Elizabeth's right shoulder, the twins were identical down to the tiny dimple in each left cheek. They were both sixteen years old, though Elizabeth was born four minutes before Jessica. Both had shoulder-length, sun-streaked blond hair, sparkling blue-green eyes, and model-slim, five-foot-six-inch figures. Even the gold lavalieres dangling around their necks were identical—presents from their parents on their sixteenth birthday.

But the resemblance between the twins was only skin deep. Elizabeth, who wrote the "Eyes and Ears" gossip column for *The Oracle*, the student newspaper at Sweet Valley High, wanted to be a serious writer one day. That was why, as she often explained to Todd Wilkins, her steady boyfriend, she tried her hardest to be objective. Organized, good-natured, and fair as possible— that was how Elizabeth's friends described her. Jessica, on the other hand, never planned more than one day at a time, though she threw herself into every project—and every new relationship—with astounding energy.

"It's eight o'clock," Elizabeth told her twin

2

firmly. "And it'll probably take you half an hour to find your closet in this mess!"

"It's cozy in here, Liz," Jessica said defensively, leaping out of bed and heading straight for the mirror over her dresser.

Elizabeth laughed. Jessica's room had always been a sore point in the Wakefield household. The rest of the attractive, split-level home was nicely decorated and tidy as a pin. But Jessica's room—which was sometimes referred to as "The Hershey Bar" because she had insisted on painting her walls chocolate brown—was always a mess. She rarely bothered to pick her clothes up from the floor.

"It feels like another world in here," Jessica told her twin proudly.

"It sure does," Elizabeth said, shaking her head as she stepped over an enormous pile of clothing on her way to the door. "Try to hurry, Jess," she called from the hallway. "I'm supposed to meet Todd before homeroom this morning."

Downstairs, in the sun-filled, Spanish-style kitchen, Alice Wakefield was mixing orange juice in a glass pitcher. "Morning, Mom," Elizabeth said, giving her mother an affectionate hug. "You look pretty today," she added, glancing admiringly at her mother's flowered dress.

"A client's coming over to look at some floor plans," her mother said, smiling.

3

Alice Wakefield worked as an interior designer. With her blond hair, bright-blue eyes, and trim figure, it was easy to see where the twins had gotten their good looks. People often mistook Alice Wakefield for the twins' older sister.

"Looks like another beautiful day," Ned Wakefield exclaimed, hurrying into the kitchen and dropping an affectionate kiss on his wife's cheek. "Where's your better half?" he teased Elizabeth, pouring himself a cup of coffee.

Elizabeth giggled. "Probably bulldozing a path to her closet," she told him.

The corners of Mr. Wakefield's eyes crinkled with laughter. Broad-shouldered and dark-haired, with warm, dark eyes, he looked to Elizabeth like an older version of her brother Steven, who was finishing his first year of college.

"Give her a hug for me, will you?" Mr. Wakefield said. "If I don't hurry I'm going to miss my meeting this morning." Ned Wakefield was a successful lawyer whose office was located in downtown Sweet Valley.

"At this rate, she probably won't be downstairs before you come home for dinner!" Elizabeth laughed as she poured herself a bowl of cereal.

Taking a last gulp of coffee and waving at Elizabeth and her mother, Mr. Wakefield hurried outside to the garage.

4

"Mom, do you mind if I take the Fiat this morning? Mr. Collins has called a meeting of the carnival committee after school today."

"The carnival committee?" Alice Wakefield looked blank for a minute.

"To raise money for handicapped children," Elizabeth reminded her. "It's not a real carnival," she added. "A group of us at school is putting it together, and I'm the chairperson. It'll just be a tent or two with games and refreshments. But Mr. Collins thinks we can raise a fair amount of money, especially now that we're getting sponsors from the community."

"Now I remember," her mother said. "When is it supposed to take place?"

"A week from Saturday." Elizabeth sighed. "That's only twelve days, and we've still got so much to do!"

"Well, you're welcome to the car," Mrs. Wakefield said. "I don't need it today. Just drive safely."

"Drive safely where?" Jessica asked, strolling into the kitchen and taking an orange from the basket on the table.

"School," Elizabeth said wryly. "Or have you forgotten?"

"I wish I *could* forget," Jessica said, flinging herself down on a chair. "That stupid term paper is giving me nightmares."

5

"Try working on it during daylight hours," Elizabeth said and smiled.

"Fifteen pages!" Jessica moaned. "How am I supposed to fit that in on top of everything else?"

"History teachers should be better organized," Elizabeth agreed. "They really should schedule homework assignments around dates and cheerleading practice."

"OK, girls," Alice Wakefield said, bringing a carton of milk to the table. "I'm going to go put my makeup on. Careful with the car, you two, and I'll see you both tonight."

"Jess, do you have any good ideas for the carnival?" Elizabeth asked, turning the red Fiat down the shady street.

Jessica shot a quick look at her twin, who was concentrating on the road in front of her. "I don't suppose you'd trade me a few pointers on my history paper for some carnival ideas?" she asked craftily.

Elizabeth checked the traffic in the rearview mirror. "You're right," she said firmly. "I wouldn't. Come on, Jess. We've got less than two weeks to get this thing organized, and we really need some help. Besides," she added, "it's such a good cause. The money we raise will be donated to a special fund at Fowler Memorial Hospital to help handicapped children."

"I'll think about it," Jessica said absently, her eyes on the lush green panorama of the roadside near Sweet Valley High. "Hey," she said suddenly, leaning forward, "isn't that Regina Morrow in Bruce Patman's car?"

Elizabeth gave her twin a quick look. "It is," she confirmed, maneuvering the Fiat into the lane next to Bruce's shiny black Porsche. "They've been seeing an awful lot of each other lately, haven't they?" Elizabeth asked, glancing at Jessica to view her reaction.

Bruce Patman was the only son of Henry and Marie Patman, one of the richest and most powerful couples in Sweet Valley. Bruce was a senior at Sweet Valley High. Dark-haired, handsome, and powerfully built, he had a reputation as a lady's man and a snob. Even his license plate number—1BRUCE1—displayed his arrogance. Elizabeth didn't like Bruce Patman one bit. He had tried to take advantage of her after her motorcycle accident when she was suffering from memory loss and wasn't herself. And she knew Jessica didn't think much of him either. At one point Jessica had fallen head over heels in love with him. Elizabeth had never seen her sister so affected by a boyfriend. The fact that things had ended badly—and that Bruce's behavior had caused the breakup—explained the stormy expression on her twin's face as they overtook the black Porsche.

"I can't understand why Regina would get mixed up with a jerk like Bruce Patman," Jessica said sullenly, pulling her blond hair back from her face.

Elizabeth was too tactful to point out that Jessica herself had once found Bruce the most fascinating male in the world. "I know," she agreed. "I have to admit I don't think much of the idea. Regina is so incredibly nice," she added, pulling into the parking lot next to Sweet Valley High.

Bruce pulled his Porsche up beside them and was leaping out to open the door for Regina.

"Good Lord," Jessica muttered. "I wonder what he's up to with the Prince Charming act."

"That's the strange thing," Elizabeth said in a low voice. "I've never seen Bruce act this way before. He seems to be killing Regina with kindness. He even meets her after every class so he can have a few minutes with her."

"I'm sure it won't last," Jessica snapped, grabbing her books and jumping out of the car. "Thanks for the ride, Liz. I'm going to find Cara before homeroom."

Elizabeth shook her head as she watched her twin bound across the parking lot. Jessica didn't seem crazy about the idea of Bruce and Regina as a couple, she thought.

It was funny, Elizabeth mused, gathering her books and getting out of the car. As far as looks

8

went, Bruce and Regina seemed like a perfect couple. But then, Regina looked perfect no matter who she was standing next to.

With her long, black hair, high cheekbones, and perfect ivory complexion, Regina Morrow was a natural beauty. The Morrows had moved to Sweet Valley just that year, and Regina's spectacular looks had caused a great deal of attention. She had even been approached by a local modeling agency, which had arranged to have her picture on the cover of a recent issue of *Ingenue* magazine.

But beauty wasn't all that made Regina Morrow special, Elizabeth thought, catching sight of Todd across the parking lot and quickening her steps to meet him. Regina had been almost completely deaf since birth. Years of training in a school in Connecticut had taught her to read lips so well that some people couldn't tell she couldn't hear them. And because Regina could distinguish tones, her voice hadn't been affected by her handicap.

The real difference, Elizabeth thought, was that Regina didn't take anything for granted as so many people did. She loved being alive and it showed in everything she did. No wonder people liked her so much and were so much happier when she was around!

"Hey, where've you been?" Todd asked, giving Elizabeth a warm hug and kissing the tip of her nose. "I've been looking all over for you. Mr. Collins wants to know how we're doing with the carnival plans."

"Sorry I'm so late," Elizabeth told him, smiling up into his coffee-brown eyes. "Jessica was in slow motion this morning. Or at least she was until she saw Bruce and Regina together. *That* speeded her up."

"I can imagine." Todd grinned and slipped his arm around her. "Hey, maybe we can get them to do a booth at the carnival," he added, laughing. "We'll call it 'Beauty and the Beast.' "

Elizabeth laughed, but she felt uneasy as she and Todd walked into the cool interior of Sweet Valley High. She wasn't sure why, but she had felt strangely protective of Regina ever since the girl had moved to Sweet Valley. As far as Elizabeth knew, Regina didn't have much experience with boys. She had lived a sheltered life, and Elizabeth felt that Bruce Patman wasn't the safest bet for a first boyfriend.

"I hope she doesn't get hurt," Elizabeth told Todd, giving his hand a warm squeeze. "You have to remember," she added softly, slipping her arm around him, "not all guys are as wonderful as you are."

"I never forget it for a second," Todd joked, kissing the top of Elizabeth's head. "You're right, though," he added more seriously. "I'm a little worried, myself. Regina's such a nice girl, and I don't trust Bruce Patman.''

"Well," Elizabeth said, opening the door to her locker and putting her books inside, "I guess we'll just have to watch what happens."

"And hope the Beast doesn't break the Beauty's heart," Todd added, a concerned expression on his face.

Two

"Don't you think the carnival committee deserves better food?" Winston Egbert joked, spearing a hot dog with his fork and raising it in the air.

Enid Rollins laughed. "We should've picked a better place to meet, Liz," she told Elizabeth, who was furiously jotting notes on a pad next to her lunch tray.

Elizabeth looked up at her best friend and grinned. "What better place for brainstorming than the eye of the hurricane?" she pointed out. Elizabeth and Todd were sitting across from Enid and Winston in the middle of the crowded Sweet Valley High cafeteria, trying to organize themselves before the meeting with Mr. Collins after school. But Winston, a tall, lanky boy generally known as the class clown, was contributing more merriment than constructive advice. He had just discovered that by pounding an empty milk carton with his fist he could fire the last drops of milk at the person next to him.

"Quit it, Egbert," Todd said cheerfully, leaning across the table to see what Elizabeth had written. "Hey, when is Mr. Collins going to announce who the parent adviser is? I think we need some fresh ideas."

"After school today, I think," Elizabeth told him, putting the cap back on her pen and looking at the preliminary list she'd drawn up. "I hope so, anyway." she said. "At the rate we're going, we'll never get this carnival together!"

"Liz! Todd! We've been looking for you everywhere," a voice called. Elizabeth turned to see Olivia Davidson and her boyfriend, Roger Barrett Patman, approaching with their trays.

"How's it going?" Olivia asked, glancing at Elizabeth's notebook as she set the tray down. Olivia was the arts editor for *The Oracle*, and she and Elizabeth had often collaborated on projects for the newspaper.

"I'm the only one who has an idea for a booth so far," Winston told her. "I'm going to let people throw pies at me for a dollar a shot."

Everyone laughed. Olivia pushed her frizzy brown hair back from her face and looked down at her lunch with a grimace. "I don't think creativity and Sweet Valley High lunches mix." Roger reached across the table and gave her hand a gentle squeeze.

Olivia had loved Roger even before his identity as Bruce Patman's cousin was discovered. Before Roger had learned he was really the illegitimate son of Bruce's uncle—dead now for many years—Roger had been the poorest boy in the class. Now he lived in the Patmans' enormous estate on the hill overlooking Sweet Valley. Elizabeth had wondered at first how Roger would react to being part of a millionaire's family, but by now it was apparent that Roger was as down to earth as he'd always been. And he and Olivia were as fond of each other as ever.

"Boy, that cousin of mine has really gone off the deep end this time!" Roger exclaimed, watching Bruce pull a chair out for Regina on the other side of the cafeteria.

"What do you mean?" Todd asked curiously, catching Elizabeth's eye.

Roger shook his head. "I don't know," he said slowly, opening his carton of milk and taking a big gulp. "But I'd say this time he really has fallen hard!"

Olivia leaned forward, her hazel eyes dancing. "It's incredible," she confided. "Bruce is like a completely new person! He actually asked me how I've been when he answered the phone last night. And"—she shook her head and giggled—"more to the point, he listened when I told him!"

"Revolutionary," Todd said, grinning.

"I've never seen him so friendly," Roger went on. "I think he's flipped over Regina."

"So you *really* think Bruce is serious about her?" Elizabeth asked.

"I'll tell you what *I* think," Winston interrupted, punching Roger's empty milk carton so the spray hit Todd on the arm. "*I* think we need to get back to the carnival."

"I guess you're right," Elizabeth said, pushing her lunch tray aside and picking up her note pad.

"Pretty romantic, don't you think?" Lila Fowler asked, waving the ice cream bar she was eating in the direction of Bruce and Regina, who were sitting across the cafeteria. There was a smirk on her pretty face.

Jessica followed Lila's gaze and shrugged. "You know Bruce," she said airily, pretending to concentrate on her lunch. "I bet it lasts about a week."

"Hmmmm," Lila said, her brown eyes narrowing as she watched Bruce kiss Regina on the cheek. "I can't imagine anyone staying interested in Regina for even that long," she said, flicking her wavy, light-brown hair behind one shoulder.

Jessica laughed. She knew there was no love lost between Lila and Regina. Lila Fowler had been the richest girl in school until Regina moved in. That in itself would have been enough to irritate Lila, who had always made a point of having the biggest or newest or best of everything. But Regina's beauty—and all the attention she got after her picture appeared on the cover of *Ingenue*—was more than Lila could bear. In fact, Lila had tried to convince The Lane Townsend Agency to put *her* on the cover instead of Regina. Lila was an attractive girl, but she wasn't model material. Or at least that was what the owner of the agency had told her. And hearing how perfect Regina was for the camera was all Lila had needed to decide that Regina Morrow was the most detestable girl at school.

"Just look at her," Lila seethed, pushing her food away in disgust. "She looks ridiculous in that purple dress. You'd think she was color blind, not deaf, the way she dresses."

Jessica turned to look across the cafeteria. "That dress isn't so bad. Bruce is the one who looks ridiculous. The way he stares at Regina you'd think he'd never seen a girl before."

"What I can't understand," Lila went on, "is how anyone could stand to be with her for more than five minutes. Regina Morrow is totally boring."

"Mmmm," Jessica muttered, opening her

notebook and scowling at its contents. She'd spent an entire period in the library, and she still wasn't any closer to finding a topic for her term paper.

"Jessica Wakefield, you're not even listening to me!" Lila cried, her mouth turning downward in a pout.

"Sorry," Jessica said, slamming her notebook shut. "I'm just worried about this stupid term paper. It counts for a third of our final grade, and I still don't have a topic."

Lila shrugged, licking the last bit of ice cream off its wooden stick. "Neither do I," she said without interest. "I can't imagine anything duller than history."

"Me either." She turned to take another look at Bruce and Regina.

"Cara told me Bruce has gone completely crazy over her," Lila confided, watching Jessica carefully to gauge her reaction. "He takes her absolutely everywhere. Cara says he can't stand to be away from her for even a *minute*."

Jessica flinched. Lila knew that one of the sorest points between Jessica and Bruce had been that he'd tried to get out of spending time with her by inventing phony excuses.

"Don't believe a word of it," Jessica said archly. "He's probably sneaking off to see those college girls of his while Regina's home studying."

Lila spread her hands out in front of her, admiring her manicure. "I don't know about that," she said, turning in their direction with a knowing smile. "Regina's even been invited up to the Patmans' house for dinner, Cara told me."

"I can't imagine anything worse," Jessica said furiously. The truth was that Jessica had always wanted to be accepted by the Patmans. She thought their house was beautiful, and she'd always pictured herself covered with jewelry, sweeping across the vast lawns of their estate. Having struck out with Bruce, she had made a play for Roger after his identity was disclosed. And it would have worked, she thought, if Roger hadn't been such a jerk about Olivia. Jessica had done her best to save Roger from social disaster, but in the end he had refused to be rescued. He'd stuck it out with Olivia, who dressed like a freak in Indian cotton dresses and funny sandals and didn't care about anything but drawing and poetry. A fate, Jessica thought, worse than death.

All in all, the Patmans were not Jessica's favorite subject these days. In her estimation, they fell even lower than history term papers, and she wished Lila would drop the topic.

"Well, dinner is one thing," Lila continued mercilessly, "but the most amazing news is that he bought her a ruby pendant. Cara saw it, and she said it's beautiful."

Jessica raised her eyebrows and said nothing, and Lila leaned forward, dropping her voice sympathetically. "Bruce never bought *you* anything expensive like that, did he?"

"No," Jessica said firmly, "he didn't. But I'll tell you something, Lila. Bruce Patman will never be serious about anyone besides himself. He'll get sick of Regina. I guarantee it. And he's so cheap, he's probably charging her rent for the necklace," she said, giggling.

Lila looked doubtful. "I don't know, Jess. I think you may be wrong."

"Trust me, Lila," Jessica said. "I give it two weeks. Tops."

Lila looked at Jessica with sudden interest. "Two weeks," she mused. "That would be about the time of the carnival, right?"

"That's right," Jessica said. "By the day of the carnival, they probably won't even be on speaking terms."

Lila gave Jessica a long look. "You sound pretty sure of yourself," she said at last. "I don't suppose you'd care to make a bet?"

Jessica thought fast. Lila's allowance was easily ten times as much as hers. She did some rapid calculation. How much did she owe Elizabeth? Not too much, she thought. Besides, she didn't want Lila to think she was backing out at this stage.

"Sure," Jessica said nonchalantly. "How much should we bet?"

Lila considered for a minute. "Let's not bet money," she suggested. "My father says it's vulgar."

Jessica looked confused. "What do we bet if we don't bet money?" she asked.

Lila's face lit up. "I've got a great idea!" she exclaimed. "We can bet term papers!"

Jessica stared at her. "Term papers? What do you mean?"

Lila laughed. "If I win, you write my term paper. And if *you* win, I write yours. How does that sound?"

Jessica swallowed. This was a lot worse than betting money. If she lost the bet, she'd have *two* term papers to write. And at this point she could barely imagine writing one!

Moreover, Jessica wasn't one bit sure that Bruce and Regina would break up. For all she knew, Bruce really *had* changed. It wasn't something she'd like to bet anything important on.

But Jessica wasn't about to let Lila see how worried she was. "You're on," she said cheerfully, reaching out to shake Lila's hand. "We'll bet our term papers."

If Lila was surprised that Jessica had accepted, she didn't show it. "Fine," she said. "We'll make the carnival the cutoff point. Just think, Jess," she added. "If Bruce and Regina break up before then, you won't have to worry about your term paper!''

And if they don't, Jessica thought uneasily, *I might as well hang myself.* She looked across the cafeteria to where Bruce and Regina were sitting, and shook her head. *This bet is too important to lose*, Jessica thought. *If Bruce and Regina don't break up on their own in a few days, I'm going to have to do my best to help them.*

Three

Lila parked her lime-green Triumph in front of her father's office and across from the new building he was having built in downtown Sweet Valley. "I hope Daddy doesn't take too long," she murmured, checking her reflection in the rearview mirror. It was a gorgeous afternoon, and Lila wanted to go to the beach with Jessica and Cara. But the message she'd received from the office after lunch had been explicit. "Your father phoned this morning," the principal's secretary had told her. "He wants you to meet him at his office at four to discuss something."

Lila glanced impatiently at her watch. It was three forty-five, and she had a sneaking suspicion her father would keep her waiting. She had at least fifteen minutes to kill and nothing to do in the meantime. And the last place Lila could imagine finding anything interesting to watch was at the site of the half-completed Fowler building. In fact, the only thing that interested Lila about the Fowler business was the hefty allowance it provided her each month.

I wonder what Daddy wants to discuss, she thought, getting out of her car and leaning against the fence enclosing the site where the construction workers were moving piles of lumber. *I hope he's not cutting my allowance.*

While she was thinking about the meeting with her father, Lila watched the construction workers struggling with sacks of concrete. Her gaze kept returning to one young man in particular. He looked different from the others. For one thing, he was much younger—not more than eighteen or nineteen, Lila guessed. And he was handsome. His honey-brown, sun-lightened hair peeked out from under his work hat, and the muscles in his strong arms rippled as he lifted the heavy bags.

Seeing her watching him, the young man looked up at Lila and smiled. It was a cool, self-confident smile.

Lila smiled back at him, slightly surprised at herself. She didn't even usually *look* at construction workers, let alone encourage them. *I must be slipping*, she thought.

The young man sauntered casually over to the fence where Lila was standing. "Hi," he said, looking her up and down with the same cool, slow smile. "My name's Jack."

"Hello," Lila said casually. She felt slightly put out by his forward manner, but she couldn't help noticing how nice his eyes were. "My name is Lila." Then, adopting her most imperious tone, she added, "Lila *Fowler*."

"Aha," he said, smiling and looking at her more closely. "Fowler, like the building?" he asked, pointing behind him to the shell of what would eventually be the world headquarters for her father's computer company.

"Of course," Lila said archly. "That's my father."

Lila expected him to be impressed, but to her surprise he didn't seem to be. If anything, he just looked slightly amused. He tipped his head back a little, shading his eyes with one tanned hand, and squinted up at the sun.

"Nice day, don't you think?" he asked her.

"It's always nice here!" Lila giggled. "Aren't you from Sweet Valley?" she demanded.

"No," Jack told her, shaking his head.

Just then a whistle blew, signaling the end of the shift, and Jack grinned. "Oh, well. I'm afraid that whistle blows for me, to ruin an old quotation. But it's nice to have met you, Lila."

"Nice to have met you, too!" Lila called after him, watching him saunter back to join the others. What a strange young man, she thought,

24

shaking her head a little as she left the fence. He didn't seem to fit her image of the average construction worker. For one thing, she had assumed that the minute he found out who she was, he'd change his manner. But he'd acted as if he and Lila were equals.

I wouldn't mind running into him again, Lila admitted to herself as she crossed the street to her father's office building. Something about him had aroused her curiosity. And Lila intended to find out more about him.

Mr. Collins was Elizabeth's favorite teacher at Sweet Valley High. And she wasn't the only one who felt that way. Everyone thought Mr. Collins looked like Robert Redford—strawberry blond hair, blue eyes. And he was still young enough to engage the interest of many of his students. Because Mr. Collins was the faculty adviser for *The Oracle*, Elizabeth had gotten to know him well. She often turned to him when she was worried about something or needed advice.

"Okay, carnival committee," Mr. Collins said now, sitting on the edge of his desk and facing the group before him. Elizabeth glanced around her to see who had shown up. Todd, of course, and Enid; Roger and Olivia; and Winston Egbert and Ken Matthews, the tall, good-looking captain of the football team. "Now, the first thing on the agenda is—"

Just then the door to Mr. Collins's room opened, and Regina Morrow walked in. "Come on in, Regina," Mr. Collins said cheerfully. "We're just getting started."

"Thanks, Mr. Collins," Regina said, slipping into an empty chair.

"As I was saying," Mr. Collins went on, the first thing we need to do is to draw up a list of booths we want, and put people in charge of them. The Sweet Valley PTA has chosen Skye Morrow, Regina's mother, to be our parent adviser," he added, looking at Regina and smiling. "Liz, as soon as you can arrange it, I'd like you to meet with Mrs. Morrow, and you two can put your ideas together. And now, I think I'll let you take over."

Elizabeth walked to the front of the room, taking her notebook with her. She flashed Todd a smile across the room. Elizabeth was delighted to be in charge of the carnival. She had a flair for organization, and this was a cause she believed in. "OK," she said, opening her notebook and picking up her pen. "Olivia, how would you like to be in charge of getting prizes and making decorations?" she asked. Aside from her role as arts editor, Olivia loved to paint and sew, and Elizabeth knew she would do a wonderful job of making the carnival festive.

"I'd love to," Olivia responded.

"By the way, Mr. Fowler has generously

donated all the lumber we'll need to make the stands," Mr. Collins told the group. "And he's dropping off a box of tools tomorrow afternoon as well."

"I can get a crew together to build the booths," Ken Matthews said.

Elizabeth scribbled in her notebook. "Regina, what would you like to do?" she asked.

Regina looked thoughtful. "I could organize all the refreshment stands," she suggested.

"I'll help with that," Enid volunteered.

"Now," Elizabeth said, consulting her list, "if Todd and Roger wouldn't mind taking charge of games, that covers just about everyone."

"What about me?" Winston demanded.

"You mean in addition to letting people throw pies at you?"

Everyone laughed, and Winston nodded.

Suddenly a flash of inspiration came to Elizabeth. "Winston, how would you like to be master of ceremonies? We'll need someone to direct people and announce prizes."

Winston looked delighted. "I'll borrow my father's old tuxedo," he said.

"OK," Elizabeth said, putting her notebook down. "It looks as though we're off to a good start. I'll arrange to meet with Mrs. Morrow, and we can meet again on Friday afternoon, if that's all right with everyone."

"Liz," Todd said, his brown eyes twinkling, "aren't you forgetting something?"

Elizabeth looked at him in confusion. "What do you mean?"

Todd laughed. "We're supposed to adjourn now to the beach!" he reminded her.

"That's right!" Enid cried.

Elizabeth laughed. "I *did* forget," she said. "Mr. Collins, how about a trip to the beach with the carnival committee?"

"No, thanks," Mr. Collins said. "You guys get out of here now and have a good time. I've got a little work to do."

"Thanks for all your help," Elizabeth told him as the group started out of the classroom. "It looks like this is going to take some work, but it'll sure be worth it if we can raise some money for those children."

"With you at the helm, Liz, I'm sure it'll be a roaring success." Mr. Collins chuckled. "Now go on and have a good time. It's too nice a day to waste inside!"

Half an hour later, Elizabeth, Enid, and Todd were lying on beach towels on the warm sand, listening to the waves crashing on the shore.

"Enid, where's George?" Elizabeth asked, rolling over on her stomach to face her friend.

George Warren was Enid's steady boyfriend,

and Elizabeth had just remembered he was supposed to meet them at the beach.

"He's at his junior flying class," she replied. "A thousand feet off the ground, as usual." For the past month or so, George had been trying to get his pilot's license, fulfilling a lifelong dream of learning to fly.

"I think I'd rather be on the ground on a day like this," Todd joked, rolling over on his back so his face could get some sun.

"I think the meeting went pretty well this afternoon," Enid commented a moment later. "I'm glad Ken Matthews is going to be helping. We need someone strong to build the booths!"

"I beg your pardon," Todd said, opening one eye. "And I suppose I'm nothing but a ninety-pound weakling?"

"You'll do," Elizabeth murmured, running her hand along the curve of his arm.

"Actually, I'm glad Ken will be around too," Todd remarked. "I thought he might miss the meeting this afternoon. I know how busy he's been with the election."

"That's right," Enid said. Ken was running for president of the Sweet Valley Centennial Student Committee, and he'd put a lot of effort into making posters and soliciting votes.

"Is anyone running against him yet?" Enid asked.

Todd shook his head. "It looks like Ken's got it

all wrapped up," he told her. "Like our friend Liz here—an uncontested victory."

"That's strange," Elizabeth said. Sweet Valley had been planning its centennial celebration for quite some time, and she would have expected the presidency of the student committee to be a coveted position. "I'll bet someone else signs up," she added, rubbing oil into her bronzed shoulders.

"Oh, yeah?" Todd said teasingly. "What would you like to bet, Elizabeth Wakefield?"

"A hot fudge sundae at the Dairi Burger," she told him.

"You're on!" Todd cried, grabbing her by the hand. "And I'll bet you an enormous kiss that I make it into the water before you do!"

"Jess, you should've seen this guy," Lila said, settling back on her enormous beach towel.

"Really? Where'd you find him?" Jessica asked, rummaging through her bag for a bottle of baby oil.

"I didn't *find* him," Lila said evasively, brushing a bit of sand off her tanned shoulder. "He was just—" She paused to think for a moment. "Just hanging around my father's office," she finished. She knew Jessica would be critical if she found out Jack was a construction worker. *Not that it matters*, Lila told herself. *At least, not that it matters yet.*

"So did you talk to this walking vision?" Jessica asked.

Lila nodded. "He's got a wonderful voice," she said. "And he really is pretty terrific looking."

"What's his last name?" Jessica asked.

Lila shrugged. "We didn't get around to that."

Jessica laughed out loud. "Oh, boy," she said. "Maybe it's Jack-in-the-box." She giggled. "Or Jack O'lantern. Or Jack the Ripper!"

"Shut up," Lila muttered, leaning forward to grab Jessica's baby oil. "He knows *my* last name. And I know I'll be seeing him again. I don't need his last name to find him!"

Jessica turned over on her stomach so she could watch people strolling back and forth in front of her. "Hey, where's Cara?" she asked, shading her eyes with one hand. "She was supposed to be here ages ago."

Lila sat up and looked around, her pretty face wrinkled in a frown. "God knows," she said. Suddenly her brown eyes narrowed. "Look who just arrived," she said to Jessica, pointing across the beach.

Jessica followed her gaze, her face darkening. Sure enough, there was Bruce Patman, tanned and muscular, in an absurdly small bathing suit. And right beside him, holding his hand as if she couldn't bear to let go of him for even a second, was Regina Morrow.

"They certainly look happy, don't you think?" Lila said brightly.

"Just give it time, Lila," Jessica said, rolling over on her back and closing her eyes. *Or give me time, I should say*, she thought. *There's no way I'm going to get stuck writing Lila's term paper. Whatever it takes, I'm going to make sure Bruce and Regina break up before the carnival.*

The only thing that remained was determining how to do it.

Four

"Roger, pass Regina the butter," Mrs. Patman said, smoothing her black hair with her hand.

Bruce glared at his mother across the table. "You don't have to treat Regina like a two-year-old," he had told her angrily while Regina was in the powder room washing her hands. "She may not be able to hear, but there's nothing wrong with her mind. Anyway, she can read lips perfectly."

"I'm sure she can," Mrs. Patman had said soothingly. But now, sitting at one end of the table in the Patmans' formidable dining room, she seemed to have forgotten everything Bruce had said. Each time she addressed Regina, she spoke very slowly and loudly, moving her lips with careful exaggeration. By the time one of the servants brought in the salad, Regina's face was red with embarrassment.

"That was such a lovely story about you in that little magazine," Mrs. Patman said loudly. "Wasn't it, dear?" she asked, looking down the table at her husband.

"Why are you shouting, Aunt Marie?" Roger asked, taking a bite of salad.

"Was I shouting? I wasn't shouting, was I?" Mrs. Patman demanded, turning with an injured look to Bruce.

"It *was* a lovely article," Mr. Patman said, smiling at Regina.

Blushing hotly, Regina stared down at her salad. Dinner was much harder than she'd expected. For one thing, the Patman mansion—though no larger than the Morrows' own—was imposing. Where the Morrows' house was warm and casual, the Patmans' was elegant and forbidding. *We could fit fifteen people at this table instead of five*, Regina thought to herself. An enormous chandelier hung over the dining room table, glinting in the candlelight. Regina thought the lighting was romantic, but it didn't make lip-reading very easy.

Still, as long as Bruce was across from her, smiling warmly and nudging her foot protectively with his under the table, Regina couldn't care less about the others. Regina thought Bruce looked more handsome than ever that evening. He was wearing a navy-blue blazer, chino pants, and a navy- and red-striped tie. *"You're* the one who belongs on the cover of a magazine," she had teased him when he'd come to pick her up earlier in the evening.

"Regina," Mrs. Patman said, twisting the heavy string of pearls around her neck, "I understand your mother has been put in charge of the carnival committee."

"Yes, ma'am," Regina said.

"I was rather hoping I would be asked to take that position," Mrs. Patman said haughtily.

"I think the PTA suggested my mother because she was new in town, and they thought she'd enjoy the opportunity to get involved," Regina said shyly. "And they knew she had experience with handicapped children. But I'm sure she'd be grateful for your help, Mrs. Patman. Mr. Fowler has already contributed lumber for the stalls."

"Oh, he has, has he?" Mrs. Patman asked, leaning back in her chair to consider this piece of news. Marie Patman hated the Fowlers. She hated them so much that she wasn't sure whether it was the *idea* of the Fowlers or the fact of them that so enraged her. According to Marie Patman, the Fowlers were nouveaux riches— newly rich. Not like the Patmans and the Vanderhorns, who were among the first families in Sweet Valley. Mrs. Patman leaned forward in her chair and smiled at Regina—her first real smile of the evening.

"Maybe I'll give your mother a call tonight and see what Henry and I can do to help," she said sweetly.

"I'm sure she'd be happy to hear from you," Regina said. *Mrs. Patman sure seems to run hot and cold*, she thought. But Bruce's smile across the table made everything worthwhile. "This soup is delicious, Mrs. Patman," she added, turning to her hostess with a smile.

"Do you think so, dear? I'm so glad," Mrs. Patman said happily, folding her hands together and beaming first at Regina and then at Bruce. Her voice had dropped back to normal, and she seemed to have forgotten that Regina was deaf. *Oh, well*, Regina thought to herself. *I guess I'm lucky that Bruce takes after his father. His mother really seems to have a few screws loose.*

"Your mother looked as if she was shouting at me the whole first half of the dinner," Regina said, sinking into Bruce's arms. They were parked in Bruce's Porsche at Miller's Point, a breathtaking spot overlooking Sweet Valley, watching the sun set.

Bruce laughed. "Try not to let my mother get to you," he said. "She means well, but she's got some pretty strange ideas."

"She really seemed to warm up after we started talking about my mother and the carnival committee," Regina pointed out.

Bruce shrugged. "She's crazy if it took her more than a minute to warm up to you," he said huskily, running his hands over Regina's silky hair.

Regina's breath caught in her throat. Bruce was the first boy who had touched her, and each time he held her, she felt almost dizzy with warmth.

Regina lay back in Bruce's arms, looking down at the sun setting over the valley. "It's so beautiful here," she murmured. She loved being alone with Bruce, away from everyone at home or at school, but her happiness was tinged with anxiety. *There's still so much I don't know*, Regina thought, closing her eyes as Bruce leaned over to kiss her. The feel of his lips on her throat made her sigh with happiness.

Suddenly Bruce pulled her up to face him. "I love you, Regina," he said softly, staring into her eyes. She stared back at him gravely and leaned forward to touch his lips with her fingers. How strange—how wonderfully strange—to see those words shaping themselves on Bruce's lips.

"I've never told any girl that I loved her before," he added seriously. "I want you to know that, Regina."

Regina blushed. "I've never even kissed a boy before," she admitted.

Bruce leaned over and tenderly—as tenderly as possible—kissed Regina on the earlobe. "I wish I could bring your hearing back with a kiss," he said softly, looking into her eyes. "You're so brave, Regina. If only there was something I could do so you could hear me tell you how much I love you!"

Regina smiled. "I'm not brave," she told Bruce quietly. "I'm happy. I have more now than I ever dreamed of having. For so many years I went to 'special' schools and 'special' camps and 'special' doctors. And it took me so long to adjust to the public school in Boston. Since I moved to Sweet Valley, I've been able to lead a normal life for the first time. And now there's you."

She pulled his face down to hers and kissed him softly on the lips. "I don't need to hear to know you love me," she whispered. "Or to know that I love you, too."

"Oh, Regina!" Bruce burst out. "What did I ever do before I met you?"

Regina shivered. It was hard to remember what life had been like before Bruce. The worst thing about her deafness was that it had isolated her from other people. Her family was wonderful—they always had been. But for years Regina had needed to be away from them so she could attend special schools. She had grown accustomed to being deaf and had come to take her handicap for granted. But it seemed her deafness had been a wall between her and other kids her age.

Bruce was the first person to break through that wall. And since she had met him, Regina felt like a different person. She wasn't isolated anymore. She could tell Bruce whatever she thought or felt, and he understood. Sometimes he even knew what she was thinking before she said anything.

"Nothing should ever keep us apart, Regina," Bruce said firmly, holding her head in his hands.

"Nothing will," Regina said, taking his hand and holding it tight. *Because I won't let it*, she thought. *Nothing in the whole world matters to me as much as Bruce does, and I won't let anything come between us. Not ever.*

Five

When Mrs. Patman called, Skye Morrow was in the living room, looking at a pile of notes Mr. Collins had given her to help her plan the carnival.

"What was that all about?" Mr. Morrow asked, taking his reading glasses off and putting down the evening paper after his wife had hung up the phone.

"The Patmans want to match the amount of money we raise at the carnival," Mrs. Morrow told him, rubbing her temples with both hands.

"That's pretty generous of them," Mr. Morrow said cheerfully. His wife stared at him unsmiling, and he wrinkled his brow with concern. "What's wrong, honey? I think that sounds like good news."

"I guess it is," Mrs. Morrow said. "But I didn't really like the way she sounded. She made it seem like some sort of contest to see who can give the most. And you should have heard the way she went on about how well Regina's adjusted to 'her little problem,' " she added indignantly. "She made it sound as though Regina's got two heads or something! And then she claims she wants to give hundreds of dollars to help the handicapped!"

"Skye," Mr. Morrow said gently, "those kids at the hospital aren't going to care where the money to help them out comes from. Even if it comes from a woman with two heads!" He chuckled.

Mrs. Morrow shook her head as she leaned back in her chair. "Maybe I should have trusted my impulses and told Roger Collins that I wasn't the right choice for supervising this project. I just can't seem to be objective about the whole thing."

"You'll be fine, Mom. You're exactly what they need," eighteen-year-old Nicholas Morrow said encouragingly.

Mrs. Morrow leaned over and rumpled his dark hair. "Thanks, handsome," she said, trying to smile. "I think I'll go upstairs and lie down for a while," she added, standing up and kneading her temples with both hands. "This project seems to be giving me a headache."

"I'm worried about Mom," Nicholas said after she had left the room. "She seems to be getting headaches again all the time now."

Mr. Morrow looked at his son and sighed. Sometimes he wished his son could remember Skye before Regina was born. As hard as he tried, it was impossible to convince Nicholas that his mother had once been a carefree, laughing young woman.

When Kurt Morrow met Skye, he was a professional football player, and she was a top fashion model who traveled on location all over the world. Sometimes Kurt had to pinch himself to prove he wasn't dreaming when she fell in love with him and agreed to marry him. They were a couple who had everything—looks, love, a perfect home, and a perfect little boy. After Kurt used his football earnings to start a computer business, Skye gave up modeling gradually, wanting to devote all her time to her husband, her home, and her son. Also, a new baby was on the way. And Skye was ready to be a full-time mother.

But a few weeks after she learned she was pregnant, one of the most glamorous magazines in New York offered her a spectacular assignment. They wanted Skye to appear in their special summer issue, modeling bathing suits and resort wear. After long discussions with Kurt, Skye decided to take the job. It would be her last modeling assignment, and she wanted it to be perfect.

There was only one catch. The magazine told her she would have to lose ten pounds in less than a month. Ignoring what her doctor told her, Skye took diet pills and lost the weight. The assignment went perfectly, and in the magazine's summer issue, Skye looked more beautiful than ever before.

But the consequences were grave. The pills Skye had taken had damaged the delicate tissue in the ears of her unborn child. After Regina was born, it became obvious that she wasn't responding to noises the way Nicholas had. The doctors' pronouncement was grave: Regina had suffered permanent damage to her ears. She would never be able to hear normally.

At first Skye refused to believe what the doctors told her. She wrote to clinics and hospitals all over the world, sending them Regina's medical files and begging them for help. Kurt had finally convinced her to accept the truth. Her children needed her now more than ever. Regina needed love from her mother, not guilt.

But Skye couldn't forgive herself. She gave up modeling completely, convinced that her work and her own selfishness had been to blame. In the past she had loved to entertain, but after Regina's condition was diagnosed, she spent more and more time alone with the children.

When Regina left home to attend a special boarding school in Connecticut, Skye began to suffer from blinding headaches. Sometimes they were so severe she couldn't leave her bed for days.

Mr. Morrow was aware that the headaches were caused by guilt and anxiety over Regina's deafness. Regina, of course, knew nothing about any of this. Whenever Regina was around, Mrs. Morrow made a special effort to act as if everything were fine.

When things went well for Regina, the headaches often stopped. Sometimes Skye felt like her old self. When Regina's picture appeared on the cover of *Ingenue*, Skye was as happy and excited as she had been in the days before Regina was born.

But over the past few weeks, Nicholas and Mr. Morrow had noticed a rapid change in her behavior. It was as if Skye had seen how close Regina could come to achieving what she herself had taken for granted. Now all the guilt and anxiety were back. Mr. Morrow sighed as he looked at the door through which his wife had disappeared. "I really hoped that moving here would make things better," he said softly. "At last we're all living together like a normal family."

Nicholas shook his head, his handsome face creasing with concern. "I don't know, Dad," he murmured. "I just wish there was something we could do!"

Mr. Morrow stood up and walked to the window, looking out at his estate as if he weren't really seeing what lay outside. "There *may* be something, son," he said at last. "I've been exploring some possibilities, and I think that now is the time to find out for sure." Without another word, he crossed the room, picked up the telephone receiver, and began to dial.

"Anyone home?" Regina called, closing the front door behind her and slipping out of her jacket. It was eleven-thirty, later than she'd thought, but the family room was still blazing with lights. *Looks like they're all still up*, she thought, hurrying to the back of the house. She could hardly wait to tell her mother about the evening. As she opened the door to the family room, she automatically reached to touch the tiny ruby pendant Bruce had given her the week before. She blushed as her fingers brushed the tiny jewel at her throat. *It's as if I don't really believe any of this can have happened*, she thought, smiling.

The scene that greeted her in the family room caught Regina by surprise. She had suspected that her mother hadn't been feeling well earlier, but Skye was still awake. And not only awake, but fully clothed, looking younger and more beautiful than ever before. Nicholas was pouring champagne into fluted glasses, and her father was smiling brightly.

"Hi!" Regina said, glancing from one happy face to the next. "What's the champagne for? Are we celebrating?"

"We certainly are!" her father boomed, coming forward and encircling Regina in his strong arms. "Nicholas, pour your sister a glass."

"Oh, Regina!" her mother cried, running forward and throwing her arms around her. "I'm so happy I could cry!"

"Wait a minute!" Regina stepped back and looked at all of them in confusion. "Can anyone explain what we're all so happy about?"

"We can indeed," her father said, reaching for a glass of champagne and passing it to Regina. "But first, I think we need a toast."

"To Regina," Mrs. Morrow said, her eyes filling with tears.

"To all of us," Nicholas added, raising his glass.

Regina laughed. "I'll drink to that," she said happily, sipping the delicious wine. She put her glass down and plopped down on the couch. "Now, what's going on?" she demanded.

Mr. Morrow took a deep breath. "Regina," he began, "what would you say if I told you there was a chance your hearing could be completely restored?"

Regina stared at him, her mouth going dry. "What?" she managed weakly.

Mr. Morrow nodded. "Completely, perfectly restored," he told her. "After approximately a year of treatments, you'll be able to hear as well as the rest of us. Concerts and birds singing and babies crying—"

And Bruce's voice telling me he loves me, Regina thought, closing her eyes in disbelief. "Are you serious?" she asked, opening her eyes and searching her father's face. "Is this some kind of joke?"

"Sweetie, do you think we'd joke about something like this?" her mother asked.

Regina stared at her and shook her head. "No," she said faintly. "It's just so hard to imagine," she added, a smile breaking across her face. "You mean there's really a doctor somewhere who thinks he can cure me?"

Mr. Morrow sat down on the couch next to his daughter and took her hand. "I would've told you months ago, but I didn't want to get your hopes up. Last year I read about a case similar to yours in which a boy from San Francisco had his hearing completely restored. I did as much research as I could and finally wrote to the doctor who invented the procedure. His name is Max Friederich. He's a brilliant Swiss surgeon. He answered several weeks later, telling me that the procedure could be used successfully only in about one case out of a thousand. Last month I had all your medical records sent to him. And tonight I got his colleague in New York City on the phone. He thinks that you're a perfect candidate for the treatment!"

Regina was trembling with excitement. The whole time her father was talking her mind was racing. *I'll be able to hear again*, she thought. *I'll hear Bruce's voice. I'll be able to talk to him on the telephone; and when we're together, I'll know what he's saying even with my eyes shut!* In her confusion and excitement, Regina could barely register what her father was telling her. All she knew was that he'd found a doctor who could make her hear again.

"We're going to come visit you, too," her mother was saying, laughing excitedly over her champagne glass. "We're not going to let this family be separated any more than we have to!"

"Come visit me where?" Regina asked blankly, turning back to her father. "Can't the procedure be done here in Sweet Valley?" A horrible, gnawing sensation began in the pit of her stomach. After a year of treatments, her father had said. A year! They couldn't expect her to go away for an entire year!

"Regina, Dr. Friederich is incredibly busy," her father told her. "We can't expect him to make house calls from Switzerland." Mr. Morrow was still laughing, unaware of the expression of growing horror on Regina's face.

"Switzerland!" she exploded. "You don't mean I'd have to move to Switzerland, do you?"

"Regina, it's only for a year," her mother said soothingly, putting her arms around her daughter. "You've been through so much already. One more year and you'll never have to worry again!"

"I'll come and visit you, Regina," Nicholas was saying eagerly. "We can go skiing together in the Alps."

"We'll *all* visit," Mr. Morrow said firmly. "And Dr. Friederich thinks you may be able to come home for two weeks at Christmas."

Regina looked from one excited face to another. "This procedure," she said slowly, trying not to burst into tears, "could it wait? Is there any reason why it has to be done right away?"

Mr. Morrow stared at her, his brow furrowing. "We thought you'd want to go as soon as you could," he told her. Obviously confused, he looked at his wife. "We'll arrange for a tutor so you can finish your schoolwork in Switzerland. But I suppose if you wanted to wait until school's out, we might try to reschedule with Dr. Friederich—if we can get you in then. He's a very busy man."

"What I meant," Regina said, "was waiting a little longer than that." She was still trembling, but she was no longer overflowing with joy.

Once again her fingers flew to her throat. The ruby pendant was still there.

"How *much* longer?" Mr. Morrow asked. "Regina, the operations should be done as soon as possible."

Regina jumped to her feet, her face blazing. "Forget it!" she cried, her eyes swimming with tears. "For the first time in my whole life, I've finally been able to live a normal life. I'm doing well in school. And I've made real friends! How can you expect me to just jump on a plane and spend the next year in a foreign country, with no one but doctors to talk to!"

Regina fought for control, but despite herself tears spilled over and trickled down her cheeks. "It's easy for *you*," she sputtered. "*You* can come visit and go skiing and then come home again! But I'm the one who has to make the decision. And I'm not going to go!"

Sobs bursting from her heaving chest, Regina ran from the room, slamming the door behind her. Her parents and Nicholas stared at one another, the color slowly draining from their faces.

Six

Regina stood in front of the mirror in her bedroom, brushing her long, black hair with automatic strokes. She examined herself critically, and, after a moment's deliberation, brushed a bit of blusher under each cheekbone. *That's better*, she thought, stepping back for a final look. She had chosen one of her favorite outfits to wear—a navy-blue cotton dress with tiny white flowers on it, and a pair of low-heeled sandals. Satisfied at last, Regina turned from the mirror. *It doesn't show*, she thought with relief. *You can't tell I've been crying or that I didn't get much sleep last night.*

Nicholas and Mr. Morrow were in the breakfast room when Regina went downstairs. They had apparently been talking about her because their lips stopped moving as soon as she walked in the room.

"Good morning," Regina said cheerfully, pouring herself a glass of milk and sitting down next to her brother. "Is Mom up yet?"

Mr. Morrow glanced anxiously at Nicholas and then cleared his throat. "She's not feeling very well this morning, Regina," he told her. "I think she's still pretty upset by what you said last night."

Regina's face became hot. "I owe you all a big apology," she said, taking a sip of milk. "I didn't behave very well last night. I guess I was too excited and then too upset to make very much sense."

Nicholas's face lit up. "You mean you've changed your mind?" he asked. "You want to go to Switzerland after all?"

Regina looked from Nicholas to her father. Both had the same hopeful expression, the same light in their eyes. Her heart melted when she saw them look at her that way. Regina knew how much they loved her, and she knew, too, that they genuinely wanted what was best for her. But she had made up her mind, and nothing would weaken her resolve. "I'm sorry," she said softly, staring down at the table. "I can't go," she added, looking up to meet her father's gaze. "If only you knew how happy I've been since we moved to Sweet Valley! For the first time in my life, I feel like a normal person."

"Regina, we know that," her father said. "And it's because we understand that we want you to undergo these treatments. Please think it over, Regina."

Regina sighed. "All right, I'll think it over," she agreed. "But I don't think I'll change my mind. Dad," she said, impulsively leaping up and throwing her arms around her father, "I know how much trouble you went through to find Dr. Friederich. And I love you for it. Please don't be angry with me if I decide to stay here in Sweet Valley."

Mr. Morrow hugged Regina. "You know we want what's best for you," he told her. "And it's not a question of being angry with you. We'll stick by you no matter what decision you come to. All we ask," he added firmly, "is that you keep an open mind about it, OK?"

"OK," Regina said softly. "That's fair enough."

The doorbell rang, and Nicholas jumped up to see who was there. "Oh, is that the door?" Regina asked. "That must be Bruce." She gave her father another kiss and hurried after Nicholas, her heart pounding. She didn't want Bruce to come inside that morning. And she didn't want Nicholas to get to him before she did.

*   *   *

"You look so beautiful this morning," Bruce said tenderly, kissing Regina softly before he started his Porsche in the Morrows' driveway.

"Thanks," Regina murmured, trying to keep her voice natural. She had promised herself the night before that Bruce would not find out about Dr. Friederich and Switzerland. *There's no point in letting him find out about it*, Regina thought. *Because no matter what Mom and Dad say, I know it would be wrong for me to go to Switzerland. I belong here.*

The whole time she was growing up, Regina had longed for the kind of life other girls took for granted. The special schools she had attended were a world away from Sweet Valley High. Tuition had been very expensive, and students had had to work twice as hard to accomplish the simplest tasks.

She had just felt comfortable in her first regular school, in Boston, when her father had announced they were moving to Sweet Valley. At first she had been worried about starting yet another school. She was afraid that no one would like her and that they would treat her differently. But week by week her confidence increased. It was easy now for Regina to do well in her schoolwork, and Sweet Valley High was quickly becoming a place to have fun as well as to learn.

For the first time in her life, Regina had a real circle of friends. She had a home she loved, and she had her family with her every single day. Sweet Valley had seemed almost magical to Regina since the day she moved in. And when Mr. Townsend had stopped her in the street and asked her if she'd like to model for a special story in *Ingenue* magazine, she *knew* it was magic.

But none of these things alone would have kept Regina from going to Switzerland. The prospect of sudden disruption and loneliness was difficult for her, but—to have her hearing restored! To be able to hear music and voices and rain falling on the rooftop at night! Where other people heard these things, all Regina could distinguish was a faint buzz.

Now, the choice was hers. The thing she had dreamed of for so many years had become a reality. She might hear again one day!

But now she had Bruce. And Bruce was the real reason why Regina knew she couldn't leave Sweet Valley. She had never dreamed that being in love could feel this way. She thought about Bruce every waking moment. The times when they couldn't be together seemed to drag on forever. *And*, Regina thought, *if a day without Bruce feels like a year to me, what would a year without him feel like?*

"Hey," Bruce said, leaning over and giving

her a hug with his free arm, "you're about a million miles away! What are you thinking about?"

Regina blushed. "I'm thinking how happy I am with you," she said shyly.

"Thank goodness," Bruce said, shaking his head. "Sometimes when you get quiet I start worrying that you may have changed your mind about me. It's funny," he added, pulling the Porsche into his usual parking place in the Sweet Valley High lot, "I never worried about a girl before. And now I'm worrying all the time!"

"There's nothing to worry about," Regina said. "You know that, don't you?"

Bruce sighed. "You're right," he said finally. "There's nothing to worry about as long as you tell me you haven't stopped caring about me. That's all that matters."

"Oh, Bruce," Regina cried, throwing her arms around him. *Thank goodness I didn't tell him about Switzerland*, she thought, breathing in the sweet smell of his after-shave. *He'd never understand. And if I were to lose him now, I'd be giving up the most precious thing of all.*

Millions of people in the world have perfect hearing, she reasoned. *But how many of them love someone with all their hearts who loves them back?*

Nothing can make me leave Sweet Valley and Bruce, she swore to herself, clinging to him as if she'd never let go. *Nothing—not even Dr. Friederich and his promise of a miracle.* And no matter what, Bruce was *not* going to learn about the treatments or her decision to forego them.

Because that's what loving someone means, Regina told herself. *It means, if you have to, you're willing to make a sacrifice for someone you really care about—like Bruce.*

"OK," Winston Egbert said cheerfully, "this is your lucky day! Your noontime meal is about to be graced with my humor and charm."

"Lucky us." Lila groaned. "Why are Jessica and I the fortunate ones today?"

"Good question," Winston said, sliding his tray next to Jessica's. "Actually, this is a business call," he added, taking a huge forkful of chocolate cake.

"You know, Winston," Lila commented, staring at his tray, "in this country, people generally eat dessert *after* the meal."

"A backward nation." Winston sighed. "I have come," he continued, gesturing grandly with his fork, "to invite you two to contribute your worthy ideas to the carnival committee."

"Carnivals are boring," Lila told him. "Besides," she added, "neither of us has time to help. We've both got these stupid term papers to worry about." She winked at Jessica.

What she means, Jessica thought glumly, *is that I've got both our stupid term papers to worry about.*

It didn't appear as though Bruce and Regina

were going to split up. In fact, they looked happier than ever. *It's enough to make a person nauseous, watching them carry on the way they do.* Bruce acted as though Regina were some kind of goddess or something.

"I'd be delighted to help you guys, Winston," Jessica said impulsively, her blue-green eyes flashing defiantly at Lila. "After all, it's silly to spend all my time in the library."

"A brilliant conclusion!" Winston declared, swallowing the last bite of cake. "Now for dessert, we have a tasty hamburger," he explained to Lila, picking his burger up with a flourish. "What kind of booth would you like to take charge of?" he asked Jessica.

"I don't know yet," Jessica said grimly, watching Bruce and Regina leave the cafeteria with their arms locked around each other.

Lila followed her gaze and turned to Winston, a malicious smile playing about her lips. "Maybe Jess should have a black magic booth!" She got up from the table and picked up her tray. "You may need some magic soon," she told Jessica. "Nothing else seems to be working!"

"What's she talking about?" Winston asked, staring after Lila as she walked away.

"Nothing," Jessica said grimly, leaning back in her chair. *Lila hasn't won the bet yet*, she told herself, chewing idly on the end of her straw. *And if she thinks I'm going to give in without a struggle, she's got another think coming!*

I wonder if I've got the time wrong, Elizabeth thought, pressing the Morrows' doorbell for the third time. *I could have sworn Mrs. Morrow said four o'clock.*

She could hear the bell echoing inside the Morrows' magnificent home, but still no one answered. "Oh, well," Elizabeth said softly, turning down the walk. "Maybe she was called away suddenly and couldn't get in touch with me."

"Elizabeth?" she heard a voice call. Spinning around, Elizabeth saw Regina's mother standing in the doorway.

"I'm sorry," Elizabeth said, hurrying up the front walk again. "I thought you weren't home."

Mrs. Morrow shook her head, her dark hair tumbling, uncombed, around her shoulders. "I was sleeping," she said flatly. "I haven't been feeling well, so I asked all the servants to leave. Come in, please," she added. "I'll put a kettle on and make us some tea."

Elizabeth looked at Mrs. Morrow with concern. "Are you feeling all right?" she asked anxiously, noticing the blue circles under Mrs. Morrow's eyes and the pained expression on her face.

"I'm all right," Mrs. Morrow replied, leading

Elizabeth through the plant-filled foyer to the sunny breakfast room. "I think some tea may help," she added, looking vaguely around as if she didn't know where she was.

"Please, Mrs. Morrow, sit down," Elizabeth urged. "I'll make tea."

To her surprise, Mrs. Morrow obeyed, sinking into the nearest chair and putting her face in her hands. "I'm sorry," she said weakly. "I should have called and canceled our appointment. But I completely forgot about the carnival."

Elizabeth went into the kitchen and put a kettle of water on the stove. Mrs. Morrow's appearance had really disturbed her. Her beautiful face had been tear-streaked, her fingers trembling as she kneaded her brow.

When Elizabeth came into the breakfast room carrying a tray with the teapot, cups, sugar, and milk, Mrs. Morrow looked up at her. "I'm sorry, Elizabeth. I hate letting anyone see me this way," she said softly. "But I get these terrible headaches."

"How often do the headaches come?" Elizabeth asked gently, pouring Mrs. Morrow a cup of hot tea. "Regina never said a word about them."

Mrs Morrow looked horrified. "You mustn't tell Regina," she said anxiously. "Promise me you won't tell her, Elizabeth."

Elizabeth sat down across from Mrs. Morrow.

60

"Of course not," she said softly. "If you don't want me to, I won't say a word to anyone. Have you seen a doctor?"

Mrs. Morrow nodded as she took a tiny sip of tea. "Thank you, dear," she said, setting the cup down again. "It's delicious. Yes," she added with a bitter laugh. "I've seen a doctor. About a dozen of them, in fact. And they all say the same thing. There's nothing wrong with me."

"I don't understand—" Elizabeth began.

Mrs. Morrow cut her off. "It's Regina," she said quietly. "I haven't felt the same since Regina was born. You see, Elizabeth, her deafness is my fault." And, taking a deep breath, she told Elizabeth the whole story, right up to the previous night and Regina's shocking outburst.

"Oh, dear," Elizabeth said, leaning back in her seat. "So Regina positively refuses to go to Switzerland?"

Mrs. Morrow nodded helplessly. "Elizabeth, do you think you could try to change her mind?" she cried. "I know how much Regina admires you."

Elizabeth bit her lip. What should she say? On the one hand, she believed Regina was making a mistake. From what Mrs. Morrow had told her, it didn't sound as though Regina had mentioned Bruce to her parents when she told them she couldn't leave Sweet Valley. But Elizabeth was convinced Bruce had a great deal to do with Regina's decision.

And try as she might to give Bruce the benefit of the doubt, Elizabeth still didn't trust him. How could Regina throw away so much for his sake? Even though Elizabeth would never betray her friend by telling her mother about Bruce, Elizabeth felt she owed it to Regina to intervene.

On the other hand, Elizabeth hated to interfere. This was a big decision, and it seemed like one that only Regina could make.

"I don't know what I can do," Elizabeth said carefully, not wanting to upset Mrs. Morrow further. "But if Regina comes to me for advice, I'll certainly do what I can to persuade her to go ahead with the operations."

"Oh, Elizabeth, thank you," Mrs. Morrow said gratefully. "We're going to do our best to change her mind," she added. "There's a boy in San Francisco who was successfully treated by Dr. Friederich last year, and we've invited him to come down this weekend to meet Regina. Maybe *he* can convince her."

"I hope so," Elizabeth said slowly. Privately, she had her doubts. Regina had fallen in love for the first time, and she'd fallen pretty hard. Elizabeth didn't think anything short of a miracle would convince Regina to leave Bruce now—however much she had to give up to stay.

Seven

"Eight days till that stupid carnival," Jessica grumbled, stretching her long legs in front of her on the lawn. It was Friday afternoon, and Jessica was sitting on the grassy slope in front of Sweet Valley High, waiting for her friend Cara Walker to emerge. Cara had said one of the shops in town had a swimsuit sale on, and Jessica had agreed to go with her to see what they had.

I wish she'd hurry up, Jessica thought grumpily. Sweet Valley High wasn't her favorite place to spend a sunny late afternoon—particularly on a Friday!

"Hi, Jess," a friendly voice called. "What are you doing here?"

"Oh, hi, Ken," Jessica said, shading her eyes

and squinting up at Ken Matthews. "I'm waiting for Cara," she said irritably. "If she's not out here in another minute, I'm going to leave."

Ken sighed, plopping down beside her on the grass. "Sounds like your mood's about as good as mine right now," he muttered, picking a blade of grass.

"Why? What's wrong with you?" Jessica asked, more out of habit than real interest. Right then Jessica couldn't care less why he was in a bad mood. All she could think about was her bet with Lila.

"It's Bruce Patman," Ken said moodily, tearing the blade of grass into little bits. "It figures he'd suddenly decide he wants to run for president of the centennial committee. The election's only a week away, and out of the blue he decides he's going to run against me!"

"No one will vote for Bruce," Jessica said automatically. "I'm sure you'll win anyway, Ken."

Ken shook his head. "I doubt it. You know the Patmans. They take things like this seriously! They'll probably hire him a campaign manager and buy him television time so he can advertise!"

Jessica couldn't believe anyone cared that much about being president of the student centennial committee, but it seemed rude to say so to Ken.

"Wait and see," she said instead, wishing Ken

would go away so she could scheme in peace. "I'll bet you still win."

Ken sighed. "I don't think so, Jess. Besides," he pointed out, "Bruce is much more popular now that he's going out with Regina. You should hear the way people talk about him! They act like he's undergone some sort of overnight transformation. He's bound to win now," he concluded bitterly. "And I'm sure he doesn't really even want to be president. He probably just threw his name in for the hell of it."

Jessica stared at Ken, her mind racing. He had just given her a wonderful idea! Ken thought Bruce was much more popular since he'd met Regina. What if Jessica could convince Regina that was the only reason he'd gotten involved with her? If she could make it seem as if this election really mattered to Bruce—one his family insisted he win—and that he'd planned to run even before he met Regina . . .

It just might work, Jessica thought, jumping to her feet. It was a long shot, but she was getting desperate. "I just remembered something," she told Ken, grabbing her jacket. "I have to meet Liz at home."

"What about Cara?" Ken asked, watching Jessica bound for the bus stop.

"Tell her I just remembered an urgent meeting!" Jessica called. *I think it's about time*, she thought, *that I really do get involved with the carni-*

val committee. It's the best way I can think of to spend some time alone with Regina.

And after all, she thought, searching through her bag for the bus fare, *it's such a worthwhile cause!*

"It looks like our committee is shrinking," Winston pointed out, shaking the water from his hair like a wet puppy.

Elizabeth, Todd, Olivia, and Winston were in the Wakefield backyard, surrounded by piles of paper.

"Winston," Elizabeth said, laughing, "you're getting our notes all wet."

"How could I resist your swimming pool on a day like this?" Winston demanded, looking injured.

"Where's Ken?" Todd asked. "We really *are* dwindling," he added.

"He said he'd try to make it later," Olivia told them. "I think he's trying to come up with a new campaign strategy, now that he has a candidate to compete with."

"I don't know how we can stand all the excitement," Winston said. "Political intrigue comes at last to Sweet Valley High."

"What do you think Bruce's chances are?" Todd asked curiously. "I wouldn't have thought he'd have much of a shot against Ken."

"Me either," Elizabeth agreed. "Ken seems the perfect candidate to me."

Olivia looked thoughtful. "I'm not sure. I know what you two think of Bruce," she said, looking at Elizabeth and Todd, "but he really does seem to have changed since he met Regina. I think he'd do a good job."

Elizabeth sighed. She had seen the way he treated Jessica, and she couldn't believe he could change so quickly. And since her talk with Regina's mother, she liked him even less. *I bet Bruce couldn't care less even if he knows why Regina isn't going to Switzerland*, she thought angrily.

"I don't know, Liv," Todd said mildly. "Regina's a terrific girl, and I'm sure Bruce has been softened just by being around her. But—"

"Once a jerk, always a jerk," Winston filled in.

Olivia laughed. "I don't blame you guys for being skeptical," she told them. "But if I were you, I'd give Bruce a chance. People *can* change," she pointed out.

Todd grinned. "Maybe you're right, Olivia," he said. "If anyone could turn a toad into a prince, it would be Regina."

Elizabeth sighed. "I hate to change the subject," she told them, "but if we're going to have a carnival a week from tomorrow, we'd better get to work."

"Hey," Winston interrupted, "look who's here!"

Jessica flung herself down at the table and wiped her brow dramatically. "Liz," she cried. "Am I too late?"

"It depends." Elizabeth giggled. "Too late for what?"

"I've got a brilliant idea for the carnival," Jessica gasped.

"In that case," Todd said and grinned, "you're just in time. What's your idea, Jess?"

"Well," Jessica began, still out of breath, "what about a mother-daughter fashion show? We would set it up in one corner of the tent or get a smaller tent for it, and charge people a dollar for tickets."

Elizabeth frowned thoughtfully. "Not bad," she mused. "Do you think Mom would do it?"

Jessica burst out laughing. "Not *me*, Liz," she said, giggling. "And you think *I'm* vain," she added.

Elizabeth blushed. "Well, who did you have in mind?" she asked her twin.

"Regina and her mother, of course," Jessica replied. "It's perfect. Regina has appeared in *Ingenue* already, and her mother used to be a model in New York."

"It's a great idea, Jess," Elizabeth said carefully, "but I'm not sure Mrs. Morrow would agree to do it."

"Oh, I can convince her," Jessica said airily.

"I don't know." Elizabeth sighed. Much as she

loved her twin, she occasionally doubted Jessica's tact. And she knew how delicate things were between Regina and her mother right then. Sending Jessica over to the Morrow household would hardly be helpful.

"Well, I'm going to try," Jessica insisted. "Honestly, Liz. How do you expect to organize a big event like this unless you're willing to take some chances?"

"OK, OK," Elizabeth said. "Go ahead, Jess. Do your worst." *Mother-and-daughter modeling show*, she wrote in her notebook, putting a big question mark beside the entry.

I'm sure Regina and Mrs. Morrow can refuse Jessica better than I can, she thought, lifting her pencil and turning to Todd. "I just hope setting Jessica loose on them won't be too terribly unfair!"

"Thanks for the ride," Regina said softly, kissing Bruce on the cheek. "What time are you coming by tonight?"

"How about seven-thirty?" Bruce asked her, getting out of the car to open the door on her side.

"Seven-thirty," Regina said, leaning forward to kiss his lips, "is perfect. I'll see you then."

She watched as he drove around the circular driveway and turned down the road to the Patman estate, waving after him. Then she walked slowly to the front door. The last few days had been very awkward around the Morrow household, and Regina could feel her steps slowing as she wondered what she would find inside.

Regina had stuck to her decision, and she could tell how worried and upset by it her parents were. Her mother, in particular, didn't seem herself. But whenever Regina asked her what was wrong she just looked sad. Even Nicholas had been unusually withdrawn.

"Regina!" Nicholas called now, hurrying forward to meet her. "Come out to the backyard for a minute. There's someone here I want you to meet."

Her curiosity rising, Regina followed her older brother out to the expansive backyard shaded by thick trees. A boy was lying in the hammock, a book in his hand. He clambered to his feet when he saw Regina.

"This is Donald Essex," her brother told her. "He's come down from San Francisco to spend the weekend with us."

"Hello," Regina said shyly, putting out her hand.

Donald looked about the same age as Nicholas. He had thick, sandy hair and green eyes.

To her surprise, he greeted her in sign language, the international language of the deaf.

"Are you deaf, too?" she asked him, puzzled.

Donald laughed. "I was," he told her. Something about his frank, easy manner made Regina warm to him at once. "But I'm not anymore. Remember the boy your parents told you was cured by Dr. Friederich last year?"

Regina stared at him. "You're the one?" she asked, astounded. "What are you doing here?"

"Your parents invited me down for the weekend." Donald grinned. "I guess I'm a surprise—a good one, I hope."

"I'll leave you two to get better acquainted," Nicholas said cheerfully. "Watch out for him, though, Regina. He plays a mean game of Frisbee."

Regina's heart melted as she watched her brother stroll across the lawn. How wonderful her family was! They had invited Donald down hoping he could change her mind. *If only there was some way I could convince them that I'm really happier as I am*, she thought regretfully. *If they knew that, maybe they'd stop worrying.*

"How about a game of Frisbee?" Donald asked her.

"No, thanks," Regina said, smiling. "From what Nicholas just said, I don't think I'd have much of a chance."

"Well, how about a walk, then? This area is beautiful."

"Sure," Regina said, falling in step beside him. She couldn't help staring at Donald. How did it feel to be able to hear again after being deaf? she wondered.

Within minutes she and Donald were talking as if they'd known each other for years. Like Regina, Donald had spent a good part of his childhood in special schools. He, too, had felt isolated and he had worked incredibly hard to win acceptance at a public high school in San Francisco. "I even tried out for the swim team," he told her, laughing. "And I did pretty well on it, too."

Regina couldn't believe it when she glanced down at her watch and saw it was almost six o'clock. "I'm sorry," she told Donald, "but we'd better turn back. I have to grab a bite to eat and take a quick shower. I have a date tonight," she added.

Donald smiled. "We'll have more time to talk tomorrow," he told her. "Don't worry, Regina," he added. "I'm not going to pressure you. That isn't why I came down here. I may not understand what you're going through, but I know it's a rough decision to make. You know," he added, "some people are more afraid of what comes *after* the treatments than the treatments themselves. They've gotten used to being deaf. Or, in some cases, they're afraid of the thought of hearing. They're afraid of what it would mean to be 'normal' all of a sudden."

Regina flushed deeply. "Donald, I'm not

afraid," she told him quietly. "If I had only myself to think of, I'd be on the first plane to Switzerland I could find." Her eyes filled with tears. How could everything be so confusing suddenly?

"We'll talk tomorrow," Donald said, squeezing her shoulder lightly.

Despite her love for her parents and her sympathy with their desire to do what was best for her, Regina was beginning to feel as if she were being pulled in two directions at once. And the tension was becoming unbearable. *It's got to get easier around here*, she thought miserably. *Sooner or later they'll forget all about Switzerland, and life will go back to normal—won't it?*

Eight

"Liz, what are you doing in there? I need to use the phone!" Jessica wailed, pounding on her sister's closed door with both fists.

"I'm working on the carnival," Elizabeth called, her voice muffled. "Why don't you use the extension in your room?"

"I can't find it," Jessica replied, opening the door and cheerfully barging in. "It's buried somewhere."

"I bet it is," Elizabeth said, laughing. "Come on, Jess—can't you see I'm busy?"

"Don't worry, Liz," Jessica said, picking up the phone and beginning to dial. "It's carnival business, anyway."

"As long as you're quick," Elizabeth mumbled, distracted.

But Jessica got Elizabeth's attention when she said into the phone, "Hello, is Regina there?" Elizabeth shot her a look. Jessica's cheeks turned bright red. "Oh, how thoughtless of me, Mrs. Morrow," she said quickly. "Of course she can't."

Elizabeth shook her head in disbelief. *Only my twin*, she thought, *would ask to speak to a deaf girl on the phone. It just figures*.

"Oh, dear. Well, actually, Mrs. Morrow, I wanted to speak to you as well as Regina. It's Jessica Wakefield calling."

"Of course," Mrs. Morrow said over the phone. "Can I give Regina a message? She's outside right now with a friend of ours."

"Well, I was wondering if I could drop by in about a half hour," Jessica said. "I wanted to talk to both of you about the carnival."

"I don't see why not," Mrs. Morrow said. "We're all going out later this afternoon, but if you come by fairly soon, you should catch us. I'll let Regina know you're coming."

"And to think I worried about your putting your foot in your mouth," Elizabeth said wryly when Jessica had replaced the receiver.

"I forgot about it for a minute, that's all," Jessica said defensively. "Actually, it's a compliment to Regina. She acts so much like the rest of us that I forgot she wouldn't be able to hear me on the phone."

Elizabeth laughed. "Jess, if you can convince the Morrows to do this modeling show, I'll clean your room," she promised.

"Don't worry," Jessica told her, glancing quickly in the mirror and charging out of the room. Jessica didn't care whether Regina modeled at the carnival or not. What mattered was making sure Regina understood that Bruce had been using her all along. It was going to take some careful planning to carry this off, but Jessica hadn't felt this good in days. *If anyone can botch up a perfect relationship*, she thought, grinning, *it's me. And right now, the stakes are high enough to make sure I give this mission all I've got!*

Regina was sitting outside on a deck chair, trying to read while Nicholas and Donald played badminton. It was a gorgeous day—too gorgeous, in fact, to concentrate on the book she was reading. She sighed, laying it face down on the table beside her. The sun caught her wrist as she moved, flashing brilliant colors through the small diamond on the bracelet Bruce had given her the previous night.

Every time Regina looked at the bracelet her face flushed. She remembered Bruce's expression as he had fumbled with the clasp, trying to put it on her wrist. "Bruce, this must have cost a fortune," she had whispered.

Bruce shook his head, his expression serious.

"Sometimes I don't think you realize how I feel about you, Regina," he had murmured. He kissed her softly then, his lips warm and gentle.

Regina had just stared at him, absolutely speechless. After Bruce had taken her home, she lay awake in bed and realized that the confusion she had been feeling that week was misguided. "This is where I belong," she whispered, turning over and pushing her face into the pillow. "As long as Bruce is here, I'm not going anywhere!"

Mrs. Morrow came out to the patio and tapped Regina on the shoulder. "Jessica Wakefield is here."

"Hi, Jess!" Regina said, sitting up and swinging her legs over the side of the chair.

"Can I get you something cold to drink?" Mrs. Morrow asked. "How about some iced tea?"

"No, thanks," Jessica said brightly. "I'm not going to stay long. I just came to ask you both if you'd be willing to do a special booth at the carnival. Liz is kind of worried," she added on impulse. "She's afraid things won't get organized in time."

"Oh, dear," Mrs. Morrow said, sitting down on a deck chair. "I'm afraid that may be my fault. What can we do to help?"

"Well," Jessica said, "how would you feel about a mother-daughter fashion show? Olivia Davidson says we can get a special tent from her uncle that we could set up near the big one. And

I can arrange to get some clothes for you two from Lisette's."

Regina looked quickly at her mother. She was sure she'd refuse. Her mother hated being reminded of her former career, and Regina was certain she'd never consent to modeling clothes in front of so many people.

"What do you think, Regina?" her mother asked slowly.

Regina stared at her. "Do you mean you'd actually do it?" she asked.

Mrs. Morrow shrugged. "Why not?" she replied. "It sounds like fun. Besides," she added, looking directly at Regina, "it's for a very good cause."

Jessica smiled. "Elizabeth will be so happy," she told them. "I can guarantee you'll draw a big crowd!"

Mrs. Morrow stood up, looking past Jessica out into the backyard. "Where have the boys gone?" she asked Regina. "I wanted to see if they could use some iced tea."

"I don't know," Regina told her. "They were playing badminton about ten minutes ago. Maybe they're out front."

"I'll leave you two, then, and see if I can find them," Mrs. Morrow said.

"Regina," Jessica exclaimed, leaning forward and staring at her wrist. "Where in the world did you get that gorgeous bracelet?"

Regina flushed. "Bruce gave it to me last night," she said softly.

Good Lord, Jessica thought. *Bruce has really gone completely mad. He'll probably thank me one day for saving his bank account.*

"You're really crazy about Bruce, aren't you?" Jessica asked innocently.

Regina nodded. "He's so wonderful, Jess," she said. "I don't think I've ever been so happy."

Jessica shook her head, her blond hair tumbling over her tanned shoulders. "It just goes to show," she murmured. "You should never listen to rumors."

"Rumors?" Regina asked, her face wrinkling in confusion. "What rumors?"

Jessica shrugged. "Don't give it another thought," she said. "People can be so stupid, Regina. The minute they see a really happy couple—like you and Bruce—they get jealous and start suggesting the most idiotic things."

Regina looked completely baffled. "What have people been saying about Bruce and me?" she demanded.

Jessica waved her hand. "Forget I even brought it up," she insisted. "They're all complete fools. It's obvious you and Bruce are perfect for each other."

Regina pleated the material of her shorts anxiously, her blue eyes darkening. "Really, Jess," she said firmly. "I want to know."

Jessica sighed. "All right," she yielded. "But remember, Regina, it's all complete nonsense."

Regina nodded, staring dumbly at Jessica as she spoke.

"It all has to do with this ridiculous election," Jessica began. "I'm sure Bruce told you all about it ages ago."

"What election?" Regina demanded.

Jessica's brow wrinkled with surprise. "Oh, didn't he tell you about it? Hmmm," she murmured. "That's strange."

"Jessica, what are you talking about?" Regina cried.

Jessica shook her head. "I'm sure it doesn't mean a thing," she said doubtfully. "You see, Bruce is running against Ken Matthews for president of the Sweet Valley Centennial Student Committee. *I* think it's a pretty silly position, but you know the Patmans. They care so much about being in charge of every last thing around here, I'm sure they pushed Bruce into it."

"But what does that have to do with me?" Regina asked, looking more confused than ever.

Jessica shrugged. "Probably not a thing," she assured her. "Regina, just forget I brought the whole thing up. It's so stupid."

Regina's face darkened. "Jessica, *please* tell me," she begged. "I can't stand having people say things about me behind my back."

"All right." Jessica sighed. "Ken Matthews is

really angry that Bruce is running against him. *He* says that Bruce wouldn't stand a chance of winning if it weren't for you. Since you two started going out, Bruce has gotten so much more popular. I guess you can sort of see Ken's point,'' Jessica concluded vaguely.

Regina stared at her. "I don't think I really understand," she said. "You mean people think Bruce has only been dating me so more people would vote for him in this election?''

Jessica nodded. "I told you it was absurd,'' she replied.

Regina laughed. "It sure is,'' she said, visibly relieved. "It's completely absurd.''

"Of course,'' Jessica said thoughtfully, toying with her lavaliere, "it *is* kind of strange that Bruce didn't mention the election to you. He probably just forgot,'' she said brightly.

"Probably,'' Regina said, her voice firmly suggesting that she'd heard enough. "I'm glad you came over, Jess. The fashion show sounds like it'll be a lot of fun.''

"Good,'' Jessica said, getting to her feet. "You two will be fabulous together. I'll get back to you later on with details,'' she added.

"Let me walk you to your car,'' Regina said, standing up as well.

Jessica wouldn't hear of it. "Stay right where you are and finish your book,'' she insisted. "I'll just walk around the side of the house.'' *And leave you alone to start wondering if there's a grain of truth in what I told you*, she added silently.

And Lila thought I needed black magic, Jessica thought, a tiny smile on her face as she hurried toward the Morrows' driveway.

"Damn!" Jessica muttered, turning the key in the ignition of the Fiat for the third time and waiting for the engine to start. Generally the car was reliable, but it seemed to be temperamental that day. Jessica was sitting in the Morrows' driveway, her pretty face screwed up with irritation. "I hate this car," she muttered, pumping the gas pedal with all her might.

"Don't flood the motor," a cheerful voice advised.

Jessica looked up with surprise. A tall, sandy-haired boy was standing beside her, resting his hands on the hood of the car. He smiled winningly, his green eyes shining.

Jessica blushed. "It doesn't seem to work," she said helplessly. "What should I do?"

"Get out," he said, laughing. "I'll see what I can do."

"My name is Jessica," she said, climbing out of the car. "Do you live around here?"

He laughed again, getting into the driver's seat. "My name is Donald Essex," he told her. "Nice to meet you, Jessica. And to answer your question—no," he said, starting the car on the first try. "I'm from San Francisco. I'm staying with the Morrows for the weekend." He got out of the car, and Jessica slid back into the driver's seat.

"Too bad you're not staying longer," Jessica said, flashing him her prettiest smile. "You're going to miss our carnival."

"What carnival?" Donald asked.

Jessica laughed. "If you decide to stick around for a while, give me a call and I'll tell you about it," she said. "Regina has my number."

"Wait a minute!" Donald cried. But Jessica, relying on a delicate sense of timing acquired through years of practice, put her foot on the gas pedal and roared around the driveway.

Not a bad morning, she thought, grinning. *I've convinced Regina and her mother to model at the carnival. I've met a mysterious out-of-towner with a fabulous smile.*

And above all, she reminded herself, *I've done what I could to start trouble between Bruce and Regina*. The rest, she figured, she'd have to leave up to the happy couple.

Nine

Regina woke up early Sunday morning. The whole house was still sleeping, and for a minute, before her mind had really cleared, she didn't know exactly what was wrong. She stretched languorously, and her gaze fell on the bracelet she had placed on the night table next to her bed. Then Regina remembered.

Everything Jessica had said the day before came flooding back to her, word for word. *It's ridiculous to distrust Bruce*, she reminded herself. *As soon as I see him again, everything will be all right. I'm only worried because I didn't see him last night.*

But Regina couldn't help feeling uneasy. She got up and dressed quickly, putting on a pair of white cotton jeans and a striped T-shirt. Crossing back to her night table, she fastened the bracelet around her wrist. Bruce was supposed to come by around noon. They were going on a picnic, and as soon as she talked to him about this silly election, she'd know nothing was wrong.

And nothing is wrong, she told herself. *Nothing at all.*

When she went downstairs, Donald was pouring himself a cup of coffee in the breakfast room. "You're up early," Regina said, surprised.

Donald laughed. "It's a carry-over from my year in Switzerland, I think," he told her. "I used to wake up before the sun rose there. Now I feel really lazy if I stay in bed after nine."

Regina took the coffee he offered her and sat down with him at the table, stirring milk and sugar into her cup.

Donald whistled softly. "Where'd you get that?" he asked her, brushing her bracelet with his finger.

Regina stared down at the table. "From a friend," she told him.

Donald smiled. "It must be a pretty special friend," he commented.

Regina smiled shyly at Donald. She liked him. Already he felt like an older brother to her, and she knew she could trust him. "It is," she admitted, taking a sip of her coffee. "A really special friend."

Regina got up to get some bread for toast. While she was popping the slices into the toaster, Donald asked her about Sweet Valley High and how she liked living in Southern California. While they ate, they exchanged memories of the transition from "special" to "normal" schools. Donald had one hilarious story after another about his high school in San Francisco, and once again Regina marveled at how comfortable she felt with him.

"This may be none of my business," Donald said awkwardly, leaning back in his chair, "but does this special friend have anything to do with your decision not to go to Switzerland?"

Regina flushed. She didn't know what to say. But Donald seemed to understand that it was hard for her to answer.

"Would you mind if I told you another story?" he continued.

"Go ahead." Regina smiled and took another sip of coffee.

He looked at her very seriously, and after a moment he began. "When I found out about Dr. Friederich's treatment I decided not to go ahead with it. That may surprise you, since I've been advocating your going ahead with the whole thing. But at the time I didn't want to leave San Francisco. You see, I'd just met a girl, and I couldn't bear the thought of leaving her."

Donald paused. "Do you want to hear the rest of this?"

"Yes," Regina said, her eyes steady on his. "Go ahead."

"Her name was Rosemary," Donald added. "She was a year older than I was and had already started college. But I saw her every weekend, and I knew if I moved to Switzerland I wouldn't see her at all. Not until Christmas, anyway. Well, I decided not to tell her about the treatments. I was afraid she'd tell me to go ahead with them. Eventually she *did* find out. But her reaction wasn't what I expected. She said she didn't want to see me anymore. She was furious that I hadn't trusted her enough to let her in on my decision. And that was that."

"So you went to Switzerland," Regina finished for him.

Donald nodded. "I wrote her several times. I was hoping she'd just staged the whole breakup so I'd go. But she wasn't that sort of girl. She meant what she said, and she stuck to it."

Regina sighed. She wished she could confide in Donald, but it didn't feel right to talk about Bruce behind his back. And though she was sorry about Donald and Rosemary, she couldn't help feeling that things were different with her and Bruce. Even if Bruce begged her to go, she couldn't bear to be without him for a whole year.

Unless, she thought uneasily, *what Jessica told me yesterday is true.*

"Regina," Donald said suddenly, "this procedure changed my whole life. I know I shouldn't interfere with your decision, but I know what you're going through, and I can't bear to see you make this kind of mistake! Promise me you'll think the whole thing through before you definitely say no."

"I promise," Regina said, and she meant it. Donald was right. This was a big decision she was making, and she owed it to everyone—especially herself—to give it serious consideration.

The first step, she thought, *is to have a long talk with Bruce.* Regina was sure Jessica had misunderstood. If Bruce was really running for president of the centennial committee, he would have told Regina about it.

Unless, she thought miserably, *there's some reason he doesn't want me to know.*

"Regina, is anything wrong?" Bruce asked, driving his car around the Morrows' driveway. "You've been awfully quiet all afternoon."

Regina sighed and pulled her long black hair off her neck with both hands. Bruce was right; she *had* been quiet. The picnic had been beautiful, but Regina couldn't relax. She wasn't very hungry, either. At one point she had steered the conversation to the subject of school and the carnival committee, giving Bruce a perfect chance to mention running for centennial president, but he hadn't responded. Even when she'd mentioned Ken Matthews, he hadn't taken the bait.

"Didn't you have a good time this afternoon?" he asked her now, parking his Porsche in front of the Morrows' mansion.

"I had a wonderful time, Bruce," Regina murmured. "It's just . . ."

"Just what?" Bruce urged, taking her hand and entwining her slender fingers with his own. "What is it, Regina? There's something bothering you. I can tell."

"Bruce," Regina began tentatively, "somebody told me something the other day about your running for president of the centennial committee. And I told them you weren't, since you hadn't mentioned it to me. You're *not* running, are you?"

Bruce thought for a minute. "Who told you that?" he asked at last.

"What difference does that make?" Regina cried, her face reddening. So maybe it *was* true!

"I don't really want to talk about it," Bruce said, shrugging. *It was supposed to be a surprise for Regina when I won*, he thought. *I could just kill whoever told her*.

"Why not?" Regina demanded. "And why didn't you mention it to me to begin with?"

"I just don't want to talk about it," Bruce said firmly. He felt a little uneasy about the whole thing. He had a feeling Ken Matthews was going to win, and he didn't want Regina to feel terrible if things worked out that way. No, better to brush the whole thing off now, keep it from turning into a big deal.

But Regina's eyes were darkening with anger as Bruce stared at the cover on his steering wheel. *I never would have believed this in a million years*, she thought furiously, *but Jessica must be right. Why else would Bruce act like such a jerk when I asked him a simple question? He's obviously got something to hide. And what he's hiding is the fact that he's only been hanging around with me until he wins that stupid election. And then I suppose he's just going to dump me—like all the others*, she thought bitterly. *I'm just like any other girl to him, and I was a fool to think that I really mattered.*

"Hey, what's wrong?" Bruce said suddenly. "Don't tell me *that's* what's been bothering you all afternoon."

Regina flinched. *He thinks I'm an idiot*, she thought furiously. *He thinks I can't figure out what's going on!* "Would you mind telling me once and for all what's going on with that election?" she demanded icily.

Bruce stared at her, his face a complete blank. "What in the world are you so angry about?" he demanded. "It has nothing to do with you!"

Regina burst into tears. *That's it*, she thought, fumbling with the clasp on her bracelet. *I can't believe I ever trusted him for a single minute.* "Bruce Patman," she sputtered, throwing the bracelet on the seat between them, "why don't you just take your expensive presents and your stupid promises and get out of here?"

"Wait a minute!" Bruce exploded. "What in the world is going on here? All I said—"

"And you can take your stupid necklace, too," Regina cried, unfastening the ruby pendant and hurling it at him. "Don't think I'm as helpless as I seem," she sobbed. "I'm wise to you, and so is everybody else!"

"I don't know what you're talking about," Bruce said angrily, his face darkening. "And apparently you don't want to tell me, either. You'd rather just throw things at me and tell me how horrible I've been. Regina, I don't think you're wise to anything. You've gone completely off the deep end. Can't you at least tell me what's—"

"If I've gone off the deep end," Regina said coldly, pulling the door handle with trembling fingers, "I won't force you to put up with my company for another minute. I never want to see you again as long as I live!" she shouted, pushing the door open and leaping out. She shot him an icy glare.

Bruce had been pushed too far to remain calm

any longer. "If that's what you want, that's what you're going to get," he said bitterly, turning the key in the ignition. "I can't believe I thought you were different," he added accusingly. "I thought you were really special. And now it turns out you're just as messed up as every other girl in this town!" He gunned the motor and drove around the circular driveway, tires squealing.

I'm sure he thought I was special, Regina thought angrily, tears streaming down her face. *Too special to figure out that he was only putting up with me so more people would vote for him in his stupid election. Well, I'm tired of being special. And I think it's time I did something so no one can ever accuse me of being "special" again.*

Dragging her feet, Regina walked up the flagstone path to the Morrows' front door. Now that Bruce was gone, there was no reason not to do the sensible thing and go ahead with Dr. Friederich's treatments.

And the sooner I go the better, Regina thought miserably. *Because the sooner I'm half a globe away from Sweet Valley, the sooner I'll forget Bruce.*

And under the circumstances, she told herself, forgetting Bruce Patman was the smartest thing she could possibly do.

"Are you sure Mrs. Morrow said to come over now?" Todd asked Elizabeth. "It doesn't look like anyone's at home."

Elizabeth looked at her watch. "She said five o'clock," she answered. "Oh, Todd, I'm afraid we'll never get this carnival together! Everything seems to be going wrong!"

"Don't worry," Todd said reassuringly. "We'll be all right. Things are bound to fall into place."

"I hope so," Elizabeth said anxiously, pressing the doorbell.

To her surprise, the door opened right away. An attractive, green-eyed boy grinned out at her, running his hand through his sandy hair. "You again!" he said, laughing. He opened the door wider to let Elizabeth and Todd come inside.

Elizabeth glanced at Todd and turned purposefully to the boy. "We've come to see Mrs. Morrow," she said firmly. "Are any of the Morrows here?"

"They've gone out for a little while. Emergency family business," he told her. Something about his expression made Elizabeth feel strange. *He looks as if he's seen me before*, she thought. *But I don't know who he is!*

"You haven't told me who your friend is," Donald added, staring past Elizabeth at Todd.

"My name is Todd," Todd told him, not sounding very happy.

"Donald Essex," the boy said, extending his hand. "I don't think we need to introduce ourselves, do we?" he said, turning back to Elizabeth. "You know, I've been thinking about your

93

carnival, and it sounds pretty interesting. Do I still have an invitation for—when did you say it was?"

"I didn't," Elizabeth said, staring at him. What was going on here? she wondered. One thing was certain—Todd didn't like it very much. He was glowering the whole time that Donald Essex was speaking.

"That's right," Donald said, laughing. "You didn't. Well, when is it?" he asked. "I wouldn't mind helping out."

Elizabeth cleared her throat. "I think you must be making some kind of mistake," she began doubtfully.

Donald looked from Elizabeth to Todd and seemed to come to a quick conclusion. "Never mind," he said cheerfully. "I guess I *did* make a mistake," he added, winking at Elizabeth. "Can I take a message for Mrs. Morrow?"

"No, thanks," Elizabeth told him. "We'll call her later."

"What was that all about?" Todd demanded, following Elizabeth down the walk. "He seemed pretty friendly, Liz. Where'd you meet him?"

Elizabeth flushed. "I never met him before in my life."

"Sure didn't look that way, did it?" Todd asked mildly, opening the car door and sliding behind the driver's seat.

"Come on, Todd," Elizabeth said lightly,

getting into the car and fastening her seat belt. "I don't even *know* that guy!"

"Well, he sure seems to know *you*," Todd said moodily.

"I'm sure there's a perfectly logical—" Elizabeth began, but Todd cut her off midsentence.

"I'm sure there is, too," he said. "But right now I'd just prefer to drop the whole thing."

Elizabeth bit her lip. How had everything turned into such a mess all of a sudden? The carnival was only six days away, and Mrs. Morrow couldn't even keep an appointment to help plan it. Even worse, Todd was angry with her now.

This is going to be some week, Elizabeth thought, putting her head in her hands. *It hasn't even started yet, and already I wish it were over!*

Ten

Elizabeth turned the dial on her locker and rummaged grumpily through the books she kept stacked neatly inside. It was Monday morning, and the world looked considerably less cheerful than it had on Friday afternoon. "Something is wrong with my favorite twin," Jessica had said earlier that morning as she cheerfully buttered a piece of toast. Elizabeth hadn't even bothered to answer. She felt completely out of sorts, and Jessica's infamous grin didn't do much to lift her spirits.

For one thing, Elizabeth hadn't gotten much sleep the night before. She'd been up well past midnight trying to finalize plans for the carnival, and when she'd finally gotten into bed, all she could think about was the unhappy expression on Todd's face when he had dropped her off at home after their visit to the Morrows'.

He hadn't kissed her goodbye, and he hadn't called her later, the way he always did. Even worse, he wasn't waiting for her in the parking lot that morning. And she'd gotten to school early just to look for him.

"Liz," a voice said shyly at her shoulder now. "Can I talk to you for a few minutes? I was hoping I'd find you alone."

Elizabeth turned, and the frown faded from her face. "Of course, Regina," she said. "Why don't we go to the *Oracle* office and sit down?" she added on impulse. Something in Regina's expression suggested she wanted to have a long talk.

"It's nice in here," Regina commented several minutes later, looking around at the typewriters and piles of paper lining the small room.

Elizabeth giggled. "It's serviceable, anyway," she said, offering Regina a chair. "Jessica thinks it's absolutely hideous."

Regina looks different today, Elizabeth thought, sneaking a glance at her as she sat down. *She looks a lot older than she did when I saw her last. More serious—as if something big has happened.*

"Liz," Regina began, "I'm afraid I won't be able to be in the fashion show this Saturday after all. Don't worry," she added hastily, seeing the expression on Elizabeth's face. "My mother's going to come up with something to take its place. She feels bad enough as it is. Things have been so crazy around our house that she hasn't been much help to you."

"That's OK, Regina," Elizabeth assured her. "I'm just sorry you won't be able to do it. Is anything wrong?"

Regina flushed. "I'm leaving for Switzerland Friday morning," she said quietly. "My mother told me about the talk she had with you, Liz. I know you know all about the treatments. And I wanted to thank you for keeping quiet about it. It's important to me that no one find out before I go."

Elizabeth took Regina's hand, squeezing it warmly. "I'm so happy for you," she said, her voice breaking with emotion. "I'm going to miss you, Regina, but it'll be exciting when you come back!"

Regina sighed. "They're not one hundred percent certain that they can completely restore my hearing," she warned Elizabeth. "And I'll have to go through a lot of tests, but the way I see it, it's certainly worth a chance. I'm going to miss you, too, Liz," she added impulsively. "You've been such a wonderful friend."

Elizabeth fiddled with a piece of paper, her gaze turning thoughtful. "How does Bruce feel about your leaving?"

Regina flushed, tears welling up in her eyes. "He doesn't know," she said at last, looking away. "We haven't really spoken since I made up my mind."

"Is everything all right?" Elizabeth asked sympathetically.

Regina shook her head, tears spilling down her cheeks. "Oh, Liz," she gasped. "I've been such a fool!" Her voice choked with tears, Regina told Elizabeth the entire story, omitting only Jessica's role as informer.

"That's amazing," Elizabeth said when she had finished. "God, sometimes I could just kill Bruce Patman!"

"Do you think I'm really gullible?" Regina whispered, reaching for her handkerchief.

"No, I don't," Elizabeth said, giving her a hug. "But now that you've told me this, I'll admit I was never crazy about you and Bruce. You're far too good for him. And I think you're doing the right thing about Switzerland. The treatments may not be guaranteed, but you'd never forgive yourself if you didn't give them a chance."

"You're right, Liz," Regina said, wiping her eyes and smiling. "Thank you so much for everything."

Elizabeth sighed, closing the door to the *Oracle* office behind them as they left the room. *So*, she thought to herself, *I guess I was right about Bruce after all*.

But this was one time when Elizabeth would have preferred to be wrong.

"Hello, Elizabeth," Mr. Collins said cheerfully, looking up from his desk as she entered his room at lunchtime. "Is something keeping you from Sweet Valley High's *haute cuisine*, or did you come to talk business?"

Elizabeth laughed. "Both, I guess," she said slowly, sliding into a desk in the front row. Elizabeth didn't feel particularly hungry. Todd hadn't spoken to her all morning. It was obvious that he was trying to avoid her.

"How's the carnival coming?" Mr. Collins asked, putting his hands behind his head and leaning back in his chair.

"Fine, I think," Elizabeth told him. "We've had a few last-minute changes."

"Like Regina Morrow?" Mr. Collins asked.

"You know about that?" Elizabeth demanded, surprised.

Mr. Collins nodded. "I've got my fingers crossed for her," he said warmly. "It takes a lot of courage for her to uproot herself again now that she's finally settled in and made some real friends."

"And some *not* so real friends," Elizabeth mumbled.

Mr. Collins got up from his desk and walked over to the window, turning around to give

Elizabeth a penetrating look. "You don't think much of Bruce Patman, do you?" he asked.

Elizabeth shook her head. "I don't like the way he treats girls," she said.

Mr. Collins sat on the edge of his desk, swinging his legs. "Well, you're entitled to your opinion," he told her. "And if I know you, Liz, it's an opinion based on good judgment. But you know," he added slowly, "people *do* change. No one is all good or all bad. That only happens in old movies."

Elizabeth shook her head. "I'm sure you're right," she answered. "But I get so angry when I think of the way Bruce treated Regina!"

Mr. Collins laughed. "You're a good friend, that's why," he said. "And I don't blame you for being angry. But you may not have all the facts yet," he warned her.

Elizabeth's brow wrinkled. "But Regina said—"

"I know," Mr. Collins said, smiling. "But I also know how easy it is for two people to have a misunderstanding."

Like Todd and me, Elizabeth thought.

"All I'm saying," he added gently, "is to try to keep an open mind. It's what you're known for around here!" he teased.

Elizabeth burst out laughing. "I'll try my best, Mr. Collins," she promised. "I just hope you'll keep an open mind while I show you the final plans for the carnival!"

*　　*　　*

"Jessica," Elizabeth complained, "you're standing in my light. I've got to get this list to Mrs. Morrow as soon as I can."

"Do you realize," Jessica pointed out, "that you've turned into a real bore ever since this carnival business got started?"

The twins were out by the pool in the Wakefields' backyard, soaking up the last rays of afternoon sun. "Sorry, Jess," Elizabeth said dryly. "If you just let me get this finished, I promise I'll be my usual entertaining self."

Jessica flung herself down on a deck chair. "You sound pretty grumpy, Liz," she commented a moment later. "Are you sure the carnival's the only thing on your mind?"

"Absolutely," Elizabeth snapped. The last thing in the world she wanted to do was tell Jessica that Todd had been avoiding her. That would be one sure way of making it a bigger deal than it was already.

"My, aren't we touchy today," Jessica said indignantly, adjusting the strings on her new white bikini top.

"I thought you had to work on your term paper," Elizabeth said, staring at her twin, who was now lolling comfortably on the lounge chair with her eyes closed.

"Oh, yeah," Jessica said, opening one eye.

"You're right. I guess I'd better go to the library after dinner."

Elizabeth shook her head. "How you've made it through school this far is beyond me!"

"I do what I can," Jessica said sweetly.

Elizabeth frowned at the sheaf of papers in her hand. It wasn't any fun planning the carnival without Todd! She remembered what Mr. Collins had said to her during lunch and straightened her shoulders purposefully. *If Todd doesn't call tonight, I'm going to call him and straighten this whole mess out*, she vowed silently.

"By the way," Jessica murmured, both eyes closed, "you didn't see Bruce and Regina today, did you?"

"Not together," Elizabeth said, surprised. "I thought you'd know by now, Jess. You must be working too hard on that term paper of yours to keep up with local gossip," she added wryly.

"What gossip?" Jessica demanded, off the lounge chair and on her feet in a flash.

Elizabeth laughed. "That's the most life I've seen in you in weeks," she commented. "Bruce and Regina had a big fight," she added. "I don't think they'll be seeing much of each other anymore."

"Thank God," Jessica breathed, hugging herself delightedly.

Elizabeth looked at her twin strangely. "Breakups aren't usually a cause for celebration, are they?"

Jessica flushed. "I'm just relieved for Regina, that's all," she said defensively. "Bruce isn't good enough for her. She deserves someone really nice, and Bruce isn't."

Elizabeth laughed. "I must admit I agree with you there."

"What was their fight about?"

Elizabeth sighed. "You'll think it's really stupid."

"I won't," Jessica promised innocently.

"Well, Regina thinks Bruce was using her to get more votes for the presidency of the centennial committee. Probably not what you expected."

Jessica raised her eyebrows. "Not at all," she demurred. "Well, whatever the reason, I'm glad for Regina. Hey," she added suddenly, her blue-green eyes narrowing, "she didn't mention anything to you about Donald Essex, did she?"

"Donald who?" Elizabeth asked, turning back to her notes.

"Donald Essex," Jessica said dreamily. "You should see him, Liz. He's absolutely gorgeous—about six feet tall, sandy blond hair, and the most amazing eyes."

Elizabeth dropped her notebook, her eyes widening. "You didn't by any chance meet this male god at the Morrows', did you?"

Jessica nodded.

"And did you invite him to the carnival?" Elizabeth went on, her voice rising.

Jessica shrugged. "How was I supposed to know Regina liked him instead of Bruce?"

"She doesn't, you jerk!" Elizabeth cried, leaping to her feet. "I've got to make a phone call," she muttered, racing for the screen door.

Jessica shook her head and flipped her blond hair behind her shoulders. *Poor Liz*, she thought sadly. *She's really lost it. She's been racing around here like crazy ever since she took over this silly carnival.*

As for me, Jessica thought lazily, *I haven't a care in the world! And since it's a cinch I'm not going to the library tonight*, she added, a triumphant grin on her face, *maybe I should try to get in touch with Donald again.* She chuckled, rolled over on her stomach, and stretched contentedly in the sun.

Eleven

Jessica had rarely been in such fine spirits. Every time she passed Regina in the hall, she felt like hugging her. Jessica had dressed, on this first triumphant day of term paperlessness, in a brand-new pair of jeans and a tight white T-shirt. "Simple but effective," she told Elizabeth. Her generous mood extended to saying hello to Winston Egbert even before he accosted her in the cafeteria.

"Hi, Winston," she said merrily, twirling a silky blond strand of hair around her finger. "You haven't seen Lila anywhere, have you?"

"No," Winston said, "I haven't. But now that you're here, Jessica, may I include you in my random poll? Which would you find more satisfying to hurl at my face—whipped-cream pie or lemon?"

"Whipped cream," Jessica told him. "Are you sure you haven't seen her? We were supposed to meet here five minutes ago."

"She may have slipped past me somehow," Winston admitted. "I've been busy tallying up the results of my poll. So far we have fifty-seven votes for whipped cream and only fourteen for lemon."

"There she is!" Jessica exclaimed, spotting Lila on the patio adjoining the cafeteria. "Good luck, Winston. I've got to go now."

"Thanks!" Winston called as Jessica hurried away.

"I've been looking for you everywhere," Jessica complained, hurling herself dramatically onto the bench across from Lila.

"I'll bet you have," Lila said grumpily.

"Cheer up," Jessica crooned. "A term paper or two will take your mind off it."

Lila frowned. "You shouldn't gloat, Jessica. It's vulgar."

Jessica giggled. "Don't be a poor loser, Lila. Admit it. I've won, fair and square. And you owe me one complete term paper, fifteen pages long—signed, sealed, and delivered by the end of next week."

"OK, OK," Lila said mildly. "I get the idea."

"So," Jessica said, a smile playing about her

lips, "are you going to the library after school today?"

Lila shrugged. "I don't know," she replied. "I was planning to stop by my father's building and see if that guy Jack is around."

"Lila! You've only got a week and a half to write two entire term papers!" Jessica shrieked.

Lila yawned, making a show of covering her mouth with her hand. "Don't be so dramatic," she said languidly. "Things get done if you don't panic, Jess. Worrying about them is useless."

Jessica stared in amazement, her high spirits suddenly dampened. It had just occurred to her that winning this bet wasn't necessarily the end of her troubles. "You'll do a good job on it, won't you?" she asked anxiously. "I really need to pull my history grade up."

"Take it easy, Jess!" Lila said, laughing. "You don't have to panic!"

Yes I do, Jessica thought, gripping the table with both hands. *If Lila doesn't get me a good grade on this paper, I'm as good as dead!*

"The best thing about arguing with you," Todd murmured, kissing Elizabeth's ear softly, "is making up again." It was lunchtime, and they were sitting under one of the oak trees on the lawn of the school.

"This was the stupidest fight we've ever had." Elizabeth laughed. "I can't believe it didn't occur to either of us that Donald thought I was Jessica."

"Poor Donald." Todd grinned and shook his head. "First your sister turns up and flirts with him like crazy. And then you turn up with me and give him the cold shoulder."

Elizabeth giggled. "I'd never seen him before," she said. "And suddenly he wanted to come to the carnival with me! Jess sure moves fast," she added admiringly.

"Well, we acted like a pair of idiots, that's for sure," Todd told her. "I can't believe we wasted a whole day feeling awful over such a stupid misunderstanding."

"And I can't believe I didn't think of Jessica the minute the whole thing came up—especially since I knew she'd been over at the Morrows' talking to Regina about the carnival," Elizabeth said.

"You've had a lot on your mind," Todd reminded her. "I think all this carnival business is wearing you out."

Elizabeth nodded, leaning against him with a sigh. "You're probably right," she said softly.

"There isn't anything else bothering you, is there?" Todd continued. "You do seem sort of preoccupied lately."

Elizabeth was quiet for a moment. "Well, I *have* been thinking about Regina," she admitted. "I know it's none of my business, Todd, but

Bruce makes me furious! Regina is incredibly vulnerable, and she really trusted him. And then she finds out that he's just been using her all along. I think it's horrible."

Todd's brow wrinkled. "It's a strange story," he said quietly. "Liz, I know you don't like Bruce, and I know you have good reason to feel the way you do. But I'm not sure I'm completely convinced that he was using Regina."

"What do you mean?" Elizabeth asked. "It sure sounds like he was."

"It's just a hunch," Todd told her. "And I may be wrong. But I've been watching Bruce the last couple of days, and he looks miserable to me. In fact, he looks like he's lost his best friend."

Elizabeth smiled. "You just think everyone's as sensitive as you are," she said, giving his shoulder a quick kiss.

"Hey," Todd said suddenly, lowering his voice. "Don't look now, but the Beast is coming toward us. And it looks as if he's got something serious on his mind."

Elizabeth turned her head. Sure enough, Bruce Patman was walking slowly toward them, his hands in his pockets and his head lowered.

"Sorry to bother you two," Bruce said, sitting down on the grass near them.

Todd's right, Elizabeth thought, taking a good look at Bruce. *He looks as if he hasn't slept in days. But that doesn't mean he really misses Regina*, she reminded herself. *He's probably just angry because his little plan got fouled up. Now no one will vote for him, and he'll lose his precious election.*

"What can we do for you, Bruce?" Todd asked cheerfully, his arm still around Elizabeth's shoulder.

"Well, actually," Bruce mumbled, a hint of red coming to his face, "it was Liz I really wanted to talk to. Do you think you might be able to come by the house later this afternoon?" he asked Elizabeth.

Elizabeth stared at him, her eyes narrowing. "Why?" she asked, trying to ignore the slight pressure of Todd's hand on her shoulder. *I don't care what Todd says*, she thought stubbornly. *As far as I'm concerned, Bruce Patman is a snake. And I don't want anything to do with him.*

"Liz, I need your advice," Bruce said, leaning forward in his chair. "I know how much Regina admires you, and I know she tells you things, too. It's not easy for me to ask for help," Bruce added, "but I'm asking now. I need to talk to you, Liz. Will you come by?"

"I'll come," Elizabeth said simply. Todd patted her arm approvingly, but Elizabeth didn't respond. *But I'm not happy about it*, she added silently. *And as far as I'm concerned, Regina is lucky to be rid of you!*

"You sure I can't get you something to drink?"

Bruce asked, drumming his fingers nervously on the table.

Elizabeth shook her head. "I can't stay long. The carnival is this Saturday, and we've still got a lot of work to do."

Elizabeth and Bruce were out on the patio overlooking the Patmans' Olympic-sized swimming pool. Late afternoon sunlight poured through the trees, glinting on the water's surface. It was a beautiful day and a beautiful setting, but Elizabeth couldn't wait to leave. She felt uncomfortable around Bruce, and the tense, distracted look on his face wasn't making her feel any more at ease.

"Liz, I'll be honest with you," Bruce said abruptly, running a hand through his hair. "I know how you feel about me, and I don't blame you. I've done some pretty obnoxious things. When things haven't gone right for me, I guess I always knew that I deserved what I got—and sometimes worse. But Regina—" He broke off, his voice choked with emotion.

"Bruce, I really don't feel comfortable talking about this," Elizabeth said quickly, getting to her feet and reaching for her purse. "I'm sorry about you and Regina, but it doesn't have anything to do with me. So I'll just get going now, and—"

"Liz, please!" Bruce interrupted, his eyes shining with tears. "Listen to me," he said desperately. "You're one of Regina's closest friends. Did she say anything to you about why she broke up with me? Did she give you any clue, any little hint? I've been up night after night trying to figure it out. I've gone back over every conversation we had, racking my brain, trying to guess what could have made her hate me. And I come up with"—he shook his head, staring pleadingly at Elizabeth—"nothing. Absolutely nothing."

Elizabeth sat back down, her eyes troubled. "You mean you really don't know?" she asked him, puzzled.

Bruce put his hands up in a gesture of despair. "Do you think I'd drag you over here and beg you like this if I knew?" he asked.

Elizabeth took a deep breath. Maybe Todd was right. What she saw before her wasn't the Bruce Patman she'd known and hated at all. He really *did* look miserable. What's more, he looked as though he was telling the truth. "Why didn't you tell Regina you were running for president of the centennial committee?" Elizabeth asked him.

Bruce stared at her. "What are you talking about?" he cried. "What does that have to do with anything?"

Elizabeth sighed. "Regina thought you kept it from her on purpose. She thinks you started seeing her to make yourself more popular so you could win the election."

Bruce looked dumbfounded. "You're kidding," he said, staring at Elizabeth as if she'd just gone mad.

Elizabeth shook her head. "She thought that was why you kept the election quiet. Because you were using her so you could win."

Bruce shook his head. "I can't believe it," he said quietly. "Liz, I signed up for that election last Thursday. That was five days ago! And I've known Regina for weeks! The reason I didn't mention that I was running was that I was going to surprise her if I won. It was just something I wanted to do at the last minute. Because I was so happy to live in Sweet Valley after I met Regina," he added softly. "I wanted to give something back to the town."

Elizabeth bit her lip. "You're telling the truth now, aren't you?" she asked quietly.

Bruce stared at her. "Liz, for the first time in my life, I had something that I really cared for. Maybe you think people are the way they are, and that's it. Well, it doesn't happen to have been true in my case. When you fall in love with someone, you change. And when you fall in love with someone like Regina, you change for the better—fast. I'm sure there's a lot of apologizing I ought to do now for the way I used to behave. But right now, Liz, I don't feel like doing anything before I apologize to Regina. I've just got to make her understand!"

"Bruce, wait a minute," Elizabeth said, putting her hand on his arm. "I'm sorry I doubted you," she added. "I was wrong. But there's something I have to tell you before you try to find Regina."

"What is it?" Bruce asked, his eyes fixed attentively on hers.

Elizabeth looked down at the table. "Regina is supposed to leave for Switzerland," she told him. "And if you explain what happened to her, she may not go."

"Switzerland!" Bruce cried, his eyes flashing with horror. "That's all the more reason to find her right away, then!" He jumped up from the table, his hands trembling.

"Bruce, wait a minute!" Elizabeth insisted. "She's going there to undergo treatments that may restore her hearing. She didn't tell you about it because she refused to leave you. And if you go find her now, she'll never go."

Bruce sank back into his chair, his face drained of color. "How long have you known about this?" he demanded.

"Not very long," Elizabeth said softly. "Regina's mother told me last week. She begged me to help change Regina's mind, but I was afraid to interfere."

When Bruce looked up again, his eyes were

soft and moist. "You mean Regina might be able to hear again—*really* hear?" he asked her.

Elizabeth nodded. "The treatments aren't guaranteed, but the doctor thinks Regina is a good candidate."

"That's wonderful!" Bruce cried. "She can go to Switzerland, have the treatments, and when she comes back, we'll have the whole summer together!"

Elizabeth sighed. "These are pretty complicated operations, Bruce. It's not just a matter of a couple of weeks."

"What are you saying, Liz?" Bruce demanded. "How long will she have to be away?"

"A long time," Elizabeth told him. "Mrs. Morrow told me it could be a year."

Bruce didn't say a word. He got up from the table and walked across the patio, where he stared out over Sweet Valley. "The poor kid," he said at last, still not looking at Elizabeth. "And she never said a word about it."

"Bruce, what are you going to do?" Elizabeth asked anxiously. Bruce couldn't go to Regina now! It would ruin everything. Regina would never leave him, and she'd never hear again.

"I don't know," Bruce said softly, turning back to face her with a look of helplessness that made her wince. "I just don't know, Liz. If I let her go now, thinking that I never loved her—" He broke off, turning away again, but not before Elizabeth saw his face.

I never would have believed it in a million years, she thought. *Bruce Patman is crying.*

Twelve

It was after midnight, but Bruce couldn't sleep. The things Elizabeth had told him earlier that afternoon kept coming back to him, mixed with the words Regina had shouted at him when they had parted. Lying on his four-poster bed with his hands behind his head, Bruce stared into the darkness, trying to decide what to do.

He wanted Regina to be with him forever. The thought of an entire year without her filled him with dread. How could he let her leave him? He couldn't, he thought to himself. He just couldn't.

Turning the lamp on beside his bed, Bruce got up and wandered over to his desk. He opened the top drawer, rummaging through the papers inside until he found what he was looking for. It was a photograph of Regina he had taken weeks ago at the beach. Her head was thrown back in the picture, her eyes were lit up with excitement, her black hair gleamed against her cream-white skin. "She's so beautiful," he said softly, putting the picture down.

For a long time he sat at his desk, holding his chin in his hand and staring down at Regina's image. He could hear the grandfather clock downstairs chiming the hour. It was one o'clock, and still he was as alert as if it were the middle of the day. Then, picking up a pen and taking a clean sheet of paper from his desk drawer, he began to write.

It seemed as though no time had passed at all before he heard the clock strike two o'clock. He leaned back, holding the sheet of paper before him, and began to read.

Dear Regina,

By the time you read this, it will be too late for you to change your mind about the treatments. And you mustn't change your mind, my dearest—not for anything. Elizabeth told me everything, and I must admit that at first all I could think of was rushing over to your house and putting things right again.

I never cared about anything but you. I signed up to run in the election last Thursday—exactly five days ago.

I was wrong not to mention it to you at once, but I wanted to surprise you if I won. I can't believe you could ever imagine my using you. I love you with all my heart, and always will.

In fact it's because I love you that I can't explain all this to you before Friday. If there's the slightest chance that you might be able to hear again one day after these treatments, you must go through with them.

I'm not selfish enough to let you stay in Sweet Valley for my sake, Regina. But I'm too selfish to let you go thinking badly of me. You must know that I've loved you with all my heart from the first.

It's not perfect, Bruce thought, *but it's how I feel*. With a great sigh, he picked his pen up again and signed his name at the bottom of the page. When the clock chimed again, Bruce was still sitting at his desk. He had a feeling it was going to be a long time before he got a peaceful night's sleep.

"Come on, you guys," Elizabeth said. "Today's Wednesday. We've got exactly three days left to pull this carnival together, and about three months of work left to do."

The committee was meeting in Mr. Collins's

room, and Elizabeth was doing her best to channel the group's high spirits.

"The prizes and decorations are all ready," Olivia told her, lifting a stuffed animal out of an enormous box.

"Actually, we're in pretty good shape as far as games go," Todd told Elizabeth, giving her a sympathetic smile across the room. Mr. Collins was almost half an hour late, and Elizabeth was getting worried.

"OK," Elizabeth said, making check marks in her notebook. "Prizes are ready. Games are ready. Ken, how do the booths look?"

"We've been setting them up today in the football field," Ken told her. "We've got one tent up already, and about half of the booths are ready."

"Good," Elizabeth said, looking relieved. "Winston, are you ready to be the master of ceremonies?"

"Never readier," Winston assured her. "I'm going to borrow a portable microphone from the office so people can hear me better."

"OK," Elizabeth said, ignoring the groans from around the room.

"Olivia, would you mind helping me at the ticket booth? Tickets will be a dollar each, and a ticket entitles you to play a game at any booth."

"Sure," Olivia said agreeably, bursting into laughter as she saw Winston throw his arms around a large stuffed rabbit and give it a passionate kiss.

"Hi, everyone!" Mr. Collins boomed, opening the door a crack and sticking his head inside. "Am I too late, or may I still come in?"

"Come in, come in!" Winston boomed, using the rabbit as a microphone. Elizabeth looked up in surprise. Mr. Collins wasn't alone, and he seemed unusually flustered as he strolled over to his desk.

"Mind if I sit in on this meeting?" Nora Dalton asked, following Mr. Collins into the room and sliding into an empty desk in the front of the room.

"You may have to buy a ticket." Olivia giggled.

Elizabeth caught Ms. Dalton's eye and smiled. She had always liked the pretty young French teacher, and she was happy to see her now. At twenty-five, black-haired, bright-eyed Ms. Dalton was the youngest member of Sweet Valley High's staff. Her bubbly personality made her a favorite with most of her students.

"We were just getting to the refreshment stands," Enid explained to Mr. Collins. "Caroline promised to make some of her disgustingly rich brownies, and Todd and I are making pizza. Does anyone else have any suggestions?"

"There's always rabbit," Winston pointed out, waving the stuffed rabbit in the air. Everyone laughed, and in the pause that followed, Nora Dalton spoke up.

"We could have an international food stand," she suggested. "If you want, Enid, I could help with it. I can make crepes."

"As long as we don't have to order in French," Todd said, grinning.

"That's a wonderful idea," Elizabeth said. "Well," she added, flipping quickly through her notebook, "it looks as though we're in pretty good shape. Mr. Collins, would you mind if I went out to the football field with Todd and Ken to see how the booths look?"

"Go right ahead," Mr. Collins told her. "I'll stay here and see how many exotic international dishes I can coax out of these chefs."

"That was kind of a surprise, don't you think?" Todd asked, putting his arm around Elizabeth as they headed outside to the field.

"You mean Mr. Collins and Ms. Dalton? It's not the first time I've seen them together," Ken said, winking at Todd.

Elizabeth flushed. She liked Mr. Collins too much to feel comfortable hearing gossip about him. "I'm sure it's no big deal," she said lightly, quickening her step.

"Liz is probably right," Todd said quickly, sensing her annoyance. "And anyway, what they do is their business. Right, Liz?"

Elizabeth was about to agree with him when she heard someone shouting her name behind them.

"Hey, it's Bruce," Todd told her, turning around and shading his eyes with his hand. "And it looks like he's trying to win the Bart again or something, he's running out here so fast."

"These days he's trying to win everything," Ken pointed out, looking annoyed.

Elizabeth followed Todd's gaze. "I'll tell you what," she said quickly. "Why don't you two go ahead, and I'll catch up with you. This looks kind of urgent."

"OK," Todd agreed, kissing her on the cheek. "But don't be too long. We need your professional opinion on our expert carpentry."

Todd and Ken went on ahead, and Elizabeth turned around to wait for Bruce. She didn't have long to wait. Bruce crossed the field a minute later, breathing heavily as he slowed down before her.

"Liz!" he gasped, wiping his forehead with his hand. "I'm glad I caught you."

Elizabeth giggled. "It would have been impossible to miss me at that pace," she told him. Her expression changed when she saw how serious he looked. "Are you all right?" she asked soberly. "I thought about calling you, but I didn't think I should butt in any further than I have already."

Bruce shook his head. "No, Liz, you were right to tell me what you did. I thought about calling you, too, but to be honest I haven't really felt like talking very much."

"I understand," Elizabeth said sympathetically. "What's that?" she asked curiously, noticing a white envelope in Bruce's right hand.

"It's a letter for Regina," Bruce told her. "That's why I came chasing after you, Liz. I was afraid I wouldn't be able to find you later, and I need to ask you a favor."

Elizabeth's heart quickened. What did the letter say? Had Bruce decided not to confront Regina and explain what had really happened? It seemed too much to hope for. Elizabeth had been thinking of little else since her talk with Bruce the day before. And all day she'd been afraid to run into Regina—afraid that Regina would say she had changed her mind about Switzerland.

"The letter explains what really happened with the election," Bruce said quietly. "Liz, I just couldn't bear to have Regina believe that I used her. I love her too much for that."

"I see," Elizabeth said quietly. *But if you* really *loved her*, she thought angrily, *you wouldn't explain a thing. That way she could still go to*

125

Switzerland—and maybe, just maybe, regain her hearing.

"The reason I need your help," Bruce continued, "is that I don't want Regina to read the letter until she's in Switzerland. And the only idea I can come up with is for you to sneak it into her suitcase—deep down where she won't find it for a while—sometime before she goes Friday morning. Liz, will you do that for me?"

Elizabeth stared at him. At first she wasn't sure she'd heard him correctly. "You mean you want Regina to go to Switzerland?" she asked doubtfully.

"Of course I don't," Bruce said fiercely. "I want her to stay right here. I've never wanted anything so badly in my whole life."

"Then why wait?" Elizabeth asked. "Why not take the letter to her now?"

"Because," Bruce said painfully, "I love her. And I want what's best for her. If there's a chance she can be cured, Regina owes it to herself to give it a try."

Elizabeth looked at Bruce wonderingly. *Mr. Collins was right*, she thought. *People can change.*

"I never could have imagined your making this kind of sacrifice before, Bruce," she said softly. On an impulse, she leaned forward and kissed him on the cheek.

"I never could have done it before," Bruce

said, clearing his throat. "You can't make a sacrifice until you love someone."

Elizabeth stared at him, resolve flashing in her blue-green eyes. "Give me the letter, Bruce," she said firmly. "I'll make sure it gets in Regina's suitcase."

Thirteen

"Elizabeth!" Mrs. Morrow exclaimed, opening the front door and smiling. "Come in, dear. Regina's upstairs getting her things together."

"I'm so glad I made it here before you left for the airport," Elizabeth said, stepping into the foyer. "I was afraid you'd leave before I had a chance to say goodbye to Regina."

Mrs. Morrow looked at her watch. "We've still got twenty minutes," she told her. Elizabeth couldn't get over the change in Mrs. Morrow. Her dark hair was swept back from her face in a neat ponytail, and her eyes were glowing with excitement. She looked carefree and happy as a girl.

"Was that someone at the door, Mom?"

Regina asked, bounding down the stairs. "I thought I saw a car coming up the drive." Catching sight of Elizabeth, Regina's lovely face clouded over briefly, then she smiled. "Liz!" she exclaimed. "It's you!"

I wonder if she was still hoping Bruce would come, Elizabeth thought sympathetically. She reached inside her book bag and brushed Bruce's letter with her fingertips. It was still there. Suddenly Elizabeth was filled with a rush of warmth and admiration for Bruce. How much easier it would have been for him to come over here, take Regina in his arms, and explain what had happened! And how incredibly hard it must be for him to stay away, knowing that within a few hours Regina would be on a plane, out of reach of his apologies!

"Will you come upstairs?" Regina was asking her. "I've still got a few things to pack, and Mom'll kill me if I'm late."

Mrs. Morrow gave her daughter a warm hug. "I couldn't care less how long it takes you," she said, her voice thick with emotion. "Go on!" She pushed Regina playfully toward the stairs. "And don't forget your passport," she reminded her.

Upstairs Elizabeth sank down on the flowered bedspread covering Regina's double bed. Watching her friend hurrying from her dresser to the open suitcase near her door, Elizabeth felt a lump come into her throat. "I'm going to miss you, Regina," she said softly.

Regina smiled at her, her blue eyes surprisingly calm. "I'm going to miss you, too," she said firmly, taking a scrapbook out of her top drawer and flipping through it. "It's funny," she added, "I don't think I've ever been as happy as I've been since I came to Sweet Valley."

"Can I see some of your snapshots?" Elizabeth asked. Regina nodded and handed her the book. "Are you taking this with you?" Elizabeth continued, reaching inside her book bag for Bruce's letter.

Regina disappeared into her closet. "I don't know," she said sadly. "It's silly to try to hang on to the past, Liz. What matters is the future."

Elizabeth tucked Bruce's letter inside the scrapbook, next to a picture of Bruce and Regina at the beach. She waited until Regina came out of the closet to answer.

"Nonsense," she told her, handing her the scrapbook. "This isn't the past, Regina. The people in this book aren't going to forget you while you're away. And I don't think you should forget them, either."

For the second time that morning, Regina's face clouded over. For a minute, Elizabeth was afraid Regina was going to break down and cry. Then, pulling her long hair back from her face and giving Elizabeth a radiant smile, she took the scrapbook and fit it into a large canvas shoulder bag next to her suitcase.

"You're right, Liz," Regina said. "I don't want to forget anything that's happened this year. Not even the bad parts," she added softly.

Elizabeth threw her arms around her and gave her a big hug. "Please keep in touch," she begged. "And I want you to know that we're all behind you. *All* of us," she added firmly.

It would be a long time, Elizabeth thought to herself, before she forgot the expression on Regina's face as she stood in the front doorway to the Morrows' estate, sadly waving goodbye.

"Where've you been?" Todd asked Elizabeth anxiously, jumping up to pull a chair out for her at the crowded lunch table. The carnival would be held the next day, and the committee had arranged one last meeting to make sure everything was in order.

"At Regina's," Elizabeth told him quietly. "She's leaving for Switzerland today, and I wanted to say goodbye." Todd didn't know yet that Elizabeth had promised Bruce to hide his letter in Regina's suitcase, but she figured there'd be time enough to tell him about it later.

Now there was something else Elizabeth was worried about. "Has anybody voted for centennial president yet?" she asked casually, looking around the table.

131

"I never vote in the morning," Winston said solemnly. "I prefer to deliberate all day and then reach my decision."

Olivia laughed. "I wish I had the same excuse," she said merrily, holding Roger's hand tightly in her own. "I haven't voted yet, either. But it's not because I want to deliberate. I just haven't had the time this morning."

"Neither have I," Roger said, grinning at Olivia.

"Pretty incriminating," Winston observed, and everyone laughed.

"Why do you ask, Liz?" Olivia inquired.

"I don't know," she said slowly. "I guess I'm just thinking out loud."

"When *I* think out loud, you can't hear a thing." Winston laughed.

"Winston!" Olivia exclaimed. "Give Elizabeth a chance to say what's on her mind."

"It's just this," Elizabeth added slowly. "I feel ashamed of the way I've talked about Bruce the last few weeks. I think I've really misjudged him."

"What do you mean?" Roger asked, leaning forward.

"I guess I just assumed that people are the way they are and can't change," Elizabeth admitted. "And that doesn't seem to be true in Bruce's case at all." Then, taking a deep breath, Elizabeth proceeded to tell the group the entire story, starting with the misunderstanding between Bruce and Regina and ending with Bruce's decision not to confront Regina, but to apologize instead in a letter so she wouldn't change her mind about Switzerland. "I'd never have expected Bruce to make this kind of sacrifice," Elizabeth concluded. "And, to be honest, I feel terrible for having been so skeptical of his affection for Regina. I know now that he really does love her. And the qualities he's exhibited these last few days have convinced me that he'd be the finest representative our school could possibly send to the centennial committee."

"That's the saddest story I've ever heard," Olivia whispered. "Do you think they'll ever see each other again?"

"I hope so," Elizabeth said. "They certainly deserve to have things work out."

"And Regina left this morning believing Bruce had used her?" Roger said, shaking his head. "Poor guy," he added. "That poor, poor guy. So that's why he's been acting so miserable this whole week!"

"What about Regina?" Olivia asked. "Can you imagine what must be going through her head right now? All by herself, having left her friends and family, going to a country where she doesn't even speak the language . . . and all the while not even knowing that Bruce still loves her?"

"One thing's for sure," Winston declared, his

cheerful face suddenly serious. "Bruce Patman *has* changed for the better. And I think Liz is absolutely right. He deserves to win this election!"

"Hear, hear!" Roger yelled. "Thank heavens we *didn't* vote this morning," he said to Olivia. "It just goes to show that tardiness has its virtues."

"My sentiments exactly," Winston agreed, taking a big bite of his sandwich.

Elizabeth looked around the table, a big smile on her face. She realized she felt much better about Bruce. And what had made her feel better was admitting that she was wrong. Mr. Collins had known what he was talking about, she thought happily, giving Todd's hand a warm squeeze under the table. People really could change, and it had been terrible of her not to give Bruce a chance.

I just hope, she thought anxiously, *that Regina's willing to give him a chance when she finds that letter.*

"Ladies and gentlemen," the stewardess announced, "Captain Rolfe has turned off the seat-belt sign. Please feel free to move about the cabin if you choose. And just sit back and enjoy the rest of your flight!"

Regina looked listlessly at the magazine in her lap. She wished she could be more excited about meeting Dr. Friederich and beginning her treatments. But deep inside Regina didn't feel excited about anything anymore.

The day she and Bruce had had their big fight, Regina felt as if a light had gone out inside her. Since then, she hadn't felt any joy about events taking place around her. She felt as though she were watching things from a great distance or as though they were happening to someone else— like a girl in a book.

Her parents had been so thrilled when she announced her decision to go to Switzerland. And at first Regina had gotten caught up in their excitement as they told her about the family Dr. Friederich had arranged for her to stay with. But for the last few days she had felt entirely numb. She had moved like a ghost from room to room in the Morrows' house, looking absently at the places where she had loved to sit and read or lie in the sun. At the back of her mind one question kept coming back to her again and again, like a refrain: would Bruce come see her before she left? He wouldn't let her go without saying goodbye! He just couldn't!

That morning, when she had seen Elizabeth's car in the driveway, a last rush of hope had flooded over her. Maybe Bruce's Porsche had broken down. Maybe he had borrowed a red Fiat from someone. Maybe he'd come at last to say goodbye, to hold her in his arms.

But it hadn't been Bruce after all. It had been

Elizabeth, and fond as she was of Elizabeth, Regina had felt almost crushed with disappointment. *I hope it didn't show in my face,* she thought. *Liz has been such a good friend to me. She was so right to insist that I bring my scrapbook—I'd be lost without it.*

Thinking of the scrapbook now, Regina felt mixed emotions. She wanted so badly to look at all the pictures she'd collected in her short time at Sweet Valley. But she knew that Bruce's pictures would be there among them. How would it feel to look down at his face, knowing she might never see him again?

With a sigh, Regina pulled the scrapbook from the bag she had stowed beneath the seat in front of her. *I don't care,* she told herself. *Bruce is part of the past, and the sooner I realize that, the better.* Flipping the album open, she saw the envelope Elizabeth had slipped inside. Curious, she took the letter from the envelope and began to read.

Anyone watching Regina as she read Bruce's letter would have seen a remarkable change in the girl's expression. At first her face turned bright red, then terribly pale, and then red again. Her lovely blue eyes, which had expressed a false serenity for the last week, filled with tears. "What a fool I've been," she said at last, laying the precious letter on her lap.

But the tears that finally flooded down Regina's cheeks had nothing to do with herself. She was thinking only of Bruce and the pain and loneliness he must have suffered. *And I thought it was hard for me*, she thought. *The whole time he was in anguish, too.*

It was hard for Regina to believe now that she had ever distrusted Bruce. *I don't know what got into me*, she thought, impatiently brushing away her tears.

Despite her remorse, Regina felt a sudden and overwhelming sensation of joy. *He still loves me*, she thought in wonder. *Enough to sit by in silence and let me go ahead with my decision. Enough to sacrifice his own happiness for my welfare.*

Regina believed now that she really had made the right decision. If Bruce, who loved her more than anyone, was willing to remain quiet so that she would go, she must have done the right thing.

"What's this?" Regina said aloud, feeling a tiny lump in the envelope. She withdrew the fine gold chain with the ruby pendant. *Elizabeth was right*, she thought, a lump in her throat. *My love for Bruce isn't part of the past. It's only just beginning.*

With a smile breaking over her face despite her tears, Regina fastened the ruby pendant around her neck. It was there, she told herself, for keeps.

Fourteen

Saturday, the day of the carnival, proved to be another beautiful day. Elizabeth, Todd, and Ken had been working all morning in the tents set up on the football field, and their efforts showed in the final results. The banners Olivia had designed snapped gaily in the breeze over the two yellow- and white-striped tents. Inside, one tent was filled with games—a ring toss, bowling pins, a wheel of fortune, as well as various booths designed by students. The other tent, much smaller than the first, was filled with refreshments.

By one o'clock the carnival was in full swing. Ms. Dalton and Enid were running the refreshment stands, serving everything from exotic French crepes to all-American brownies.

Winston Egbert, looking particularly lanky in his father's oversized tuxedo and red suspenders, was booming into a microphone before the large tent.

"Step right up, ladies and gentlemen! Welcome to the first ever Fowler Memorial Hospital/Sweet Valley High fund-raising carnival! Tickets are on sale right at the door, ladies and gentlemen, right at the door! For just one dollar—for one dollar only—you can take your chances in one of our challenging booths. Or you can take your chances at the refreshment stand. As you choose!"

"Don't you think he's going to drive everyone crazy in about an hour?" Jessica said grumpily, coming up behind Elizabeth and Todd.

"Jess! I've been looking for you everywhere," Elizabeth said happily. She couldn't believe how well everything was working out. The carnival seemed to be a roaring success. The field was crowded with familiar faces, both from school and from the community. "Look, there's Mrs. Patman," Elizabeth said to Todd, looking over at the small tent, where Marie Patman was presiding over a group of her friends. "Haven't the children done a *lovely* job?" she was saying loudly. "Of course you know that Henry and I are matching whatever money they raise today. It's the very *least* we can do for such a worthwhile cause."

"I wonder where Bruce is," Elizabeth mused. "Jess, you haven't seen Bruce anywhere, have you?"

Jessica grimaced. "No," she said sourly, "I haven't. And with luck I can keep things that way."

"What's eating her?" Todd asked, watching Jessica walk away.

"I don't know." Elizabeth sighed. "It's hard to keep up with her these days. I'm sure it's nothing very important."

"Hey," Todd said suddenly, starting to laugh, "Winston's setting up his booth. Let's go take a look, Liz."

Sure enough, Winston was transporting himself, microphone and all, into the large tent. Once inside he put his head through a hole in a board, and cajoled the crowd to throw pies at him.

"A dollar a throw! A dollar a throw! It's the bargain of the century, ladies and gentlemen. For merely one hundred copper pennies you have the satisfaction of hurling a large, fresh whipped-cream pie at my face! Step right up, ladies and gentlemen!"

Elizabeth burst out laughing as Mr. Collins stepped up to throw the first pie. Taking careful aim, he hurtled the pie, hitting Winston square in the face. For a minute the class clown looked completely dumbfounded as he reached out from behind the board to wipe the cream from his eyes. But the next minute he was laughing as hard as the crowd that had gathered to watch him. "Leave it to Winston." Todd grinned. "He even looks happy with pie all over him."

Later, Elizabeth and Todd were at the refreshment stand with Enid when Winston made a surprise announcement. "Ladies and gentlemen," his voice boomed. "We have a special speech this afternoon from our parent adviser for the carnival, Mrs. Skye Morrow. If you could all file into the large tent in ten minutes, you'll be able to hear what she has to say."

"Did you know about this?" Enid asked, looking puzzled.

Elizabeth shook her head. "Not at all," she replied, obviously surprised. "She did say something about finding a way to replace the mother-daughter fashion show, but with Regina leaving and all, I thought she forgot."

"Let's go," Todd said eagerly. "I want to hear this."

Several minutes later, the big tent was filled with attentive faces. All the game booths were left vacant as Mrs. Morrow climbed up on a small platform at the rear of the tent. Winston passed her his microphone, and she coughed nervously into it, caught the reassuring glances of Nicholas and her husband, and smiled.

For the first time, Elizabeth was able to envision Mrs. Morrow as she must have been in her youth. Wearing a simple green silk dress and a pair of low-heeled pumps, she looked so beautiful and poised it was hard for Elizabeth not to stare. Mrs. Morrow's black hair was brushed back from her face, and her high cheekbones and luminous eyes reminded Elizabeth of Regina. Looking around the tent for Bruce, she wondered if he saw the resemblance, too.

"The story I've chosen to tell you today is a true one," Mrs. Morrow said, her voice clear and strong. "It's about a little girl with a handicap and what she was able to do to overcome that handicap and live a normal life."

In the same rich, confident voice, Mrs. Morrow went on to tell the audience about Regina. She didn't seem to have prepared a speech, because her words were so natural and spontaneous. She told the audience about Regina's defect at birth and the difficulties she faced while she was growing up. Then Mrs. Morrow described the things Regina had been able to learn with the help of special schools and teachers. Finally, she told the audience about Dr. Friederich and his treatments in Switzerland. "We don't know yet what will happen to Regina," she concluded. "But what we do know is that children like her need help. Regina was very lucky to have a family who had the means to get all the help for her she needed. The chil-

142

dren at Fowler Memorial Hospital aren't all so lucky. With your help we can overcome their handicaps and give them the opportunities that so many of us take for granted."

A hushed silence followed this speech. Elizabeth had never seen her classmates so moved. After a moment or two, scattered applause broke out across the tent, until everyone was clapping as loudly as possible. Mrs. Morrow raised her hand. "Just one more thing," she said into the microphone. "I'm afraid my own child has kept me so busy this week that I haven't been able to help the children at the hospital. In fact, I've been a very neglectful adviser," she admitted. "I'd just like to take this moment to thank Elizabeth Wakefield, who has done a phenomenal job of bringing all of us together today."

To her surprise and embarrassed pleasure, the whole tent went wild with applause. "You deserve it," Todd said warmly, giving Elizabeth a big kiss. "I'm so proud of you."

"While we're all in the same place," Mr. Collins said with a smile, taking the microphone from Mrs. Morrow, "I'd just like to announce the results of the students' centennial presidential election. The winner," he said with a big smile, "is Bruce Patman."

Once again the audience burst into applause. "Oh, Todd, I'm so happy for him," Elizabeth said warmly.

"He's right over there," Todd told her, pointing across the tent. "Why don't you tell him so yourself?"

"OK," Elizabeth said, giving Todd a quick hug. "I think I will."

"Congratulations, Bruce," Elizabeth said shyly, coming up from behind and putting her hand on his shoulder. Bruce whirled around to face her, his eyes lighting up when he saw who it was.

"I think I should say the same to you," he said quietly. "You've done a great job with all this, Liz. Regina would have loved it."

Elizabeth flushed. "I guess I didn't just mean congratulations on the election," she told him softly. "I never would have guessed I'd be saying this, but I'm proud of you, Bruce. And it's not because you won the election. I think you won something much more important."

"So do I," Bruce said solemnly, looking past Elizabeth at the Morrow family. "I just hope Regina knows how I feel," he added.

"I have a feeling," Elizabeth told him, "that she does."

"Whoever heard of having a reunion party for something that took place just two weeks ago?" Jessica grumbled to Elizabeth. It was Friday afternoon, and the twins were sitting out on the green lawn in front of Sweet Valley High.

144

"It was Todd's idea, and I think it's a good one," Elizabeth told her sister.

"Just because you were the star of the carnival," Jessica muttered, "you want to drag it out forever."

"Jess!" Elizabeth exclaimed indignantly. "That isn't true at all. It so happens that today's the day Mr. Collins is making the donation to the hospital. We raised over eight hundred dollars! Isn't that cause enough to celebrate?"

"I suppose so." Jessica sighed. She was scanning the lawn for someone, and Elizabeth could tell her mind wasn't really on their conversation.

"What's wrong with you today, anyway?" Elizabeth asked her. "Since when do you turn your nose up at the chance for a good party?"

"Nothing's wrong," Jessica said shortly, swatting at a mosquito with the paper she'd rolled up into a tube.

"What's that?" Elizabeth asked. "Is that your term paper?"

"Sorry, Liz," Jessica burst out unceremoniously. "I've got to go." She had just spotted Lila across the lawn, and within seconds she had sped over to confront her.

"Lila Fowler," she said angrily, "don't you feel the tiniest bit sorry about what's happened?"

"What's happened where?" Lila asked innocently, brushing a bit of nonexistent dirt from the front of her new white trousers. Lila was planning to drop by her father's building again this afternoon, and she wanted to make sure she looked her best.

"Here!" Jessica shrieked indignantly, unrolling the paper in her hand and waving it in front of Lila's eyes. "*This* is what I'm talking about!"

"Oh, dear," Lila said, looking down at the big red D marked on the top of the paper. "Jessica, please see me" was written under the grade.

"Is that all you can say?" Jessica muttered. "Did you get yours back yet?"

Lila hesitated. "Of course," she admitted finally. "We all got them back today, Jess. You know that."

"And how'd you do on it?" Jessica demanded.

"OK," Lila said noncommittally. "Come on, Jess—I'm really in a hurry. Can't we talk about this later?"

"No," Jessica fumed, "we can't. Just how good is 'OK'?"

"I got a B-minus," Lila admitted. "But I still can't see why you're making such a fuss, Jessica. I *tried* my hardest. I just—"

"If you tried your hardest and got a D on my paper, how'd you manage to get a B-minus on your own?" Jessica demanded.

Lila shrugged, her eyes wide with innocence. "I guess I was just tired," she said apologetically.

"You know how it is, Jess. I did mine first, and by the time I got around to yours—"

"That's great, Lila," Jessica snapped. "Really great. Do you realize that term paper could keep me from passing history?"

Lila shrugged. "It won't, will it?" she asked sweetly.

Jessica stared at her. "It won't, if I do OK on the final, but—"

"Good," Lila said firmly. "Then it's all right."

Jessica didn't look convinced.

"Who cares about history, anyway?" Lila said airily. "Guess where I'm going right now?" she asked, dropping her voice.

"Where?" Jessica asked. *As if I care*, she thought moodily. Jessica didn't share Lila's nonchalance about her term paper. She'd had a harrowing talk wtih Mr. Fellows about it, and now she'd have to work extra hard on the final exam or she'd fail for sure.

"I'm going over to my father's building to see if Jack is around," Lila told her. "I'm almost positive he'll ask me out this time," she added.

"Maybe he'll ask you to help him write a term paper," Jessica suggested, irritated by Lila's smugness. Jessica just wasn't in the mood for Lila. Aside from the rotten grade she'd gotten on her paper, she was depressed because she'd gotten a letter from Donald the day before, apologizing for not getting in touch with her before

147

the carnival. He hadn't wanted to lead her on, the letter said. *Lead me on!* Jessica thought sadly. I'm all washed up. Sixteen years old and over the hill.

"Jess, I'm telling you, he's fabulous," Lila said.

Jessica stared at her, the sparkle coming back to her blue-green eyes. "Tell me more about him," she said impulsively.

Her face brightening, Lila leaned forward, launching into a lengthy description of Jack's charms.

And Jessica listened avidly. It had just occurred to her that Lila might need a dose of her own medicine. And maybe—if Jessica could get to know this Jack character herself—she just might be able to get that smirk off Lila's face for good!

Fifteen minutes later, Lila parked her car in front of her father's new building. Frantically checking her appearance in the rearview mirror, Lila bounded out of the car and strolled casually over to the fence closing in the construction site.

"Jack!" she called, waving at the group of men moving iron girders with heavy machinery. A minute later Jack separated himself from the group and sauntered over to the fence.

"Lila Fowler," he said lazily, grinning down at

her with his green-flecked eyes. "What brings you back to this territory?"

"Oh, I don't know," she said coyly, shrugging her shoulders and looking up at him with her most flirtatious smile. "I was just thinking about my plans for the summer. I wanted to talk to Daddy about going to Europe," she lied.

"Really?" Jack said, folding his arms on top of the fence and putting his chin on his arms. "Where in Europe?"

"Oh, I don't know," Lila said, thinking quickly. "Maybe the Riviera."

Jack smiled. "I used to go sailing off the south of France," he told her.

Lila's breath caught in her throat. That absolutely settled it as far as she was concerned. Whoever this Jack was, he wasn't *really* a construction worker. He was far too sophisticated, too refined.

"Do you have a boat? It's been so hot," she added softly. "I'll bet it feels just terrific out on the water."

"It sure does," Jack agreed, half-closing his eyes. "I *do* have a boat," he told her. "And I wouldn't mind being out on her right this minute," he added.

Why aren't you? Lila wanted to ask him. *What are you doing here, dragging these heavy pieces of lumber around on such a beautiful day?* But she controlled herself. First things first. Once Jack had fallen in love with her, he'd reveal his real identity to her. Then maybe he'd whisk her away to the south of France and introduce her to his family. Lila was convinced by now that he was only working here as a disguise. His *real* family was probably filthy rich.

But first she had to get him to ask her out. And he didn't seem to be jumping at the bait for some reason. "They say the weather's supposed to be perfect for sailing tomorrow," Lila said, trying again.

"That's good news," Jack said, smiling that mysterious, slow smile.

Lila thought quickly. Jack didn't seem to be taking a hint, so she'd have to try the direct approach. "You know," she said suddenly, "a bunch of us have been planning a swimming party at my place on Sunday. You wouldn't want to drop by, would you?"

"Sure," Jack said. "That sounds nice."

Lila flushed. She felt strangely insecure with Jack, though she couldn't tell why. He couldn't possibly know that she had just decided to have a party right then, but something in his eyes made her feel that he was looking right through her. His smile had a slightly ironic look that made Lila's heart beat faster.

"Here," she said quickly. "Let me give you directions to my house. Can you come by around two o'clock?" she asked, taking a piece of paper from her purse and frantically writing on it.

"I'll be looking forward to it," Jack said, grinning as he took the piece of paper Lila handed him through the fence.

"Happy sailing!" Lila called after him. Jack wriggled his fingers in a backward wave, not turning around. *What a stupid thing to say*, Lila thought. *He's going to think I'm too dumb to talk about anything but boats.*

Whirling around, Lila almost bumped smack into Marcia Forbes, her father's secretary. "Marcia!" she exclaimed, trying to retain her composure.

"How are you, Lila?" Ms. Forbes asked, looking at Lila a little strangely. "Did you want to see your father?"

Lila nodded, too surprised to speak.

"He's upstairs," Ms. Forbes said. "I have to run an errand, but I'm sure you two won't need me."

Lila knew that she had no choice now; she would have to stop in at her father's office. *I wonder if she saw me talking to Jack*, Lila thought, hurrying toward the office. *Not that it would matter if she did. It won't be long now before the whole world knows!*

Lila felt as if she were floating as she opened the door to her father's office. She had no idea what excuse she could give for visiting him. All she knew was that she was falling head over heels in love and that she had to wait until Sunday before she got to see her mysterious prince again.

Will Jack destroy Lila and Jessica's friendship? Find out in Sweet Valley High #19, SHOWDOWN.

A LETTER TO THE READER

Dear Friend,

Ever since I created the series, SWEET VALLEY HIGH, I've been thinking about a love trilogy, a miniseries revolving around one very special girl, a character similar in some ways to Jessica Wakefield, but even more devastating—more beautiful, more charming, and much more devious.

Her name is Caitlin Ryan, and with her long black hair, her magnificent blue eyes and ivory complexion, she's the most popular girl at the exclusive boarding school she attends in Virginia. On the surface her life seems perfect. She has it all: great wealth, talent, intelligence, and the dazzle to charm every boy in the school. But deep inside there's a secret need that haunts her life.

Caitlin's mother died in childbirth, and her father abandoned her immediately after she was born. At least that's the lie she has been told by her enormously rich grandmother, the cold and powerful matriarch who has raised Caitlin and given her everything money can buy. But not love.

Caitlin dances from boy to boy, never staying long, often breaking hearts, yet she's so sparkling and delightful that everyone forgives her. No one can resist her.

No one that is, but Jed Michaels. He's the new boy in school—tall, wonderfully handsome, and very, very nice. And Caitlin means to have him.

But somehow the old tricks don't work; she can't

seem to manipulate him. Impossible! There has never been anyone that the beautiful and terrible Caitlin couldn't have. And now she wants Jed Michaels—no matter who gets hurt or what she has to do to get him.

So many of you follow my SWEET VALLEY HIGH series that I know you'll find it fascinating to read what happens when love comes into the life of this spoiled and selfish beauty—the indomitable Caitlin Ryan.

Thanks for being there, and keep reading,

Francine Pascal

A special preview of the exciting
opening chapter of the first book
in the fabulous new trilogy:

CAITLIN

BOOK ONE

LOVING

---

by Francine Pascal,
creator of the best-selling
SWEET VALLEY HIGH series

"That's not a bad idea, Tenny," Caitlin said as she reached for a book from her locker. "Actually, it's pretty good."

"You really like it?" Tenny Sears hung on every word the beautiful Caitlin Ryan said. It was the petite freshman's dream to be accepted into the elite group the tall, dark-haired junior led at Highgate Academy. She was ready to do anything to belong.

Caitlin looked around and noticed the group of five girls who had begun to walk their way, and she lowered her voice conspiratorially. "Let me think it over, and I'll get back to you later. Meanwhile let's just keep it between us, okay?"

"Absolutely." Tenny struggled to keep her excitement down to a whisper. The most important girl in the whole school liked her idea. "Cross my heart," she promised. "I won't breathe a word to anyone."

Tenny would have loved to continue the conversation, but at just that moment Caitlin remembered she'd left her gold pen in French class. Tenny was only too happy to race to fetch it.

The minute the younger girl was out of sight, Caitlin gathered the other girls around her.

"Hey, you guys, I just had a great idea for this year's benefit night. Want to hear it?"

Of course they wanted to hear what she had to say about the benefit, the profits of which would go to the scholarship fund for miners' children. Everyone was always interested in anything Caitlin Ryan had to say. She waited until all eyes were on her, then hesitated for an instant, increasing the dramatic impact of her words.

"How about a male beauty contest?"

"A what?" Morgan Conway exclaimed.

"A male beauty contest," Caitlin answered, completely unruffled. "With all the guys dressing up in crazy outfits. It'd be a sellout!"

Most of the girls looked at Caitlin as if she'd suddenly gone crazy, but Dorothy Raite, a sleek, blond newcomer to Highgate, stepped closer to Caitlin's locker. "I think it's a great idea!"

"Thanks, Dorothy," Caitlin said, smiling modestly.

"I don't know." Morgan was doubtful. "How are you going to get the guys to go along with this? I can't quite picture Roger Wake parading around on stage in a swimsuit."

"He'll be the first contestant to sign up when I get done talking to him." Caitlin's tone was slyly smug.

"And all the other guys?"

"They'll follow along." Caitlin placed the last of her books in her knapsack, zipped it shut, then gracefully slung it over her shoulder. "Everybody who's anybody in this school will just shrivel up and die if they can't be part of it. Believe me, I wouldn't let the student council down. After all, I've got my new presidency to live up to."

Morgan frowned. "I suppose." She took a chocolate bar out of her brown leather shoulder bag and began to unwrap it.

Just at that moment, Tenny came back, empty-handed and full of apologies. "Sorry, Caitlin, I asked all over, but nobody's seen it."

"That's okay. I think I left it in my room, anyway."

"Did you lose something?" Kim Verdi asked, but Caitlin dismissed the subject, saying it wasn't important.

For an instant Tenny was confused until Dorothy Raite asked her if she'd heard Caitlin's fabulous new idea for a male beauty contest. Then everything fell into place. Caitlin had sent her away in order to take credit for the idea.

It didn't even take three seconds for Tenny to make up her mind about what to do. "Sounds terrific," she said. Tenny Sears was determined to belong to this group, no matter what.

Dorothy leaned over and whispered to Caitlin. "Speaking of beauties, look who's walking over here."

Casually Caitlin glanced up at the approaching Highgate soccer star. Roger Wake's handsome face broke into a smile when he saw her. Caitlin knew he was interested in her, and up until then she'd offhandedly played with that interest—when she was in the mood.

"And look who's with him!" Dorothy's elbow nearly poked a hole in Caitlin's ribs. "Jed Michaels. Oh, my God, I've been absolutely dying to meet this guy."

Caitlin nodded, her eyes narrowing. She'd been anxious to meet Jed, too, but she didn't tell Dorothy that. Ever since his arrival as a transfer student at Highgate, Caitlin had been studying him, waiting for precisely the right moment to be introduced and to make an unforgettable impression on him. It seemed that the opportunity had just been handed to her.

"Hey, Caitlin. How're you doing?" Roger called out, completely ignoring the other girls in the group.

"Great, Roger. How about you?" Caitlin's smile couldn't have been wider. "Thought you'd be on the soccer field by now."

"I'm on my way. The coach pushed back practice half an hour today, anyway. Speaking of which, I don't remember seeing you at the last scrimmage." There was a hint of teasing in his voice.

Caitlin looked puzzled and touched her fingertips to her lips. "I was there, I'm sure—"

"We were late, Caitlin, remember?" Tenny spoke up eagerly. "I was with you at drama club, and it ran over."

"Now, how could I have forgotten? You see,

Roger"—Caitlin sent him a sly, laughing look—"we never let the team down. Jenny should know—she's one of your biggest fans."

"Tenny," the girl corrected meekly. But she was glowing from having been singled out for attention by Caitlin.

"Oh, right, Tenny. Sorry, but I'm really bad with names sometimes." Caitlin smiled at the girl with seeming sincerity, but her attention returned quickly to the two boys standing nearby.

"Caitlin," Dorothy burst in, "do you want to tell him—"

"Shhh," Caitlin put her finger to her lips. "Not yet. We haven't made all our plans."

"Tell me what?" Roger asked eagerly.

"Oh, just a little idea we have for the council fund-raiser, but it's too soon to talk about it."

"Come on." Roger was becoming intrigued. "You're not being fair, Caitlin."

She paused. "Well, since you're our star soccer player, I can tell you it's going to be the hottest happening at Highgate this fall."

"Oh, yeah? What, a party?"

"No."

"A concert?"

She shook her head, her black-lashed, blue eyes twinkling. "I'm not going to stand here and play Twenty Questions with you, Roger. But when we decide to make our plans public, you'll be the first to know. I promise."

"Guess I'll have to settle for that."

"Anyway, Roger, I promise not to let any of this other stuff interfere with my supporting the team from now on."

At her look, Roger seemed ready to melt into his Nikes.

Just at that moment Jed Michaels stepped forward. It was a casual move on his part, as though he were just leaning in a little more closely to hear the conversation. His gaze rested on Caitlin.

Although she'd deliberately given the impression of being impervious to Jed, Caitlin was acutely aware of every move he made. She'd studied him enough from a distance to know that she liked what she saw.

Six feet tall, with broad shoulders and a trim body used to exercise, Jed Michaels was the type of boy made for a girl like Caitlin. He had wavy, light brown hair, ruggedly even features, and an endearing, crooked smile. Dressed casually in a striped cotton shirt, tight cords, and western boots, Jed didn't look like the typical preppy Highgate student, and Caitlin had the feeling it was a deliberate choice. He looked like his own person.

Caitlin had been impressed before, but now that she saw him close at hand, she felt electrified. For that brief instant when his incredible green eyes had looked directly into hers, she'd felt a tingle go up her spine.

Suddenly realizing the need for an introduction, Roger put his hand on Jed's shoulder. "By the way, do you girls know Jed Michaels? He just transferred here from Montana. We've already got him signed up for the soccer team."

Immediately the girls called out a chorus of enthusiastic greetings, which Jed acknowledged with a friendly smile and a nod of his head. "Nice to meet you." Dorothy's call had been the loudest, and Jed's gaze went toward the pretty blonde.

Dorothy smiled at him warmly, and Jed grinned back. But before another word could be spoken, Caitlin riveted Jed with her most magnetic look.

"I've seen you in the halls, Jed, and hoped you'd been made welcome." The intense fire of her deep blue eyes emphasized her words.

He looked from Dorothy to Caitlin. "Sure have."

"And how do you like Highgate?" Caitlin pressed on quickly, keeping the attention on herself.

"So far, so good." His voice was deep and soft and just slightly tinged with a western drawl.

"I'm glad." The enticing smile never left Caitlin's lips. "What school did you transfer from?"

"A small one back in Montana. You wouldn't have heard of it."

"Way out in cattle country?"

His eyes glimmered. "You've been to Montana?"

"Once. Years ago with my grandmother. It's really beautiful. All those mountains . . ."

"Yeah. Our ranch borders the Rockies."

"Ranch, huh? I'll bet you ride, then."

"Before I could walk."

"Then you'll have to try the riding here—eastern style. It's really fantastic! We're known for our hunt country in this part of Virginia."

"I'd like to try it."

"Come out with me sometime, and I'll show you the trails. I ride almost every afternoon." Caitlin drew her fingers through her long, black hair, pulling it away from her face in a way she knew was becoming, yet which seemed terribly innocent.

"Sounds like something I'd enjoy,"—Jed said, smiling—"once I get settled in."

"We're not going to give him much time for riding," Roger interrupted. "Not until after soccer season, anyway. The coach already has him singled out as first-string forward."

"We're glad you're on the team," Caitlin said. "With Roger as captain, we're going to have a great season." Caitlin glanced at Roger, who seemed flattered by her praise. Then through slightly lowered lashes, she looked directly back at Jed. "But I know it will be even better now."

Jed only smiled. "Hope I can live up to that."

Roger turned to Jed. "We've got to go."

"Fine." Jed nodded.

Caitlin noticed Dorothy, who had been silent during Jed and Caitlin's conversation. She was now staring at Jed wistfully as he and Roger headed toward the door.

Caitlin quickly leaned over to whisper, "Dorothy, did you notice the way Roger was looking at you?"

Her attention instantly diverted, Dorothy looked away from Jed to look at Caitlin. "Me?" She sounded surprised.

"Yeah. He really seems interested."

"Oh, I don't think so." Despite her attraction to Jed, Dorothy seemed flattered. "He's hardly ever looked at me before."

"You were standing behind me and probably couldn't notice, but take my word for it."

Dorothy glanced at the star soccer player's retreating back. Her expression was doubtful, but for the moment she'd forgotten her pursuit of Jed, and Caitlin took that opportunity to focus her own attention on the new boy from Montana. She knew she only had a moment more to make that unforgettable impression on him before the two boys were gone. Quickly she walked forward. Her voice was light but loud enough to carry to the girls behind her.

"We were just going in your direction, anyway," she called. "Why don't we walk along just to show you what strong supporters of the team we are?"

Looking surprised, Roger said, "That's fine by us. Right, Jed?"

"Whatever you say."

Caitlin thought he sounded pleased by the attention. Quickly, before the other girls joined them, she stepped between the two boys. Roger immediately tried to pull her hand close to his side. She wanted to swat him off, but instead, gave his hand a squeeze, then let go. She was pleased when Diana fell in step beside Roger. Turning to Jed, Caitlin smiled and said, "There must be a thousand questions you still have about the school and the area. Have you been to Virginia before?"

"A few times. I've seen a little of the countryside."

"And you like it?"

As they walked out the door of the building, Jed turned his head so that he could look down into her upturned face and nodded. There was a bright twinkle in his eyes.

Caitlin took that twinkle as encouragement, and her own eyes grew brighter. "So much goes on around here at this time of year. Has anyone told you about the fall dance this weekend?"

"I think Matt Jenks did. I'm rooming with him."

"It'll be great—a real good band," Caitlin cooed. In the background she heard the sound of the others' voices, but they didn't matter. Jed Michaels was listening to *her*.

They walked together for only another minute, down the brick footpath that connected the classroom buildings to the rest of the elegant campus. Caitlin told him all she could about the upcoming dance, stopping short of asking him to be her date. She wasn't going to throw herself at him. She wouldn't have to, anyway. She knew it would be only a matter of time before he would be hers.

It didn't take them long to reach the turnoff for the soccer field. "I guess this is where I get off," she said lightly. "See you around."

"See you soon," he answered and left.

Caitlin smiled to herself. This handsome boy from Montana wasn't going to be an easy mark, but this was an adequate beginning. She wanted him—and what Caitlin wanted, Caitlin got.

"You going back to the dorm, Caitlin?" Morgan asked.

"Yeah, I've got a ton of reading to do for English lit." Caitlin spoke easily, but her thoughts were on the smile Jed Michaels had given her just before he'd left.

"Somerson really piled it on tonight, didn't she?" Gloria Parks muttered.

"Who cares about homework," Caitlin replied. "I want to hear what you guys think of Jed."

"Not bad at all." Tenny giggled.

"We ought to be asking *you*, Caitlin," Morgan added. "You got all his attention."

Caitlin brought her thoughts back to the present and laughed. "Did I? I hadn't even noticed," she said coyly.

"At least Roger's got some competition now," Jessica Stark, a usually quiet redhead, remarked. "He was really getting *unbearable*."

"There's probably a lot more to Roger than meets the eye," Dorothy said in his defense.

"I agree. Roger's not bad. And what do you expect," Caitlin added, "when all he hears is how he's the school star."

The girls started crossing the lawns from the grouping of Highgate classroom buildings toward the dorms. The magnificent grounds of the exclusive boarding school were spread out around them. The ivy-covered walls of the original school building had changed little in the two hundred years since it had been constructed as the manor house for a prosperous plantation. A sweeping carpet of lawn had replaced the tilled fields of the past; and the smaller buildings had been converted into dormitories and staff quarters. The horse stable had been expanded, and several structures had been added—classroom buildings, a gymnasium complete with an indoor pool, tennis and racketball courts—but the architecture of the new buildings blended in well with that of the old.

"Caitlin, isn't that your grandmother's car in the visitors' parking lot?" Morgan pointed toward the graveled parking area off the oak-shaded main drive. A sleek, silver Mercedes sports coupe was gleaming in the sunlight there.

"So it is." Caitlin frowned momentarily. "Wonder what she's doing here? I must have left something at the house last time I was home for the weekend."

"My dream car!" Gloria exclaimed, holding one hand up to adjust her glasses. "I've told Daddy he absolutely *must* buy me one for my sixteenth birthday."

"And what did he say?" Jessica asked.

Gloria made a face. "That I had to settle for his three-year-old Datsun or get a bicycle."

"Beats walking," Morgan said, reaching into her bag for another candy bar.

"But I'm dying to have a car like your grandmother's."

"It's not bad." Caitlin glanced up at the car. "She has the Bentley, too, but this is the car she uses when she wants to drive herself instead of being chauffeured."

"Think she'll let you bring it here for your senior year?"

Caitlin shrugged and mimicked her grandmother's cultured tones. "'It's not wise to spoil one.' Besides, I've always preferred Jaguars."

Caitlin paused on the brick path, and the other girls stopped beside her. "You know, I really should go say hello to my grandmother. She's probably waiting for me." She turned quickly to the others. "We've got to have a meeting for this fundraiser. How about tonight—my room, at seven?"

"Sure."

"Great."

"Darn, I've got to study for an exam tomorrow," Jessica grumbled, "but let me know what you decide."

"Me, too," Kim commented. "I was on the courts all afternoon yesterday practicing for Sunday's tennis tournament and really got behind with my studying."

"Okay, we'll fill you guys in, but make sure you come to the next meeting. And I don't want any excuses. If you miss the meeting, you're out!" Caitlin stressed firmly. "I'll catch the rest of you later, then."

All the girls walked away except Dorothy, who lingered behind. Just then, a tall, elegantly dressed, silver-haired woman walked briskly down the stairs from the administrative office in the main school building. She moved directly toward the Mercedes, quickly opened the driver's door, and slid in behind the wheel.

Caitlin's arm shot up in greeting, but Regina Ryan

never glanced her way. Instead, she started the engine and immediately swung out of the parking area and down the curving drive.

For an instant Caitlin stopped in her tracks. Then with a wide, carefree smile, she turned back to Dorothy and laughed. "I just remembered. She called last night and said she was dropping off my allowance money but would be in a hurry and couldn't stay. My memory really *is* bad. I'll run over and pick it up now."

As Caitlin turned, Dorothy lightly grabbed Caitlin's elbow and spoke softly. "I know you're in a hurry, but can I talk to you for a second, Caitlin? Did you mean what you said about Roger? Was he really looking at me?"

"I told you he was," Caitlin said impatiently, anxious to get Dorothy out of the picture. "Would I lie to you?"

"Oh, no. It's just that when I went over to talk to him, he didn't seem that interested. He was more interested in listening to what you and Jed were saying."

"Roger's just nosy."

"Well, I wondered. You know, I haven't had any dates since I transferred—"

"Dorothy! You're worried about dates? Are you crazy?" Caitlin grinned broadly. "And as far as Roger goes, wait and see. Believe me." She gave a breezy wave. "I've got to go."

"Yeah, okay. And, thanks, Caitlin."

"Anytime."

Without a backward glance, Caitlin walked quickly to the administration office. The story about her allowance had been a fabrication. Regina Ryan had given Caitlin more than enough spending money when she'd been home two weeks earlier, but it would be all over campus in a minute if the girls thought there was anything marring Caitlin's seemingly perfect life.

Running up the steps and across the main marble-floored lobby that had once been the elegant entrance hall of the plantation house, she walked quickly into the dean's office and smiled warmly at Mrs. Forbes, the dean's secretary.

"Hi, Mrs. Forbes."

"Hello, Caitlin. Can I help you?"

"I came to pick up the message my grandmother just left."

"Message?" Mrs. Forbes frowned.

"Yes." Caitlin continued to look cheerful. "I just saw her leaving and figured she was in a hurry and left a message for me here."

"No, she just met on some school board business briefly with Dean Fleming."

"She didn't leave anything for me?"

"I can check with the part-time girl if you like."

"Thanks." Caitlin's smile had faded, but she waited as Mrs. Forbes stepped into a small room at the rear.

She returned in a second, shaking her head. "Sorry, Caitlin."

Caitlin forced herself to smile. "No problem, Mrs. Forbes. It wasn't important, anyway. She'll probably be on the phone with me ten times tonight."

As Caitlin hurried from the main building and set out again toward the dorm, her beautiful face was grim. Why was she always trying to fool herself? She knew there was no chance her grandmother would call just to say hello. But nobody would ever know that: She would make certain of it. Not Mrs. Forbes, or any of the kids; not even her roommate, Ginny. Not anyone!

Like it so far? Want to read more? LOVING will be available in May 1985.* It will be on sale wherever Bantam paperbacks are sold. The other two books in the trilogy, LOVE DENIED and TRUE LOVE, will also be published in 1985.

---

*Outside the United States and Canada, books will be available approximately three months later. Check with your local bookseller for further details.

☐	25033	**DOUBLE LOVE #1**	$2.50
☐	25044	**SECRETS #2**	$2.50
☐	25034	**PLAYING WITH FIRE #3**	$2.50
☐	25143	**POWER PLAY #4**	$2.50
☐	25043	**ALL NIGHT LONG #5**	$2.50
☐	25105	**DANGEROUS LOVE #6**	$2.50
☐	25106	**DEAR SISTER #7**	$2.50
☐	25092	**HEARTBREAKER #8**	$2.50
☐	25026	**RACING HEARTS #9**	$2.50
☐	25016	**WRONG KIND OF GIRL #10**	$2.50
☐	25046	**TOO GOOD TO BE TRUE #11**	$2.50
☐	25035	**WHEN LOVE DIES #12**	$2.50
☐	24524	**KIDNAPPED #13**	$2.25
☐	24531	**DECEPTIONS #14**	$2.50
☐	24582	**PROMISES #15**	$2.50
☐	24672	**RAGS TO RICHES #16**	$2.50
☐	24723	**LOVE LETTERS #17**	$2.50
☐	24825	**HEAD OVER HEELS #18**	$2.50
☐	24893	**SHOWDOWN #19**	$2.50
☐	24947	**CRASH LANDING! #20**	$2.50

Prices and availability subject to change without notice.

Buy them at your local bookstore or use this handy coupon for ordering:

Bantam Books, Inc., Dept SVH, 414 East Golf Road, Des Plaines, Ill. 60016

Please send me the books I have checked above. I am enclosing $_____
(please add $1.25 to cover postage and handling). Send check or money order
—no cash or C.O.D.'s please.

Mr/Mrs/Miss _____

Address_____

City_____ State/Zip_____

SVH—6/85

Please allow four to six weeks for delivery. This offer expires 12/85.

SPECIAL
MONEY SAVING
OFFER

Now you can have an up-to-date listing of Bantam's hundreds of titles plus take advantage of our unique and exciting bonus book offer. A special offer which gives you the opportunity to purchase a Bantam book for only 50¢. Here's how!

By ordering any five books at the regular price per order, you can also choose any other single book listed (up to a $4.95 value) for just 50¢. Some restrictions do apply, but for further details why not send for Bantam's listing of titles today!

Just send us your name and address plus 50¢ to defray the postage and handling costs.

DARK ENCHANTMENT

"Please take me back—"

"Not yet, Sybilla."

She tried to protest, but the words would not come. The night breeze was heavy with the spicy scents of the great tree ferns and the damp moss that spread a velvet carpet around the pool at the bottom of the falls. In the tangle of vines and shrubs she saw the flickering green and gold of the fireflies.

"Say you don't want me to take you back," he urged. "Say it . . ."

Even as she heard his words, muffled against her hair, she sensed the danger of giving in to her aching need for him.

Gavin's mouth moved from her palm to her lips. She felt his kiss, hot and urgent.

Now there was only Gavin and this moment. So brief a time to discover what it was to give herself in passion.

He drew her down on the soft moss beside the pool and buried his face in her hair. The thudding of her heart, the sound of his breath, harsh and a little unsteady, blended into the dark enchantment of the night.

DIANA HAVILAND

Pirate's Kiss

PINNACLE BOOKS
WINDSOR PUBLISHING CORP.

PINNACLE BOOKS

are published by

Windsor Publishing Corp.
475 Park Avenue South
New York, NY 10016

First printing: June, 1992

Printed in the United States of America

Chapter One

Sybilla Thornton stood for a moment at the head of the gangplank. Her golden eyes glowed with warm anticipation as she looked down at Montego Bay, with its low white buildings, its waterfront teeming with sailors, merchants, and street vendors, its cobblestone quays piled high with crates and bales of cargo from every corner of the world.

After all these endless months of waiting and her long voyage across the Atlantic, she and her brother Lance would be together again. Her slender fingers tightened around the small purse in which she carried his letter asking her to come and join him in their new home in Jamaica. Now she lifted the skirt of her amber velvet dress, smoothed her silk shawl around her shoulders, and hurried down the gangplank, followed by the sailor who carried her trunk.

Ever since she had caught her first glimpse of the island she had been enchanted by its exotic beauty—the tall blue-green mountains, their rounded tops lost in the silvery morning mist; the turquoise waves breaking in creamy foam against the palm-fringed coves. And she had savored the offshore breeze, fragrant with the scent of tropical flowers, ripening sugarcane, and spices.

But she could not quite overcome her homesickness for her native Somerset, with its ancient, towering oaks, its apple orchards and hedgerows. Her throat tightened as she remembered her family's manor house, the mellow red-brick walls and mullioned windows. She stepped onto the quay, sternly reminding herself that England was lost to her forever. Jamaica was her home now. The sailor set down her trunk. She gave him a coin and turned to watch him go back to the deck of the *Bristol Belle*.

Catching sight of Dolores de las Fuentes, the plump, pretty young Spanish girl who had come aboard at the Canary Islands, Sybilla raised her hand in a gesture of farewell. Dolores was going on to Panama to marry a man chosen for her by her family—a bridegroom she had not seen since she was betrothed to him at the age of eleven, back in Cádiz.

The prospect did not trouble her. "It is our custom," she told Sybilla. And she added with pride that her future husband was a most important official, the lieutenant governor of Panama.

For a moment, Sybilla wanted to go back aboard the now-familiar frigate. Then she straightened her slender shoulders, raised her chin, tucked a loose strand of her dark auburn hair back under the brim of her velvet hat, and looked about her. Somewhere in the milling crowd Lance would be waiting for her.

She reminded herself that her brother was lucky to be alive. So many of the bold young men who had ridden out on that July morning in 1685 to fight for the Duke of Monmouth had been condemned to death as traitors against His Majesty, James II. Others had been sentenced to a life of slavery to be driven by the overseer's whip here in the sugar cane fields of these Caribbean islands.

But Lance had managed to escape after the disastrous defeat of Monmouth's army at the battle of Sedgemoor and had reached Jamaica safely. He had found a home at Acacia Hall, their uncle Oliver's plantation.

And then, six months ago, he had written to Sybilla,

telling her that Oliver Thornton was making him plantation manager. It was a most important position, Lance had explained. She must sail out at once to join him.

Sybilla's soft red lips curved in a smile as she remembered the parting words of her shipboard friend, Dolores. "No doubt your family will arrange a fine marriage for you. Before the year is out you will be the wife of a wealthy English planter."

"Perhaps," Sybilla had said. Useless to try to convince the Spanish girl that she would never submit to an arranged marriage. Not that such marriages were unheard-of back in England. But Sybilla knew that she would have to fall in love with a man before she could give herself in marriage.

And this certainly was no time to be thinking about such matters, she chided herself. She searched the bustling crowd, but she could not see her brother anywhere.

She felt a bit unsteady on her feet after all these weeks at sea; and now the fierce, humid heat and the unending clamor of the waterfront added to her discomfort. Muscular black stevedores shouted to each other as they unloaded their cargoes; women of every hue from pale coffee to ebony called out to the crowd to buy their fruit, their carved wooden trinkets, and their woven baskets.

Sybilla's velvet dress—far too heavy for this climate— clung damply to her body. She went on looking over the crowd with rising uneasiness. The captain had assured her that her brother, like everyone else in Montego Bay, would have gotten word of the arrival of the *Bristol Belle* long before the frigate dropped anchor.

Why wasn't Lance here to meet her?

She drew in her breath sharply as she realized that she had caught the attention of a stranger. He was tall, over six feet, and dressed with the elegance of a gentleman of means. His open jacket revealed a spotless, white cambric shirt and a scarlet sash. From under the wide brim of his hat, with its curling black ostrich plume, she caught the bold gleam in his dark gray eyes. As his gaze locked with hers his lips curved in a smile of frank, sensuous approval.

How dare he look at her that way? All at once, she felt vulnerable—a girl of eighteen, alone in these unfamiliar surroundings. If only she, like Dolores de las Fuentes, had been accompanied by a stern-faced, hawk-eyed duenna.

Her velvet gown was not only too warm, it was also far too conspicuous here on the waterfront, for it was cut low at the neckline, and the tightly fitted bodice accented the high, firm curves of her breasts. She had put it on this morning because it was the only fashionable new garment she owned; she wanted to look her best for her reunion with Lance.

She drew her black and amber silk shawl more closely around her shoulders—a moment too late.

The gray-eyed man who had been looking at her, made no move toward her. But a burly dockside idler, his soiled shirt open halfway to his waist, came sauntering over, his wide grin showing broken yellow teeth.

"Lookin' for somebody, Miss?"

Sybilla's icy stare did not discourage him.

"Ain't right to keep a pretty little lady like you waitin' all alone," the man persisted. He put a sweaty paw on her arm. "Come on along with me."

She tried to pull away.

"My brother is coming to meet me."

But he ignored her words. "Why don't we wait in the tavern over there? A bottle of wine'll liven you up, and then—"

"Let me go!" Her heart began to race with fear, and her voice rose shrilly, cutting through the noise of the crowd. "My brother—Lance Thornton—will be here at any moment!" She hoped the Thornton name might carry some weight with him.

"I don't see this brother of yours," he told her. "I'll wager there ain't no brother—you're here on your own with nobody to look out for you."

"You are mistaken." The words held the ring of cold steel. It was the tall, gray-eyed man who spoke. He had come striding over, and Sybilla now saw that, in spite of his elegant appearance, his face showed the hard, ruthless look of an adventurer.

He bowed to Sybilla. "I am Captain Gavin Broderick," he said, his voice deep and resonant.

The other man shot an uneasy glance at Broderick and took a backward step. "I didn't mean the young lady no harm. . . ."

But Captain Broderick's cold stare, from under straight, black brows, silenced him and sent him slinking off into the crowd. Looking up at Broderick, Sybilla saw the self-assurance in the captain's bronzed face, with its sharply defined cheekbones and firm jawline.

Her gaze moved from his face to his broad chest and shoulders—the powerful muscles clearly outlined beneath his shirt—to his lean waist, bound by the scarlet sash, and his long, hard thighs encased in close-fitting breeches. His booted legs were planted apart, and as he looked down at her she felt an unfamiliar, tingling sensation coursing through her.

"My name is Sybilla Thornton—I've only just arrived from England, aboard the *Bristol Belle.*" She managed to speak with calm control, in spite of the tumult inside her.

"Lance Thornton's sister?" the captain asked.

Sybilla nodded, feeling a surge of relief. "Do you know him?"

"We've met," said Broderick.

"I was sure he'd be waiting for me when my ship docked—do you know where I might find him?"

"If you'll wait here, I'll bring him to you," Broderick offered. He gestured to a red-bearded giant of a seaman, who quickly responded, shouldering his way through the crowd to join them. "Mr. Pascoe's my first mate. He'll see that

9

you're not bothered by any of the waterfront scum again."

Then, turning to the huge, bronzed man, he said: "Abiathar—take Mistress Thornton over into the shade. We don't want her passing out, here on the quay."

"I've never fainted in my life," Sybilla told him indignantly. "And if you know where Lance is, I wish to go to him at once."

"It may be a while before he's in any fit condition to meet you."

Sybilla tensed at his words. Was Lance ill, or injured? All the more reason she should go to him now. Her heart began to thud against her chest, but she held herself erect and spoke with the manner of an outraged duchess giving orders to a servant. "You will take me to my brother, at once."

"He's in the Blue Dolphin," Broderick told her, gesturing in the direction of a two-story white building nearby. "You better wait for him out here."

Sybilla hesitated briefly, then started for the tavern, with its painted sign overhanging the street. Swiftly, she reached the weathered oak door, only to hear the captain's booted footsteps close behind her. He stepped around her, his tall, wide-shouldered body blocking her way. "You must not go in here alone."

"Stand aside," she ordered, her chin set at an imperious angle, her eyes flashing defiance.

"As you please, Mistress Thornton."

He stepped away with a bow and opened the door for her. "No doubt you'll find your brother in the back chamber," she heard him say.

She swept past him into the dark, noisy taproom, with its low, oak-beamed ceiling. Even now, at midday, the room was crowded. Barmaids moved swiftly from one table to another, carrying beakers of ale or bottles of rum.

She managed to stop one of them long enough to ask directions. The girl eyed her doubtfully. "I don't remember seein' you in here before."

10

"I am Mistress Thornton," she said. "I was told that I might find my brother in the back chamber."

The girl hesitated, then shrugged. "Through that side door, then down to the end of the passage. But I don't think you should—" Before she could say more, a sailor at one of the tables shouted to her for service. She hurried off about her duties.

Sybilla followed her directions as quickly as possible, and found herself in a narrow passageway. Reaching the door at the end, she tapped softly. "Come on in," an unfamiliar male voice called, and after a moment's hesitation, she obeyed.

"Stubborn female, ain't she?" Abiathar Pascoe remarked, as he and Broderick lingered outside the tavern.

The captain nodded. "All the same, the Blue Dolphin's no place for a young lady like her."

"You tried to warn her," Pascoe reminded him. "Now it's up to her brother to look out for her."

"Lance Thornton's in no condition to look out for himself by now, I'll warrant," the captain said. "Somebody should be on hand, in case she gets herself into trouble." His concern for the girl surprised and annoyed him.

Pascoe grinned. "I don't mind wetting my whistle. And a joint of hot roast lamb would be a rare treat, after all those weeks on salt beef and ship's biscuits."

They went inside and Broderick led the way to a table in a secluded corner, close by the archway opening into the hall. Pascoe ordered the lamb, with plantains and rice, and a mug of ale. Broderick contented himself with a beaker of rum.

He glanced around the taproom, and when he did not catch sight of Sybilla Thornton he felt somewhat reassured. At least she'd taken his advice and headed straight for the back chamber. Otherwise, a girl with her looks—hair like gleaming russet silk, those tawny golden eyes, and that seductive shape—might have started a riot in here.

He wrenched his thoughts away from the girl, reminding himself that he had far more important concerns at the moment. "It's time we got the *Condor* careened in Hobart's cove," he told his first mate. "The crew'll have their work cut out for them, getting her back in seaworthy condition."

"We kept her from port too long this time," Pascoe remarked, digging into his steaming food with his usual lusty appetite. "Her hull needs a good scraping, and we got to replace most of the sails. She handled heavy when we closed with that galleon." His eyes shone at the memory of the recent encounter. "I don't know another captain who could've swung her into position to fire the first broadside, then veered off again, out of the line of the Spaniard's guns. Sink me, if I do!"

"It was a close fight," Broderick agreed. "But the prize was worth the risk."

"Can't deny that, Captain," said Pascoe. "Why, them pearls alone are worth a fortune, and the silks—"

Gavin Broderick's face grew sober. "We got a fine haul from the *Valladolid,*" he said. "But it'll look paltry to our lads, when we divide the shares from our next voyage."

"You're still set on going through with that daft scheme of yours?"

Broderick nodded, his eyes dark and remote. He was looking past the red-bearded mate now, at the vision of unspeakable horror that had haunted him for so long. Over the past few years he and his men had already captured a fortune in Spanish cargoes, and he had taken his shares along with the rest. But the gold and pearls, the silks and spices, meant little to him.

He was driven by an insatiable need for revenge. So far, he had fed that hunger by taking one Spanish galleon at a time. But when the *Condor* was seaworthy again, he would embark on a venture no other buccaneer had dared to attempt. Nothing would stop him from exacting full

12

retribution from the Spanish for the wrong they had done him.

Sybilla stepped inside the back chamber of the tavern. Although the shutters were closed, an overhead oil lamp lit the faces of the well-dressed men seated around a card table, intent on their game. She went weak with relief as she caught sight of her brother. "Lance!" she called to him.

He looked up, startled, then dropped his cards. A moment later, he was on his feet, swaying slightly. His tawny hair was disheveled, his hazel eyes unfocused. His light jacket lay crumpled over the back of his chair and his shirt was stained with liquor. Sybilla's heart sank. No wonder Captain Broderick had tried to keep her outside. He had wanted to give her brother time to sober up and make himself presentable.

But she reminded herself that at least he was well and safe; that they were together again. He stumbled over to her, and she threw her arms around him.

"Sybilla—I'm sorry—"

His speech was slurred. "Your ship—I didn't expect it would drop anchor so soon . . ." He gave her the familiar, boyish smile she remembered. "I guess I lost track of the time."

Before Sybilla could speak, she was startled by a burst of shrill, feminine laughter from a shadowy corner of the room. She turned her head and caught sight of the two women lounging on a cushioned bench. Dockside trollops, by the look of them, wearing sleazy silk skirts, their bodices unbuttoned nearly to the waist to display their ample breasts, their faces heavily powdered and rouged.

Trying to ignore them, Sybilla gripped her brother's arm. "Please, Lance—take me out of here."

She kept her arm around his waist to steady him and

somehow they got as far as the taproom. At the back of the room, Lance stumbled against a table, and lurched forward, almost dragging her down with him.

Then she saw Captain Broderick spring up from the table. With one swift movement, he gripped Lance by the shoulder. Pascoe sighed and stared longingly at the juicy meat, plantains, and rice before him.

"You stay here and finish your meal," Broderick told the red-bearded mate.

He shifted Lance's weight from Sybilla to himself, and guided the unsteady young man through the taproom while she followed close beside them. Once outside, she paused in the purple shade of the balcony that jutted over the street.

"I am most grateful, Captain," she began, but before she could say anything more she heard someone calling to her brother from the crowd.

"You, Thornton! Come here!"

Sybilla caught sight of a stocky, glowering man who was making himself heard over the uproar of the waterfront. "Let me go—I'm all right," Lance muttered. Broderick released him.

"Thornton! Get yourself over here, I say—and be quick about it!" Somehow Lance managed to keep his balance, and obey the harsh command. The man confronted him with an angry glare. "Do you think those cargo manifests will get themselves copied while you laze away the afternoon in the Blue Dolphin with your card-playing friends and your doxies?"

Although Lance's slender body tightened with outrage, he did not reply. Sybilla saw his hands close into fists, but he rammed them into his pockets. It wasn't possible, she thought. How could Lance accept such a humiliating reproof and not respond?

Sybilla looked more closely at the stranger who had dared to rail at her brother out here on the street where any passerby could hear. The man wore a pale blue taffeta suit

14

and a yellow doublet. His hat was heaped with blue and yellow plumes. A pearl gleamed in the foam of lace at his throat. In his hand he carried a gold-topped ebony cane. But all his finery could not lend distinction to his chunky figure or his flushed face with its thick features and bulldog jaw. Beads of sweat trickled down from under his elaborately curled periwig. He dabbed at his forehead with a lace-trimmed handkerchief and glared at Lance.

"Do you suppose I pay you to take your ease in the tavern?"

Sybilla felt her insides start to churn as she stood there, an unwilling witness to her brother's humiliation. But now Gavin Broderick took her arm, led her forward, and introduced the man who was upbraiding her brother.

Sybilla inclined her head slightly, as she acknowledged the presence of Mr. Nicholas Hobart. But Hobart was not put off by her cool, distant manner. He stared at her for a long moment; then, removing his hat, he made her a deep, formal bow.

"Mr. Thornton left his duties to meet his sister," Broderick remarked. "She has just now arrived from England aboard the *Bristol Belle.*"

Hobart's eyes were lingering appreciatively on Sybilla's delicately molded cheekbones, her full, red lips, and small square chin. Then his gaze swept downward, and he stared avidly at the proud, firm lift of her breasts, the curve of her slender waist.

"Your pardon, Mistress," Hobart said, with an ingratiating smile. "If your brother had told me the reason for his absence, I would have been more than willing to give him the time off."

Sybilla, her slender body taut with dislike for Hobart, made no reply, but her silence did not discourage him. "That's my carriage over there. I should be honored to drive you to Acacia Hall."

She cast an urgent glance at her brother, hoping that he

15

would refuse Hobart's offer on her behalf and suggest other arrangements for taking her to her uncle's plantation. But Lance remained silent, and it was Gavin Broderick who came to her rescue.

"We've not yet settled the matter of repairing my ship," he reminded Hobart. "The cove on your beach will be suitable for careening the *Condor*."

Before Hobart could protest, Broderick jerked his head in the direction of the Blue Dolphin. "You'll find Mr. Pascoe in there. He can tell you all you need to know about the supplies you'll have to provide for the job."

"But surely, you do not expect me to keep Mistress Thornton waiting out here on the dock—"

"Certainly not." Broderick spoke with cool assurance. "If I may have the use of your carriage, I'll drive the lady to Acacia Hall, myself."

Without giving Hobart a chance to discuss the matter further, the captain signaled to a black porter nearby, and ordered him to put Sybilla's trunk in the back of the carriage—an elegant open landau, gleaming with polished brass trimming.

Sybilla and Lance exchanged hasty farewells. As her brother assured her that he would join her at the plantation that evening, she could not help but notice the uneasiness in his eyes.

"And now it's off to the warehouse with you, young man," Hobart told Lance. "There's work to be done." But he spoke with a forced heartiness, quite different from the manner in which he had berated her brother only a few minutes ago.

And to Sybilla, he said, "Indigo—my own plantation—is right alongside Acacia Hall—we will be neighbors, and I trust we may soon become friends."

Sybilla nodded and managed a faint smile, but her golden eyes held no trace of warmth. Then Broderick was escorting her to the open landau. He helped her onto the seat and they went rattling off over the cobbled street leading away from the dock.

They soon left the crowded waterfront far behind and started up the steep road out of Montego Bay. Sybilla drew a deep breath, welcoming the touch of a cool breeze against her face. Under other circumstances she might have enjoyed the beauties of the countryside—the majestic height of the palms, with their rustling emerald fronds, the brilliance of the hibiscus flowers, the jewel-colored parrots, and glowing blue butterflies. But now she sat, tense and unmoving, her hands clenched in her lap.

"Is something troubling you, Mistress Thornton?" Broderick asked.

He spoke with genuine concern. Sybilla hesitated, then turned to him. "It's my brother," she told him. "When he sent for me to come and join him at Acacia Hall—he said in his letter that he was managing my uncle's plantation. Now I find him working as a clerk in Mr. Hobart's warehouse."

"I think that's not all you're concerned about," Broderick said. She thought she saw a flicker of compassion in the depths of his gray eyes.

Filled with growing uneasiness, she put her hand on his sleeve in an unconscious gesture and drew strength from the hardness of his arm, beneath her fingers. "When I found Lance there, in the back chamber of the tavern, I could scarcely believe the change in him." She flushed slightly. "I understood then why you wished to keep me from seeing him like that."

"Try not to judge your brother too harshly. I should think he's had a bad time of it, working for Hobart."

"But what on earth could have possessed Lance to give up managing Acacia Hall, to take employment with a man like Mr. Hobart?"

"Perhaps your brother should tell you that, himself."

"But you do know something about it, don't you, Captain Broderick?" She raised her face to his, her jaw set, her golden eyes demanding an answer. He nodded. "Please tell me now," she persisted.

"As you wish," he said. He closed his hand around hers, as if to steady her. "Your uncle died of fever, a little over a month ago."

She drew in her breath sharply. Her uncle, dead. And there had been no way for Lance to get word to her, for she had already set sail aboard the *Bristol Belle*.

"I never knew Uncle Oliver," she said slowly. "I was so looking forward to meeting him."

"He was a fine old gentleman," Broderick said, "respected by all who knew him, here on the island." Then his lips tightened. "Madeleine Thornton is mistress of Acacia Hall now."

"Madeleine Thornton? Who is she?"

"Your uncle's widow. They were married less than two months before he died."

Sybilla struggled to adjust to all Broderick was telling her. Uncle Oliver had passed away. Acacia Hall was now the property of a woman she'd never heard of. Lance, her proud, quick-tempered brother, was toiling as a clerk in a warehouse.

What other changes faced her, here on the island that was to be her new home? She must learn as much as she could from Gavin Broderick, before she reached the plantation, so that she might cope with whatever lay ahead.

As she braced herself to question him further, she felt a kind of reassurance that seemed to radiate from the warmth of his powerful body so close beside her, and from the hard grip of his strong fingers, still tightly closed around her own.

18

Chapter Two

"Lance must have given up managing Acacia Hall soon after Madeleine inherited the plantation," Sybilla said. "I wonder if there was some connection—"

"He didn't leave by choice, Mistress Sybilla. Madeleine dismissed him and gave his job to Tom Yates, who'd been one of the overseers."

How could Lance go on living there after Uncle Oliver's widow had treated him that way? It wasn't like her brother to accept favors at the hands of anyone who had dealt with him so shabbily. Sybilla's eyes were troubled and her brows drew together in a slight frown.

"You needn't worry about your own reception at Acacia Hall." Broderick spoke with assurance. "Madeleine may not welcome you with open arms, but she won't turn you away. She can't."

"You know a great deal about Jamaica, don't you? Were you born here?"

He shook his head. "I come from a town called Boston, up in the Massachusetts Bay Colony. But I've been sailing these waters for years, and I've often dropped anchor here."

"You are a—a kind of trader?" she asked.

She caught a flicker of amusement in the depths of his gray

eyes. "I suppose you might say that."

"But your ship's called the *Condor,*" she said, remembering his conversation with Hobart, back in Montego Bay. "That's a bird of prey, isn't it?"

His dark brows lifted slightly in surprise. "So it is, Mistress Sybilla," he said. "You're a well-informed young lady."

"You chose a curious name for a peaceful trading vessel, Captain Broderick."

"Perhaps I did."

Plainly, he did not care to pursue the matter. Instead, he looked out over the rolling green hills below, and beyond them, to the sea. All at once he was seized with a longing to be aboard his frigate again, to feel the roll of the deck beneath his feet, to hear the crack of the sails overhead.

The *Condor* was, indeed, a bird of prey. And soon she would be off to hunt down the galleons of Spain, to strike with a swift fury, taking a toll that the proud Castilians would never forget.

Sybilla glanced at him, then drew away, bewildered by the swift flash of anger in his eyes, the grim lines that bracketed his mouth. But a moment later, when he turned back to her, the look had vanished.

And when he spoke his voice was quiet, his words casual. "No doubt it will take time for you to adjust to living here in Jamaica," he said. "I should think it's quite different from what you're used to back home."

She felt an ache of homesickness. With all her heart she longed to be back at the manor in Somerset. Now, early in December, the leafless oaks would be etched against a frosty gray sky. She would rise early for a gallop over the familiar fields and roads, the wind fresh and damp against her face.

Broderick's voice brought her back to the present. "Under the circumstances, your brother may decide he's had enough of Jamaica. Perhaps you may be returning home with him soon."

20

"We can't go back to England—not ever!" The words sprang to her lips unbidden. What was she thinking of, to set aside caution, even for a moment?

After the disastrous battle of Sedgemoor, she had hidden her brother from the King's troopers and had helped him to escape. Under the harsh laws of James II, anyone giving aid and comfort to a rebel was considered a traitor. She shared her brother's guilt, and if they were denounced to the authorities here in Jamaica they both would face swift and terrible punishment.

Quickly, she went on, "I would not wish to stand in the way of my brother's plans for the future. My uncle came out here to Jamaica and made his fortune. Since Lance has chosen to do the same, I must help him all I can."

"Your brother isn't likely to make a fortune working as one of Hobart's clerks."

"Lance won't remain a clerk for long—"

"You may be right about that," he agreed. "If Hobart catches him once more, drinking and amusing himself with the tavern sluts during business hours, your brother is likely to find himself without work again."

Sybilla's golden eyes narrowed with indignation. If only she were free to tell Broderick of Lance's courage at Sedgemoor—of how her brother had risked his life, charging into the thick of battle to lift an unhorsed comrade onto his own mount. How he had gone on fighting long after most of Monmouth's other followers had fled before the King's forces.

"My brother is brave, honorable—"

"I don't question his courage, or his honor. But I suspect he lacks caution and foresight. They're also valuable qualities."

She wanted to deny the truth of his words, but how could she? If Lance had not gone off to fight for a hopeless cause, they would both be safe in England right now.

Tears stung her eyelids, and she turned her face away. But

she wasn't fast enough to hide her distress. Broderick pulled the horse to a stop.

"Look there, Mistress Sybilla. I warrant you've never seen anything like that back in England, have you?"

She heard a rushing sound, and then her lips parted in wonder. By the side of the road, a great waterfall cascaded down from the rocks high above. Tiny drops of spray glittered along the fronds of the giant tree ferns and sparkled on the crimson hibiscus petals.

"It's beautiful," she said softly.

He closed his fingers around her chin, and turned her face to his. "Beautiful," he repeated, his voice deep and husky, his eyes fixed on hers.

"Captain Broderick, you mustn't—" she began, shaken by his touch.

"Make it Gavin, won't you—since I've already taken the liberty of calling you Sybilla." She felt the warmth of his body touching hers. "Right now, you're feeling lost and a little afraid. I don't suppose this was the sort of arrival you were expecting."

Sybilla was comforted by his closeness, his soothing voice. "A girl as lovely as you could make an excellent match here in the islands. Any man would think himself fortunate to win so lovely a bride."

He spoke softly, his eyes locked with hers. Her taut body relaxed gradually, lulled by the rush of the waterfall, the scents of the ferns and the damp, mossy earth.

Gavin tossed his hat aside. His thick, dark hair glowed in the sunlight. His arm went around her and she felt his mouth against her cheek. His lips parted, tracing the curve of her jaw, the line of her throat.

An unfamiliar, strangely exciting sensation stirred deep within her loins. When she made no move to draw away, he bent his head. His mouth found the cleft between her breasts and he touched it lightly with his tongue.

She went weak and clung to him, her hands closing

22

around his shoulders. Her breathing was unsteady, and she was lost in the tumult of sensations that surged through her. The green of the foliage and the deep blazing blue of the island sky blurred together. "How could any man hold you this way, without wanting to possess you?" he said softly, his breath hot against her flesh.

What was happening to her?

"Let me go!" She was afraid now—not only of this stranger who held her, but of her own unbridled response. Gavin relaxed his embrace.

"You're quite safe with me, Sybilla—if you're sure you want to be." His eyes sparkled with a teasing light, and her fear gave way to indignation.

"Perhaps you've been in the Indies too long," she told him. "I think you've learned your primitive style of courtship from the pirates hereabouts. I've heard of their lawless ways. No doubt they capture their women, and force them into marriage—"

He released her so swiftly that she fell back against the seat of the carriage. Staring up into his face, she was shocked to see his mahogany skin drawn taut across his high, sharply cut cheekbones. She shrank before the bleak stare from the depths of his gray eyes.

"I fear you've misunderstood me, Sybilla. When I spoke of marriage I was not offering myself as a prospective suitor."

She sat up, her back ramrod straight, her cheeks burning with embarrassment. How could she have made such a fool of herself?

"Any man would be tempted by your charms," he assured her. "But as for me—I'm not seeking a wife."

He flicked the reins and the horse broke into a trot.

"Acacia Hall's right around that next bend in the road," Gavin said. A few minutes later, she saw the tall, wrought-iron gates of the plantation. Beyond the gates lay the cane fields, their green stalks rustling in the breeze, and in the distance, set high on a hill, stood the Great House itself,

23

glowing brilliant white in the tropical sunlight.

Gavin drew the carriage to a stop, got down, and strode to the gates. Before he could open them, he was confronted by a wiry, sandy-haired man mounted on a brown mare.

"Captain Broderick—the mistress wasn't expecting company today." Tom Yates, the plantation manager, sounded unsure of himself.

"I've brought Mistress Sybilla Thornton up from Mo' Bay," Broderick told him.

Yates hesitated, holding his mount in check.

Gavin flung the gates wide. Then he was back in the carriage beside her. He cracked his whip and drove forward so swiftly that Yates was barely able to turn his startled mare out of their way.

The carriage rolled along the wide road between the cane fields. Sybilla glanced back. Yates was glowering at them, but he made no move to stop them.

"Tom Yates is doing a good job since he replaced your brother as manager," Gavin remarked. He looked out over the fields, where half-naked black men, their powerful bodies gleaming with sweat, worked at a furious pace, cutting the ripe stalks with their machetes. "Acacia Hall will have a fine harvest this season."

But Sybilla's thoughts were not on the harvest. She glanced at Gavin, her gaze lingering on his strong profile, with its straight nose, high cheekbones, and jutting chin. Yates was in command here, but Gavin had not hesitated to override his authority.

"Look there," he said. "The Great House. Impressive, isn't it?"

Sybilla stared up at the mansion, set against a grove of acacia trees, their branches heavy with fragrant yellow blossoms. Wide stone steps led from either side to the massive mahogany door. A broad balcony stretched along the length of the second-story facade.

Gavin got down, then lifted Sybilla from the high seat. As

she felt the slight friction of her rounded breasts brushing against the hardness of his chest, her breath caught in her throat. How was it possible that even such brief contact with this man could send flickers of heat darting along every nerve of her body?

Gavin tossed the reins to a small black boy who came hurrying forward. Then he took her arm and escorted her up the steps to the door, where they were admitted by a female servant in a starched calico dress, with a white kerchief tied about her head. "Cap'n Broderick, suh," she said, with a curtsey. "An' the lady?"

"Mistress Sybilla Thornton. Your late master's niece."

"Ah go tell the mistress yuh be heah," she said.

Gavin and Sybilla were left to wait in the drawing room. She looked about her, impressed by the elaborately furnished chamber. Polished silver candelabra stood on tables of mahogany and ebony. The couches that flanked the great fireplace were covered in pale yellow silk; their frames were heavily gilded and ornately carved. The tall windows were draped in the same shade of silk.

"No wonder you call it the Great House," Sybilla said to Gavin.

"That's what all Jamaican plantation houses are called," he explained. "Although few are quite so magnificent—"

He broke off, as Madeleine Thornton came sweeping into the room. She was a tall woman, in her early forties, with silver-blond hair and sapphire blue eyes. The taffeta skirt of her midnight blue gown made a delicate, rustling sound.

Gavin introduced Sybilla to her uncle's widow. "Nicholas Hobart was most eager to bring Mistress Sybilla here himself. However, he was detained in Mo' Bay on business. He has assured the young lady that you would be delighted to welcome her and to do everything possible to make her feel at home."

"My ship arrived a few hours ago," Sybilla began.

"You've been on our island so short a time, and you've

already made a friend of Nicholas Hobart." Madeleine spoke as if Sybilla had somehow arranged the meeting for her own advantage.

"Scarcely a friend," Sybilla told her. "I met Mr. Hobart purely by chance."

Madeleine shrugged her plump shoulders, as if dismissing the matter, but now she eyed Sybilla more closely. "Had I known you were coming, my dear, I would have ordered a suitable room to be prepared."

"Surely Lance told you he had sent for me," Sybilla said.

"He mentioned it—but that was months ago. Since he is no longer employed on the plantation . . ."

Sybilla looked at her in surprise. "My brother still lives here in the Great House, doesn't he?"

Madeleine shook her head. "Lance prefers a house of his own, so that he may come and go as he pleases."

"I will share his quarters," Sybilla said firmly.

"But, my dear—I would be happy to have you here with me. You have only to choose one of the guest chambers, and it will be prepared for you immediately."

"That is kind of you, madam, but it won't be necessary." She was not deceived by Madeleine's pretense of hospitality. "So much has changed since my brother sent for me. We must make plans for the future."

If Sybilla's words caught Madeleine off guard, the older woman quickly recovered herself. "No doubt you were deeply distressed to learn of your uncle's passing," she said. "What a shock for you, so soon after your arrival. Dear Oliver was such a fine man—and so generous. His will states that you and Lance may live here on the plantation for as long as you wish."

As Gavin and Sybilla rode away from the Great House, she kept her eyes fixed straight ahead, her hands clasped tightly in her lap.

"Perhaps you should have accepted Madeleine's offer," Gavin said.

"She doesn't want me there. No doubt she'd have turned Lance off the plantation, if it weren't for our uncle's will."

"Lance, perhaps—but not you," Gavin said, with an ironic smile. "I made it plain enough that Hobart expects her to treat you well."

"Why should she care what Mr. Hobart wants?" Sybilla demanded.

"He's the most influential man on the island. Many other planters are in debt to him. Your uncle was one of them. Madeleine has inherited her husband's debts, along with his property."

"You're well-informed about Mr. Hobart's affairs," Sybilla observed. "Are you a friend of his?"

"We have certain mutual business interests. As a matter of fact, I'm staying as a guest at his plantation."

"Is it as large as Acacia Hall?" she asked.

"It's larger by far. And he owns a thriving export company as well. He deals not only in sugar, but in spices, lumber, and other profitable commodities. But enough of Hobart."

Gavin slowed the carriage. "I'll have to ask directions to your brother's house from the overseer at the mill."

Even as he spoke, she caught the heavy, sickeningly sweet smell of the boiling cane. As they approached the long, low building, a blast of heat from the open door assaulted them. Black men unloaded heavy piles of cane from a line of oxcarts, while an overseer stood, whip in hand, urging them on.

"Which way to Lance Thornton's house?" Gavin called to him. The overseer mopped his forehead with his grimy shirtsleeve. "Straight ahead, Captain. Then left at the ceiba." The man gave Sybilla a brief, curious glance, before turning back to his work.

"What is a ceiba?" Sybilla asked, as they went moving on.

"Look over there," he told her.

27

She stared at the huge tree, its heavy branches shading the road. "That one's about fifty feet around the trunk. The natives can carve a dugout canoe from a single tree."

They turned onto a dirt path. Sybilla stifled a sound of disbelief as she caught sight of a wretched little shack, with its paint streaked and peeling, a deep crack across the sloping roof, and a few splintered boards nailed together for a porch.

"Surely Lance isn't living here."

"I don't see any other houses about, do you?"

"But—how dare that woman send my brother to live in this hovel?" Her voice shook with indignation.

"She did offer you a room in the Great House," Gavin reminded her.

"I'd sleep in a ditch, before I took a favor from Madeleine."

"That would scarcely be practical in the rainy season," Gavin remarked lightly.

But he was moved by Sybilla's spirited reply, by the proud tilt of her head and the look of outraged dignity in her golden eyes. He sensed the core of strength within her, untested as yet, perhaps. It would sustain her through whatever trials might lie ahead.

"I will stay here with Lance until we can find lodgings in Montego Bay," she told Gavin.

"You're determined to remain on the island?"

"I have no choice."

He removed his jacket, lifted her heavy trunk onto his shoulder, and carried it inside. Returning to her, he said, "Since you'll be staying here, no doubt we'll meet again." He took her hand in his, and she tingled at the warmth of his touch.

But she was on guard now, remembering what had happened back at the waterfall. "It was most kind of you to drive me here," she said. "However, I don't think there will be any need for us to see each other in the future."

"A prim and proper little speech, Sybilla," he said with a half-mocking smile. His fingers stroked her palm. "I think you have much to learn about a man's needs—and your own."

She took a step back, shaken by his words and the look that accompanied them. Before she could rebuke him, he caught her up in his arms. Cradling her against his chest, he strode to the house, kicked open the door, and carried her inside.

Although she was stirred by the swift, answering response of her body, she tried to cling to her self-control. "You've got to leave—at once—"

"Not yet, my sweet." His deep, vibrant voice was sweeping her up in a warm tide of longing. He set her on the frayed cushions of a bamboo couch, and then he was beside her. With one tug, he pulled open the bow beneath her chin, removed her velvet hat, and tossed it aside.

His fingers thrust deep into the soft waves of her auburn hair. He tilted her head back, and his mouth possessed hers. Her lips parted in a wordless cry of protest, muffled by his tongue as it slid inside. Her tongue met his in a kind of sensuous, primitive dance. She felt a hot current racing down along her spine.

Without quite knowing how it happened, she found that she was pressing her hands against his back, her fingers seared by the heat of his flesh beneath his light shirt. She should be trying to push him away, but instead she was drawing him closer. Bewildered by her response, she had no will to resist. Pride, modesty, all were swept away before the fierce need that surged up inside her.

His mouth lifted from hers, then pressed against the pulse at the side of her throat. His weight bore down on her until she lay back, looking up into his eyes, which had darkened to a deep smoky gray. Her hair fell across his arm in a cascade of russet silk.

He began to undo the buttons of her bodice. His gaze

lingered on the upward-thrusting breasts scarcely hidden by her thin shift.

"No, you must not—"

Her protest stopped him, but only for a moment. "Don't be frightened, Sybilla," he said softly. He touched one of her nipples, flicking at it lightly, teasingly. Then he began to roll the pink bud gently, between thumb and finger, until it rose and peaked. She gasped as the rhythmic waves of desire surged through her, spreading, deepening, until they engulfed the hidden core of her being.

"Gavin—please . . ."

What was she asking of him? She was no longer sure.

All at once, through the folds of her gown, she felt the hard urgency of his maleness, pressing against her thigh. She sensed instinctively that she had stirred this fierce need in him. Pride in the power of her untried womanhood warred with her fear of surrender. She became aware of the answering hunger deep inside her, the void that only he could fill. She arched upward, her thighs parting.

But a moment later, Gavin's body tensed and drew away. She stared up at him, shocked and bewildered. Then she, too, heard the thud of hoofbeats, far off at first, then moving steadily closer.

Gavin took his arm from around her. Although his powerful body shook with the force of his need, he managed to get to his feet. He set his jaw and tried to ignore the fiery ache of protest deep in his loins.

Sybilla lay against the cushions, struggling to regain her control, to quiet the tumult inside her. Shakily, she sat up and buttoned her bodice, then smoothed her skirt. She pushed her hair back from the white oval of her face.

By the time Gavin reached the window, the hoofbeats had stopped abruptly. "It's Yates," he said. "He must have caught sight of Hobart's carriage out there." He swore softly under his breath.

The plantation manager reined his mare to a halt under

the branches of the ceiba tree. While the horse pawed at the ground and tossed its head impatiently, Yates sat staring in the direction of the house. Then he wheeled about and rode off out of sight, the hoofbeats fading away.

As Gavin turned back to Sybilla, he was stirred once more by her loveliness: her delicate features framed by her shining hair, the seductive curves of her slender body.

He tried to convince himself that the interruption had been for the best. Sybilla, warm and ardent though she was, had little experience with men. He would wager that she was still a virgin, taught by a careful mother to guard her innocence until she might surrender it to her husband, in the sanctity of the bridal chamber. For a gently reared girl of good family, marriage was the only acceptable destiny.

Gavin's mouth curved in self-mockery. For him there would always be the tavern wenches of the Jamaica waterfront or the light ladies of Tortuga, that island known throughout the Caribbean as a haven for pirates. On Tortuga any man could find a doxy, experienced in her trade and ready to offer herself for a few bright pieces of eight or a glittering trinket looted from a Spanish galleon.

"Is Yates gone?" Sybilla was asking uneasily.

Gavin nodded. "He has little time to waste during the harvest season."

"But he must have seen the carriage—and he'll guess that we're in here—together—" He caught her uneasy look, and heard the tension in her voice. It was natural enough, he thought. A respectable young lady must be on guard at all times, to avoid even the slightest appearance of immoral conduct.

"Yates'll keep his mouth shut. You can count on it." Gavin spoke with a hard self-assurance that left no room for doubt. Instinctively, she trusted him to protect her from gossip.

But now, for the first time in her life, she did not trust herself to control her unruly emotions. Her cheeks burned as she remembered how close she had come to yielding herself completely to a man she scarcely knew.

Quickly, she rose and said, "You must leave at once." She glanced around the shabby little room. "I've much to do, if I'm to have the house in decent order when Lance comes home." She tried to sound brisk and efficient, but she could not meet Gavin's eyes.

"As you wish, Mistress Sybilla," he said. "I'll be staying at Indigo until my ship is made ready to sail. If you should need me, you've only to send word."

Before she could speak, he turned and left the house, striding back to the waiting carriage. She followed him as far as the doorway, where she stood for a moment, looking after him. In spite of herself, her eyes lingered on his hard, powerful back, his muscular thighs.

She watched him drive away, but after the carriage had disappeared from sight and she had gone back inside she could not shake off the restless longing that possessed her. She paused to smooth the rumpled cushions on the couch, and the memories, vivid and disturbing, came flooding over her. Gavin Broderick had shown her a side of her nature she had never known until now.

Moving quickly, purposefully, she went through the rooms—three of them, if she counted a small cubicle, scarcely more than a shed. She'd find plenty of hard work to keep her occupied during the next few hours. First she must check the food supply. Although she had never cooked a meal, she would manage somehow. And she would also have to scrub the floor and dust the furniture with her own hands.

But it wouldn't do to ruin her one presentable garment. After a brief search of her trunk, she found a striped muslin morning dress, worn and a little too tight, but still serviceable.

Stripping off her velvet gown, she folded it away carefully. Then she paused for a moment, clad only in her shift. She brushed her fingertips over her nipples, lightly, wonderingly. No man had ever touched her there before. Or kissed her as

Gavin had, with sensuous intimacy.

Forget Gavin Broderick, she warned herself, her delicate features tightening with determination. He had given her fair warning that he had no intention of marrying her. Soon he would go sailing off, bound for his next port of call.

She was no trollop, to surrender herself to the first man who stirred her passions. She was Sybilla Thornton, daughter of a proud family bred in the tradition of honor and dignity. The Thornton name commanded respect here in Jamaica, as it had back in England. Hadn't Gavin himself said that there would be more than one planter, who would be proud to claim her for his bride?

Yet even now, in spite of all she told herself, she still ached with longing to feel his arms around her, his body strong and demanding against her own.

Chapter Three

Lance frowned as he pushed away the serving of golden brown mutton pie Sybilla offered him. Reaching for the jug of rum he had brought home from Montego Bay, he refilled his tall wooden tankard. Sybilla cast an uneasy glance at him.

"There's more than enough dinner for two," she said. "A maidservant brought a basket of food from the kitchen of the Great House a little while before you returned." She forced a smile and kept her voice light. "It's lucky she did, too, because all I was able to find in your cupboard was half a bag of mildewed cornmeal."

"I usually dine at the Blue Dolphin after I'm finished at the warehouse." Lance drained his cup, and filled it again.

Sybilla's spirits plummeted. She had been looking forward to her brother's return, but as soon as he seated himself at the table he had begun drinking.

Hadn't he noticed all she had accomplished that afternoon? The splintery floors were freshly scrubbed, the few sticks of cast-off furniture were dusted, and she had picked up his scattered garments and hung them on the pegs in his bedroom. She had decorated the table with a few scarlet hibiscus blossoms from the bush beside the porch, using a chipped tumbler as a vase. But her brother had not offered a word of appreciation for her efforts.

Restraining her disappointment, Sybilla poured a mug of strong black coffee for herself. She would have preferred a pot of tea, but this was no time to be finicky. She moved a platter of fruit to his side of the table.

"I've never seen so many oranges all at once," she said. "And look—a whole pineapple." Such imported delicacies might appear in the mansions of the wealthy in London, but they were rarely available at the Thorntons' manor house in Somerset.

"You may take dear Aunt Madeleine's charity, but I don't choose to," he told her.

"You're still living here on her plantation," she interrupted, with a touch of asperity. "No doubt you could have found other quarters."

"Hobart allows his clerks to sleep in the loft, over the warehouse." His mouth twisted with distaste. "It smells of molasses and mouse droppings."

She understood now, why he went on staying here. Bad enough he had to work in the warehouse, without having to live there, too. She felt a quick flood of sympathy for her fastidious brother, trapped in such disagreeable surroundings. But it would do him no good to wallow in self-pity.

"Gavin—Captain Broderick—told me that Madeleine dismissed you after she took over, and I can imagine how that must have made you feel. But brooding won't help, you know. Or drinking yourself into a stupor, either."

"Rum's cheap enough here," he told her. "And when I've emptied a bottle or two, I can forget Somerset—the manor house—the friends I'd known all my life. Richard Gordon, Arthur Markham and the rest—slaughtered like cattle at Sedgemoor . . ."

He lifted his tankard again. But Sybilla's hand shot out and the wooden vessel went clattering to the floor.

Lance's hazel eyes darted angry sparks. At least she had managed to jolt him out of his apathy.

35

"What the devil—who gave you the right—" he sputtered.

Ignoring his protest, she seized the jug and made a dash for the door, her skirts billowing around her. Leaning over the porch railing, she poured the rum into the tall shrubbery, then set down the empty jug.

She turned to see Lance close behind her, his face tight with fury. "I won't put up with your high-handed ways—I'm not a child!"

"Then don't behave like one," she told him, as she brushed past him and returned to the table. "I don't like Madeleine any more than you do. But since she's provided us with a good dinner, I'm not about to go hungry."

"A good dinner." His voice shook with indignation. "She should have offered you a chamber in the Great House!"

"As a matter of fact, she did. But I chose to live here and keep house for you. And it looks as if I haven't arrived a moment too soon."

Her eyes met Lance's squarely. "If we're going to make a fresh start here on the island, you've got to take hold. Stop addling your wits with rum and gambling at the Blue Dolphin. I doubt you can afford to lose a farthing."

She did not speak of those waterfront trollops she'd seen lounging about the back chamber of the tavern. A well-bred young lady was supposed to ignore the existence of such females.

"Captain Broderick should never have brought you into a place like that."

"He tried to keep me outside," she said, with a faint smile. "I was too stubborn to heed him."

Lance's shoulders slumped and his hazel eyes darkened with self-reproach. "It's my fault for not having come to meet your ship. For keeping you waiting alone on the dock." His brief flare of anger had burned itself out, but to Sybilla, his hangdog look was even more distressing. "I'd never have sent for you, if I'd known how little I'd have to offer when you got here."

36

"I wasn't all that safe back in Somerset," she reminded him. "If one of our servants had denounced me to the law . . . But that's all past now."

"And what sort of a splendid future do you see ahead? You'll have to go on living in this shack while I ride down to Mo' Bay to sell my services to Hobart. To swallow his insolence in exchange for the wretched pittance he doles out to me."

Sybilla could control herself no longer. "You're better off than those rebels who were hanged. Or shipped out here to the Indies as bond slaves," she reminded him.

Lance stared at her for a moment. Her words had shocked him out of his maudlin self-pity. When he spoke, his voice was bleak. "Those poor devils might've been better off if Judge Jeffreys had sentenced them to the gallows during his Bloody Assizes. They don't last long out here, cutting cane or working in the mills. Sunstroke or fever soon put an end to their suffering. Or they're flogged by the overseers. I've seen men with their backs cut to shreds. And when they die at last, their bodies are left tied to the whipping post as a warning to the others—"

Sybilla made a choking sound, and a shudder ran through her.

"Forgive me," he said quickly. "How could I speak of such horrors to you?" Then, in an attempt to console her, he added, "Uncle Oliver bought no English convicts to work here at Acacia Hall."

At least Lance sounded more like himself, moved by the fate of his fellow rebels, protective of his sister's feelings. Sybilla told herself that it was only his sense of isolation and his resentment at being forced to work at such a menial position that had driven him into this depressed state. But now that she was here she would change all that. She filled his cup with steaming black coffee, hoping it would clear away the lingering effects of the rum.

"Did Uncle Oliver know why you left England?" she asked.

"It was only fair to tell him," Lance said. "He gave me a proper tongue lashing and made me promise to settle down. He taught me to keep the accounts for the plantation. I did my best, and he was satisfied with my work."

"But why did Madeleine dismiss you?"

"She wanted Yates in my place."

Sybilla looked at him with a puzzled frown.

"Uncle Oliver was an old man," he told her. "Tom Yates was only too willing to give her what she needed—" Lance broke off, and looked away quickly. "You wouldn't understand," he muttered.

His words brought a warm flush to her cheeks. Only a few hours ago, here in this room, she had lain in Gavin's arms, her breasts bared to his touch. Lance never would have believed that his virginal young sister could have behaved so shamelessly.

She could scarcely believe it herself.

Later that night, as Sybilla tossed restlessly on her pallet, she tried to tell herself that she was unable to fall asleep because of her unfamiliar surroundings. Ignoring her brother's protests, she had insisted on taking the smallest of the three rooms for her bedchamber. The humid air was heavy with the smell of boiling cane from the mill, the clanking of the machinery, the creaking of the oxcarts. During the harvest season, the mill was kept going day and night, Lance had told her.

She shifted her body, and felt her skin tingling, her muscles taut. Her thin nightdress, already damp with perspiration, clung to her breasts and thighs. She closed her eyes, only to see each plane and angle of Gavin's bronzed face behind her lids.

Before he had left her that afternoon, he'd said that if she needed him, she was to send word. She turned over on her stomach and pressed her face against the coarse cotton

38

pillow. She had to forget Gavin Broderick. As soon as his ship was repaired, he would sail away, and she was not likely to see him, ever again.

"So you invited Lance and that pretty young sister of his to the house for dinner tomorrow night." Tom Yates, seated at the foot of Madeleine's canopied bed, finished buttoning his shirt. "You think they'll come?"

"Lance can't afford to insult Nicholas Hobart by staying away." Madeleine smoothed back her silver blond hair from her face. "I've had one of the front chambers prepared for Sybilla. From now on, I want her here in the house with me."

Yates threw her a quick, wary look. "And Lance—you want him here, too?"

"Don't worry about him," she said. "I'm not about to give him back his position as manager." She sat up and leaned forward, her blue silk robe revealing her plump white shoulders and her ample breasts. Her skin was still smooth and enticing, for she kept her maids busy, for hours at a time, massaging her body with fragrant lotions. "Lance is of no importance to me," she assured Yates.

"But his sister is?"

"I was speaking to Hobart, a few days ago. He made it plain that he wished to see Sybilla again." Her full, sensual mouth curved in a wry smile. "It would appear that he's taken quite a fancy to my little niece."

"Perhaps she may not care for him," Yates remarked, pulling on his boots.

For a moment, he considered telling Madeleine that Broderick and Sybilla Thornton had spent some time in the shack together, right after she'd arrived here. But he quickly dismissed the thought.

He remembered his recent conversation with Broderick, when the captain had stopped him near the mill. Broderick had not mentioned Sybilla by name. "I'm surprised you have time to be idling during harvest season," he'd remarked.

"What business is it of yours?" Yates blustered. The captain's gray eyes glinted dangerously, and the hard stare sent a chill through Yates's insides.

"I thought I saw you wandering around near Lance Thornton's place a short while ago." There was a steely edge to Broderick's voice.

"You're mistaken—it wasn't me, Captain Broderick," Yates assured him hastily. "I don't go poking around, meddling with what don't concern me. Or talking out of turn, neither."

"That's wise of you." Broderick gave him a curt nod, and drove off.

Yates was no coward, but he wasn't one to go looking for trouble. And his instincts told him that Captain Broderick could be a dangerous enemy.

Madeleine's voice jerked Yates back to the present, and to the silk and lace elegance of her bedchamber. "If Hobart is attracted to Mistress Sybilla," she was saying, "why shouldn't I bring them together?"

Madeleine had never been troubled by conscience. It was essential for her to stay in Hobart's good graces, and if she could do so by offering him Sybilla's ripe young body, she would not hesitate for a moment. "I'll be doing the girl a favor, too," she went on. "Poor creature—left without a farthing."

Yates gave her a knowing grin and went straight to the heart of the matter. "A few more profitable harvests and you'll be able to pay off the last of old Oliver's debts."

Really, she thought, the manager was getting above himself. He ran the plantation efficiently. And he came to her bed whenever she sent for him, hot and eager to please her. She ran a plump, white hand over the rumpled sheets, still heavy with the musky smell of his wiry body. She was not the sort of woman who could get along without a man to share her bed.

But she must not allow him to go beyond the boundaries she'd set in their relationship. She was the mistress of Acacia Hall, and she'd make sure he didn't forget that he was only her paid subordinate.

"What about young Lance?" Yates asked. "Suppose he don't relish the notion of Hobart taking liberties with Mistress Sybilla?"

Madeleine's blue eyes narrowed. "That's no concern of yours, Yates," she said. "If you've nothing better to do than meddle in my family affairs, I must see to it that you're kept busier."

It was as if she had not been lying under him on the wide bed only a little while ago, clutching at his naked, sweating body, tossing her head from side to side, urging him on, then crying out when he satisfied her at last.

"You are to go to the mill, right now. Stay there for rest of the night, and keep your eyes on the overseers as well as the slaves. I want the grinding speeded up, the trash burned. And you had better look over all the wagons. I don't want a broken wheel or a split axle on the next trip down to Mo' Bay."

At sunset the following evening Sybilla arrived with Lance at the Great House. Madeleine greeted her with an effusive show of pleasure, then led her upstairs to one of the guest chambers, leaving the young man to sip his wine in the drawing room below.

"How charming you look, my dear," Madeleine said. No wonder Hobart hungered to possess the girl; she was a rare beauty, with her glowing auburn hair and her topaz-colored eyes. Even the worn muslin gown, which had been altered none too skillfully, could not detract from the curves of her seductive young body.

Perhaps it did not really matter that Sybilla's gown looked completely unfashionable compared with Madeleine's elegant black satin, which was cut daringly low in the bosom and trimmed with gold lace. Still, it might be a sensible investment to provide the girl with a becoming new wardrobe to set off her looks to their best advantage.

"Do try a touch of this frangipani scent," she said. She dabbed Sybilla's wrists with perfume from a flask on the ornate dressing table. "And a bit more here—" She touched the stopper to the hollow at the base of her slender white throat.

"I fear you've had an uncomfortable few days in Lance's house, but from now on, you'll be living here with me."

Sybilla stared at Madeleine, baffled by this complete reversal. On the day of her arrival, her uncle's widow had been cold and aloof. What on earth had happened to change her?

The older woman went on quickly. "I've sent one of the servants for your trunk. You'll find your clothes here, pressed and hung away, by the time you are ready for bed tonight."

How dare the woman make such an arrangement without consulting her. "I have no intention of coming to live with you, while my brother remains in that wretched shack!"

"Maybe you can persuade him to move back here," Madeleine said, but she did not bother to mask her indifference to Lance Thornton's comfort.

She took Sybilla's arm and led her out through the tall, louvered doors to the balcony. "Look out there, beyond the fields. A most delightful view, isn't it? You can see all the way down to the beach."

For a moment, Sybilla was caught up in the magic of the prospect spread out before her. The setting sun tinted the clouds to soft rosy glow and struck glittering sparks from the surface of the blue-green sea. Closer to the Great House, the cane fields glowed a deep emerald green, and the regal, towering palms cast their shadows across the drive.

But Madeleine's voice broke the spell. "Look, there's Mr.

Hobart's carriage now," she said.

Sybilla leaned forward to get a better look. As the carriage drew closer to the house she caught sight of another man seated beside Hobart.

Her fingers gripped the balcony railing so tightly that the wrought iron cut into her flesh. Her topaz-colored eyes widened, and she found it difficult to draw a deep breath. Even at such a distance, she had no difficulty in recognizing Hobart's companion.

"I didn't know that you'd invited Captain Broderick to dinner," Sybilla said. Her voice sounded a trifle breathless, and she could not make herself look away. The carriage drew to a stop. Gavin swung himself down, and then, as if he were aware that he was being watched, he tilted back his head. The sunlight glowed on the lines of his strong chin and angular cheekbones. She felt herself enveloped, overwhelmed by the man's physical presence.

"Since the captain is staying at Indigo, I thought it only common courtesy to include him in my invitation," said Madeleine.

She cast a quick, alert glance at Sybilla. Was the silly young creature attracted to Gavin Broderick? That would never do. The man was a handsome devil, and he had a dashing, self-confident way about him. Such qualities might well attract a young girl who was inexperienced with men. But Madeleine did not doubt her own ability to guide her niece in the right direction.

"Come along, my dear," Madeleine said. "We must not keep the gentlemen waiting."

Chapter Four

"This is excellent turtle soup," said Nicholas Hobart. He smiled at Sybilla across the polished table. "I don't suppose you've ever seen one of our big turtles."

She shook her head.

"The waters hereabouts are swarming with them. But they're not easy to catch. Sometimes a few of my blacks drown or get themselves smashed up against the rocks, trying to land one."

He shrugged his beefy shoulders and went on spooning up his creamy turtle soup with obvious enjoyment. "Few Englishmen back home eat as well as we do here, Mistress Sybilla. Lobsters, crayfish, groupers. The hills are teeming with game—and all sorts of luscious fruit to be had for the plucking. Compared with England, our island's a paradise."

"I wonder if your slaves think it so," Sybilla said quietly.

Hobart laughed. "The blacks don't think," he told her. "Not if they know what's best for them. We have them shipped here to cut cane, work the mills, and breed more of their kind."

"And the white bond slaves—what of them?"

"A sorry lot, they are. I'm not sure His Majesty did us any great kindness by sending us his rebel scum."

He wiped his thick lips and went on. "I grant you, a white

44

slave cost far less at auction than one of the blacks. But they die off before a man can get his money's worth from their labor. The climate doesn't suit them, you see." He shook his head. "A successful planter's got to take the long view."

Sybilla repressed a shudder at his callous words. "You are speaking of Englishmen, Mr. Hobart, who fought for a cause they believed in."

"Rebels and malcontents, my dear young lady." He gave her a slightly patronizing smile. "But I'm forgetting that you're new to the islands. Our ways take a bit of getting used to."

She glanced over at Gavin and wondered if he shared Hobart's opinions on slavery. For an instant, she thought she saw a flicker of revulsion in his gray eyes, but then it was gone. He sipped his wine in silence, his tanned face inscrutable.

"But you must start thinking of Jamaica as your home now," Hobart went on. "Your uncle certainly did. He made his fortune on the island and built himself this fine house. Acacia Hall's most impressive, don't you agree?"

"My sister hasn't seen much of the Great House," Lance said. "She's been sharing my quarters near the mill."

"I was completely unprepared for Sybilla's arrival," Madeleine said quickly. "It was thoughtless of Lance not to tell me he'd sent for her. But she will be moving here tonight."

Gavin's eyes met Sybilla's, and a corner of his mouth lifted in an ironic smile. She'd assured him less than a fortnight ago that she would sleep in a ditch before she would live under Madeleine's roof. She told herself that his mocking glance should not trouble her.

But even now, with Madeleine chattering on, Sybilla was disturbingly aware of Gavin Broderick. The sight of his fingers on the stem of his wine goblet brought back the vivid memory of his touch. It was as if she could feel his hand cupping her breast . . . her nipple tingling against his palm. . . .

45

"You said nothing to me about moving into the Great House, Sybilla," Lance interrupted.

"Surely you wish your sister to live in comfort, under her aunt's protection," Hobart said, without giving her a chance to explain.

"I'm perfectly capable of protecting my sister," her brother told his employer.

Hobart grinned, as if relishing some private joke. "No doubt you are—but you won't be here much longer, young man."

Sybilla remembered Gavin's warning that Hobart might dismiss her brother from his position at the warehouse. But surely, even this gross, crude man would not choose the occasion of a dinner party to do so. Such behavior would be unthinkable.

"Your brother was never meant to be a clerk," Hobart told Sybilla. "I confess that I was mistaken when I offered him such work. An adventurous young gentleman of good family deserves far better—a fitting opportunity to show what he can do. I've no doubt that, given the chance, he'll be able to make his fortune here in the Indies, as his uncle did."

He turned to Lance, who looked a little dazed. And no wonder, Sybilla thought.

"You are offering my brother a different sort of work?" Sybilla asked.

"That's right, Mistress Thornton. He'll have to leave Jamaica for a time, but it'll be well worth the trip."

Although she disliked Hobart, she was prepared to try to overlook his faults, if he would give her brother a chance to make good. Lance needed a challenge to shake him out of his apathy. He wasn't meant to sit hunched over a ledger in a warehouse.

Lance leaned forward, and Sybilla saw that his eyes had begun to glow with excitement. "Where am I to go, Mr. Hobart?" he asked.

"I'm sending you to the Isle of Pines, off the coast of Cuba.

46

You're exactly the right man to handle my business affairs there. You'll have nearly forty men working under you. You'll give the orders and make certain they're carried out. It will be a heavy responsibility, but if you succeed I'll see that you're well rewarded."

Sybilla's lips tightened. Lance looked as he had that night, more than a year ago, when he had met with his friends at the manorhouse in Somerset. The night he'd pledged himself to go off and fight for the Duke of Monmouth.

"I'll succeed," he was saying. "You may count on me, sir."

Sybilla stared at Lance with dismay. She wanted to share his newly awakened enthusiasm, but she couldn't. For she had not forgotten how contemptuously Hobart had spoken to him only a few weeks ago, on the waterfront in Montego Bay.

Now he was offering Lance an important position, and a chance for advancement. What had caused him to change his opinion of her brother's abilities in so short a time? Hobart did not strike her as the sort of man who would act on impulse, where his business was concerned.

"Exactly what sort of work will Lance be doing, Mr. Hobart?" she asked.

"That need not concern you, my dear," he said expansively. He spooned up the rest of his soup. "I'm confident that he has a fine future ahead. I'm sure that's what you'd wish for him, isn't it?"

"But you've not answered my question," Sybilla persisted. She saw a glint of respect in Gavin's eyes, as they met hers. "I must admit you've aroused my curiosity, Hobart," he said. "Let us all know more about this new enterprise."

Hobart's bulldog jaw tightened. He shot Gavin a warning glance, but the captain chose to ignore it.

"Are you going to put Thornton in charge of a turtle-hunting expedition, perhaps? Or are you sending him out to the Isle of Pines in search of bigger game?"

Sybilla gave him a grateful smile, for she decided that, in

spite of his offhand manner, Gavin was trying to help her get the information she wanted.

But Lance interrupted impatiently. "Mr. Hobart and I will discuss our business venture at a more suitable time, Captain," he said.

"Surely you will," Madeleine agreed. "I must confess that I understand little about business matters and no doubt such talk would bore Sybilla to tears."

"You needn't worry about your brother," Hobart told Sybilla, with what was meant to be a reassuring smile. "He's capable of looking out for himself. Naturally you will miss him, but while he's away, I'm sure I can rely on your aunt to keep you pleasantly occupied."

"Yes, indeed! It is time that Sybilla met some of the other ladies here on the island."

"An excellent idea," Hobart agreed. "Our Jamaican ladies have their tea parties and musicales, as they do back in England. They go on little excursions, and make sketches of the scenery."

"And no doubt Sybilla will wish to see more of island," Madeleine chimed in. "The trails in the Blue Mountains are most picturesque, and the air is so invigorating. Do you ride, my dear?"

"Why, yes—"

"Capital!" Hobart exclaimed. "I've bought a new chestnut filly—a spirited little animal, but well-trained. I'll have her sent over here tomorrow morning."

One of the maids removed the soup plates, while others carried in platters of roast quail, heaping bowls of yams, beans, rices, boiled greens, and baskets of hot biscuits. A butler followed, with an assortment of wines—Malaga, Burgundy, Port, and Canary.

It was plain to Sybilla this wasn't the time to find out about her brother's new position. But if Hobart thought he could go on dodging her questions, he was mistaken.

Although she was two years younger than Lance, she had

always been the one to look out for him, to help him to control his impulsive nature. True, she had not been able to prevent him from going off to fight for the Duke of Monmouth. But this time she would not fail him. She would wait for her chance to get him alone, and then she would try to reason with him.

Somehow, she managed to take part in the light conversation through the rest of the dinner. Madeleine's cook had prepared so many elaborate dishes—ham cooked in wine and surrounded with slices of pineapple, platters of succulent baked fish seasoned with unfamiliar herbs. In addition to the frosted cakes and the small silver baskets of marchpane candies there was also an elaborate dessert made of cream, almonds, and an exotic kind of fruit called a "banana"—a delicacy unknown in England. Although she had little appetite, she tasted each dish, and made a pretense of enjoying it.

But before Madeleine could give the signal to rise, Sybilla began to flutter her fan in an agitated way.

"I fear I am still not quite used to the climate," she said. "Lance—would you accompany me out to the terrace for a breath of air?"

Her brother gave her an anxious look and hurried over to take her arm, and together they left the candle-lit dining room.

Once outside, she led him away to the far end of the terrace. "I needed to speak to you alone," she said. "You mustn't even think of leaving Jamaica, before you find out as much as possible about this new venture of Hobart's—"

"So that's what is troubling you," he interrupted, with an indulgent smile. "Look here—I don't want to leave you behind, after you've come all the way from home. And I would rather you did not have to stay here with Madeleine. But you can't live alone—it would be most unsuitable."

"I'm not concerned for myself. It's you—"

"I can take care of myself." She caught the impatience in

49

his voice. "You said I'd find a way to make my fortune, but I never expected Hobart to offer me this splendid opportunity!"

"What sort of opportunity?" she demanded.

"Why—I'll be managing his business on the Isle of Pines— he's putting me in charge—"

"For heaven sake, Lance, didn't you notice how he avoided answering my questions?"

"Because he knew you wouldn't understand. What do you know about business?"

She refrained from reminding him that before his arrival in Jamaica he'd had nothing to do with any sort of business, either. He had lived in comfort at their manor house, riding, hunting, gambling with his friends, and had left the day to day care of the property to their estate manager.

"Mr. Hobart didn't give Captain Broderick an answer, either." Sybilla was trying hard to keep her temper.

"I thought you'd be pleased to see me gain advancement," he said sulkily.

"I would, if I could be sure of why Mr. Hobart's offering you a better position. Maybe you've forgotten how he spoke to you that day outside the Blue Dolphin. But I haven't."

"He realizes that I'm not suited to the work I'm doing now. But he has confidence in me. He is convinced I can handle this new position—and I won't disappoint him."

"Lance, if you'll only wait, and listen to reason this time—"

She stopped a moment too late. She was remembering the uprising, the vain attempt to put the Duke of Monmouth on the English throne—and the terrible defeat at Sedgemoor. And Lance knew it. During the uneasy silence that stretched between them, she sensed how deeply she had wounded his pride.

"Why should I care precisely what Hobart has in mind? I know I can make good. Just think, Sybilla! With a decent sum to make a new start, I can buy land, build a house and plant my own crop of sugarcane."

"That's the kind of talk I like to hear!"

Sybilla started violently. How had Hobart managed to slip up on them without her being aware of his presence? She must have been too intent on her talk with Lance to hear him until he was beside them.

"You may be sure I'll explain your new duties before you set sail for the Isle of Pines. And I can promise you all the adventure you could wish for, once you get there."

He turned to Sybilla with an ingratiating smile. "Have no fear, Mistress Thornton. I'll do all in my power to see that you have no time to fret, while your brother's away."

Chapter Five

Mistress Fanshawe rolled out the bolt of silk with a flourish, turning it this way and that, so that it gleamed like burnished copper in the sunlight that slanted through the shop window. "This came in a shipment from France only last week," the dressmaker told Sybilla. "The color will be perfect, with your hair and eyes."

Sybilla stroked the delicate material and nodded, but her thoughts were not on her new wardrobe. She glanced uneasily toward the door of the small shop.

She had sent a letter to Gavin yesterday, and Poppy, her maidservant, had carried back his reply. He had written, promising to meet her at Mistress Fanshawe's shop in Montego Bay this afternoon.

But perhaps he had encountered some unexpected difficulty while overseeing the repairs to his ship. Or maybe he had simply changed his mind.

"With such fine silk, I can create a magnificent ball gown," the dressmaker was saying. She held the material up against Sybilla's body. "It should be draped low at the bosom, I think. With the overskirt of gold lace, caught up on one side with a cluster of silk roses. Or perhaps a large bow."

Sybilla smiled, and tried to concentrate on Mistress Fanshawe's running comments, but her thoughts were elsewhere.

"Perhaps you will wish to have a fan trimmed with matching lace—and gloves, scented with orange flowers or Neroli."

The small, sharp-featured dressmaker kept up a steady flow of chatter as she displayed her merchandise. Madeleine Thornton was one of her best customers, and she was anxious to please the lady's young niece. And besides, Mistress Fanshawe thought, with a girl as attractive as Sybilla to display her handiwork, no doubt she would get many more new customers.

"Perhaps you will also want a new riding costume." The dressmaker held up a length of fawn-colored broadcloth. "A fitted jacket, I think, to accent the waist and bosom. I might trim it with russet braiding, or dark brown if you prefer."

She glanced at the well-worn, black garment Sybilla had donned for the ride down to Montego Bay. It was over two years old and, like her other dresses, this one was too short and stretched too tightly over her breasts. During the intervening time, she had changed from a slight adolescent with narrow hips and budding breasts to a young woman whose firm, rounded bosom thrust seductively at her bodice and whose graceful walk hinted at the lush hips and long legs beneath the folds of her skirts.

"I suppose I could do with a new riding outfit," Sybilla agreed. Since Nicholas Hobart had sent over the chestnut filly she had spent the early morning hours in the saddle. And as for the ball gown, she would be needing one soon.

"Mr. Hobart insists on giving a ball at Indigo, to present you to our local society," Madeleine had said. "And, if I may speak frankly my dear, the wardrobe you brought from England is scarcely suitable. You must go to Mistress Fanshawe's shop in Montego Bay, as I do. Your new dresses are to be made of her finest goods, regardless of cost."

Sybilla had managed to delay her visit to the dressmaker for nearly a week after she had moved into the Great House. Madeleine had already provided her with a luxurious bedchamber and given her Poppy, a pretty young quadroon girl, for her personal maid. Sybilla was reluctant to accept any more favors from her uncle's widow.

But yesterday, when Madeleine again urged her to order a new wardrobe, it occurred to Sybilla that a visit to Montego Bay might offer her a chance to arrange a private meeting with Gavin Broderick. She had to see him soon—without anyone else around.

"There's no need to accompany me to Montego Bay," Sybilla assured Madeleine. "I'll ride the new filly."

"But my dear, you cannot possibly go riding about the island alone. It would be most unseemly. One of the servants must go with you."

And early this morning she had set out, accompanied by a young groom mounted on a mule. It was good to get away from Madeleine for a few hours, to ride along the road, past groves of coconut palms and now and then a great ceiba tree, its heavy branches dark against the sky. Beyond the fields stretched the broad expanse of the Caribbean, the water shading from purple to azure, and then to a pale, translucent green nearer to the shore.

The groom had proved useful after all, for he had guided her down into Montego Bay by the shortest route. She glanced at him now through the shop window; he was standing patiently in the shade of the overhanging balcony.

For the past hour, she had lingered inside, prolonging her visit by examining an endless assortment of luxurious fabrics, and nodding politely at each of Mistress Fanshawe's suggestions. She examined the dressmaker's poppets—the fashionably dressed dolls with heads of porcelain, created in Paris and shipped out to the distant ports of the Caribbean and South America so that the wives and daughters of the wealthy might keep up with all the latest styles.

"If you will allow me to show you these gloves—no doubt you'll wish to have a pair to go with each of your new gowns," the dressmaker was saying. She reached for a polished satinwood box, but before she could display the contents, the shop bell tinkled.

Sybilla turned swiftly, her heart thudding against her ribs. Gavin stood framed in the narrow doorway, an impressive figure in his steel gray suit, his linen shirt open to reveal his strong, deeply bronzed neck, his long legs encased to the thighs in black boots of fine cordovan leather.

"Mistress Thornton." He swept off his hat, with its scarlet plume, and made her a formal bow. "I chanced to see you through the shop window as I was riding by. This is an unexpected pleasure, indeed."

The dressmaker was not deceived by his pretense that this was a chance meeting. Over the years, she'd known many ladies who had used a visit to her shop for a secret encounter. She glanced from Sybilla to the towering, dark-haired man, broad-shouldered, lean-hipped, his booted feet planted apart. Although he was an incongruous figure in these feminine surroundings, he appeared to be completely at ease.

But young Mistress Thornton was not so self-possessed; her skin flushed to her hairline. And her slender hand, resting on the counter, trembled slightly.

"I would be pleased to wait upon you at Acacia Hall, at your earliest convenience," the dressmaker said, her thoughts turning back to business. "I shall bring you a selection of sketches, if you wish. And whatever materials you choose."

"Yes, indeed," Sybilla said automatically. "I'll have the russet silk and the cinnamon broadcloth and—" She could no longer remember the other fabrics she had seen. "And the gloves," she managed to say. She was already hurrying toward Gavin.

"When would you like me to come, Mistress Thornton?" the dressmaker called after her.

"Tomorrow afternoon, if you please."

The groom raised his head as he saw Sybilla coming out. He straightened up, awaiting her orders.

"I've got to speak to you alone," she told Gavin in a whisper. He nodded, helped her up onto her chestnut filly, then mounted his own horse, a black stallion with white star on its brow.

"Wait here," he ordered the groom.

Then he and Sybilla went riding off side by side, at an easy pace. The street of small shops was some distance from the bustle of the waterfront; it was deserted now, and its heavy-scented flowering shrubs offered patches of deep shade. A perfect place for a private talk, she thought with satisfaction.

But she had not seen Gavin since the evening of the dinner party, and now it was difficult for her to fix her mind on the reason she had arranged this clandestine meeting, for she was caught up in the dizzying whirlpool of her sensations. She kept her eyes fixed straight ahead, and her hands tightened on the reins as she struggled to conceal her inner turmoil.

Unsure of how to begin, she found herself making aimless small talk. "I didn't wish to accept Madeleine's offer of a new wardrobe," she said. "Although I do suppose she is right—the dresses I brought from England are hopelessly out of fashion. Except for the amber velvet, and that is—" Her eyes met his and all at once she could not go on.

Was he, too, remembering how he had opened the bodice of that velvet dress, to stroke her back and shoulders and caress her breasts, with only the thin shift a tenuous barrier between his hands and the warmth of her skin? Did he think that she had asked to see him so that they might arrange a lovers' tryst?

"Since Madeleine has planned a whole round of entertainments for me, I suppose I must choose at least a few gowns. And Nicholas Hobart's giving a ball, to introduce me to his planter friends and their ladies."

"You didn't send for me because you wished to discuss your new wardrobe, or Hobart's ball," Gavin interrupted. "Just why did you write that note, Sybilla?"

When she did not answer, he drew rein, turning his stallion

so that it blocked the narrow street, and she, too, was forced to halt. "You said in your note that I was to tell no one about this meeting," he persisted. "Why the need for secrecy?"

"It's about Lance," she told him. "Oh, Gavin, I'm so concerned for him—"

A corner of his mouth went down in self-mockery. "And here I was hoping that you could not do without seeing me another day."

"You flatter yourself, sir."

She tried to keep her tone light and bantering, but even as she spoke, she felt her cheeks grow hot. She had known that she was taking a risk, asking Gavin to meet her in secret. But her growing fear for her brother gave her no choice.

"You have business dealings with Nicholas Hobart—you told me so," she began. She hoped that she sounded brisk and impersonal. "You are staying at Indigo, repairing your ship on his beach."

"That particular stretch of beach is convenient for careening the *Condor*." Seeing her puzzled look, he explained. "What that means is turning her on her side and scraping her hull free of barnacles and weeds. The cove shelves up smooth and easy from the lagoon. Once my crew lightened the ship and warped her ashore, they left the hull to dry in the sun, and now they've almost finished that part of the task. But they've still got to replace some of the sails and rigging."

He broke off and searched her face, his eyes alert and probing. "Surely you've no interest in the methods by which ships are kept seaworthy," he said. "Why did you send for me, Sybilla?"

She hesitated for a moment, then answered with equal directness. "Nicholas Hobart's offered my brother an important position, one with great responsibilities, and the chance to make a fortune. I've got to know what reason he had for such a complete about-face."

"You don't trust Hobart, do you?"

Sybilla shook her head. "He avoided answering my questions about exactly what he expects Lance to do on the Isle of Pines."

"Have you told your brother how you feel?"

"I've tried, more than once. But he wouldn't listen."

"That doesn't surprise me. No doubt Lance was caught up in his glorious visions of the future. All those splendid prospects Hobart spread out before him."

"I tried to reason with him, on the night of the dinner party. But I only made him angry. I slipped out of the Great House and went to see him twice after that. But he wasn't there. I waited until long past midnight—he still hadn't returned from Montego Bay."

"No doubt he was enjoying the diversions of the Blue Dolphin."

Sybilla chose to ignore Gavin's remark and its implications. "I finally found him at home, on the night before last. But even then, each time I tried to question him about his new position, he put me off. I don't believe he knows much about it even now."

"That's possible," Gavin conceded. "Or perhaps he's resentful, because you don't trust him to manage his own affairs."

Sybilla's voice shook with indignation. "I never said that!"

But her eyes wavered under his hard gaze. "You didn't have to, in so many words. Sybilla, don't you think it is high time you stepped aside, and allowed your brother to make his own decisions?"

The black stallion pawed the ground impatiently and tossed its head, but Gavin held the animal in check with no difficulty. "Tell me, have you always looked after Lance and tried to save him from the consequences of his folly?"

"Someone had to. Mama died when he was twelve."

And she had been only ten, a thin, long-legged little girl who went tagging along after her brother whenever he would allow her to. Her throat tightened, and she felt the familiar ache at the memory of that dreadful winter. Mama had gone to the village to nurse some of their tenants through the cholera and had caught the disease. In less than a week she was gone.

"After that, Papa stayed away from our home in Somerset for months at a time," she told Gavin. "He was either in London, or traveling on the Continent. And when he did return, he brought a great many guests with him. It was as if he could not face the loneliness; often Mama was gone."

Her golden eyes darkened. "Sometimes he'd send for me to come to the drawing room. I hated being put on display before all those strangers. He would order me to play the spinet or sing a ballad, to entertain his guests. But he paid no attention to Lance except to punish him severely for the most trifling escapade."

"Was Lance often disobedient?"

"Most boys take foolish risks and get themselves into scrapes. Didn't you?"

"At every opportunity," Gavin said with a grin. "But we were speaking about Lance."

"He was reckless—I think maybe he wanted to get Papa to notice him, any way he could. Once, he found an abandoned skiff, and took it out on the bay. I went along. He was Sir Francis Drake, and I was the crew."

"The whole crew?" Gavin's eyes danced with amusement. "Quite a responsibility for one small girl."

"It wasn't a laughing matter," she assured him. "The current was strong that day. I was afraid—I tried to persuade Lance to wait for another time, but he wouldn't listen. A rainstorm came up and we were lucky to get back to shore, both of us soaked to the skin. Papa had been home for over a month, and there were no guests to keep him distracted.

"We slipped into the stable to try to get dried before he could see us, but we got caught. Papa was furious. He grabbed Lance by the collar and took down a horsewhip."

"And you tried to protect him from a thrashing, I'll warrant."

"I convinced Papa that I was the one who'd taken the skiff

59

out, all by myself. I said that Lance followed, and saved me from drowning."

"Weren't you afraid your father would beat you instead?"

She shook her head. "Not Papa. He believed that all girls were foolish, fragile creatures, who couldn't be expected to have a particle of common sense."

"Did he, indeed? I suspect he was mistaken, where you were concerned."

"Never mind about that," she interrupted impatiently. "Gavin, I need your help now."

"If you mean to go on questioning me about Hobart's plans for Lance, it'll do you no good."

"You mean you don't know. Or is it that you refuse to tell me?"

"What I'm saying is, it no longer matters. You're too late. The *Trelawney*—one of Broderick's merchant ships—is about to set sail for the Isle of Pines right now. Lance has already gone aboard."

Sybilla stared at him in disbelief. "But that can't be. My brother wouldn't leave Jamaica without saying good-bye to me."

"He had no choice," Gavin told her. "Another of Hobart's ships is leaving ahead of time, and it'll be safer if the two of them travel together."

"Safer?"

"There's danger to ships in these waters."

"From pirates—is that what you mean?"

Gavin nodded. "They're always on the lookout for a merchantman. One of Hobart's vessels can be a rich prize. But they might hesitate to take on two of them at once."

She shuddered. "The captain of the *Bristol Belle* told us all about the pirates. He said they were ruthless monsters, without the slightest trace of compassion, or common humanity!"

"No doubt there are some among the Brotherhood of the Coast, who fit that description," Gavin said. For an instant she thought she saw a glint of amusement flickering in the depths of his gray eyes.

But surely she must have been mistaken, for what sort of man could be amused by the actions of sea robbers who attacked ships, who plundered cargoes and killed helpless victims, or held them for ransom?

"Come along," Gavin urged. "If we hurry, perhaps you'll at least have time to say good-bye to your brother." He spurred his horse to a brisk canter and she kept pace. But as they approached the waterfront they were forced to slow down because of the crowd. They had to make their way around heavily laden drays, carriages, and handcarts.

Several times, Sybilla had to rein in the filly, to avoid the stevedores carrying crates and barrels onto the ships, or vendors who haggled with sailors over the price of a gaudy neck cloth or cheap trinket.

A line of lumbering, ox-drawn wagons stopped, cutting them off completely. Sybilla gave a little cry of dismay.

"It looks as if you're too late, in any case." She heard a touch of sympathy in Gavin's voice, as he pointed toward the quay.

She had to narrow her eyes against the glitter of the sunlight on the water. "No—to the left," he said. "The schooner with the crimson pendant."

She caught sight of the ship with Hobart's house flag snapping in the breeze. The masts and rigging were etched against the brilliant blue sky. Even now, the sailors were preparing to take away the gangplank.

"That's the *Trelawney*," Gavin told her. "The *Pembroke* is larger, and carries forty guns. There she is, farther out on the bay. She'll accompany Lance's vessel as far as the Cuban coast and then go on alone."

Sybilla could only stare in dismay at the smaller of the two ships. "Gavin—please help me get down to the end of the quay."

He gave her a reassuring smile, then spurred his powerful

stallion forward, forcing his way between two of the wagons. Sybilla followed close behind him. The little filly tossed her head uneasily, as if she could sense the tension in her rider. But Sybilla, who had been bred to the saddle, kept her mount under control.

When she was close to the edge of the quay, she gave a cry of dismay, for the gangplank had already been removed. She heard the mate shouting orders and saw the sailors climbing swiftly up the rigging and out onto the yards. The white sails unfurled and hardened as the strong breeze filled the canvas.

"There's Lance at the taffrail," Gavin said. She followed the direction in which he was pointing.

Sybilla called out to her brother, but he could not hear her at this distance. Then Gavin's voice rang out with all the force and resonance of a man used to shouting orders over the roar of the gale, the pounding of the waves.

"Thornton! Lance Thornton! Over here!"

Now Lance stared down across the strip of water that was growing wider by the minute. Catching sight of Sybilla, he smiled and raised his arm in a gesture of farewell. His light cloak whipped about his shoulders. She waved back, her eyes fixed on him. She was scarcely aware of the breeze that loosened the strands of her auburn hair and sent them whipping across her cheeks. At least she'd had a chance to see him once more before he set sail.

But the distance between the quay and the hull of the *Trelawney* grew wider. She went on waving as Lance's ship sped off to join the *Pembroke*. How long would it be before she saw him again? Then she felt Gavin touch her arm. She looked down at the white linen handkerchief he held out to her, and she realized that her eyes were brimming with tears.

She dabbed at her cheeks, angry at having allowed herself to lose control and show her weakness.

"Come along," Gavin said. He turned his mount and led the way back, away from the quay and into one of the narrow side streets. There she reined to a halt. If only she had a few moments alone, to give way to her feelings. Instead, she held herself erect and lifted her chin.

"Lance probably will be back soon," Gavin said. "And with any luck, he'll have earned a great deal more than he would if he'd stayed at the warehouse."

"I don't care about this fortune Hobart's promised him. At least he was safe at the warehouse."

"Maybe you'd better start thinking about yourself," he said.

"Surely I'm in no danger from pirates, here in Jamaica."

"It seems the captain of the *Bristol Belle* made a deep impression with his talk of those fearsome devils," Gavin said.

His mouth curved in the trace of a smile. "Your girlhood hero, Sir Francis Drake was a pirate," he observed.

"You are mistaken! He was a privateer—Queen Elizabeth bestowed a knighthood upon him."

"She rewarded him for looting Panama and sharing his booty with her. You see, a privateer is only a pirate sailing under a letter of marque, a royal commission that allows him to plunder with the consent of his sovereign."

Then his voice grew sober. "There are other dangers beside pirates, and closer to home, Sybilla."

"So long as I'm living at Acacia Hall, I've nothing to fear."

"Are you sure?" He spoke brusquely. "You don't trust Hobart, and you're wise not to. But what about Madeleine? She's no more scrupulous than he is."

"What has that to do with me?"

"The man was attracted to you from the first day he met you. You aren't too naive to have noticed that," he said.

Sybilla grimaced. "You surely can't imagine that I have the slightest interest in such a crude, unfeeling lout. I was revolted by his indifference to the suffering of his slaves. I must be civil to Nicholas Hobart, I suppose. But as for his feelings toward me, you must know that I have done nothing to make him believe I care for him."

"You accepted that handsome little filly—"

"Madeleine insisted. She explained that he would be offended if I sent the animal back."

She turned a searching look on Gavin. "You do know something of Hobart's business on the Isle of Pines, don't you?"

Gavin shrugged. "What does it matter, now that your brother's ship has sailed?"

"Tell me—you must!" Her golden eyes were filled with urgency.

"Hobart uses the Isle of Pines as a base for trade with the Cubans. The wealthy planters there are desperate for all sorts of goods from Europe."

She looked at him in surprise. "I should think the Cubans would prefer to do business with Spain."

Gavin threw back his head and laughed, his white teeth flashing against the deep tan of his face. "The Spanish government certainly wants the Cubans to trade only with the mother country. In fact, their laws set down by the *Casa de Contratación*—that's a kind of board of trade—prohibit any of their colonies here in the New World from dealing with the merchants of other nations."

"Then why do the Cuban planters risk dealing with Mr. Hobart?"

"They have little choice," Gavin explained. "Spain doesn't produce nearly enough manufactured goods to supply the planters' needs. And the government back in Seville has put a prohibitive tax on what they do ship out here. Men like Hobart provide the same goods—or better—with no tax at all."

As she took in the full import of his words, Sybilla's body went taut in the saddle, and her hands tightened on the reins. "But you're talking about smuggling. That's Hobart's business on the Isle of Pines."

Icy fear swept through her, as she realized that her misgivings had not been unfounded after all. "And he's involved Lance in his lawless trade. Sweet Jesú! Lance could be captured, imprisoned in some dreadful Cuban dungeon. If only I had known before he sailed."

"Calm down," Gavin interrupted. "Surely the situation's not so bad as all that."

"Not so bad! To trick my brother into joining a band of smugglers? I should have stopped Lance from taking Hobart's offer. And now it's too late . . ."

Gavin held up his hand, as if to stem her frantic outburst. "You're taking an exaggerated view of the situation, aren't you, Sybilla? Smuggling's common enough. There are plenty of moonrakers plying their trade back in England. I'll warrant you've never stopped to wonder how you sometimes were able to buy your fine French silks and laces at bargain prices, have you?"

"I don't care about that now—it's Lance I'm thinking of!"

But Gavin ignored her interruption and went on calmly. "No doubt those goods were smuggled over to the Cornwall coast—or carried over the Romney marshes on a moonless night. And I'm sure your father and his friends were pleased enough to buy their French brandy and Holland ginevra without paying your English tariffs."

Sybilla's voice shook with outrage. "I assure you that no one in my family ever had anything to do with such illicit trade. If you knew anything about the Thorntons, you would realize how impossible that would be."

A corner of his mouth went up in a teasing smile. "Smooth your ruffled feathers, my sweet. I haven't suggested that your Papa was a smuggler by trade. Only that he and other respectable gentlemen help to fuel a demand for such goods. And if it comes to that, our stiff-necked Massachusetts colonists are eager to buy smuggled goods from England, rather than to hand over the excise tax."

But Sybilla could take no comfort from his words. She could only think about Lance, whose headstrong disposition and eagerness to build a fortune had drawn him into

Hobart's web.

Then a new thought struck her, sending cold anger surging through her. She glared accusingly at Gavin. "That night at Madeleine's dinner party, when Hobart first spoke of sending Lance to the Isle of Pines—you knew what sort of work he was offering my brother. Yet you never told me."

Gavin looked at her, his gray eyes impassive. Her voice began to shake, but she went on. "All the while you were asking your friend, Hobart, if he meant for Lance to lead a hunt for those—those giant turtles—I was foolish enough to believe you really were trying to . . . that you cared enough about me to help me."

She was breathing quickly now, her breasts rising and falling in her agitation. Her throat tightened until she felt that she would choke.

"I did care, Sybilla. I still do."

"Do you? I don't believe it. I doubt you know what it means to care for anyone. That afternoon when we were alone in Lance's house you would have taken all I had to give. And afterward, you'd have flattered yourself on how easily you'd robbed a foolish little virgin of her—of the—"

"The jewel more precious than life," he said, a hint of a smile tugging at his lips. "Isn't that what proper young ladies call it?"

Her eyes burned with indignation. How dare he humiliate her so, to make a mockery of all she'd been taught to believe?

"As I recall," he went on, "you were not exactly fighting to preserve that jewel."

Shame gave way to blind fury. Her hand tightened around the handle of her riding crop. She drew back her arm, but Gavin wheeled his horse beyond her reach.

"If you're ashamed of what happened that day, you've no need to be." His eyes rested on the crop in her upraised arm. "And you won't have to defend yourself against me, Sybilla. You're perfectly safe—if you want to be."

She dropped her arm, and turned the filly around, driven

by the need to get as far from Gavin Broderick as possible.

"Sybilla, wait."

In spite of herself, something in his voice made her hesitate. "No matter how you feel about me, don't ignore what I said—as long as you remain under Madeleine's roof, be on your guard."

"Spare me your advice, Captain Broderick! You care nothing about what happens to me. I only hope we don't meet again, before you sail."

She spurred her horse forward and Gavin made no move to stop her. Pausing for a moment at the end of the street, she heard the clopping of his horse's hooves moving in the opposite direction.

Somehow, she found her way through the maze of narrow streets to the dressmaker's shop, where her groom waited. "I wish to return to Acacia Hall—at once," she told him.

But as she rode back to the plantation, with the groom jogging along behind her on his mule, she could not shake off her uneasiness. From time to time, she turned her head and looked out at the sea. The *Trelawney* had already carried Lance far from Jamaica.

But he would come back safely—he had to.

Maybe you'd better start thinking about your own safety.

Gavin's words echoed in her mind. They were all the more troubling because she had no hint of their meaning.

Impatiently, she told herself to forget him. She had trusted him and he had betrayed her. He knew all about Nicholas Hobart's illegal dealings, and perhaps he had even taken part in some of them.

Why couldn't she banish the memory of his gray eyes, his strong, sensuous mouth? She spurred her horse to a gallop and went pounding along the road, between the rolling green fields, trying to lose herself in the swift motion—to put all thought of Gavin from her mind.

Chapter Six

Nicholas Hobart lifted the velvet-covered jewel case from his desk and opened the lid. "What do you think of this, Broderick? Fine enough to grace the throat of a queen, isn't it?"

Gavin, who was standing on the other side of the desk, in the mahogany-paneled library at Indigo, glanced down at the magnificent yellow topaz-and-diamond necklace mounted in an elaborate gold setting.

"It's a fine piece," he agreed. He examined it more closely. "It's part of the loot my men and I took from the *Valladolid*, I believe."

"I thought you'd recognize it. No doubt you're wondering why I didn't turn it into hard cash."

Gavin glanced impatiently toward the door. He had been about to leave the plantation when his host had stopped him and invited him into the library. Now Hobart lifted the yellow topaz necklace from its case and held it up, turning it this way and that. His small, raisin-colored eyes gleamed with satisfaction.

"You mean to give it to some lucky female, no doubt," Gavin said, without taking the trouble to conceal his indifference. He had little interest in his host's personal affairs.

"I am going to present it to Mistress Sybilla Thornton at the ball tonight."

Although Gavin was caught off guard by the unexpected reply, he kept his voice carefully expressionless. "You think she'll accept it?"

"And why shouldn't she?" Hobart demanded.

"Because she is not one of the doxies of Tortuga, who'd be all too willing to get her hands on such a splendid bauble." He sounded casual enough, but even as he spoke, a cold rage stirred in his vitals. The violence of his reaction took him by surprise. "A gently bred young lady like Mistress Thornton would not take such a gift from a man she scarcely knows."

"She'll soon come to know me much better," Hobart interrupted. His thick lips curved in a self-confident smile. "I mean to make her my wife."

The words struck Gavin like a blow. A red haze swam before his eyes. The muscles of his powerful shoulders tensed, and he fought against the overpowering urge to smash his fist into Hobart's flushed, perspiring face.

But he managed to control the impulse by reminding himself that he needed the other man's backing in order to carry out his new enterprise. Although he had managed to amass a considerable sum of his own, he would not be able to embark on the venture without the additional funds Hobart had promised him.

Even so, the prospect of Sybilla marrying Nicholas Hobart, and sharing his bed, filled Gavin with uncontrollable revulsion. He flinched inwardly as he pictured her surrendering her slender white body to Hobart in a conjugal embrace.

He took a step backward. If he didn't get away from Hobart quickly, he might forget the dictates of common sense and endanger their joint venture.

"You'll have some hard riding to do, if you mean to return from Mo' Bay in time for the ball," Hobart went on. Gavin forced himself to keep his eyes fixed on the tall louvered window. He stared out across the broad, rolling acres of sugarcane, where the sweating black men swung their machetes, chopping at the tall green stalks while the overseers urged them to speed up their pace.

"It'll be the greatest event of the year," Hobart was saying. "I've given orders to my cook to prepare a spread they'll be talking about for the rest of the season. And you'll have your choice of good-looking females to dance with."

Gavin cut him short. "I'm meeting Abiathar Pascoe down in Mo' Bay," he said. "We're going to look over the new guns for the *Condor*. I want twelve-pounders. And I'll be needing a new figurehead. The other one was badly damaged by a round of grapeshot from *Valladolid*." His lips tightened. "The Spaniards will pay for that—" *And for a great deal more.*

"Can't wait to get back to sea, can you, Captain Broderick?"

"That's where the profit lies—for both of us," Gavin reminded him.

Hobart's small eyes gleamed with naked greed. He was taking a risk by investing so great a sum in the new venture, to be sure; but past experience had given him confidence in Broderick's seamanship, and in his his hard, ruthless daring.

And something more, that Hobart could not quite fathom. Gavin Broderick was driven by an insatiable need to seek out and destroy every galleon that crossed his path. Occasionally, Hobart had wondered at the obsessive force that possessed his partner. But the captain of the *Condor* was a close-mouthed sort, and he had made it plain from the start that he did not welcome any probing into his personal affairs.

"Surely you can make it back to Indigo in time for tonight's festivities," Hobart persisted. "Bring Abiathar Pascoe along, if you want to. I grant you he's a rough sort, with that great red beard of his and the gold hoop he wears in his ear. But I've known more than one fine lady who had an itch to bed down with a man like that."

"Maybe so. But Abiathar Pascoe prefers the company of wenches at the Blue Dolphin, or Cora Lawson's place—as I do."

Hobart shrugged. "Time was, I'd have said the same. But since I first saw Mistress Thornton, all that's changed. Even you'll have to admit she's out of the ordinary. Young and innocent, but ripe for bedding. You can see it in the way she moves."

Gavin started for the door, driven by the urgent need to get away from Nicholas Hobart as quickly as possible. Another minute here in the library and no power in heaven or hell would stop him from breaking the man's bulldog jaw.

"Aren't you going to congratulate me?" Hobart's voice pursued him.

Gavin paused in the doorway. "Congratulations aren't in order until the lady has agreed to marry you."

"Do you doubt she will?" Hobart sounded outraged at the very thought that Sybilla might refuse him.

"How should I know? These overbred young ladies can be skittish and unpredictable. That's why I prefer to take my pleasure with Cora Lawson's girls, when I'm ashore here. They give a man what he pays for. And when he's ready to weigh anchor, he doesn't need to waste his time drying their tears. Or crossing swords with an outraged brother or jealous husband."

"That's all well enough for you, Broderick. But a man in my position has much more to consider. I've decided that it's time I found myself a suitable wife to preside over this house. A lady who will be an asset to me in the future." A smug expression spread over his heavy features. "She'll need to be good-looking and come from an excellent family. Young and healthy, as well—I'll be wanting strong sons, to carry on my name."

71

Hobart flicked a bit of dust from the broad, gold-embroidered cuff of his satin jacket, and his thick lips curved in an indulgent smile. "Mistress Thornton will bring no dowry. But I'm willing to overlook that. She has other assets to offer the man she marries—if you take my meaning."

One more minute, and I'll kill the bastard.

Gavin turned and left the library. He strode swiftly down the long hallway and out into fierce embrace of the blazing sun. But even the noonday heat of Jamaica could not melt the icy knot of tension in the pit of his stomach.

What the devil did a crude swine like Hobart know about Sybilla? She would never agree to marry the master of Indigo, not even if he decked her in diamonds from head to foot. Gavin's face hardened, and he reminded himself that Sybilla's future, her choice of a husband, did not concern him.

Hadn't he already told her, that first day she came to Jamaica, that she would need a husband to care for her? But not Nicholas Hobart! The man was thoroughly ruthless and unscrupulous.

Then Gavin's mouth twisted, and his gray eyes filled with self-mockery. When it came to scruples, was he any better? Certainly, Sybilla had made it plain enough that she no longer thought so. If he hadn't moved out of the way fast enough, he'd be carrying the mark of her riding crop across his face right now.

He felt a twinge of remorse as he thought of their last meeting. If she was foolishly protective of her brother, who could blame her? Even the little she had told him of her lonely childhood helped him to understand her deep attachment to Lance. He could imagine what it had been like for her, growing up in that lonely Somerset manor house, without her mother and with a father who was away much of the time.

Gavin's thoughts were interrupted by the appearance of

72

one of Hobart's stable boys leading his black stallion. He swung himself up into the saddle and grasped the reins. But even as he rode along the gravel path and out through the ornate iron gates of Indigo he found that he could not stop thinking of Sybilla.

She wasn't likely to forgive him for not warning her of the real nature of Lance's new position out there on the Isle of Pines. He doubted that she would have been able to dissuade her hotheaded brother from joining Hobart's smugglers in any case, but at least he'd have given her a chance to try. Why hadn't he told her what he knew, that night at Madeleine's dinner party, or even the following day?

He knew the answer well enough; and it hardly did much for his own self-respect. He had not wanted to become involved, even though he had known that Hobart was attracted to Sybilla and might be sending her brother away so that he could pursue the girl without interference. He had kept silent because his partnership with Hobart was too important to risk.

This glimpse of his own motives did little to enhance his self-esteem. Sybilla had accused him of not being able to care for any woman. She had reminded him that although he would have taken her without a twinge of conscience he would have felt no responsibility for her afterward.

But he had not always been this way. Once there had been a girl with light brown hair and wide, guileless blue eyes. . . .

His mouth clamped into a hard line, and he spurred the stallion forward, away from Indigo and down the winding road, past mangrove swamps and cane fields. After he and Abiathar had completed their business in Montego Bay they would go to the Blue Dolphin or Cora Lawson's place.

But somehow, the prospect of such a night seemed singularly uninviting. What the devil was happening to him? He needed to get back to sea, to feel the canting deck beneath his feet, and see the *Condor*'s canvas snapping out

73

before the wind.

The sooner he sailed, the better it would be for him. And for Sybilla, too.

The ballroom at Indigo ran the whole length of the right wing in the Great House. At one end of the room, on a raised platform banked with orchids and ferns, the musicians played for the planters and their ladies. The dancers, decked out in silk, taffeta, and lace, moved through the measures of a lively gavotte.

Some of the older ladies sat in groups, fluttering their fans and exchanging choice bits of local gossip. They had looked over Sybilla Thornton when she made her entrance with her aunt; and now they had begun to whisper that it was scarcely proper for a young lady to dance all evening with only one man.

As for Sybilla, she wished fervently that Nicholas Hobart had not insisted on being her partner ever since she had arrived at Indigo over an hour ago. Other men had glanced her way, but they had not approached her. Was it possible that they were afraid of offending him?

Gavin had told her that many of the local planters were in debt to Hobart; perhaps they thought it wise to keep their distance. But Sybilla's patience was wearing thin, and as the gavotte drew to a close, she made up her mind to put an end to this intolerable situation.

Looking up at him from under her long, thick lashes, she gave him a forced smile. "I am quite out of breath," she said. "I believe I should sit out the next dance, and make the acquaintance of some of the ladies." The last notes died away, and she started toward the nearest group, but a moment later, she discovered that she could not rid herself of her insufferable host so easily.

He took her arm and led her in the direction of the terrace. "It was thoughtless of me to keep you dancing so long," he said. "But you don't want to waste your time with those clucking females. I've a much better idea."

She caught a glimpse of Madeleine, who had decked herself out for the evening in a new gown of shimmering black satin, with an elaborate design of jet beads on the bodice and an overskirt made of row upon row of black lace. But she quickly realized that she would get no help from that quarter; her aunt glanced away from her own partner for a moment and smiled approvingly at Sybilla.

She sighed and allowed Hobart to escort her outside. The orchestra began to play again, and Sybilla heard the music of the violins and flageolets drifting out of the ballroom. Perhaps it would have been better if she'd gone on dancing, for she was even more uncomfortable to find herself out here with Nicholas Hobart.

How could she forgive him for having involved Lance in his smuggling venture on the Isle of Pines? Surely he must have deceived her brother as to the exact nature of his business there. No matter how casually Gavin had spoken of smuggling, it was still a criminal offense.

But her common sense asserted itself, and she was forced to admit that by the time her brother had sailed, he'd known what Hobart expected of him. Why, then, had he agreed to go? Perhaps because he was determined to get the money to set himself up on a plantation of his own, even if it meant flouting the law. And there was his sense of responsibility toward her, too. No doubt he considered it his duty to provide his sister with a suitable dowry, so that she might make a good match.

She pressed her lips together tightly and shielded her face with her fan. No matter what Lance's reason for turning smuggler, she blamed Hobart for talking him into taking such a risk. It was scarcely possible for her to hide her intense dislike for the man. She searched for an excuse to return to inside without having to dance with him again.

But her companion had other ideas, and he lost no time in

leading her to one of the marble benches against the railing of the piazza. Close by a torch, set in an ornamental sconce, burned against the velvet blackness of the night. The glowing light turned Sybilla's hair to a blaze of red-gold splendor and flickered across the delicate contours of her oval face. It shimmered over the clinging silk of her low-cut bodice, accenting the firm roundness of her breasts and the tapering line of her narrow waist. Hobart's small eyes shone with unconcealed lust, and his thick lips spread in a wide, possessive smile.

With an instinctive movement she smoothed the skirt of copper-colored silk, spreading its folds out around her to keep him as far away as possible. But her efforts proved futile. Leaning closer, he drew a velvet box from the pocket of his purple satin jacket.

"I had a special reason for wanting you to come out here with me," he said.

She took the box, but she felt a twinge of uneasiness as she lifted the lid. Her golden eyes widened as the torchlight caught the dazzling brilliance of the diamond-and-topaz necklace inside.

"When I looked at this for the first time, I knew it was meant for you and no other woman," he told her. "It suits you perfectly, my dear." He reached out and touched one of the soft curls that fell forward across her bare shoulder and the curve of her breast. She drew back, repelled by the close contact, but he went on speaking as if he hadn't noticed. "I'll be hanged if I've ever known a female with hair like yours. And your eyes—"

He moved closer. She was uncomfortably aware of the touch of his hot breath against her cheek and the overpowering scent of the musk-and-sandalwood pomade he used on his elaborate black periwig.

"Let me fasten this around your pretty neck right now," he urged.

"No! I don't want it!" She had not meant to speak so

bluntly, but the words came unbidden. In an attempt to soften her refusal, she added, "Surely you know that no lady could accept such a valuable gift from a gentleman unless—"

"Unless she is betrothed to him." Hobart took her hand in his, and stroked her palm. "Look here, Mistress Sybilla— maybe your idle Somerset gentry have time for a long drawn-out courtship. But I'm a man of affairs, with all manner of pressing business to attend to. There're over five hundred acres of cane still to be harvested. As for my warehouse, those good-for-nothing clerks would slack off if I didn't go down there and keep them at their duties. And now that the repairs to the *Condor* are nearly finished I am undertaking a new enterprise that will require still more of my time."

"I do understand, Mr. Hobart," Sybilla said. A more perceptive man might have caught the hint of irony in her voice. "And you may be sure that I won't keep you from your duties."

"That's the way I hoped you'd feel," he said, with an approving grin. "You're a sensible female, thank heaven. All the better."

Her arched brows drew together in a puzzled frown.

"You've seen something of my house," he went on. "And I can show you the rest of it whenever you like. We'll take a ride around the plantation, too—as soon as the harvest's over."

"I assure you, that isn't necessary," she began. But he went on as if he had not heard her.

"Meanwhile, you may ask your aunt—or any of those planters and their ladies inside—about my present assets and future prospects. No man on the island has more to offer his bride than I do."

His bride. All trace of color drained from Sybilla's face. For a moment she could not make a sound. She felt as if an iron band had closed around her throat. She had known the man was arrogant, but this was too much.

But she drew a deep breath, and spoke firmly, her eyes fixed on his. "I cannot understand what reason I've given you to suppose I would consider marrying you, sir. But I fear that I must refuse the honor of your proposal."

He smiled indulgently, as if he found her words amusing. "No doubt your mama taught you that a certain reluctance on the young lady's part makes her more desirable to a gentleman. But I swear I couldn't want you more than I do right now. Not if you kept me running after you, prating a lot of poetical nonsense, and showering you with gifts until next harvest season."

Sybilla sprang to her feet, her silk skirt billowing around her. "I don't wish to hear your pretty speeches, Mr. Hobart. And as for your gifts, I've no intention of accepting a single one." She snapped the jewel case shut, and thrust it into his hand. "You may offer this to another lady, one who will appreciate it."

"But it's you I want." He sounded less like a prospective suitor than a man of business, determined to get possession of a piece of valuable merchandise. "And I mean to have you for my wife, Sybilla. Make no mistake about that."

Then, as if realizing the incongruity of his words and the tone that accompanied them, he gave a harsh bark of laughter. "If you wish me to serenade you, as the Spanish gentlemen do their ladies, I'll try it—though I warn you, I have no skill with the lute or guitar."

"Please don't go on," she said. "I do not wish to marry you, and nothing you can say or do will change my mind."

"And why not? You aren't likely to get a better offer." He thrust out his jaw, and his face went deep purplish color.

"I don't love you—and I never will. I trust that is reason enough for you." Under other circumstances, she would have chosen her words more tactfully, but she was determined to rid herself of her unwelcome suitor once and for all.

She wheeled about and took a few steps in the direction of

the tall, half-open doors leading to the ballroom. But his hand caught her wrist in a hard grip, so that she could not free herself without an unseemly scuffle.

"Not so quickly, Mistress Sybilla." He swung her around to face him. "You say you aren't in love with me. I never supposed you were. But you do love that hotheaded young brother of yours, don't you?"

She looked at him in bewilderment. "What has my feeling for Lance to do with my marrying you?"

Hobart's voice was soft and silky now. "You want him to come back safely from the Isle of Pines. You are looking forward to his return."

Although the words were commonplace enough, she felt her nerves go taut. Her heart began to thud in a queer, erratic way. Hobart's eyes held hers with a cold, ominous stare, but somehow she found the strength to defy him.

"You tricked my brother into joining your smuggling venture on the Isle of Pines. I'm not sure exactly how you were able to convince him to accept a part in such an unsavory venture, but—"

"The young fool promised not to tell you," Hobart interrupted. "How the devil did you find out?"

"That's no concern of yours," she shot back. "I only wish I'd known the truth soon enough to keep him from leaving." Anger rose up in her, fierce and hot, and it gave her the strength to go on. "I've never liked you, Mr. Hobart—not from the first time we met. And now I can feel nothing but loathing and contempt for you." She tried to free herself from his grasp but it was useless.

His voice grated harshly. "Feelings are a luxury you can't afford, Mistress Sybilla. You'd do well to understand your position—and to accept my offer of marriage, before I change my mind."

She glared at him, her golden eyes narrowing, like those of an angry cat. "I'll see you in hell, first!" She drew back her foot and drove it into his shin, then twisted free from his grasp and ran the length of the piazza. She was trembling with relief when she found herself back inside the candle-lit ballroom.

She longed to get away from Indigo as quickly as possible. But she was sure that it would do no good to try to persuade Madeleine to accompany her home. She tried to collect her whirling thoughts. Perhaps she could order one of Hobart's servants to have the carriage brought around for her so that she might return to Acacia Hall alone.

But at that moment a planter's son, a plump, fair-haired young gentleman resplendent in a suit of apple green taffeta, bowed before her. "Allow me to introduce myself," he said. "I am Clive Howard, of Fairview plantation. I hope you have not promised all your dances to our host tonight," he added with a smile.

"No, indeed, sir." She managed a graceful curtsy and took his arm, so grateful for this brief reprieve that she gave him her most dazzling smile.

After that, she found herself surrounded by gentlemen eager to be her partners, and she tried to lose herself in the rhythms of the coranto, the gavotte, and the saraband. She fluttered her lids and flirted shamelessly, and somehow she managed to keep up her part in the conversation.

Yes, indeed, she found the climate of Jamaica far different from that of England, but she was becoming accustomed to the heat. And, no—she had not yet had the opportunity to go riding up to the highest peaks in the Blue Mountains. But even as she offered the correct responses, as she laughed at her partners' witty remarks, her thoughts were fixed on Hobart's veiled threat.

How far would Hobart go to keep her brother from returning to Jamaica? Lance was surrounded by smugglers, hard-bitten criminals paid by Hobart. Men who might stop at nothing, if they were offered a high enough payment.

Sybilla had no doubts about her brother's courage. Whatever his other faults, he had fought valiantly for

Monmouth's cause; and he was resourceful as well. After the battle of Sedgemoor he had managed to evade the King's troopers and had made his way across the countryside, hiding by day and traveling by night, until he reached the port of Bristol. There he had slipped aboard a ship bound for the West Indies.

Sybilla was sure that even now, if she could find a way to get word to Lance, he would move heaven and earth to return to Jamaica. But how could she possibly manage that? And even if she could find someone to carry such a message, what chance would he have against Hobart's men if they had orders to keep him there?

A pang of fear shot through her. Was it possible that Hobart had given orders to have her brother held prisoner on the island unless she consented to the marriage? But she thrust the thought aside. She must not allow her imagination to run away with her.

It was close to midnight when two liveried servants opened the doors to the adjoining room, where a lavish supper had been spread on long tables. Hobart's cook, assisted by his large kitchen staff, had outdone themselves in providing an impressive feast for his guests: ornate silver platters held a whole boar surrounded by sliced oranges and pineapples. There were roasted doves and quail, ducks, snipes, and pigeons, baked in brown sugar and spiced with cloves; prawns, crayfish and conch swimming in rich butter sauce. These were flanked by trenchers laden with yams, beans, squash, and rice; and others still, piled high with tropical fruit.

Dark-skinned servants offered cups of wine posset to the guests from a glittering silver bowl, while others kept the goblets filled to the brim with port, burgundy, malmsey and rhenish. Sybilla was quickly surrounded by the planters' ladies, and she heard herself accepting their invitations to a bewildering variety of coming events: afternoon teas, musicales, riding parties, and a masked ball.

These ladies of Jamaica's plantation society were a charming, pampered little group, accustomed to being waited on hand and foot. A few had been born on the island, while others had come from England. Sybilla, the niece of Oliver Thornton, was welcomed into their circle.

But she could not help noticing that they were somewhat cool toward Madeleine. Had they, too, heard the rumors about Madeleine's liaison with Tom Yates?

Although Sybilla feared that Hobart might seek her out during supper, he stayed a little distance away. But even as he and the other planters discussed the harvest, the shocking rise in the price of slaves, and the difficulties of importing equipment for the sugar mills, she caught his eyes darting quick glances at her.

After dinner, she was relieved to see him leading a group of gentlemen into the drawing room, where gaming tables had been set up. Nevertheless, she was deeply disturbed each time she thought of their encounter out on the piazza. Perhaps another man would have accepted her cold refusal of marriage and turned his attentions elsewhere. But Nicholas Hobart was not the sort to give up so easily.

Chapter Seven

You do love that hotheaded brother of yours, don't you?
On the short drive home, those words kept nagging at
Sybilla.

"My dear, what a triumph!" Madeleine put a hand on her
arm, and she stiffened. "Why, what's wrong?"

"I am not used to such large gatherings," Sybilla said,
drawing her arm away. "And I fear I'm not yet accustomed
to the climate, after all." She closed her eyes, and rested her
head against the leather back of the carriage seat, to
discourage Madeleine from engaging her in conversation.

But after they arrived at Acacia Hall, she could not stop
her aunt from accompanying her upstairs and taking up the
conversation where she had left off. "You were a great
success tonight, my dear," she said.

Sybilla smiled politely and opened her bedchamber door,
hoping to get away from the other woman as quickly as
possible.

"From the moment you made your entrance, Nicholas
Hobart did not spare a glance for any of the other ladies,"
Madeleine gloated.

If only she could be alone in her room, to try to sort out
her thoughts. But Madeleine showed no sign of leaving her.

"You were out on the veranda with Mr. Hobart for some

time." She slanted a knowing half-smile at Sybilla. "Isn't there anything you wish to tell me?"

Sybilla hesitated, wondering whether it would do any good to confide in her aunt. Perhaps Madeleine might be able to shed some light on Hobart's remarks. There had certainly been a threat of some kind behind those seemingly casual words.

But Gavin had cautioned her not to trust Madeleine, and she could not dismiss his warning. He had even suggested that she herself might be in danger.

"I hope you've recovered enough so that we may have a little chat?" Madeleine said, her blue eyes alert and eager. Without waiting for a reply, she opened the door to Sybilla's chamber, and led the way inside. The quadroon maid, Poppy, was waiting up , to help her new mistress get ready for bed. "Leave us," Madeleine ordered the girl.

Then, seating herself on a small, silk-cushioned settee, she drew Sybilla down beside her. The candlelight flickered on the jet beads of her black bodice as she leaned forward. Sybilla moved back slightly, but nevertheless she was enveloped in the heavy scent of her aunt's perfume.

"You looked quite ravishing tonight, I declare. And wasn't I right to persuade you to have a new gown? No London dressmaker could have provided you with a more fashionable costume."

"I am most grateful for your generosity," Sybilla said, trying to keep the impatience out of her voice. If only the woman would go to her own room.

"Even the prettiest young lady needs the proper clothes to enhance her charms." Madeleine bent a little closer. "Now, do tell me—what did Mr. Hobart say to you, out on the piazza?"

"He offered me a valuable topaz-and-diamond necklace, and then he said he wished to marry me."

Madeleine's cornflower blue eyes widened, and she caught her breath. "I knew he was taken by you. He hinted at his attachment more than once. But a proposal of marriage! I scarcely expected that."

She gave Sybilla an approving smile. "You are a most fortunate young lady—and a clever one, for all your touch-me-not airs," she said. Her shrill little laugh set Sybilla's teeth on edge. "When I think of Theodora Gilbert, Prudence Worthington, and the rest, who have marriageable daughters—I can't wait to see their faces, when I tell them that you snatched Nicholas Hobart away from all of them, and so soon after you arrived here on the island." Her eyes gleamed with malicious pleasure. "They will be quite overcome with envy when they hear of your betrothal."

"There's no need for them to envy me," Sybilla said dryly. "I refused Mr. Hobart's offer."

"You refused him!"

Sybilla spoke with quiet but unshakeable determination. "I accepted his loan of the filly, and his invitation to Indigo tonight, only because I am living under your roof, and because you made it plain that I was not to offend the man. But if you think for a minute that I am about to wed a man I despise, to please you, you're quite mistaken."

Madeleine gripped her closed fan so tightly that one of the ivory sticks snapped. "You little idiot! And to think I gave you credit for having more good sense than your brother. How could you have behaved so foolishly? A girl without so much as a farthing for her dowry. Living in luxury, at my expense—"

Sybilla's lips tightened. "No doubt when Lance returns, he will be able to repay you, madam." She held her head high, and spoke with cool dignity. "In the meantime, if you wish, I can return to his house. I'll ring for Poppy, to pack my trunk at once."

"Now, Sybilla—there is no need to be hasty. I confess I was carried away—and who can blame me? I only wished to remind you of your situation. You must allow yourself to be guided by my advice. I've had a good deal more experience than you—"

"No doubt you have. But I'm not completely unworldly, I assure you. If you want me to wed Mr. Hobart, it isn't out of concern for my future."

"My dear child, what other possible reason could I have for wishing you to make such an excellent match?"

"I believe you owe him a good deal of money, do you not?"

In the silence that followed, Sybilla heard the harsh rustling of the palm fronds in the garden below and the far-off cry of a bird from the mangrove swamp.

"I don't know how you managed to find out about my debts. But since you have, and you choose to speak so bluntly, I'll do the same," said Madeleine. "When your uncle brought me to Acacia Hall, I found the house was far from what I had expected. It had grown shabby over the years—an elderly bachelor pays little heed to such details, I suppose. And the furnishings were hopelessly old-fashioned. I needed a large loan to turn the place into one of the most elegant homes on the island."

"And so you drove my uncle into debt, to satisfy your whims!"

"What if I did? A newly married man will go to any lengths to please his wife. She only has to make use of the advantages nature gave her. No doubt you'll learn all about that, once you're married to Nicholas Hobart. You won't regret taking him for a husband, I promise you."

"I thought I'd already made it plain that I have no intention of marrying him."

"Spare me your foolish dithering," Madeleine said impatiently. "You're lucky he wants you for a wife. I expected that a man as practical as Nicholas Hobart would make you his mistress—and nothing more."

Sybilla's face burned with outraged pride. She clenched her hands in her lap, scarcely feeling her fingernails cutting into her palms. "And would you have urged me to accept such a degrading offer, madam?"

"Why, certainly," the older woman said. "But it is much better for both of us this way. As Nicholas Hobart's wife, you may have a more splendid future than you ever hoped for."

She tapped Sybilla's arm lightly with her fan. "I've heard rumors that King James may honor Nicholas Hobart by appointing him governor of Jamaica. Only think of it, Sybilla—one day you could be the governor's lady."

Sybilla rose to her feet, her silk and lace skirt swirling about her. "Since I cannot convince you that I will never marry Mr. Hobart, I see no point in continuing our talk. If you will send Poppy back, I'll make ready for bed."

"Not before we've settled this, once and for all."

"I believe we already have." Sybilla looked at her coldly. "I'll return to my brother's house at once, and wait there until he comes back."

"If he comes back."

A cold pang of fear shot up Sybilla's spine. "At the ball, Mr. Hobart said—"

"Do go on," Madeleine urged.

"He spoke of my devotion to Lance, and said he knew I wanted to see him come back safely. It sounded like a— threat."

"A warning, perhaps."

"But Gavin assured me that Lance was in no great danger from the Cuban authorities. He said they did not take a serious view of smuggling, since they needed the goods that were brought in—"

Madeleine started slightly. "And when did you discuss your brother's new position with the dashing Captain Broderick?"

"I happened to meet him in Montego Bay, when I went to the dressmaker's shop."

"I should not have allowed you to go roving about unchaperoned," Madeleine said. "Hobart will want a virgin bride. He won't settle for damaged goods."

Sybilla flinched at her aunt's choice of words, but she went on quickly. "I care nothing about Hobart—it's Lance I'm thinking of—"

"The Cuban authorities aren't likely to be a problem, so long as they get their bribes." Madeleine paused, and her eyes held Sybilla's. "But there are our own laws to be considered. His Majesty has a long arm—it stretches all the way to these islands."

She rose from the settee and stood confronting Sybilla. "What do you think would happen if Hobart were to denounce your brother as a traitor to King James?"

Sybilla took a step back. For a moment, she was too shaken to speak. Then she managed to recover herself. "That's not true—he didn't—"

"Your brother fought for the Duke of Monmouth. Yes, I know all about it."

"I don't believe you. My uncle was a Thornton. A man of honor. He would never have—"

"He wouldn't have betrayed your brother. Isn't that what you were about to say? And no doubt you are right. But poor Oliver went quite out of his wits, when his fever was at its height. I remained at his bedside all through his illness. At first, I could scarcely make sense of his ravings—but then I caught a word here and there, about the rebellion. And I listened more closely."

Sybilla knew it would be useless to try to deny Madeleine's accusations. She stared at her uncle's widow accusingly. "And you told Hobart what you knew."

"He expressed a certain interest in you. I felt it only right to tell him, since he is my friend."

"Your creditor," Sybilla corrected her.

Madeleine shrugged. "As you wish. But don't worry, my dear. Once you're his wife, Lance will be safe enough. Nicholas Hobart's not going to run to the authorities, proclaiming that his brother-in-law is a traitor."

Sybilla considered speaking out in defense of her brother.

He had not thought of himself as a traitor when he'd gone to fight for Monmouth. He and his friends had been convinced that the handsome, rebellious young Duke was the legitimate heir to the throne. They had believed what they'd been told of a secret marriage, years before, between Charles II and Monmouth's mother.

But Sybilla was no longer concerned with the rights and wrongs of the young Duke's lost cause; he had been defeated, and his plea for mercy denied. He had been executed as a traitor. King James sat secure upon the English throne.

And Madeleine was not likely to be moved by Lance's motives in joining the uprising. Her uncle's widow had found a way to manipulate Sybilla, and she would be completely ruthless in getting what she wanted.

Now Sybilla realized, with a start, that Madeleine was speaking to her. "Unless you agree to this marriage, your brother will pay dearly, I promise you. He'll be brought back to Jamaica and denounced to the authorities. If he isn't hanged for his crime he'll be sold into slavery."

Sybilla sought frantically for a way out, but she was too shaken to gather her thoughts. Madeleine went on, her voice hard and pitiless. "How long do you suppose that brother of yours would survive, working in the cane fields? If the hard labor and the climate didn't kill him, he'd not survive the overseer's lash. I've seen the strongest black men die, after a few floggings. Their backs were slashed to ribbons and the bones showed through."

"No! Sweet Jesú . . ."

She felt Madeleine's hand on her arm again, and the touch of those plump fingers filled her with revulsion. But she couldn't pull away. The bedchamber, with its gilded furniture and silk draperies, began to swim before her eyes. A moment later, she was sitting beside Madeleine, who held a tiny glass vial of smelling salts.

"Take a deep breath—that's right. Too bad you forced me

to speak so plainly. But it's as well that you understand what's at stake. When you're formally betrothed to Hobart, you'll have nothing to fear." Sybilla was unable to speak. Her mind was numb with despair. "Think of the future, Sybilla," Madeleine went on. "Your brother's as well as your own. With Hobart's backing, Lance could go far."

"But how can I marry such a man? The very thought sickens me."

"God's teeth! Don't go on blathering like some silly creature just out of the schoolroom. I know Hobart's not the sort of man a young girl dreams of. But no doubt it's your youthful innocence that appeals to him. That, and your gentle breeding."

Sybilla shuddered. To wed Nicholas Hobart, to lie beside him at night. To feel the weight of his gross, sweating body on hers, and to force herself to submit to him as a dutiful wife.

"Once you and Hobart are married, you can manage to have a certain freedom, a life of your own," Madeleine said.

Sybilla stared at her without comprehension.

"Mr. Hobart's often away on business. If you're discreet, there's nothing to prevent you from amusing yourself with another man. Like the handsome Captain Broderick, perhaps."

"I am no trollop, madam. I will not marry one man and pleasure myself with another."

Madeleine's laughter was soft and suggestive. "You say that because you've not yet lain with a man. Although I'll wager that our gallant captain has made an attempt on your virtue."

Sybilla felt the hot blood burn in her cheeks. "Get out," she said, and the cold rage in her voice made Madeleine move back hastily.

"As you please, my dear," she said. "No doubt you need your rest after such an eventful evening." She paused for a moment at the door. "Remember what I've told you, Sybilla.

Don't wait too long to give Nicholas Hobart the answer he wants—or you'll have cause to regret it. You, and your brother."

But long after Madeleine had gone, and Sybilla lay in her bed, sleep would not come. Was this the danger Gavin had hinted at during their last meeting? Perhaps he had known that Hobart planned to propose to her tonight. But surely he had not suspected that the master of Indigo had such a powerful weapon to use in persuading her to become his wife.

As for Gavin himself, maybe Madeleine, with her greater experience, understood him all too well. He would have no scruples against carrying on a brief affair with a married woman. But he would stay free of any permanent attachments.

Forget Gavin Broderick.

Sybilla rose from her bed, thrust her feet into her slippers, and began to pace her darkened bedchamber. It was Lance she had to think about now. Lance who was in mortal danger, unless she agreed to marry Hobart.

Chapter Eight

The *Condor* lay at anchor in the cove off Indigo. The frigate's hull had been scraped and caulked, and the new masts had been set in place. The crew had labored all that afternoon, and then they had gone ashore.

But although it now was close to midnight, Gavin and Abiathar Pascoe still remained on board. They stood beside the quarterdeck rail, looking out across the lagoon to the shore.

"I suppose we'll have to take Hobart to Cuba," Pascoe said. "And like as not, he'll be wanting to bring his pretty young bride along on a honeymoon."

"The devil he will!"

Abiathar, startled by Gavin's vehemence, turned and stared at him. "It's but a short voyage from here to Cuba," he said. "And once we've got that over with, we'll lose no more time in setting out about our own business." Abiathar grinned, showing strong white teeth. "A lucky fellow, Nicholas Hobart is. He's found himself a fine-looking young wife."

"He's not married yet."

Abiathar shrugged. "The betrothal ball's goin' to be held tomorrow night at Acacia Hall, isn't it?"

Gavin nodded brusquely, his mouth clamped in a thin,

hard line.

"And like as not you've been invited."

"As a matter of fact, he invited both of us," Gavin said. "But we've no time for such doings, and I told him so."

Abiathar raised his bushy brows. "You might have asked me first," he said. "No doubt we could've eaten our fill of the finest victuals and downed as much good wine as we could hold."

"We've got more important matters to attend to, here aboard the *Condor*," Gavin interrupted. "The crew has to set those new twelve-pounders in place. And see to the gun trucks, as well. There's the shot and powder to be stored. As for the new rigging, I want you to examine every foot of it before we set sail."

"I know my trade well enough to manage all that, and more, with time to spare," the red-bearded mate said dryly.

"I don't doubt it, Abiathar," Gavin told him. "But all the same, I'm in no mood for another social evening here on the island. I've had my fill of Nicholas Hobart's company. It's bad enough he's decided to take passage on the *Condor*."

"I don't relish having him sail with us, either," said Abiathar. "Nor his bride, come to that. A female's an accursed nuisance aboard ship. Even one as fine and trim as young Mistress Thornton." He gave a rumbling laugh from the depths of his barrel-like chest. "I doubt we'll be seeing her often, though. Hobart'll keep her busy in their cabin, training her in her wifely duties. No doubt he means to get his money's worth from this marriage—like he does from all his other investments."

Gavin wheeled about, his features tight with rage. "That's enough!" In the light of the lamp that swung overhead, his gray eyes glittered coldly. "Hobart's backing our venture with his cash. That gives him the right to passage aboard this ship. But as for Sybilla Thornton, she'll not set foot aboard the *Condor*."

"Easy there, Gavin. When you lead us into battle against

93

the damned Spaniards, you'll have a chance to give vent to that devil's temper of yours."

Gavin nodded brusquely. He turned and started down the steps leading to the deck below. "Come along, now."

Abiathar followed. "Where're we bound for?"

"We're going ashore. With that full moon, we'll have light enough to work by. We'll pick up some of the supplies from the shed and carry them aboard."

"It'll be near dawn before we get them stowed away," Abiathar pointed out.

Then, catching a glimpse of his captain's set face and the steely look in his eyes, the mate shrugged and followed.

Sybilla spurred her filly to a brisk canter. Leaning forward, she rode along the beach as though she were being pursued by demons. Overhead, the stars blazed in the night sky, and the moonlight turned the sand to shimmering silver.

An hour ago Sybilla had risen from bed, put on her new riding habit, and slipped out of the Great House. She had gone to the stables where she had saddled the filly herself, not wanting to rouse any of the sleeping grooms.

Perhaps the long, hard ride through the cane fields and down to the sea would leave her tired enough to fall asleep. Anything was better than lying wide-eyed in the darkness, staring at the ornate brocade canopy over her bed and trying to shut out all thought of tomorrow night.

Two weeks had passed since Hobart had asked her to marry him. Even after Madeleine had told her that he knew about Lance's part in the rebellion and was prepared to use that information as a weapon to force her into marriage, she held out as long as possible. She shrank from the thought of trading any chance of happiness, even for her brother's safety.

At first she told herself there must be some other way of escape. If only she could put Hobart off until she figured out a plan to get word to Lance.

But Madeleine never relaxed her vigilance, accompanying her to every small social function, riding along with her to Montego Bay to order more finery from Mistress Fanshawe. And even on those rare occasions when she had a few moments to herself, she could not think of a way to let Lance know what was happening.

She could not manage it alone. She would have to take more than one person into her confidence. Back home in Somerset she had known which servants she could trust. But here at Acacia Hall, how could she take such a risk?

In her growing desperation, Sybilla had even considered sending Poppy with a note to Gavin at Indigo, as she had before. But she had decided against it.

Even if she were willing risk asking him for help, it wasn't likely that Gavin would care to become involved. Why should he?

She remembered how she had turned on Gavin, before they'd parted in Montego Bay. She had accused him of having kept silent and allowing Lance to become involved with Hobart's smugglers. She had struck out at him with her riding crop and had told him that she hoped never to see him again.

Most likely, if she could get word to him, he would ignore her plea for help. Or worse yet he might show her letter to Nicholas Hobart.

During the past fortnight, while she had struggled with her doubts and fears, Madeleine had not missed a single opportunity of reminding her that the time for decision was growing short. And Nicholas Hobart was not a patient man. He would not wait indefinitely for Sybilla to set a date to announce their betrothal.

"And he'll want to have the wedding soon after that," Madeleine had said, one afternoon a few days ago. She had summoned Sybilla to the drawing room for tea, and then she had dismissed the maid.

"I believe we ought to start Mistress Fanshawe working on your wedding gown at once," she said, nibbling on a small, frosted cake. "Ivory satin, I think. With rows of Brussels lace, and tiny seed pearls."

"I've not said I would marry Mr. Hobart," Sybilla reminded her.

"You're not a fool, my girl. You know well enough what is at stake if you persist in these useless delaying tactics."

"No matter what it cost Lance, he would not want me to marry a man I don't love—or even respect."

"Never mind the cost to Lance," Madeleine said, setting down her delicate china cup. "Unless you tell Hobart you'll marry him, you'll be in serious trouble, yourself. If you expect to go on living here in luxury another day, you're quite mistaken. My patience is at an end."

"I've lived in Lance's house before and I can do it again—" Sybilla began.

"I don't think you quite understand," Madeleine interrupted. "I have only to give the order to Yates, and you'll find yourself turned off the plantation at once."

"My uncle's will provides that I may remain here as long as I wish." But even as she spoke, Sybilla began to realize the full extent of the danger that threatened to engulf her.

If Madeleine should inform the authorities that her niece had helped a fugitive traitor to escape, she would have no rights at all. Icy fear coursed through her at the thought of being arrested and brought to trial for treason. What was the punishment for a female who had aided in the escape of one of Monmouth's followers?

"I'll leave the plantation at once," she said hastily. It took all her willpower to keep her voice from shaking. "I'll go to Montego Bay."

"And how do you plan to provide for yourself, once you're there?" Madeleine finished the last of her frosted cake, and patted her lips daintily. "Too bad you were foolish enough to refuse that necklace Hobart offered you. Perhaps you might have sold it for a tidy sum."

"I'll find some sort of employment."

"No doubt you will. Mo' Bay has several taverns and bawdy houses, as all seaports do. And there'll be plenty of sailors, hungry for the company of a good-looking young female."

Sybilla stared at Madeleine with disgust. In spite of her fashionable gowns and her thin veneer of elegance, the woman was as coarse as any common slut. How could such a creature have cozened Oliver Thornton into marrying her?

But Sybilla had little time to consider the question, for she had to deal with the problem of her immediate future. She had spoken of finding employment, but she had never earned a penny piece in all her sheltered life.

Even back in England she'd have had considerable difficulty finding any sort of work, however menial. And here in Jamaica, the house servants were all slaves, shipped from Africa and sold on the auction block. She could not pay the fee for an apprenticeship with a dressmaker or milliner, nor could she provide the necessary references.

Madeleine's voice cut through her whirling thoughts. "I don't believe you'll be running off to Mo' Bay, will you? Not that you would starve. There are plenty of men who'll offer a handsome sum for the satisfaction of deflowering a virgin." Her lips curved in a derisive smile. "I've never understood what possible satisfaction a man hopes to get, when he beds an inexperienced young creature."

Sybilla's insides tightened into a cold knot at the picture conjured up by Madeleine's words. The woman was completely ruthless, intent on gaining her own ends. She would stop at nothing to force Sybilla into submission.

But even so, she was probably speaking the truth. Fear clawed at Sybilla, driving every other emotion from her mind. Sweet Jesú! If she left Acacia Hall and fled to Montego Bay, she would find herself in exactly the situation Madeleine described.

She remembered the two trollops she had seen in the back room of the Blue Dolphin on the day she had arrived in Jamaica. Her heart thudded against her ribs, and she pressed her closed fist to her lips, to fight back the sickness that rose inside her.

"It's too bad if I've wounded your delicate sensibilities," Madeleine said. "But you should understand the sort of future you may expect, if you persist in refusing Hobart's offer."

Numb with despair, Sybilla nodded slowly. Then she drew a long breath.

"You may tell Mr. Hobart that I will marry him," she heard herself saying. Her voice was toneless, drained of all emotion. She felt much older than that hopeful girl who had walked down the gangplank of the *Bristol Belle,* to make a new life for herself in Jamaica.

As Madeleine began to speak with enthusiasm of the splendid betrothal ball she would arrange here at Acacia Hall, Sybilla scarcely listened. Instead, she tried to find what comfort she could in her own thoughts.

Once she married Nicholas Hobart, Lance would be safe from punishment as a traitor. And as Hobart's lawful wife, at least she would be respected and looked up to by Jamaican society. But what about her brother? How could she explain to him why she had agreed to become Hobart's wife?

It wouldn't be easy to convince Lance that she had somehow developed a fondness for Nicholas Hobart. But surely, by the time her brother returned to Jamaica, she would have managed to concoct a plausible explanation.

Nearly a week had passed since Sybilla had agreed to the marriage. She had little time to brood, for her days had been crowded with activity.

Mistress Fanshawe, flushed with triumph at having

gained such a profitable order, had visited the plantation and had kept Sybilla occupied with choosing materials for the gown she would wear at the betrothal ball, the delicate shifts of silk and lace, and, most important, the wedding gown.

But now, as Sybilla rode along the beach, she fought off a growing tension. Once she had announced her betrothal, the marriage would follow quickly. She spurred the filly to a gallop as she crossed an inlet; she was scarcely aware of the few inches of water that covered the inlet's rocky bottom.

She rode close to the shoreline with the sea breeze tugging at the loose strands of her hair. Lost in her unhappy thoughts, she did not realize that she had crossed the boundary between Acacia Hall and Indigo, until she saw the graceful silhouette of the *Condor,* the sails and rigging gleaming silver in the moonlight.

How long would it be before Gavin sailed from Jamaica? Pain gripped her throat, as she told herself that it could not possibly matter to her now.

She tore her eyes from the ship and forced herself to look away from the sea. Beyond the beach stretched the cane fields, acres and acres of dark, rustling stalks; and the mills, with their machinery clanking and grinding, day and night, producing enormous wealth for their owner. And far off, white in the moonlight, stood the house, tall and ornate, brooding over the rest of the plantation.

My house, she thought with a shudder of revulsion. *I will live at Indigo soon, with Nicholas Hobart. My husband. I'll sit across the table from him each night at dinner. And later, we will climb the great stairs to the bedchamber together. I will share his bed and bear his children.*

No! I can't do it—I can't! There has to be a way out. I could run away, back to England.

But almost at once, her brief surge of rebellion ebbed away. Even if she could somehow raise the money for her passage back to England, Lance would surely be made to pay dearly for her escape. Hobart would see to that. If he could not manage to have Lance sent to the gallows, he would use his influence to get her brother sold as a bond slave.

She wheeled the filly about and started back in the direction of Acacia Hall. She would have to return and try to get a few hours' sleep. It would take all her strength and poise to carry her through tomorrow night's festivities. The yellow topaz necklace would encircle her throat, with the huge glittering center stone resting cold and heavy between her breasts.

Sybilla's thoughts were cut short as her mount reared back so suddenly that she was nearly flung from the saddle. She heard the sound of rushing water, and as she tightened her grip on the reins she saw that the tide had turned. The inlet she had crossed a short while ago was now filling up rapidly, so that the water rose almost to her stirrups.

She looked about, seeking another way back. But the inlet was far wider than she had realized and was shaped like a rough crescent. On her right, the encroaching waves lapped at the horse's legs, and on her left lay a steep rocky ledge.

The filly tossed her head and whinnied shrilly, refusing to take another step. Sybilla tried to coax her across, bending low in the saddle and speaking softly. But the frightened animal did not respond.

Although Sybilla realized how risky it would be to try to cross even now, she knew that she had no time to lose. Reluctantly, she applied the spurs, but the terrified filly only reared up, pawing the air. Sybilla's determination started to ebb away. Why not remain where she was, while the tide rose, deep and dark around her? It would not be long before she was swept out to sea. . . .

Then she felt the salt spray strike her face, and sting her eyes, and she was shocked out of her numb despair. She drew a deep breath and her cry for help echoed along the beach.

*   *   *

100

"Hear that?" Abiathar said. "Sounds like one of them spirits the black folk fear—duppies, they call 'em."

"That's no duppy! It's a woman, scared out of her wits." Even as Gavin spoke, he climbed over the side of the small boat and headed for shore, a few yards off.

"Want me to go with you?" the red-bearded mate called.

"No need of that. You beach the boat and get the supplies aboard."

As he gave the orders, Gavin was already out of the water, the soles of his boots squelching in the wet sand. He had left his stallion tethered to a palm tree. Now he unfastened the reins, and, vaulting into the saddle, he spurred the animal forward. Even before he came near enough to see her clearly, he recognized Sybilla's voice.

"Hold on!" he shouted. "Stay where you are!"

Then he was beside her. He quickly appraised the situation, and he knew he could not try to force the filly across the rising water—not yet. The terrified animal might rear and throw Sybilla against the rocky ledge.

Instead, he maneuvered his stallion beside Sybilla's mount. Then, reaching across the narrow space between them, he lifted Sybilla clear of her saddle and set her in front of him.

The stallion responded to the pressure of Gavin's hard-muscled thighs and the touch of his spurs. Obedient to the will of its rider, the stallion breasted its way through the strong current and galloped up the other side of the inlet.

Sybilla pressed herself against Gavin's chest, her hands clutching at his doublet. "You're all right now," he assured her. He got down and set her on a flat rock, a safe distance from the inlet.

"Don't leave me!"

"I've got to see to your horse," he reminded her. Then he mounted again and went back for the filly.

Although the skittish young animal was still reluctant to cross the water, Gavin moved his stallion beside her and seized her reins. His voice was low and steady as he gentled her. After a brief hesitation the filly submitted and allowed him to lead her through the rising water and across the stretch of sand beyond.

Gavin drew in his breath sharply as he looked at Sybilla, standing in the moonlight, her damp skirt flattened against her body by the sea breeze. He caught an enticing glimpse of her rounded hips and long, shapely thighs. Under the trim, tightly fitted jacket of her riding habit, her high, firm breasts rose and fell quickly, for she had not yet recovered from her fright. Her hat had been carried away and her hair swirled in loose waves about her face and over her shoulders.

He got down and helped her back onto her velvet-covered sidesaddle. "You're trembling," he said softly.

"The breeze is chilly this time of night."

"Why the devil were you riding about the beach after midnight? And on that skittish beast?"

"She's not skittish—not usually. As for my being here so late, I might ask you the same question."

"Abiathar and I were bringing supplies aboard the *Condor*. The sooner she's made ready, the sooner we can weigh anchor."

"You're so eager to leave Jamaica?"

"There's nothing to keep me here." He spoke brusquely. "Come along, now. I'll see you get back to Acacia Hall."

"Don't let me keep you from your duties."

"Abiathar can load the supplies himself."

"But there's no need for you to accompany me."

"You're not afraid to be alone with me, are you?" he mocked her. "You had no such maidenly scruples that day when you arranged our meeting in Mo' Bay."

"I was concerned for my brother."

"Are you sure that was the only reason you ignored the conventions?"

"You flatter yourself, Captain Broderick."

"So we're back to those formal terms again. There's no need—"

Then she saw his gray eyes harden. The skin drew tightly across the angular slash of his cheekbones, and a hard ridge of muscle stood out along his jaw. "But I'm forgetting—a young lady, betrothed to Nicholas Hobart, must be careful of her behavior. Caesar's wife must be above reproach. Isn't that how the quotation goes?" Sybilla caught the cold mockery in his voice. And the anger that surprised and bewildered her.

"Nicholas Hobart's no Caesar," she snapped. "And I am not yet his wife."

She spurred her horse to a canter. He urged his stallion to match the filly's pace.

"No," Gavin agreed, "you're not wed to him yet. But the marriage day is not far off, is it? Tomorrow night your aunt will announce your betrothal. The gentry of Jamaica will be drinking to your happiness and showering Hobart with congratulations." His laugh was brief and mirthless. "I'd have thought you'd be safely in bed right now, dreaming of your bridegroom and your glorious future together."

Sybilla's throat tightened so that she could not answer. She became aware of the sound of the surf, faint and far-off. They had left the beach and now they rode along one of the roads leading to Acacia Hall. The night breeze rustled the fronds of the slender coconut palms that rose on either side. A small mongoose went darting across their path into the underbrush.

"No doubt your wedding will be a splendid affair," Gavin went on. "Hobart likes to make a fine show to impress his neighbors. He'll deck you out in the costliest jewels. By the way, Sybilla—have you been fitted for your wedding gown yet?"

Why was he taunting her this way—as if he were trying to wound her deliberately? Or was the cutting lash of his words directed against himself?

She gave a wordless cry of protest. Then she bent forward and spurred her mount to a gallop, in an effort to escape from his mocking voice. The road was filled with deep ruts, and was slippery in places.

The stallion's hooves came thundering up beside her, and she heard Gavin shout, "Slow down, Sybilla! You'd better mind how you go, if you want to get home safely."

"Acacia Hall is not my home! I hate the place—and Madeleine! And—"

She stopped herself before she could speak Hobart's name. She urged the filly to a furious gallop, for she knew she must get away from Gavin, and quickly. His voice, his very presence, awakened all those tumultuous emotions she had resolved to put aside forever.

Rounding the bend in the road, she caught her breath. Directly ahead, she saw the great waterfall plunging down over the rocks. Here Gavin had stopped the carriage on the way to Acacia Hall, on the day she had arrived on the island. Here he had embraced her for the first time.

The glittering silver cascade, the stretch of road ahead, blurred before her eyes. Forced to draw rein, she bent her head forward, so that her long hair fell about her face. She could not let Gavin know how much she loathed the thought of marrying Nicholas Hobart.

She fought back her tears, but it was already too late. She heard Gavin dismount with a jingling of spurs and harness. And now he was beside her. He reached up and his hand closed around hers.

"Sybilla—look at me."

She turned, her body shaking as she gave way to the feelings she had been holding under control so long. She clutched at his arm, and he lifted her from the saddle, holding her against him. She felt his warm breath on her cheek, and she drew in the now-familiar scents of salt, brandy, and the clean, male odor of his flesh itself.

"Why did you agree to marry Nicholas Hobart?" She heard his voice above the rush of the waterfall, the erratic thudding of her pulses. "You're not in love with the man— you can't be."

"You know nothing about it," she managed to say.

"I know you nearly got yourself drowned, roving about the beach tonight. Then, you went tearing off down the road as if the devil himself were after you. And now—" He cupped her chin, his fingers pressing hard so that she could not look away. "Now you're crying."

"Brides often get these vaporish moods—Madeleine told me so."

"Madeleine's no better than any bawdyhouse madam, for all her airs and graces." He gave her a sharp, searching look. "I'll warrant she's been pushing you into marrying Hobart."

"That's no concern of yours."

"Isn't it?"

"Certainly not." Gavin must not even guess at her reasons for agreeing to the marriage. "Madeleine wishes to see me make a good match. And you yourself said I'd do well to marry one of the island's planters."

"Not Hobart! Surely you know the kind of man he is. You've never made any secret of how you dislike and distrust him. That day we met in Mo' Bay, you said—"

She put her hand over Gavin's lips. "Please—don't say any more. Just take me back to Acacia Hall."

But a moment later his mouth brushed her wrist. Deftly, he drew off her riding glove, and she felt her pulses leap beneath the touch of his tongue. He turned her hand over, and bent his head. Now his tongue slowly caressed her palm, sending long, delicious shivers through her whole body.

"Please take me back—"

"Not yet, Sybilla."

She tried to protest, but the words would not come. The night breeze was heavy with the spicy scents of the great tree ferns and the damp moss that spread a velvet carpet around the pool at the bottom of the falls. In the tangle of vines and shrubs she saw the flickering green and gold of the fireflies.

"Say you don't want me to take you back," he urged. "Say it. . . ."

Even as she heard his words, muffled against her palm, she sensed the danger of giving in to her aching need for him.

From somewhere in the past, she heard a girl's voice saying, "No doubt your relations will find you a good match, here in Jamaica—a wealthy planter—" It had been Dolores de las Fuentes, her shipboard companion.

Now the words came back with a cruel irony. Madeleine had, indeed, arranged a match for her, one that even Dolores would consider most satisfactory. And Sybilla had promised herself that, once she went through with the marriage, she would keep her vows.

Gavin's mouth moved from her palm to her lips. She felt his kiss, hot and urgent. Her lips parted and his tongue found hers. And now there was only Gavin, and this moment. So brief a time to discover what it was to give herself in passion and tenderness.

He drew her down on the soft moss beside the pool and buried his face in her hair. The thudding of her heart, the sound of his breath, harsh and a little unsteady, blended into the dark enchantment of the night.

Nothing could stop the rushing waters from surging down over the rocks to the earth below. And no force was strong enough to keep Sybilla's from reaching out to Gavin. With one swift, sensuous movement, she embraced him, molding her body to his.

Chapter Nine

Sybilla lay in Gavin's embrace, her slender arms wrapped tightly around him, her hands stroking his thick, dark hair, then lingering along the hard tendons at the back of his neck.

The delicate spray from the high, rushing waterfall wove a moon-silvered cloud around the two of them. Gavin's damp linen shirt molded itself tightly against his body. As her questing fingertips moved lower, she was stirred by the feel of the powerful ridge of muscle across the width of his shoulders.

When he bent his head and covered her full, soft mouth with his, she parted her lips to welcome the first thrust of his tongue. Stirred to the depths of her being by a swift and overpowering urgency that left no room for modest hesitation, she touched her tongue to his, darting, withdrawing, teasing. . . .

She gave a faint sound of protest as his lips lifted away from hers, only to trace a line of fire along the slender, graceful curve of her neck. With a deep sigh that came from the innermost recesses of her being, she let her head fall back, resting it against the curve of his arm. The heavy, silken waves of her auburn hair fanned out over the velvet softness of the moss beneath her.

Gavin's dark head moved downward, and she felt the

107

pressure of his cheek against the rounded swell of her breasts. He gave a wordless groan of frustration, and a moment later he drew away. His fingers were moving quickly, expertly, as he began to unbutton the close-fitting jacket of her riding habit.

She lay still, gazing up at him with wide golden eyes, as he stripped away the jacket and the cambric blouse underneath it. He shifted his position, kneeling so that he could pull off her riding boots. Now her legs were sheathed only in her silken hose.

He raised himself once more, and her pulse speeded up when he unfastened the ribbons of her shift. But as she felt the light spray from the waterfall flicking over her bare breasts, she drew back; for all at once she was gripped by a brief reluctance to allow him to go on.

She was remembering that other time when they had embraced on the shabby couch in the shack near the mill. Then, Gavin had caressed her body through the protecting folds of her shift. But tonight she knew, without the slightest trace of doubt, that he meant to possess her completely.

For here they were hidden from view by the deep shadows of the towering tree ferns and the delicate branches of the tall bamboos, and no chance passerby would intrude on their privacy. In the lush, heavy-scented depths of the island night, Gavin would bare her body completely. He would strip away each of her fragile, lace-trimmed undergarments. And after that, nothing would stop him from satisfying the hard, driving urgency of his need.

She was tormented by her longing to know the complete fulfillment he was offering her; but at the same time, she felt restrained by all that she'd been taught of right and wrong. A respectable young girl might entice a man, up to a point; indeed, she was encouraged to fire his passion with countless flirtatious maneuvers, like the steps in an intricate dance. But she must not surrender her virginity to anyone except her husband.

Once Gavin had told her that she knew little of a man's need. And he'd been right. How could she know? No one had ever explained what she could expect the first time she lay with a man. She had no elder sister, no close female confidant, to prepare her for this moment.

Somehow Gavin must have sensed her hesitation. He paused for a moment, and brushed his lips lightly against her cheek and along the line of her jaw. "Don't be afraid of me, love. Not now—not ever."

His voice was warm and reassuring. She felt some of the tension go out of her and she made no protest as he finished unfastening her shift. He drew it down, and his mouth burned against the shadowy cleft between her breasts. He burrowed deeper into the warm softness, and she was stirred, touched by his deep sigh of satisfaction.

He turned his head and captured one nipple between his lips, then drew the rosy point deep inside his mouth. He released it, drew it in again. And now he was suckling, laving her, sending swift waves of sensuous excitement rippling through her.

Her fears began to fall away as she felt herself caught up in a tingling rush of anticipation. The sweet-hot current within her grew and grew until it became a fierce pressure, filling the deepest part of her being. Gavin's hands rested on her thighs. "Part your legs for me," he said softly.

And now he was drawing her silk stockings down. His hands moved more slowly, and he paused from time to time, to caress the sensitive skin of her inner thighs. She felt her body arch upward as though it had a will of its own. He touched the satin softness of her flat belly, and began stroking lightly. She drew in her breath as a hot jolt of desire went to the very core of her being.

But when his fingers slipped lower still, and he began to toy with the triangle of russet silk at the apex of her thighs, she could not hold back a cry of protest.

"Easy, my sweet Sybilla," he said softly. "Yes, here,

too . . ." His voice gentled her, for she heard the tenderness in his husky tone. He seemed to understand her uncertainty, her reluctance to surrender herself completely. He went on stroking the soft, damp curls of her womanhood, until she was able to accept this new intimacy.

Then he rose to his feet and moved away. Quickly, he stripped off his own clothes. She watched as he dropped his shirt atop a broad, flat rock near the pool. His fingers worked swiftly at the heavy buckle of his belt. She turned her face away, and fixed her gaze on the glittering flow of the waterfall, and breathed the scent of the night-blooming jasmine, mingled with the spice of the ferns and the primeval odor of damp earth and moss.

Little by little, the last of her fears ebbed away, and she looked up to see Gavin standing beside her. The angles and planes of his face stood out sharp and distinct in the moonlight. She no longer felt the need to restrain herself, and she allowed her eyes to move down, to know more of this man who was about to take her.

Her lips parted in wonder. For the first time, she realized that a man's body could have a beauty all its own. Her gaze went from the magnificent width of his bare shoulders to his powerful chest, with its dark tangle of hair, its flat nipples. And lower still, to his lean hips, and his taut belly.

Only then did she give a slight gasp and look away. But not before she had caught a glimpse of his male arousal, proud and erect.

With lithe animal grace, he dropped down at her side, and brushed her hair back from her face. Taking her chin in his hand, he bent and kissed her. Then he stretched out at full length and drew her against him once more. She clung to him and the heat of his body enveloped her.

The crisp hair on his chest was rough against her nipples. All at once she realized that she had begun to move against him, wanting to heighten the exciting friction. The pink tips of her nipples peaked and hardened.

Gavin slid his arm under her. Raising her, he bent his head and, taking one of her breasts in his hand, he kissed the soft swell. She could scarcely bear the aching heaviness engendered by his mouth. And gradually she became aware of a throbbing in another, deeper part of her. She pressed her thighs together, as if to subdue her response, but the movement only seemed to intensify the pulsation down below.

His fingers were moving now, in a light motion, tracing the arc of her ribs. He was circling the flat of his palm against her belly. The pulsing inside her speeded up, and she found herself clutching at his shoulders, driving her fingers into his flesh, to communicate the growing fierceness of her need.

Swiftly, surely, he dropped his hand to her virgin mound, parted her and found the moist, hidden place within. He touched the peak of her womanhood, then took it gently between his fingers. The incessant surging of the waterfall blended with the growing rush of sensation that possessed her.

She pressed herself upward against his hand, her body pleading for release. She drew up her knees, and felt the damp velvet of the moss beneath the bare soles of her feet. He took his hand away and spread her thighs. His breathing was harsh and unsteady and she saw, through her half-closed lids, the rise and fall of his chest.

He parted her legs wider, and knelt between them. He was nudging at her, pressing into her and she drew in her breath, trying to prepare herself for what was to follow. The first swift, burning stroke of his entry sent a lance of pain driving into her. She cried out and tried to pull away, but his hands cupped her buttocks, holding her firmly against him.

He did not move, but allowed her to get used to the hardness of him, buried deep within her. She raised her eyes to his face, and saw his skin drawn tight across the slashes of his cheekbones and the line of his jaw.

She sensed his fierce inner battle to hold himself back; to allow her to overcome her fears and completely accept the unfamiliar sensation of their joining. He would not take his own pleasure without consideration for her feelings. And the realization filled her with a new understanding of the man. . . .

She reached out, her hands stroking his back, and even now she felt the pain begin to ebb away. His palms cupped the silken rounds of her buttocks as he raised her closer to him. And he was moving again, and she was moving with him, and they were part of the night and the warm, flower-sweet, earth-scented darkness.

Beyond the line of his shoulder, she caught a dazzling glimpse of the stars. The blazing points were touching her . . . burning into her. . . .

Gavin began to thrust again, slowly at first, then faster. Plunging deep inside her, and deeper still, taking her with him. She felt as though they were moving upward in ever-quickening spirals. She cried out for release and found it, somewhere between the dark, lush earth and the wide, overarching sky.

He was exploding in one fiery burst, filling her with himself, sending shock waves into her muscles and down along every nerve of her body. She tightened around him, her moist, dark sheath contracting again and again, as they shared the timeless moment of fulfillment.

Sybilla lay on her side and felt the pressure of Gavin's body molded against hers. He stroked her hair, her shoulders, her slender, tapering back.

"Look, my love," he said softly. "Over that way. It'll be dawn soon."

She raised her eyes and, with a swift ache of regret, she saw that even now the stars were growing paler. A faint light burnished the rocks at the top of the waterfall. Here in

Jamaica the dawn came on swiftly in a blaze of rose and gold.

On other mornings she had found it soothing to stand on the balcony outside her bedchamber at Acacia Hall, and drink in the cool, fresh beauty of the coming day. But now she reached out and drew closer to Gavin, and her arms tightened fiercely around his shoulders, as if her embrace could weave a spell to keep back the first rays of the sun.

A light breeze stirred the branches of the bamboos; already she could see the hibiscus flowers begin to take shape on the bushes nearby. Slowly, reluctantly, she took her arms away.

She sat up, reached for her clothes, and began to dress. She smoothed her thick, tangled hair, twisted it into a loose chignon at the back of her head, and fastened it in place with the few gold-tipped bodkins she had left scattered about on the damp moss.

"My hat," she said absently. "It must have blown away back there on the beach."

Gavin rose and went to the flat rock where he had piled his own garments. "It doesn't matter, Sybilla. I'll take you home by one of the back roads near the mangrove swamp. No one must know that you haven't spent the night in your own bedchamber."

He pulled on his breeches and his boots. Then he returned and put out a hand to help her rise.

"I don't want to go back to Acacia Hall," she protested. "Not ever."

"Sorry, love—but you'll have to stay there for a little while longer."

Reality began to flood in once more, filling her with dismay. Her whole being shrank frm the thought of what lay ahead. She knew, beyond any doubt, that she loved Gavin completely. But how brief a time she'd been given to glory in the discovery of that love.

Gavin peered down into her face. "Surely you're not afraid

113

of Madeleine," he chided. "I don't doubt she'll make quite a scene when you tell her that she'll have to call off the betrothal party. She'll have a devil of a time breaking the news to Hobart. His lips curved in a faint smile. "He's used to getting his own way. Once he knows you aren't going through with the wedding—"

A wave of pain gripped Sybilla, tightening the muscles of her chest and making it difficult for her to get the words out.

"I am going through with it."

Gavin stared at her in disbelief. "You don't mean that. Not now!"

She swallowed and moistened her lips, then made herself look directly at him. "What happened here hasn't changed anything." Even if it tore her apart inside, she would have to convince him that she meant what she said.

In the first gray light, she saw his features harden. The muscles of his bare chest and shoulders went taut. He stood immobile for a moment, then picked up his shirt and thrust his arms into the full sleeves.

"I'm sorry, Gavin."

He drew in his breath, and she braced herself for an angry tirade. But when he spoke, his voice was even and matter-of-fact.

"Why should you be sorry?" He threw a glance at the mossy bed where they had lain together. "I found a willing young girl, and we shared a few hours of pleasure. That's all a sailor hopes for, when he goes ashore. And as for the future—" He buttoned his shirt and pushed it into the waistband of his breeches. Were his hands a bit clumsy when he fastened on his broad leather belt? Or was it a trick of the light, she wondered?

"As for the future, you've charted a safe course for yourself, Sybilla." His laugh was brief, harsh. "Nicholas Hobart has more land than any other planter on the island. He can offer you wealth and social position. The Jamaica gentry may not like him, but they'll court his favor by fawning over you."

"Gavin, no! That's not why I'm marrying him."

"Isn't it? He boasted that you wouldn't be able to bring yourself to refuse his gift." Although Gavin spoke softly, she could not mistake the savage irony in his voice, the contempt in his eyes. "Lord, what a fool he must have thought me. I said you were not the sort to be won with such baubles. But he knew better. He dangled that splendid topaz before you, like a fisherman out after a prize catch. And you snapped at the bait."

Sybilla's lips parted in surprise. "What do you know of the necklace?"

"I found it for him."

"You mean—Nicholas Hobart sent you to select such a valuable gift?"

"You might put it that way." He gave her a mirthless smile. "It would seem he understands the secrets of a woman's nature better than I do. You're not so different from the wenches of Tortuga, after all. A man only has to toss a glittering jewel into your lap and you're willing to give yourself in exchange."

Slashed by the merciless lash of Gavin's contempt, she could keep silent no longer. "I didn't take the necklace!"

"Indeed? You're even more shrewd than I suspected, my sweet."

"And what is that supposed to mean?"

"You refused the necklace because you were holding out for a wedding ring. You knew that once you were Mistress Hobart of Indigo plantation, you'd have all the rest—all the jewels, all the fine clothes and handsome carriages you could wish for. A houseful of slaves to do your bidding."

"Damn you, Gavin Broderick! You know I'm not like that—" Her eyes burned deep amber. "There's little enough you don't know about me, not now—not after we—"

He seized her by the shoulders and searched her face. "Then why are you going through with the marriage,

115

Sybilla?" His strong fingers tightened on her shoulders in a fierce grip, but she was scarcely aware of the pain. Only grief possessed her now, and brought the sting of tears to her eyes.

Soon, Gavin would set sail. Somehow, she would have to learn to be without him, through all the empty days to come. But how could she let him go, believing the worst about her?

"Tell me why you're marrying Hobart." Now his voice was no longer cool and mocking. "Give me one reason!"

She writhed in his grasp. "Let me go—" She had to get away, before it was too late.

"Hobart can't force you to marry him against your will."

"Gavin—for the love of heaven—" A treacherous weakness rose within her and she slumped forward.

"You're not leaving until you've told me the truth."

He pulled her against him. The barrier of her self-control was swept away like a fragile seashell before the outgoing tide.

"It's because of Lance," she said. "Hobart knows all about my brother—why he had to leave England—Madeleine told him everything."

"Told him what?"

He was holding her against him now, his arm around her shoulders. Her legs felt unsteady as he led her to the flat rock nearby and drew her down beside him.

"Lance didn't come out to the West Indies in search of adventure," she began. "Or a fortune, either. He fled from England one step ahead of the King's troopers."

"He arrived in Jamaica in '64, didn't he? Not long after Monmouth's rebellion," Gavin said. "Your brother chose the losing side."

Sybilla nodded. "If he'd remained in Somerset, he'd surely have been captured and tried for treason before the Bloody Assizes."

With these few words, she had put her trust in Gavin, for now he, too, had the power to denounce her brother, if he chose to. She glanced at him anxiously. His hand closed

116

around hers. "I should have guessed it was something like that," he said, with the trace of a smile. "You want to save him from another well-deserved thrashing, as you did when you were both children."

Her face flushed slightly. "How can you make light of this?" she demanded. "If I don't go ahead with the marriage, Hobart will denounce my brother to the English authorities here on the island. Lance will be hanged, or sold as a bond slave—"

He drew her head against his chest, and felt him stroke her hair, his touch gentle, reassuring. "You won't marry Hobart," he said. "I won't let you."

She drew back and raised her face, her eyes searching his. "Why should it matter to you?" Even as she asked the question, she felt hope flare within her. He had told her that he had no intention of marrying. He'd said that a wife could have no place in his roving way of life. But she pushed the memory aside.

For surely the passion they'd shared had changed everything. She was not the girl who had ridden away from Acacia Hall last night. And he, too, must be different. If only he would tell her so.

"Why don't you want me to marry Hobart?"

In the growing light of dawn, she could see the harsh lines at the sides of his mouth; the implacable anger that smoldered in the depths of his eyes. Instinctively she drew back.

Then she realized that he was looking past her, and it was as if he no longer saw her. She rose and stood before him, and still he did not speak.

Squaring her shoulders, she lifted her chin and walked toward the tree where her horse was cropping at the dew-soaked grass. A moment later he came after her, and caught her by the wrist.

"Wait, Sybilla."

"For what?"

"I can't blame you for trying to save your brother. Even at the cost of your own future."

These were not the words she'd been hoping to hear, but nevertheless, her spirits lifted slightly. She saw the quick, shrewd intelligence behind his eyes. "There's got to be another way to keep Lance out of danger." His straight black brows drew together. "Too bad you couldn't manage to hold Madeleine off a little longer."

"I tried. But she's determined to please Hobart, any way she can. She said if I didn't agree to the marriage at once, she'd have me thrown off the plantation. And she meant it, Gavin—I know she did."

Forcing herself to speak with a calm she did not feel, she told him of her talk with her uncle's widow, a few days ago. "She said I'd have no choice but to go to work in a tavern or a—a bawdy house."

"She missed her proper vocation," Gavin interrupted harshly. "She'd have done well as the keeper of a brothel."

"All the same, what she said was true. How else could I have survived in Montego Bay, without money or friends?"

"You should have come to me at once." Gavin looked at her, his eyes warm and reassuring now. "When I think what hell you must have gone through, these last few days! Little wonder I found you riding out there on the beach, too dazed to know what was happening."

His arms went around her, and he held her tightly, as if he were afraid she might be taken from him. "Good Lord! You could have drowned, with the tide coming in. . . . But you're all right now." He cradled her body against his. "You're safe, Sybilla."

His voice, tender and protective, convinced her that he *had* changed. Of course he had. She loved him. She knew it with a calm certainty. And he returned her love. Hadn't he proved it when he taught her the ways of passion, holding his own needs in check, arousing her with gentleness and patience, as if she had been his cherished bride?

118

The fear that had shadowed her days, and tormented her through the long, sleepless nights, melted away now. Gavin would marry her. He would take her aboard the *Condor,* and together they would sail the waters of the Indies. She would share his wandering life willingly, gladly.

But what about Lance? If she fled with Gavin now she did not doubt that Hobart would swiftly move to seek his revenge; not only because of his frustrated desire to possess her, but also because her disappearance would humiliate him in the eyes of his neighbors. Even though the betrothal had not been announced formally as yet, Madeleine had lost no time in spreading the news among the plantation gentry.

But she pushed her doubts away. Hobart would be no threat to her, or to Lance—not any longer. Gavin would protect them both. He was strong and determined, and he had a crew of tough, hard-bitten sailors who would follow his orders without question.

"How long will it be, before the *Condor* is ready to set sail?" she asked eagerly. "I don't have to go back to Acacia Hall, not even for my clothes. Let's go aboard the frigate and leave Jamaica right away—today—"

He gave her an affectionate smile, but shook his head. "You know nothing about ships, my love. It'll be at least a fortnight before we've put her in fit condition to weigh anchor."

"But Madeleine's going to announce my betrothal at tonight's ball." She could not hide her consternation.

"And you will play your part as she expects you to," Gavin went on calmly. "You'll smile sweetly and blush, and thank the guests for their good wishes. You'll wear that topaz necklace with a show of pride, so that every other lady in the room will envy you."

"Gavin, you're not making sense. You said I wouldn't have to marry Nicholas Hobart. You promised to find another way—"

"And I have. I give you my word, your brother won't be

charged with treason. And there'll be no need for you to marry that self-important bastard in exchange for Lance's safety."

She opened her lips to speak, but he went on, "Be still and listen carefully. Hobart has made plans to sail to Cuba aboard the *Condor* as soon as she's ready to put to sea. He has business to attend to in Havana. When you have a few moments alone with him at the ball tonight, you must persuade him to take you along."

"But what possible excuse can I offer? He's not a fool— he'll never believe that I've grown so fond of him that I can't bear to be separated from him, even for a short time."

"Say you have your heart set on being married in Havana. And that you want him to lay over off the Isle of Pines, to take Lance aboard. As your nearest male relative, it's only proper that he should be there, to give you away in marriage."

"But even if Hobart agrees, what will happen once we reach Havana?"

"Leave that to me," Gavin said.

Chapter Ten

The setting sun sent a glittering path of gold across the blue-green waters of the Caribbean and touched the low clouds with a soft rosy light. Sybilla stood beside the towering foremast, on the main deck of the *Condor,* looking out to the west, in the direction of Cuba.

Soon they would weigh anchor off the Isle of Pines, and then, once Lance had come aboard, the frigate would proceed to Havana. It would be good to see her brother again, although she could only wonder how he would receive the news that she and Hobart were to be married. Later, when Gavin had carried out his plans to help her and Lance get away, there would be time enough to explain the situation.

The freshening breeze that heralded the coming-on of evening, ruffled the full skirt of her gown. The traveling costume was a new one; it had been delivered by Mistress Fanshawe shortly before Sybilla's departure from Acacia Hall. The dressmaker had been proud of her creation, and even Sybilla, distracted though she was by the ordeal that lay ahead, had been sincere in her praise of Mistress Fanshawe's skill.

The bodice of yellow and black striped silk fitted snugly, and the neckline was cut low and trimmed with black lace to set off the whiteness of Sybilla's curving bosom. Over the gown she wore a light traveling cloak of black, lined with yellow satin.

Sybilla tried to find what solace she could in having this brief time to herself. All too soon, Nicholas Hobart would emerge from his cabin to join her. She would have to listen politely, once more, to his plans for their wedding, which was to take place in Havana on the day after tomorrow. And she would keep an acquiescent smile fixed on her lips, even when he placed his heavy arm about her waist, and held her body tightly against his.

Ever since the night of the betrothal ball he had taken every opportunity for physical contact with her. When he came to visit Acacia Hall and Sybilla played a few simple melodies on the wing-shaped harpsichord, he insisted on leaning close to her, and brushing against her, on the pretext of turning the pages of the music album.

And when they were seated at the card table, she was unable to concentrate on a game of hazard or ombre, for she could not ignore the purposeful pressure of his leg against hers. It was as if he needed to prove to her, and to himself, that before long he would take complete possession of her body.

Sybilla sighed as she braced herself for this evening's ordeal. Under different circumstances, she might have lost herself in the beauty of the sea and sky and taken pleasure in the swift movement of the frigate, the light touch of the breeze that brushed her cheek and played with a few loose strands of her auburn hair. But now she was distracted, as her thoughts returned to the fortnight just past.

On the evening of the betrothal ball she had come down the stairs and into the lavishly decorated ballroom, which was banked with masses of flowers. Hobart, flushed with satisfaction, stood waiting for her. And less than an hour later her hand had rested on Hobart's arm while Madeleine, her blue eyes aglow, had announced the betrothal of her niece.

She remembered the planters and their ladies, decked out in all their finery, crowding around, smiling and raising their glasses in a toast. And the ladies had, indeed, looked envious, when they saw the topaz-and-diamond necklace glittering on her bosom.

Later that evening, still following Gavin's instructions in every detail, she had managed to get Hobart out into the garden. There she urged him to take her along on his voyage to Cuba.

At first he hesitated, obviously puzzled by her insistence.

"Please humor me in this," she said softly, looking up at him from under her lashes and shielding her face with her fan. "Surely it is not so difficult for you to understand that I should wish my brother to give me away."

"But I've been planning to have the ceremony at St. Ann's church, here in Jamaica, with all our neighbors present," Hobart protested. "And I've already started making arrangements for a splendid reception afterward."

"You've said that you cannot put off this trip to Havana," she persisted. "I don't want to stay behind."

He gave her a swift, suspicious glance. "Surely you don't expect me to believe that you cannot wait a few weeks longer, until after my return from Cuba, to marry me."

Sybilla had already decided that it would be useless to try to convince Hobart that she was eager to become his wife; for all his enormous conceit, he never would have believed that she'd had such a complete change of heart.

"Since I have agreed to the marriage," she said with quiet dignity, "I see no point in further delay." She raised her eyes to his. "I won't rest easy until I am your wife, since that's the only way I can be sure of my brother's safety."

"Sybilla, you wound me," he protested. "I've already given you my word that, since you've decided to be reasonable, no harm will come to your brother." He put his thick arm around her waist. "A betrothal's as good as a marriage."

"Not quite, Mr. Hobart," she told him, her body stiffening in his grasp.

"If that's the way you feel, maybe it's as well to move up the date of our wedding," he said. His hand cupped her breast and she had to set her teeth to force back a sound of revulsion. His fingers tightened around the soft mound beneath the thin silk of her gown. "You won't regret marrying me, Sybilla. Wait and see."

She searched her mind, seeking for a way to distract him. "Tell me, Mr. Hobart—"

"Nicholas," he corrected her.

"Is it true that you may be appointed governor of the island?"

"So Madeleine told you that, did she? Yes, my dear, it's likely enough. And you're not averse to the notion of being the governor's lady, as well as mistress of Indigo, are you?"

"I see no reason to deny it," she said. If only he would take those fat fingers away from her breast. But she made herself speak in a soft, coaxing tone. "And you won't refuse to allow my brother to take off a little time to come to our wedding, will you, Nicholas? The Isle of Pines is so close to Havana."

"Why not?" He kneaded her breast, and she was thankful for the shadows that concealed her expression of overpowering distaste. "You'll find me a most indulgent husband, Sybilla. Though I must say, it's as well you don't have half a dozen relations scattered through the islands. Or no doubt you'd want me to send out ships to bring them all to the wedding."

He let his hand fall from her breast. "What about Madeleine? If we're to be married in Havana, are we to take her along?"

"I don't want her there," Sybilla told him. Then, to soften the blunt response, she added, "I don't believe she will mind. She's taken up with her duties here. The harvest—" And no doubt Madeleine would welcome the opportunity to entertain the overseer in relative privacy.

"As for our neighbors," she went on, "there will be no need to cheat them out of the festivities. Why not hold a great reception at Indigo soon after we return—one that will be the talk of the island for months to come?"

"That's what I like to hear!" He gave Sybilla an approving smile. "It proves I was right in choosing you to be my wife. I'll be the envy of every man in Jamaica."

Warming to his subject, he went on. "There'll be a great deal of responsibility for you, but I've no doubt you'll do me credit. I have many plans for the future."

"Indeed, Nicholas?" She fluttered her fan and feigned a deep interest. "If you're to be governor, I should think that would occupy most of your time."

"Hardly," he assured her. "I'll have a staff to take care of the routine duties at Government House." He puffed out his chest, under his tightly fitted satin coat. "I've taken possession of a smaller plantation, high up in the Blue Mountains. The improvident fool of an owner borrowed money from me and couldn't pay it back. The climate up there should be ideal for cultivating a coffee crop. Why go on importing the beans all the way from Africa, when I can grow the plants right here on the island?"

"You are sure to succeed—you're an enterprising man. And no doubt such a venture will help to get you appointed governor—"

"So you do look forward to being the governor's lady."

She lowered her eyes. "For a dowerless girl like myself—it is more than I ever hoped for, Nicholas."

"No doubt. I'm sure when you sailed from England, you didn't expect to make such an advantageous marriage—and so soon after your arrival here."

"I shall do my best not to disappoint you."

"Now you're being sensible," he said with an approving look. "It's taken you a while, but obviously you've come to see that it's in your best interests—and your brother's—to be a dutiful wife to me."

"Certainly, Nicholas." She dropped her thick curving lashes, to hide the distaste in her eyes. "Once I'm your wife, I'll try to please you—in every way."

As she spoke, she felt the topaz necklace, cold and heavy against her flesh. She had all she could do to keep from tearing it off, but she reminded herself that she would not have to go through with the wedding. She had Gavin's word on that.

Gavin had not attended the betrothal ball, and she had not had even a glimpse of him in the days that followed. No doubt he was keeping busy, supervising the rest of the repairs on his frigate.

He had not told her what he planned to do, once he got Lance away from the Isle of Pines and out of Hobart's reach. And what of her own future? Perhaps it should be enough that she would not be forced to marry Hobart. But after that night when she had lain in his arms, she knew she wanted so much more. Why had Gavin ridden back with her in brooding silence and then left her near the gates of Acacia Hall with only a swift embrace, a deep, lingering kiss?

This morning, when she and Hobart had come aboard the *Condor* at dawn, Gavin had been waiting on deck to greet them. Seeing him for the first time since their night beside the waterfall, she felt her senses come alive with a warm, dizzying rush. But she managed to conceal her soaring joy at being near him and to smile with formal courtesy, as she acknowledged his greeting.

He had provided separate cabins for the betrothed couple, and Hobart had appeared satisfied with the arrangement. The voyage, first to the Isle of Pines, and then on to Havana, would take no more than two days, at the longest.

"And after that, my dear, you will belong to me," Hobart

had said softly, when he had taken leave of her outside her cabin door.

But now, as the sun dipped toward the horizon, she stiffened at the sound of his heavy footsteps. She had to force herself to turn to him with a smile. How soon would it be before Gavin could get her away from him? If only he had confided all of his plans to her, on their ride back to Acacia Hall.

"The sea air agrees with you, I see," Hobart said with a smile. "That touch of color in your cheeks is most becoming." He slid his arm around her waist and drew her against him. She flinched as she felt the heat of his thick, stocky body through her silk gown.

Instinctively, her gaze moved upward to the quarterdeck, where Gavin was standing. Even at this distance, the sight of him stirred memories of the hours they'd shared near the waterfall. If only he'd been able to give her a word, a sign, that he was remembering, too.

"We'll be approaching the Isle of Pines in a few hours," Hobart said. "It'll be dark by then, and we may have to lay off the island until dawn." His arm tightened possessively about her waist. "But by tomorrow night we'll be man and wife."

His insinuating laugh made her stomach muscles tighten. "It will be most agreeable to instruct you in the ways of pleasuring a husband," he added. "You need not be concerned by your lack of experience—I prefer it that way."

She clenched her jaw. If he went on speaking much longer, she would not be able to conceal her feelings. Even now, her muscles ached with her effort at self-control.

But he was interrupted by the shout of a sailor, perched high in the rigging. "Vessel sighted, west, nor'west, Captain!"

All along the deck, men stopped in their tracks, to stare out over the water. "She's movin' under full sail!" the lookout shouted. "She's a Spanish galleon! A ship o' war!"

Hobart released Sybilla. She shaded her eyes with her hand, and caught sight of a sliver of white in the distance. It appeared to grow larger as she watched. Now she could make out the great white sails, the rhythmic rise and fall of a row of oars, as they caught the gleam of the setting sun.

Instinctively, she turned to look up at the quarterdeck. Gavin, his long legs braced apart, raised his telescope to his eye.

And now, from all parts of the deck, the sailors came running; they jostled one another, pointing out over the sea, and exclaiming noisily.

"She's a warship, right enough!"

"Sink me if she ain't!"

Not one of them seemed the least uneasy at the sight of the great vessel approaching the *Condor* at such speed. Instead, the unexpected appearance of the Spaniard stirred a growing anticipation through their ranks.

"Looks to be five miles off—"

"Six is more like it!"

"Movin' fast, she is—like she's got the devil snappin' at her heels!"

Sybilla, her eyes fixed on the quarterdeck, saw Abiathar Pascoe approach Gavin. The red-bearded mate gestured, and Gavin nodded.

"Gunners to your stations!" the mate roared out, his powerful voice rumbling like thunder down the length of the deck. "Jump to it, you buggers!"

Sybilla moved out of the way, to keep from being jostled by the crew. She heard the slap of bare feet on the scoured planks, and watched as the gunners hurried to obey. Two young boys, no older than twelve, came staggering after them, lugging heavy buckets of sand.

Sybilla felt a shiver run through her. She tried to keep her voice steady, in spite of her fear. "Surely we are not under attack."

"Certainly not, my dear." But even as he reassured her, she

saw that he looked up anxiously, his eyes fixed on Gavin, who was rapping out a barrage of orders to the crew.

"Hands aloft. Prepare to loose top'ls! Padgett—break out cutlasses, pikes and boarding axes. Jenkins! To the forward carronade."

Hobart seized Sybilla's hand in a tight grip, and hurried her to the foot of the steps leading to the quarterdeck. "Captain Broderick," he called. "I want a word with you at once."

"Stay where you are," Gavin ordered, in a tone that discouraged any further discussion.

"Ferguson! Hold her steady as she goes. Muskets to the rigging."

Then he descended to the maindeck, moving without any particular haste. But although he appeared calm enough, Sybilla caught the hint of a frown between his straight, dark brows, tension in the set of his jaw.

"She's the *San Bartolomé,*" Gavin told them. "She's back from Cadiz, sooner than I'd have expected."

"But why have you ordered those men to their guns?" Hobart demanded. "We're not under attack."

"The hell we're not! I'll warrant her captain's already recognized the *Condor.* He'll have forty guns to our thirty-six. And almost twice as many men—not counting the galley slaves." He gestured toward the great hull bearing down on them, under a tall cloud of white sail. "She got every stitch of canvas set."

Sybilla, following the direction of his arm, squinted at the blaze of gilding on the galleon's broad bows. The red and gold flag of Spain streamed from the masthead.

"But we're not at war with Spain," she protested. "If the captain of the galleon has identified our ship, he must know she's a merchantman, bound on a peaceful errand."

For one instant, Gavin's gray eyes held her. She knew he was about to answer. But Hobart spoke first. "We should have sailed aboard one of my own trading vessels, damme!"

129

Gavin shrugged. "Too late for second thoughts, now."

He turned to Abiathar, who had come up beside them, unnoticed. The mate grinned, and nodded. "Right enough, Captain! There's nothing for it, but to stand and fight," he said.

Even as the man was speaking, he started stripping off his shirt. He bared his powerful bronzed torso, with its heavy thatch of carrot-colored hair, then wrapped a scarf around his head and stroked his great red beard. The prospect of imminent battle did not appear to trouble Abiathar Pascoe in the least.

"We're ready to run out the guns, soon as you give the word, Captain," he said calmly. "Meanwhile, them powder monkeys had better be spreadin' plenty of sand around the gun trucks."

A ray from the setting sun glinted on the large gold hoop in his ear. He shoved his cutlass into his belt and caressed the handle, as if he were stroking a favorite hound.

"Couldn't we head for that fogbank, and try to shake off the Spaniards?" Hobart pointed hopefully to the thickening whitish fog that lay to the west.

"And smash the ship on a lee shore, or run her onto a hidden reef and tear the bottom out of her?" Gavin did not bother to hide his contempt for the other man's ignorance. "No, Mr. Hobart. We'll go about and lay the *Condor* beside the galleon."

"And what then?" Hobart demanded. "You can't hope to take a Spanish ship of war with this frigate. We're outgunned—outmanned! You said so yourself!"

"The *Condor*'s size has always given us the advantage of greater mobility than any galleon. The more so, now that we've had a chance to scrape her and make her seaworthy again." It was plain that Gavin was keeping a tight rein on his temper. "You'd better hope the wind holds," he added.

Then turning to the mate, he said, "Abiathar, pass the order to the helm to wear ship. We'll turn her about and move in fast, to intercept the *San Bartolomé*. And we'll fire off the first broadside. If we can dismast her before she returns our fire, we've a good chance of taking her."

"Wind's dropping," Abiathar observed, glancing up at the sails. "That blasted galleon can keep moving in the lightest breeze. The Spaniards have plenty of galley slaves aboard, pulling at the oars. Those poor buggers'll keep her on course—or have their backs torn to shreds by the lash!"

"We'll take her all the same." His gray eyes narrowed, and his face went hard as granite. Deep lines bracketed the sides of his lips.

"But this is sheer madness!" Hobart's bluster could not mask his mounting uneasiness. "Surely there must be some other way to deal with—"

"I give the orders here. We'll stand and fight." Gavin spoke softly, but there was no mistaking his unshakeable determination.

"Never fear, Mr. Hobart," the red-bearded mate said, and his big white teeth flashed in a mocking grin. "We ain't expecting you to man one of the guns or go climbing aloft. Or is it the young lady you're worried about?"

"Mistress Thornton's perfectly safe," Hobart said. "The Spaniards won't harm a respectable female. If you knew the Spanish code of chivalry, you would understand that it forbids them to molest any lady."

Gavin turned on Hobart. "What the devil do you know about it, you pompous jackass!" His voice held the warning of imminent danger. Hobart took a step back.

Abiathar moved with surprising speed to interpose his giant body between the two.

"Hold your tongue, Mr. Hobart," the mate said.

He put his speaking trumpet to his lips, and shouted to the helmsman. "All hands! Wear ship! Get her about!"

More men went scampering aloft. Sybilla heard the creak of rigging, a flapping of sails, as the seamen did their part to carry out the maneuver.

Gavin spoke directly to Sybilla, as if there were no one else on deck. "Try not to be frightened. We've beaten the Spaniards before—and against greater odds than these," he assured her. His gaze locked with hers, his eyes steady under his straight black brows. She drew strength from his words and the look that accompanied them. If only she could go into his arms, for only a moment.

"Now come along." His look took in Hobart. "Both of you," he said.

Hobart's usually ruddy face had taken on a grayish pallor. His skin glistened with sweat, but he made no move to wipe it away. Gavin led the way up to the quarterdeck, with Hobart and Sybilla behind him and Abiathar bringing up the rear.

Chapter Eleven

"Get inside, and be quick about it," Gavin ordered, throwing open the door of his cabin. A lantern was swinging from an oaken beam overhead, but the candle had not yet been lit. Only a few rays of sunlight still slanted through the wide stern window.

"Abiathar—fetch a sword for Mr. Hobart!"

"God's teeth, Broderick!" Hobart protested. "If you expect me to take part in the battle—"

"You'd only get in the way," Gavin said. "But if the Spaniards board us, it'll be up to you to protect Mistress Thornton." He gave the man a long, measuring look. "With your life, if necessary."

Abiathar shoved a rapier into Hobart's hand. "Hope you know enough not to cut yourself."

"I've handled a blade before," Hobart said with what dignity he could muster. "And I've given my opponent cause to wish he had not met me on the field of honor. But what chance can one man have, against a crew of bloodthirsty Spaniards?"

Abiathar dismissed Hobart's protest with a shrug of his massive shoulders. Sybilla watched in anxious silence, as Gavin stripped off his coat, tossed it aside, then wrapped a scarlet sash about his lean waist.

He buckled a baldric of tooled Cordovan leather across his chest and thrust a matched set of heavy pistols into the sling in front. He fastened on a sword belt, drew his rapier. His gaze ran down the glittering blade with grim satisfaction.

Sybilla watched his swift preparations with growing bewilderment. His air of calm assurance surprised her and stirred a vague suspicion. She had no doubt that Gavin was experienced in sea warfare—that he had fought other such battles and triumphed.

Gavin started for the door, with a swift, easy stride. For one instant, he turned to throw Sybilla a reassuring look. But it was to Hobart that he spoke. "Bar the door behind us. And the moment you hear the first cannons, get down and stay down."

"But if the Spaniards board us—" Hobart's voice betrayed his mounting fear.

"It may not come to that," Gavin said quietly. "If it does, you must make ready to defend Mistress Thornton—and yourself."

He left the cabin with Abiathar at his heels.

Hobart stood motionless, staring at the closed door. His face glistened. A few beads of sweat dripped down, and left dark splotches on his gold-trimmed blue satin coat.

"Hadn't you better bar the door now?" Sybilla prompted him.

"If the *Condor*'s taken, no iron bar will keep the Spaniards out of here."

"Even so, we'd better do as Captain Broderick said."

He shrugged, but went and heaved the bar into place. Sybilla hurried to the broad stern window, and knelt on the padded windowseat to look out.

The Spanish galleon was approaching swiftly, her massive cloud of sails tinged bloodred now, by the setting sun. The burnished rays played over her figurehead, which was carved in the shape of a great gilded lion, with painted teeth bared in a fearsome grin. The water dripped from the oars as they rose and fell, still keeping their steady rhythm.

Sybilla bit down on her lower lip, to hold back a cry of fright. Her eyes were enormous in her white face. It looked to her as if the *Condor* was on a collision course with the galleon.

Then the frigate heeled and the space between the two vessels seemed to have widened slightly. But she still felt the erratic thudding of her heart, the knot of ice in the pit of her stomach.

Only an hour ago, she had been confident that she would soon be free of Hobart. Gavin had laid his plans carefully—she'd been sure of that. And she had followed his orders as best she could. He couldn't have foreseen the appearance of the Spanish vessel.

But why was the *Condor,* a merchant ship, under attack? As she had watched Gavin's men running to take up their stations, she had felt a stirring of doubt. These half-naked sailors with cutlasses thrust into their sashes, with axes or pikes in their hands and silk scarves around their heads, looked like a horde of savages, eager to do battle with the galleon's crew, no matter what the odds.

The order came so quickly that Sybilla was more shocked than frightened. She heard Gavin shout, "Prepare for close action!"

She slid off the window seat, and dashed to a small square window that gave her a view of the main deck below. The gunners stood at their stations like leashed hounds, ready to run out their weapons at Gavin's command. The powder monkeys spread their sand around the gun trucks. Her stomach lurched as she guessed the reason for this precaution—it was so that a man might not slip on the blood-soaked planks, once the battle began.

Gavin stood beside the mizzenmast, a tall, impressive figure, with his leather baldric across his powerful chest, his booted feet set apart.

He drew his sword and raised it so that it flashed in the

light of the setting sun.

"Load and run out!"

Two rows of great guns thrust out over the glassy-smooth water.

Gavin brought his sword down with a swift motion. "Fire as you bear!"

His words rang out above the creak of spars and rigging, the squeals of the gun trucks. Sybilla kept her eyes fixed on Gavin. Even now, in the face of dangers she had not reckoned with and could scarcely understand, she was reassured by the sight of him, the sound of his voice.

Hobart grabbed her by the shoulder, shoved her to cabin floor, and hastily dropped down beside her. A moment later, she heard Gavin shout, "Aim high. Go for her masts!"

Then came a deafening boom, another and yet another as each of the guns fired in succession. Sybilla clapped her hands over her ears.

Hobart's muttered oath was drowned out by an answering volley from the Spanish vessel. If only she could see what was happening on deck. Her throat contracted with sheer terror as she thought of Gavin out there, confronting the enemy's fire.

"Fresh charges!" Pascoe was bellowing an order. "Sponge out!"

She started to raise herself, but Hobart pulled her down again. His mouth was close to her ear. "If Broderick can't dismast the Spaniards at once, they'll soon have us wallowing helpless under their guns," he said.

"And after that?"

"God's teeth, girl! I'll protect you as best I can, but I won't be able to stand off their whole crew."

"As you bear, fire!"

Hobart's volley of oaths was lost in the thunder of the *Condor*'s guns. But a few moments later, Sybilla heard him saying, "I should have sailed aboard one of my trading vessels!"

136

"But the *Condor*'s a merchant ship—"

She was silenced, taken aback by Hobart's harsh bark of laughter. "That Spanish captain knew better!"

A volley of musket fire smashed through the stern window, showering glass down around them.

"We can't stay here—" she cried out.

"We've no choice now. Don't move—keep your face covered!" Hobart ordered.

Sybilla buried her head in her arms. She caught the rank odor of fear from Hobart's sweat-soaked body. Thick, black smoke came billowing through the shattered window. The acrid fumes invaded her nostrils, and filled her throat.

She feared she would strangle, and then she heard Hobart coughing and gasping beside her. Once again, she lifted her head and tried to peer through the smashed stern window. The window seat where she'd been kneeling was covered with glittering shards.

How much time had passed since the lookout up in the rigging had sighted the galleon, she wondered. Had the night already fallen on the sea?

She buried her face in her arms again, too dazed to think coherently. The shouts of the men still fighting, the screams of the wounded, the crack of gunfire and the clash of steel all blended together in a senseless, terrifying din.

"Hold your fire!"

The guns fell silent, and somehow that was more frightening than the uproar had been. But it was Gavin's voice that had given the command. He was alive, and preparing to carry the battle to the enemy's own decks. "Prepare to board her!"

"Broderick's never lacked for courage—I'll have to say that for him." Hobart muttered. "But to make such a mad attempt! He must put little value on his life—or the lives of his men."

"What do you mean?"

When Hobart did not answer at once, Sybilla tugged

137

fiercely at his sleeve. "Answer me!"

"We're outmanned," Hobart said. "Broderick and his crew don't have one chance in a thousand! Even if they can board the galleon without being cut down by musket fire, they'll be slashed to pieces as soon as they reach the deck."

No! Sweet Jesú, no! Hobart was wrong—he must be!

And all at once, Sybilla felt a surge of guilt. If Gavin were killed, she would be to blame. Why had she given way to her weakness, and told Gavin the truth back there in Jamaica? It would have been far better if she had let him go on believing that she was a mercenary, conniving female, who was planning to marry Hobart for his wealth.

He'd have remembered her with contempt, no doubt. But at least he would not have sailed into this trap because he'd been trying to help her. Right now, he might have been far off in some distant port of call, enjoying a drink with Abiathar and looking about for a promising wench to give him a few hours of pleasure. Better that, than to have sent him to his death . . .

Gradually, she became aware of the silence outside the stifling cabin.

"The Spaniard's stopped firing," Hobart said. "It's all over."

"Gavin—"

"Broderick and his men had no chance. They were destroyed as soon as they set foot on the deck of the *San Bartolomé.*"

Sybilla was too stunned to cry. She lay still, as she tried to deal with the terrible impact of Hobart's words. For a moment, it was as if she could feel Gavin's arms around her, his body joined with hers, that night at the waterfall.

Then nothing . . . only a terrible black void that opened beneath her and grew steadily wider, deeper. Another moment and it would swallow her up.

But now Hobart was dragging her to her feet. "You hear that?"

Boots came thudding along the deck. Men were shouting in savage triumph. "The Spaniards have come aboard. The *Condor*'s been taken."

Sybilla understood every word, but she felt no response. No fear for herself. Only a dazed numbness that kept her immobile.

Now she heard a mighty crash against the cabin door. It shook on its hinges. Hobart pushed her behind him, but he did not draw his sword.

"I must deal with the Spanish captain," he told her. "Let me handle this. You stay where you are, and don't try to interfere."

She stared at him, her golden eyes blank. "Do you understand?" he demanded impatiently. She ran her tongue over her smoke-parched lips, but no words would come.

He spoke slowly, distinctly, as if to a simple-minded child. "I shall tell the Spanish captain who I am, and I'll offer him a generous ransom in exchange for our safe return to Jamaica—"

His voice was drowned out by the din of axe blades against the door. The massive oak boards shook violently, and then split apart. Sybilla saw a muscular bronzed arm reaching in. A moment later, the iron bar crashed to the floor.

The door swung wide on its iron hinges. Sybilla moved back behind Hobart. Then, peering through the smoke that still darkened the cabin, she caught sight of a tall, lean young gentleman in a suit of black taffeta laced with silver; a wide-brimmed hat, with a curling ostrich plume shaded his features. He carried himself with an air of authority, his gloved hand resting lightly on the jeweled hilt of his sword. Behind him stood a few half-naked seamen, armed with cutlasses and pistols, their faces blackened with the grime of battle.

The elegant young Spaniard swept off his hat and bowed to Sybilla with the grace of a courtier. "A thousand pardons for this rude entrance into your quarters, señorita." He spoke English with a marked Castilian accent.

"Are you the captain of the *San Bartolomé?*" Hobart interrupted with a trace of his familiar blustering tone.

"I have the honor to be his first officer." The young gentleman turned again to Sybilla. "Don Diego de Lorcha y Fernandez, at your service, señorita."

"Please, señor—por favor—What has happened to Captain Broderick?"

Hobart glared at her and without giving the Spaniard time to answer, he introduced himself hastily. "I am Mr. Nicholas Hobart of Jamaica. I'm a gentleman of wealth and property. I own Indigo—the largest plantation on the island. And a fleet of merchant ships as well. Mistress Thornton and I are betrothed."

"My congratulations, señor," said the Spaniard, with a slight inclination of his head. "You are indeed most fortunate."

Hobart brushed the gallantry aside. "I am prepared to offer a substantial payment in exchange for our release."

"Are you not concerned with the fate of the *Condor's* captain?" asked the young officer. Sybilla thought she detected a note of irony in his voice.

"Broderick?" Hobart shrugged his thick shoulders. "Why, I never met the fellow until I booked passage aboard his ship. Mistress Thornton and I were bound for Havana, to be wed." He forced an ingratiating smile. "Surely a gallant gentleman like yourself would not wish to harm a helpless, gently bred female."

"The young lady will come to no harm."

"And you'll put in a word for me with your captain? Tell him I'll meet any reasonable demand." Hobart persisted. "I'll make it worth your while, if you do."

The lean young Spaniard drew himself up, his hand tightening on his sword. "Let us have no more tradesman's talk of ransom, señor! Don Diego de Lorcha y Fernandez does not haggle over money with such as you." Then he inclined his head in Sybilla's direction and added, "As for the lady, I shall take her aboard the *San Bartolomé.*"

"But—what about me?"

The Spanish officer laughed softly. "I leave you to the tender mercies of my men."

He advanced toward Sybilla. "Come along, if you please." She drew back instinctively. "You'll be quite safe aboard the *San Bartolomé*—have I not given my word?"

Hobart was too badly shaken to be prudent. "The word of a Spaniard—what's that worth?"

The young officer frowned, his eyes narrowing dangerously. He motioned to his seamen. "Silence this English dog," he commanded.

He brushed past Hobart, and reached for Sybilla's arm. Hobart bellowed with outrage, and now, at last, he reached for his sword. But before he could draw it from the sheath, a hulking sailor leaped forward and struck him a powerful blow squarely on the point of his chin. Hobart staggered and fell to the cabin floor, his periwig askew.

Sybilla tried to get to him. No matter how much she disliked him, she could not bring herself to leave him lying there unconscious in the hands of the Spanish sailors. But Don Diego was already lifting her in his arms. "My captain's waiting, señorita. He is a most impatient gentleman, with a ferocious temper."

Sybilla writhed in his grasp, and tried to strike at him, but he only smiled at her futile efforts. With a swift motion, he tossed her over his shoulder and strode out on deck.

The strength drained out of her, and she lay limp and motionless, her head dangling forward, as he carried her down to the maindeck. The sky was a blue-black bowl overhead, and a chill breeze blew across the dark waters.

Then she gave a cry of horrified disbelief. Although her sight was blurred by the thick pall of smoke that still shrouded the deck, a few lanterns burned dimly. By their faint, wavering light she was able to catch a glimpse of the havoc left in the aftermath of the battle. The maindeck was a tangle of fallen spars and rigging and pieces of canvas from the torn sails. A seaman lay sprawled beside one of the guns, with a sliver of wood through his throat and his lifeless eyes turned up to the sky.

Sybilla gave a strangled cry and tried to free herself from the Spaniard's grasp.

"Calm yourself, señorita. I hope you won't make it necessary to have you hauled aboard the *San Bartolomé* in a cargo net—like a barrel of rum. Allow me to spare you such humiliation, if you please."

She thought she heard a trace of amusement in the young man's voice. But there was no mistaking the strength of the iron grip in which he held her. He reached out with his free hand and seized a rope that was fastened to the rail. Sybilla stiffened with alarm as she realized how he meant to get her across to the other ship.

"Have no fear, señorita—I'd never allow so beautiful a lady to fall into the sea."

The sky, with its few flickering points of silver, and the dark waves began to whirl before her dazed eyes, as she lay, head down, clutching at his coat. She felt a sheer animal terror as he mounted to the rail with her. Using his free hand, he grasped the heavy hempen rope more firmly. He pushed off, and for one awful moment, they were swaying across the narrow expanse of water between the two ships.

Then she heard a thud as his boots struck against the side of the galleon. He sprang down onto the deck with incredible ease. "Welcome to the *San Bartolomé*," he said.

She struggled to catch her breath. "Put me down— please!"

"Not until I have taken you to the cabin and presented you to my captain. He'll be pleased with such a rare prize."

And what would become of her then? She did not dare to ask. She remembered what Hobart had said about the Spanish code of chivalry. But suppose he had been mistaken? Perhaps such gallantry applied only to the ladies of

142

Spain, and not to an English girl. She lay still, as he carried her along the wide deck. At last he stopped and kicked open a heavy carved door.

The candlelight was blinding after the darkness outside. Carefully, the officer set her down on her feet, supporting her with a muscular arm.

"Here's the young lady, sir. Safe and sound. But she is a trifle shaken up, I'm afraid."

Sybilla stared at him in surprise. The young officer no longer spoke with the accent of Castile.

"And Hobart? Trussed up like a prize pig by now, I'll warrant."

Even as Sybilla cried out with relief, she was running to the man who stood next to the massive, candlelit table. Although her sight was still blurred, she could never have mistaken his voice—Gavin's voice.

A moment later, he reached out and gathered her into his arms.

Chapter Twelve

Later there would be time for questions. But now, Sybilla could only surrender completely to her overwhelming relief, at seeing Gavin again. She hadn't lost him. An upsurge of thankfulness, of joy, went coursing through her.

She pressed her face against his shoulder, and tightened her arms about him, as if to convince herself that he was really there. He gave a sound of protest, and she felt his muscles tense.

She drew back in bewilderment. Tilting her head, she looked into his face and saw his grimace of pain, the deepening lines around his mouth. His coat, which had been draped over his shoulders, slipped to the floor.

"Sweet Jesú—you've been wounded!" She stared fearfully at the scarlet splotch beneath the jagged hole in the sleeve of his shirt.

"A Spanish sharpshooter up in the rigging. It's lucky for me that his aim wasn't better," Gavin told her. "Abiathar got the bullet out and bandaged the wound." Then, seeing her agitation, he added, "I'll mend soon enough."

"Abiathar's not a physician," Sybilla protested.

"He's dug out more bullets and sewed up more sword cuts than most of your pompous London physicians, I'll warrant," Gavin told her.

"What if the wound should mortify?"

Sybilla remembered one of Lance's friends, who'd been wounded in a duel. Although the most well-respected physician in Somerset had removed the pistol ball, mortification had set in. The patient's arm had swollen and reddened. Wracked with fever, he had come close to dying, before his distraught family had given permission for his arm to be amputated.

"The captain'll be well enough, Mistress Thornton," said the tall young officer who had brought her aboard. "Mr. Pascoe seared the wound with the red-hot blade of his cutlass."

Sybilla went pale, and she felt her insides tighten as she thought of the ordeal Gavin had endured. She realized that she was part of him now and would always share his suffering as well as his pleasure.

"Enough, Jeremy," Gavin said. "Can't you see you're frightening the wits out of Mistress Thornton?"

Jeremy?

The tall young fellow smiled at her. "I am Jeremy Randall, of Tiverton, in Devonshire. Your humble servant, ma'am. Sorry I had to make you believe I was one of those Spaniards."

"You were most convincing," Sybilla said, with a slight smile.

"If you're quite finished," Gavin told Jeremy sternly, "you may go and take off that elegant frippery."

"Aye, Captain."

"I want the decks cleared, fast. Get together a working party to cut away the fallen rigging and a couple of sailmakers to mend that torn canvas. Check the gun trucks. I'll have no loose cannon careening about the decks. And send extra men to guard the hatches, in case those Spaniards get any notions about retaking the ship."

"Right away, Captain," the young man said earnestly.

Gavin gave him a brisk nod of approval. "You've done

145

well, Jeremy. You may keep that handsome taffeta and silver suit as booty. It'll set the wenches in Tortuga fighting for your attentions."

Jeremy Randall's face reddened under his dark tan. He bowed hastily to Sybilla, and hurried out of the cabin.

She stared at Gavin in dismay. "Tortuga!" Had she heard correctly? "Surely you don't mean to take us there."

"I do."

"But Tortuga's a refuge for pirates. They come to the island from every corner of the Indies."

Gavin's brows shot up. "How did you happen to hear about that?"

"The captain of the *Bristol Belle* told us that no law-abiding master of a merchant vessel would drop anchor there."

"He was right about that." She caught the flicker of amusement in Gavin's eyes and saw that he was smiling slightly.

"Then why should you . . ." Her voice trailed away. She had already guessed the answer to her question. Her lips parted in dismay and the color drained from her face as she tried to cope with this shattering discovery about Gavin Broderick.

She'd sensed a certain ruthlessness in him even at their first meeting, a capacity for violence just below the surface. She knew he was a rover, a man who would never settle down to a conventional way of life. But the truth was worse—far worse.

"A pirate," she stared at him, unable to conceal her feelings. The very word repelled and frightened her.

"I hoped you wouldn't have to know. Now that you do, perhaps I can make you understand. But this isn't the time. Come here to me, love." He held out his arms to her.

Although she hungered to feel his embrace and the warmth of his body enfolding hers, she could not make the slightest move toward him. She fixed her golden eyes on his

146

face, and spoke accusingly. "The Spanish captain recognized the *Condor* as a pirate ship." Her voice began to shake with indignation. "That's why he attacked us."

Her face was still pale, except for two spots of color burning on her cheeks. Her eyes hardened. "I know now why you named your frigate for a bird of prey. How many unarmed merchant vessels have you sent to the bottom? How many men have you slaughtered?" Her hands were clenched into tight fists. "And how many helpless women have you—"

"That's enough!"

The cold fury in his voice silenced her. "I would have hoped you knew me better. The only ships I've attacked have been those that were flying the flag of Spain. I had my reasons for that." He paused, his eyes locked with hers. "And I've never taken any woman against her will."

Then all at once, the anger drained out of him and she saw that he was leaning heavily against the massive table for support. Perhaps he was more badly wounded than he had admitted.

She hurried to him, but he held her off. "Surely you aren't about to offer aid and comfort to a pirate, Mistress Thornton."

"Gavin—let me help you."

"Take care, my sweet." Even now, his eyes glinted with the mockery she had come to know so well. "Aren't you afraid of the indignities you may suffer, at the hands of a brute like me?"

"Spare me your sarcasm," she told him. "Maybe you've forgotten how you accused me of agreeing to marry Hobart for his money. You said all he had to do was to dangle that necklace before me, and I'd leap for the bait. You compared me with the doxies of Tortuga, as I recall—"

He put up his hand. "Truce, Sybilla."

His eyes were no longer hard. "We make a strange pair, don't we?" A hint of a smile touched his lips. "Both of us quick-tempered, ready to jump to the worst possible conclusions about one another."

"I don't know that we are a—a pair. Not the way you mean it."

Even as she tried to deny it, she felt a swift, hot tide stirring deep inside her. How could she forget the mossy bed beside the rushing waterfall, where he had taught her what it meant to give herself freely, to hold nothing back? In that timeless moment she had known beyond all doubt that they were one.

But now she saw him move unsteadily. His hand tightened on the heavy, elaborately carved side of the table. He reached for the wine that stood nearby, and nearly knocked the heavy goblet over. In an instant, she was beside him, helping to steady the goblet. He drank quickly. Even now he might be parched with fever, she thought.

"You're going to lie down, before you collapse. It takes time and rest for a wound to heal properly."

"Such concern for a pirate! Do you feel a sense of duty to every abandoned wretch you chance to meet or have you singled me out for your special attention?"

"Damn you, Gavin Broderick—I've had enough! I was frightened out of my wits during the battle." Even thinking about it made her go cold inside. "Those dreadful cannon balls slamming against the hull. Smoke pouring through the stern window—it nearly strangled me." Her voice faltered slightly, but she went on. "I was sure you'd be killed when you led your boarding party onto this ship."

Her breasts rose and fell with her growing agitation. "And as for sending Jeremy Randall to act out that idiotic charade—"

"I had my reasons for that bit of mummery," Gavin told her. "It was necessary to convince Hobart that the Spaniards had taken the *Condor*. I gave you my word that I had a plan to get you and your brother safely away. Jeremy's charade was part of it—"

"Can you imagine how I felt when he carried me aboard

this ship like a—a lamb to the slaughter?"

"More like a squalling, clawing cat, I'll warrant!"

She decided to ignore his words. Her eyes moved quickly around the spacious cabin, with its fine, thick carpet and handsome furniture.

"Surely there must be a bed somewhere in these elegant quarters. I'm going to get you into it, right now."

"The devil you will! I won't have you making a great pother over nothing. My wound's already been taken care of. It'll heal." But he tightened his grip on the edge of the table.

"If you won't do as I say, I'll have to get Abiathar to help me!"

"He's aboard the *Condor*. I put him in command of her until we get to Tortuga."

Gavin's voice was a trifle unsteady. Maybe his wound hadn't stopped bleeding.

Why must a man be so stubborn, as if he dared not show any sign of weakness no matter how badly hurt he might be? Papa had been that way. And Lance, too. Sybilla had considerable experience in handling such mulish behavior.

"I'll call Jeremy, then!"

"You'll do no such thing. Jeremy Randall's acting as my second-in-command aboard this ship. Every man out there on deck has his duties." His eyes darkened. "We've freed the galley slaves—English, most of them. But they've suffered such vile treatment at the hands of the Spaniards that they won't be of much use for awhile."

"And neither will you, until you get your strength back. Now, do I get Jeremy in here or—"

"You've made your point, Sybilla." He managed a rueful smile. "The Spanish captain's sleeping quarters are through that door. He's a nobleman with a string of titles a yard long—and his accommodations are worthy of his exalted rank."

Until now, sheer willpower had kept Gavin on his feet. But

it would not sustain him much longer. Sybilla put one arm about his waist. She felt his weight resting heavily against her. He needed proper care, and she would see that he got it.

She took a candelabrum from the table. The flaring candles gave a steady glow. She would need as much light as possible in order to examine the wound properly. Keeping her arm tightly around Gavin, she led the way to the adjoining chamber.

"Such elegance, aboard a ship of war," she remarked in surprise.

She set the candelabrum on a large, marble-topped nightstand beside the huge bed. With a swift gesture, she drew aside one of the heavy, purple velvet bed curtains that hung from the massive canopy. Then she drew back the satin-covered bolster, revealing the fine linen sheets beneath.

She barely had time to complete these preparations before Gavin sank down on the side of the bed. A sigh of relief escaped his lips. He tugged at his boots.

"I'll do that," she told him, kneeling in front of him. As soon as she got his boots off, she eased him down on the bed. He lay back against the pillows, watching her. The candlelight glowed on her auburn hair, now loose and tangled over her shoulders.

"This bed's much too large for one," he said, and his eyes glinted wickedly. "If you really want to comfort me, come and lie beside me."

She stared at him. Really, this man could be impossible. "You are in no condition for—"

"But you're wrong. In my condition, a chill could be dangerous," he said. "Since you've decided to take care of me, it's no more than your duty to make sure I'm kept warm."

She put her hand over his mouth. "That's enough of your foolish talk," she told him sternly.

She drew in her breath, as she felt his tongue flick against her palm. But even as the first flurry of response stirred inside her, she rebuked herself silently. He drew one of her fingers between his lips.

"Gavin! This isn't the time for indulging in such foolishness."

"Later, then?"

She gave him what she hoped was a suitably reproachful look. Then she pulled her hand free, and went about her duties. A basin of water stood on the nightstand. She opened the cabinet underneath.

"There are plenty of towels," she said with satisfaction. "I'll be needing them. Soap, too. And a—" She stared into the depths of the cabinet. "I don't believe it!"

"What've you found there?" Gavin asked. "A hidden treasure?"

"It's a silver—a silver utensil. . . ."

"If it's a solid silver chamberpot, say so. I'm scarcely surprised. I suppose it's got the captain's family crest engraved on it." He managed a faint smile. "These Spaniards choose their ship's officers from the ranks of the nobility. A great mistake—an ancient title doesn't qualify a man to command a ship. . . ."

But she was only half listening, for she had more important matters at hand. She filled the basin and placed the towels and soap beside it. Then she moved the candelabrum nearer.

She unbuttoned Gavin's shirt and slid it down over his arms as carefully as possible. When she eased off the bandage, stiff with dried blood, she managed to hold back a cry of dismay.

"Lie still. I'll try not to hurt you." She kept her voice under careful control. She tried to tear a towel in half, but the linen was too thick and heavy for her.

"I'll need a pair of scissors," she said impatiently. She did not want to lose time searching through the tall, polished chest of drawers.

"You'll find a knife in the sheath of my boot," Gavin told her.

After she had torn the towels into long strips, she bent over him and bathed the wound carefully. Although it still oozed a little blood, it had been well-cleansed. She saw no traces of cloth, that otherwise might have been left to fester in the wound.

She cringed inwardly as she thought of the pain Gavin must have endured when Abiathar had seared his torn flesh with a heated cutlass.

She went on washing the wound and the surrounding skin, her touch light and deft. But there was no way she could spare him completely. She saw him wince and felt his muscles tighten.

"You seem to know what you're about," he said through gritted teeth. "Where did you get your experience?"

She placed a thick pad over the wound, then started wrapping long strips of cloth about his chest to hold the bandage in place. "I cared for Lance, and his men—those who managed to escape the King's troopers," she said. "After the battle of Sedgemoor, I kept them in a concealed passage in our house. After the hunt died down, I made arrangements for them to get to Bristol."

"And you were sixteen at the time—or seventeen, perhaps? I suppose you knew the penalty for harboring traitors."

Sybilla shrugged slightly. "I had no choice."

She put his bloodstained shirt aside and covered him with the sheet and then the satin bolster.

She laid her hand against his forehead. The skin was not burning with fever, as she'd feared. She smoothed back the hair that clung damply to his forehead, and her fingers lingered for a moment. Then she straightened and glanced about the cabin.

"What're you looking for now?"

"No doubt the Spanish captain kept a well-stocked medicine chest among his belongings."

He gave her a suspicious frown. "What the devil do you mean to dose me with?"

"There is a certain sleeping draught, made with poppy syrup and Peruvian bark. We always kept a bottle in the stillroom back home. It eases pain and brings sleep."

She stroked his broad chest with a soaped cloth. "After you've slept, I'll bathe you properly."

"Now that might be an enjoyable experience," he told her. "But as for the syrup, you needn't bother. If you really want me to have a restful sleep, and sweet dreams, you'll lie here beside me."

"If you imagine I'd endanger your recovery by encouraging you to—exert yourself that way—"

"You do have a suspicious turn of mind, Sybilla. I'm only inviting you to share comfort of this fine bed," he said. He looked at her closely in the candle glow. "You're about ready to drop. And you're pale, under all that soot—"

"Soot!" She soaked the corner of a towel, rubbed it with soap, and scrubbed at her cheeks. Then she stared at the blackened cloth. "I must look awful."

"You're a positive fright," he agreed. She pushed her hair back from her face. "No man could possibly be tempted by you. So you see you'll be quite safe lying beside me."

A smile tugged at the corners of her mouth. Really, the man was impossible.

"Now I think of it," he went on, "I do believe I feel a chill coming on."

"Liar! You've got that thick bolster to warm you."

But she could not ignore the deep weariness creeping over her. If she was to go on taking care of Gavin, she, too, must rest. Stripping off her soiled gown, she let it fall to the floor. She sat down on the edge of the bed to remove her shoes and stockings.

Clad only in her shift, she slid under the bolster. She

153

reached over and snuffed out the candles. Then she stretched out and lost herself in the joy of being so near him once more. Her taut muscles began to relax, and her eyelids started to close.

But she started slightly when she felt him tugging her shift, his fingers fumbling awkwardly with the ribbons at the low neckline. His movements were usually quick and expert, and she found herself touched by these clumsy efforts. Pushing his hand aside, she undid the shift herself. Moved by an instinct too compelling to resist, she bared her breasts to him without a trace of shame.

He rested his cheek on one warm, silken mound. "Stay with me, love . . . don't leave me. . . ." His lips moved against her skin, and she drew him closer. Drowsily, he buried his face in the shadowed cleft between her breasts. His body relaxed and in a few moments his deep, even breathing told her that he slept.

But although she, too, was in need of rest, she could not let herself fall asleep, not yet. Too many doubts tormented her, too many unanswered questions about the future.

When she'd believed that Gavin had been killed in battle, she had been torn apart by grief. But here he was, lying beside her, his head resting against her, his breath warm against her skin.

Only a little while ago, he'd made it plain that he meant to make love to her again. With his vitality, his great strength to sustain him, it would not take him long to recover.

And what then?

She had heard the truth about him, from his own lips. She must decide what to do.

Gavin Broderick was a pirate, an outcast who would surely be shunned by any female with the slightest claim to decency. Even now, Sybilla told herself, she should be filled with shame and remorse at having given herself to such a man. She ought to be figuring out some means of getting as far away from him as possible, when the *San Bartolomé* dropped anchor off Tortuga.

Not that there was much chance of finding a haven of safety in such a nest of sin. Even if she could persuade him to take her ashore, who would be there to help her?

If she remained with Gavin, as his mistress, if she surrendered herself to his desires—and her own—what sort of life awaited her? She knew the answer, well enough. She'd be a pirate's woman, unable to go back to decent society ever again.

There could be no future for her with such a man. But even as she told herself so, she drew him closer, resting her head against his uninjured arm. Her hand reached out, her fingers stroked his hair, and moved down to caress the hard tendons at the back of his neck. Curving her body against his, she let herself drift into sleep.

Chapter Thirteen

At sunset on the following day, Sybilla stood near the window of the *San Bartolomé*'s bedchamber, brushing her hair. Gavin lay sleeping in the wide, velvet-curtained bed, his head resting on his uninjured arm.

A few hours before, he had awakened and summoned Jeremy Randall. He had listened carefully to the young officer's report and given him further orders for repairs to the galleon. Then he had dismissed Jeremy, eaten a light repast, and fallen asleep again.

Sybilla, convinced that Gavin was out of danger, occupied her time by taking care of her own needs. First she washed away every trace of soot and grime. She used the fine castile soap left behind by Don Alfonso de Talvera, the former captain of the galleon.

Back in England most people, if they bathed at all, scrubbed themselves with rancid-smelling whale oil soap. But at Thornton manor, Sybilla's mother had kept the stillroom supplied with castile, made with the finest olive oil and much prized as an aid to the complexion.

After finishing her basin bath, Sybilla washed her hair until it glowed; then she put on a fresh shift and over it a white silk dressing gown. Silently, she blessed Abiathar Pascoe for taking time from his many duties to have her trunk sent across from the *Condor*. She was determined that by the time Gavin woke and looked at her again her own appearance would be more in keeping with these impressive surroundings.

Don Alfonso had provided himself with all the amenities that could be fitted into his private quarters. The thick carpet had been chosen to match the purple bed curtains, and the ceiling was painted in white and gold.

Such regal decorations would have been better suited to a nobleman's palace in Seville than to a ship of war, she thought with a smile. Her mirrored image smiled back at her, reflected in a long mirror set in the door of the polished, mahogany armoire.

Her dressing gown, which she wore tightly belted about her slender waist, emphasized her firm, rounded breasts and the curving contours of her hips. The fetching garment, embroidered with tiny bunches of primroses and lavishly trimmed with lace, was to have been part of the trousseau for her wedding to Nicholas Hobart. But now she would not be forced to wear it for him. He must have been furious when he'd regained consciousness only to find that the "Spanish officer" had carried off his future bride!

It was no more than he deserved, she told herself. And although his neighbors back in Jamaica might commiserate with him, secretly they would not feel the slightest trace of sympathy.

How dreadful it would have been if she had been forced to spend the rest of her life with such a man. Now, as she savored her freedom, she threw back her head and drew a deep breath. The long, slanting rays of sunlight played over her hair, framing her face in a glowing, red-gold halo.

"Now that's what I'd call a real improvement."

Glancing toward the bed, she saw that Gavin was awake and watching her. Quickly, she tied a ribbon around her hair and hurried to his side.

The pallor had disappeared from his face, and his skin was a warm, healthy tan once more. He sat up, his appreciative gaze moving over her. "Last night you looked like one of the gunner's powder monkeys. But now—" He reached out to her. "Now you're a treat to the eye."

The hours of sleep had restored his vitality, and when he closed his fingers around her wrist she felt the renewed strength in his grasp. He drew her closer and lifted a long strand of her hair; pressing it to his cheek, he breathed in its clean fragrance. "You're a delight to all the senses," he said.

"I'm afraid I can't return the compliment." She gave him a teasing smile. "But since you're feeling better, it's time you had a proper bath."

"Don't I have anything to say about that?"

"You have some objection, perhaps?" she challenged him.

He pretended to be considering his answer carefully. "I've not decided yet." But she caught the gleam of anticipation in his eyes.

"You've certainly made a remarkable recovery," she said as she filled the wash basin. "But still you must save your strength." She looked down at him a bit warily, then began to soap his chest with light, swirling movements. When she felt the hard muscles beneath her fingers, a tremor of excitement stirred inside her. But she kept at her task, laving the dark crisp hair, before moving down to the arc of his ribs, and then to the place where the hair narrowed into a straight line.

She went on washing him, and saw the warm, coppery glow of his skin emerging from under the coat of smoke and grime left behind after the battle. The sight and the feel of him struck deep inside her, so that her fingertips began to tingle. She caught her lower lip in her teeth and forced herself to concentrate on her duties.

She unfastened his scarlet sash and laid it on a carved, high-backed chair beside the bed. Then she hesitated, her fingers on the top button of his breeches.

"Enough," he protested. "I can do that for myself." He slanted a smile at her, as he pulled off his one remaining garment. Her cheeks flushed as she caught a brief glimpse of his masculinity.

158

"Turn over," she said hastily.

"I feel as if I were back in the nursery," he said. "Although, if I remember rightly, Nanny Pringle was not nearly so attractive as you." But he obeyed by turning over on his stomach.

She had always thought of the colonists as a lot of humble merchants or backwoodsmen, struggling to build a life for themselves in a hostile wilderness. But Gavin's remark caused her to reconsider. Perhaps in some ways, his upbringing had not been so different from her own.

She resumed her task, and started to wash his back. Then stopped abruptly, her fingers tightening around the soapy cloth. The lingering rays of the sun sent golden shafts through the cabin window. They lay across Gavin's back and touched a pattern of crisscrossed white lines that stood out against his deeply tanned skin.

Sybilla's forehead furrowed in a puzzled frown. She had caught a glimpse of those scars last night, as she was fastening the bandage in place. But then she had been far too preoccupied with caring for his wound to give more than a passing thought to less immediate matters.

"Don't stop now," Gavin said. Then, with mock severity, he added, "I expect you to do a thorough job." When she did not respond, he turned his head to look at her. "What's wrong?"

"These scars on your back. How did you get them?"

"It was an accident." There was something in his voice that made her faintly uneasy.

"What sort of an accident?"

He raised his head and she saw a shadow pass over his face. "I took a fall from the rigging, that's all. It was on my first voyage, and I was clumsy and inexperienced. Such mishaps aren't uncommon."

His gray eyes darkened and his lips clamped together so tightly that the muscles sprang out along the line of his jaw. Then almost at once, he turned away, pressing his face into the pillow. Although Sybilla was not convinced by his

159

explanation, she saw that he did not want to discuss the subject any further. No doubt a boy's first time at sea was a difficult, perhaps frightening experience. How old had he been, she wondered. The cabin boy aboard the *Bristol Belle* had looked to be no more than twelve.

She went on washing his back, stopping to rinse the cloth from time to time. She began stroking the sensitive spot at the base of his spine, and he gave a soft groan of sensuous pleasure. As she moved the cloth lower, she felt the muscles of his hard buttocks tighten suddenly under her fingers.

Abruptly, he turned over onto his back. She looked away—but not quickly enough to keep from seeing the thrust of his hardening manhood.

"Go on," he said sternly. "We can't have you slacking off now." His gray eyes challenged her to refuse.

With one quick movement, she pulled the sheet up to his waist: but it was impossible for her to ignore the unmistakable evidence of his arousal as it thrust against its linen cover.

"Come now, my sweet. Surely there's no need for such maidenly modesty," he said.

How could she deny it? She had seen all of him when she had made love with him in the moonlight beside the waterfall. And even last night, although their bodies had not been joined in the act of passion, she had lain beside him here in this bed, with his head pillowed on her breast.

Yet somehow she could not meet his eyes. Quickly she rinsed the last traces of soap from his skin. "That's enough for now," she said, but her voice was unsteady.

He caught hold of her hand. "You aren't finished yet, Sybilla," he said. Although he spoke like a stern schoolmaster, his gray eyes glinted, teasing her—daring her to protest. "Whatever is worth doing, is worth doing well," he told her. "A most useful maxim, don't you agree?"

Determined not to shrink from his challenge, she set her jaw, and reached under the sheet. His manhood went rock-hard beneath her touch. With one swift movement, he pulled the cloth from her fingers, and tossed it into the basin, so that the water sprayed in all directions.

His uninjured arm shot out and closed around her waist. Then, somehow, she found she was lying beside him. She tried to free herself from his grasp but it was no use.

"You mustn't struggle with me, my love," he teased her. "You said I should save my strength, remember?"

She went warm and melting inside; she had no desire to escape, and he knew it.

"But you might hurt yourself if you—if we should—Gavin, do be sensible."

"I'm not feeling particularly sensible at the moment." He reached over and stroked the curve of her hip.

"Do stop—" But she could say no more, for his touch, firm and lingering, silenced her. Her breathing quickened as she felt the heat of his hand burning through the soft silk of her dressing gown.

Her body ached for his caresses, but even now she hesitated, out of concern for him. Perhaps it was too soon. . . . As she tried to draw away, her gown fell aside, revealing the length of her shapely legs up to her thighs.

He held her close, and she felt his powerful body tremble with the force of his desire. His fingers stroked the satin skin on the inside of her thigh.

She grasped his wrist and tried to pull his hand away, but it was useless.

"Don't worry, my love. There are so many other ways we can give pleasure to each other."

Her golden eyes widened in bewilderment. "Other ways?"

He stroked her cheek and she was moved by the swift uprush of tenderness in his face. "My sweet Sybilla," he said softly, "this is still so new to you, isn't it? You have much to learn about loving."

He drew off her robe and let it fall to the carpet. "There, that's better," he said.

He levered himself upward on the bed, so that his back rested against the pillows. She gave a small, wordless exclamation of surprise, as he drew her head against his hard, muscled thigh.

"Easy, my love." He reached down and pushed back the glowing russet curtain of her long hair, then touched her cheek. "There's nothing to fear. You need not do any more than you want to."

His voice soothed her. She let herself relax, and rubbed her cheek against his thigh. As she caught the clean, intimate male scent of him, a sensuous warmth enveloped her.

Taking her hand, he closed it around his hardness. To her surprise, she discovered that the skin of that part of him was smooth as velvet. He kept his hand on hers, guiding her until she had learned the motion. Then he lay back against the pillows.

Raising her head, she saw that his eyes were half-closed, his lips parted. A sense of triumph flowed through her, as she watched the expressions that moved across his strong, mobile features, in response to her every stroke. To think that she had the power to stir him so.

But all at once, he pushed her hand away. She felt his leg muscles tighten. "What's wrong?" she asked anxiously.

"I want to pleasure you, too—but a man can hold back only so long—" His chest began to rise and fall, as he drew in long, deep breaths. She sensed that he was striving to control himself until he could take her with him—to fulfill her urgent need, even while he satisfied his own.

"Take off that shift."

She hesitated, then pulled the shift over her head and dropped it beside her discarded robe. He drew her to him once more, but now her head rested on the pillow next to his. Her lips parted and his kiss sent a swift current of desire racing through her. He turned over, supporting his weight on his uninjured side.

His eyes held hers and she understood. It wasn't enough that she should ease his need. He wanted her to join him in the pleasures of loving, to take as well as give. The realization filled her with a deep tenderness.

He raised her thigh, so that it rested on his hip. Her legs parted, and she was open to him now. She could feel how completely she had aroused him, and a surge of fire went through her, as she waited, anticipating the first thrust of possession.

But he delayed, while he kissed her mouth deeply, searchingly, his tongue flicking at hers, seeking to explore the moist sweetness. Then his lips moved to her throat, her shoulder, her breasts. His fingers traced the length of her back, leaving a line of silken fire wherever they touched her. He cupped his palms around her buttocks, pressing the soft, flesh. Stirred by the sweet-hot urgency deep in her loins, she moved her inner thigh against his hip in a wordless plea for release.

He played with the russet curls that shadowed the cleft of her womanhood. Then he probed deeper, stroking the dewy peak of her sensations, rubbing it gently between his fingertips. Tiny sparks raced along every nerve of her body and converged in that one exquisitely sensitive spot.

When she thought she could bear the waiting no longer, he shifted slightly, then thrust himself deep inside her. His hard, swollen manhood filling her, pressing at the sides of her sheath.

He kept himself motionless, embedded to the hilt in the depths of her femininity. Even now, although her senses were dazed with passion she realized that this was another kind of lovemaking, slow and sensuous . . . and infinitely pleasurable. Gavin was teaching her to savor each subtle variation in the tide of rapture that was carrying them along.

She did now know how long they lay joined together this way. Although neither of them was moving, she gradually became aware of the steady motion beneath them, around them. In some distant corner of her mind, she realized that she was feeling the rise and fall of ship. Cradled by the tides of the sea as it moved with a ceaseless rhythm, timeless, unending . . .

Sybilla's body took up the primeval rhythm of the tide,

and moved along with it. She pressed herself against Gavin, as if to draw him more deeply inside her. Her hips began to rotate, slowly at first. And now Gavin was moving, pausing between each long, slow stroke, then thrusting again, to bury himself deep inside her.

Her fingers pushed hard against the muscles of his buttocks. Deeper he drove, and still deeper. He thrust more quickly now, and she felt herself contract around him, her moist sheath gripping his powerful manhood. She threw her head back, and cried out as she sensed the approach of their shared climax.

A shattering explosion of fulfillment sent her rocketing upward, caught on the crest of a wave of liquid fire. And upward again. And again. Until she cried out and clung to him, and universe burst into a shower of burning sparks all around them . . .

Later—much later—Sybilla saw that the sunlight had long since disappeared. She and Gavin lay close together, enfolded in the shadows of the tropical night, lulled by the sound of the wind and the waves. A breeze stirred the velvet curtains of the bed and stroked her bare skin. She brushed a lock of dark hair from Gavin's forehead, then held him against her. It was good, so good, to feel his even breathing as he slept.

For a moment, she remembered the aching despair that had engulfed her last night, when she had believed that he had fallen in battle. But she quickly dismissed the memory. She hadn't lost him. He was warm and alive beside her.

Letting her eyelids close, she rested her head on his chest, and, with a sigh of perfect contentment, she drifted off into darkness.

Early the following morning, Abiathar Pascoe arrived aboard the *San Bartolomé,* and came striding into the bedchamber, without pausing to knock. His coat of fine bottle green velvet and gold lace was unbuttoned, but nevertheless it strained across his huge shoulders as if it might burst at the seams. No doubt he'd found this impressive garment in the sea chest of one of the Spanish officers and was determined to wear it, even though it was not nearly large enough for his towering, massive frame.

If he was surprised to find Sybilla, clad only in her shift and perched on the edge of Gavin's bed, he did not show it. Tactfully he turned his head away and fixed his eyes on the stern window to give her time to thrust her feet into her satin slippers and to retrieve her robe. She slid her arms into the full sleeves and belted the garment tightly about her.

Flushing, she withdrew quickly to the other side of the sleeping quarters and began to busy herself, unpacking her trunk and hanging her clothes away in the tall armoire. But her attention was fixed on Gavin and Abiathar, as they talked of the progress that had been made in repairing the ships.

The *Condor* would set sail by the following day, the bronzed giant assured Gavin. "And Jeremy says that the *San Bartolomé* will be in condition to sail with her. The lad's done well," Abiathar went on. "I don't doubt he'll be master of his own ship, one of these days."

"He'd have made a good strolling player, if it comes to that," Gavin said, with a reminiscent smile. "I wish I could have been there when he smashed his way into my cabin, after the battle. He convinced Sybilla that he was a Spanish grandee. You should have seen the look on her face when he dropped his Castilian accent afterward, and she realized he was one of us."

Sybilla's thoughts went back to the jumble of confusing events following the battle. At the time, she had been too shaken to question the reason for Jeremy's charade.

"Why was it necessary to convince Hobart that the Spanish had captured the *Condor?*" she asked Gavin. "I can understand that you would not want him to find out that you are a—" How difficult it was for her to speak the word, even now. "That you are engaged in an unlawful trade."

Abiathar's laugh boomed out across the spacious cabin. "Hobart knows all about that, Mistress Thornton. He's invested in our 'unlawful trade' before—and he will again."

"But he is a respected planter and merchant. He's received by the gentry of Jamaica."

"They tolerate him, because they can't afford to risk his displeasure. And as for his respectability, that's no more than a convenient facade. He would not hesitate to deal with a pirate—or the devil himself—if there was enough profit in it for him. He made a tidy sum when he disposed of the loot from the *Valladolid*. That's the Spanish galleon we captured a few months ago. Hobart's export business provides the perfect cover for his illegal sideline. And his customers don't ask questions so long as his prices are right."

"And you want him to go on receiving your loot and disposing of it," Sybilla said slowly. "You don't want to break off your partnership with him. That's why you let him believe that the Spaniards had captured the *Condor*. So he'd be convinced that it was a Spanish sailor who knocked him unconscious, and a Spanish officer who carried me away."

"The ruse worked well enough, considering that I had to figure it out on the spur of the moment," said Gavin. "When we were forced into battle with the *San Bartolomé*, I had to change my original plans on short notice."

And he'd succeeded in doing so, even after he'd fought and conquered the Spanish galleon against overwhelming odds and been wounded himself. For a moment, she felt a glow of admiration for the man she loved. Gavin was not only a strong, courageous fighter, he was shrewd and quick-witted, too. How else could he have survived in such a dangerous way of life?

But almost at once, Sybilla's pride in Gavin gave way to uneasiness over her future and that of her brother. So long as Lance was out there on the Isle of Pines, she would have cause to fear for his safety. "Suppose Hobart finds out that you weren't killed in the battle?"

Abiathar grinned broadly. "He'll find out soon enough. Gavin will get word to him, soon as we drop anchor in Tortuga." Then, seeing her puzzled frown, he went on, "We've got to have Hobart's backing for our next enterprise. We'll need half a dozen new ships and tons of supplies, before we're ready to set out again."

Gavin shot him a warning glance. "Mind your tongue, Abiathar."

"Then you do intend to go on doing business with Hobart?" Sybilla asked. She hoped that Gavin would deny it, but he only looked at her in silence. "And this new enterprise Abiathar speaks of?" she persisted.

"That is no concern of yours."

She went hot with humiliation. Surely he should understand that his future plans concerned her deeply. How could he shut her out, as if she were no more than some dockside trollop with whom he'd spent the night?

"I gave you my promise that you would not have to marry Hobart. And that your brother would not be arrested, and denounced to the authorities in Jamaica. You may trust me to keep my word."

"But what's to become of us after that? We can't return to England, as long as King James sits upon the throne." Heedless of Abiathar's presence, she ran to Gavin and grasped his arm.

"There's no need for you to go back there." He covered her hand with his own, but his touch gave her little comfort. For even now she felt that they were being swept apart by an unknown force as powerful, as inexorable, as the sea itself.

"You'll be safe enough here with me, Sybilla," he told her. "And although Lance must remain where he is for a few more months, you'll both be on your way to Boston as soon as I can make the necessary arrangements."

"Boston?" Her heart sank at the prospect. The very name had a cold, alien ring to it. "What will become of us there?"

"My family will help you both to get established." He

smiled wryly. "The Brodericks are a most respectable clan, I assure you. You mustn't judge the rest of them by what you know of me."

Before she could question him further, he spoke brusquely. "Abiathar and I have not finished our business." He jerked his head in the direction of the adjoining quarters. "Get yourself dressed, and I'll join you later."

Sybilla stared up at him, unable to move. With growing despair, she sought a way to get through to him. But no words would come.

He gestured impatiently. "What are you waiting for?" he demanded.

Surprisingly, it was Abiathar who, sensing her hurt feelings, tried to cheer her in the only way he knew. "Don Alfonso's cook is hard at work in the galley, Mistress Thornton, and I'd wager that the larder's crammed with the finest fare you'd find aboard any ship afloat. A good, hearty breakfast—that's what you need."

Sybilla was touched by the mate's clumsy kindness. Although the muscles of her face felt frozen, she forced herself to smile at him. Then she hurried back to the armoire, took down an elaborate gown of apricot silk—the first that came to hand—and carried it into the adjoining chamber. But in her haste, she neglected to shut the door firmly.

"Go easy with the lass," she heard Abiathar saying. "She's not used to such rough use."

"I've no time to waste, satisfying her curiosity. We've more important matters to deal with."

"You mean those Spaniards penned up below? Most of the lads are for tossing the lot overboard. Jeremy's had no easy time holding them back."

"The Spaniards will stay where they are, for the present. They may prove useful to us later—particularly our noble Don Alfonso."

"You could be right," Abiathar conceded.

"Now, as to those galley slaves. They're to have all the meat and drink they need. Have those filthy rags they've

168

been wearing tossed overboard, and see that they're given decent clothes from the slop chest."

"Aye, Gavin. Though I'll wager Jeremy Randall's already given the orders. But there's a couple of 'em who're likely to be buried on Tortuga, if they last that long. Whipped and starved, and worked like beasts—some of them been down below in that hell for months."

"You've no need to speak of—" Gavin stopped short. And the next moment, the heavy door to the sleeping quarters was slammed shut.

Sybilla's fingers felt stiff and cold as she buttoned the bodice of her dress. She had deceived herself into believing that Gavin was falling in love with her, but now she must accept the truth. Nothing had changed for him. He could make love to her with passion, and deep tenderness, too. But he was not willing to share his thoughts or his plans with her.

Let him send her away to Boston, then. And the sooner the better. She did not question what he had told her of his family there. No doubt they were a decent, respectable clan. Certainly Gavin had been given a gentleman's upbringing. That much was plain from his speech and manners.

Why had he chosen to turn his back on his own class, she wondered. What had driven him to embark on his outcast's way of life? He was one of a company of violent, dangerous men, who flouted the law and were feared and shunned by every honest seaman. Even now, he could scarcely wait to embark on his next voyage, to swoop down on some rich merchant ship, seize its cargo, and make a run for cover.

He made no secret of his distaste for Hobart, but he would not break off his partnership with the man, so long as it was to his advantage. He was a ruthless adventurer, an opportunist. Surely not the sort of man with whom she could ever find the secure, honorable life for which she had been bred.

Her thoughts went back to the manor house in Somerset. How serene and well-ordered she had thought her future would be. Although she had not fancied herself to be in love with any of the young men she knew, she had expected that sooner or later she would marry. What other possible future could there be for a young lady like herself?

Even if she never felt any overwhelming passion for her husband, she would respect him, and perhaps in due course she would learn to love him. She would bear his children, take care of his home, and carry out her duties as mistress of his estate, as her mother had done.

If Lance had not ridden out to join the rebellion that summer day, if he had not drawn her into danger, she would never have left England for Jamaica. And her path would never have crossed that of a man like Gavin Broderick.

But though she tried to summon up a feeling of shame, of self-reproach, for having yielded to him, she knew it was useless. He had not seduced her. She had wanted him to make love to her. And he had responded to the desire he had felt in her.

She would have to leave him, for he had given her no choice. She must resign herself to his plans. But how could she? It was not enough for her that they had shared a few nights of passionate lovemaking.

No doubt that had been all he'd wanted from her. He would sail away, and think of her from time to time, until the memories faded from his mind. But for her, it was different, for she had given him not only her body, but all of her being. And even now she could not bring herself to face a future without him.

Chapter Fourteen

"What a dreadful experience it must have been for you, Mr. Hobart!" Madeleine Thornton exclaimed. She took a sip of sherry, then set her glass down on the small ebony table beside the satin-covered sofa in her drawing room. The evening breeze rustled the heavy, yellow silk drapes. She fluttered her fan and sighed. "If only Sybilla had agreed to have the wedding here in Jamaica, as I wanted her to. But no, she had to go traipsing off to Havana to be married."

"Your niece was far too willful and spoiled for her own good," said Nicholas Hobart. "You should have been more strict with her."

Madeleine pressed a plump white hand against her ample bosom, which was encased in a bodice of sky blue taffeta trimmed with Brussels lace. "You must not speak as if our poor Sybilla were—as if she'd passed away."

"She may be wishing she were dead by now, instead of living as the whore of that misbegotten swine of a Spaniard." He did not bother to choose his words carefully, for he was thoroughly infuriated every time he thought of Sybilla yielding up her slim, white body to Don Alfonso's lustful embraces. After all his waiting and scheming, another man had come along and cheated him out of the long-anticipated pleasures of his bridal night.

"You can't be sure she was taken by the Spanish captain,"

Madeleine protested.

"What reason would Broderick's sailors have had to lie about it?" Hobart drained his wineglass, and Madeleine quickly refilled it. "They were right there, aboard the *Condor*, when she lay anchored in Havana harbor. They were imprisoned below decks, until most of the Spanish crew went off to carouse ashore. And the rest—those who were ordered to stay aboard and keep watch, had drunk themselves into a stupor. Then Broderick's men made a break for it."

"No doubt you fought bravely alongside the others," Madeleine murmured. Long ago, she'd learned that a little flattery could work wonders in dealing with any man. But this time, her remark did not have the desired effect. Instead, Hobart glowered at her.

"I only wish I'd had the chance," he said. "But I was unconscious at the time—laid low by a savage beating from those damned Spaniards, while I was attempting to protect the honor of your niece, ma'm. When I came back to my senses, I found myself in an open boat that pitched about like a cockle shell, heading for Jamaica. The sun was glaring into my face, I had a devil of a headache, and I felt as if my jaw had been smashed in a dozen places."

Madeleine nodded sympathetically. "Such a harrowing ordeal! But still, it was fortunate that the sailors were able to get you out of the hands of your captors," she added by way of consolation.

"Luck had nothing to do with it," he said. "They expected an ample reward for their help. And they were not disappointed."

Unable to restrain herself any longer, she asked, "But what of Sybilla? Didn't they attempt to rescue her, too?"

"It was too late for that. Don Alfonso, the captain of the galleon, carried her to his cabin. She was struggling and pleading for mercy. Then, as soon as the *San Bartolomé* dropped anchor in Havana harbor, he took her ashore with him."

"But how could Broderick's men know all that?" Madeleine leaned forward, her china-blue eyes filled with dismay. "If they were imprisoned below deck, as you say—"

Hobart's lips twisted in an ugly semblance of a smile. "They are not deaf, ma'm. They overheard the lewd talk and the foul jokes of the Spanish crewmen. Surely there's no need for me to go into greater detail, is there?"

She shook her head. "No—no, indeed, Mr. Hobart. It is only that I've been trying to believe that Sybilla might have managed to get away from her captors, as you did."

Madeleine had convinced herself that after the marriage, Hobart could have been persuaded to defer payment on her debts, or perhaps have canceled them completely. A bride as young and enticing as Sybilla, guided by an experienced female relative, could have done much to influence Hobart.

Why had she allowed the girl to go junketing off aboard the *Condor*, instead of remaining here at Acacia Hall until Hobart returned? And all because the headstrong little fool had been set on the sentimental notion that her brother must be present at the wedding to give her away.

But Madeleine was a born survivor and she was not about to give way to despair even now. She had to find a way to salvage what she could from this unexpected disaster.

"You declared your betrothal to my niece before all those guests," she reminded Hobart. "You cannot blame the poor, innocent child for this unfortunate turn of events."

"It's not a question of blame," he said. "The girl's been taken away by that Spaniard, and there's an end to it."

"Mr. Hobart, you gave your word that you would marry Sybilla. Perhaps she may yet contrive to escape and return here. If that should happen—"

But Hobart did not allow her to go on. "Your niece is no longer the innocent young lady I promised to wed. Even if she were to return—and I consider it most unlikely she ever will—she would be shunned by every respectable lady on this island. Her name would be bandied about in every waterfront tavern in Mo' Bay. Surely you don't expect a man

173

in my position to marry such a—degraded female!"

Madeleine sighed. "I suppose not," she said. But still she refused to acknowledge defeat. "You have so many business connections throughout the islands—you might be able to get word of her whereabouts. If you did, you could have her brought back to Jamaica."

"For what purpose?" Hobart demanded. "You have enough experience to know that Sybilla's presence could only be a source of embarassment to me now."

"Really, sir! Consider what she may be suffering. It's possible that Don Alfonso—the wretched beast—might have tired of her and abandoned her in Cuba or one of the other Spanish colonies. I can scarcely bring myself to think of what her future might be."

Madeleine sighed and shook her head. The candlelight shimmered over her silver-blond hair and caught the sparkle of her sapphire earrings. "Even now, it would be my duty to take her back into my home. I am sure that my late husband would have wished me to do no less, regardless of the embarrassment it might cause me."

Hobart gave her a long, icy stare. "You may do as you please," he said. "As for me, I've no intention of neglecting my business affairs like some lovesick idiot, to undertake a search for that unfortunate niece of yours. I've far more important matters to attend to, and they won't wait."

Hobart stared moodily at the window. As the breeze ruffled the silken draperies, he caught the salty tang of the sea. But it brought him no consolation. For it reminded him—as if he needed reminding—that in a shipyard down the coast, the half a dozen fine new frigates he'd ordered on Broderick's instructions were almost completely ready to set sail. Crates of weapons—cutlasses, boarding axes, pikes and swivel guns, along with casks of salt pork and biscuits, were piled high in his warehouse in Montego Bay. Only yesterday he had stood on the dock and watched the stevedores unloading a shipment of flintlock pistols from the finest gunsmith's shop in London.

All that hard cash laid out, and for what? Without Gavin Broderick to command the expedition, it would never become a reality. To think of all that profit, slipping out of his grasp! Hobart's thick fingers tightened on the delicate stem of his wineglass. How could he have allowed himself to be drawn into such an undertaking, only to see it fall apart before his eyes? For so many years, he had gone from one success to the next. Surely his luck could not desert him now.

"Maybe he wasn't killed?" Hobart spoke so abruptly that Madeleine nearly spilled her wine. "He's clever and resourceful. Maybe he managed to escape."

Madeleine's carefully plucked eyebrows drew together in a puzzled frown. "Who are you speaking of?"

"Gavin Broderick, of course. Not one of the sailors who brought me back to Jamaica in that accursed, pitching shell of a boat could say he'd seen Broderick fall in battle. He's managed to get out of tight places before."

Madeleine fixed her eyes on her lap and smoothed the elaborately draped skirt of her sky blue gown while struggling to conceal her annoyance. God's teeth! Why should she care what had become of Gavin Broderick?

"We were speaking of my niece," she reminded Hobart.

He made an abrupt, dismissive gesture, for he was already pursuing a new line of thought. If Broderick had escaped unharmed, he'd lose no time in getting word to Indigo. And then the enterprise could go forward as they had planned.

Hobart's spirits began to rise. All great business ventures involved a certain amount of risk. But if only luck were with him once more, this expedition would make him one of the wealthiest men in the West Indies. Five hundred thousand pieces of eight! That was what Broderick had estimated that the loot would be. Even more, perhaps, once all that fabulous treasure had been turned into gold.

Why, with such riches, he'd be besieged by every parent on the island who had a marriageable daughter. He'd have no trouble finding another bride, one who was well-bred, pretty, and docile. And a virgin.

But she would not be Sybilla.

Damn the golden-eyed little witch! She had cast her spell on him, and even now he could feel the heat stirring in his loins at the mere thought of her. Why had he been so circumspect during the days following their betrothal?

His hand curved as he remembered those brief moments when she had allowed him to cup her breast through all those layers of silk and lace. How firm and round she'd felt beneath his fingers. He'd been a proper fool. If he had taken her then, without regard for her protestations that a betrothal was not the same as a marriage, she would not have dared to refuse him. Not with her brother's life at stake.

Even if he found her again, he certainly could not marry her. That would be entirely out of the question, and a woman as experienced as Madeleine Thornton knew it. But he might still possess Sybilla, one day. He set down his wine glass and got to his feet.

"Surely, you do not have to leave so soon, Mr. Hobart."

"I've told you all I know of your niece's unfortunate mischance, ma'm." He smoothed the folds of his brocaded coat. "You must excuse me now." He bowed and took his leave.

On his drive back to his own plantation, he stared out over the dark fields. He would order the shipwrights to have those new vessels ready on schedule. While overseeing his many other business affairs, he would continue with all his preparations. Then, in case he received word from Broderick, he'd be ready to go ahead.

And afterward . . . Perhaps there was a chance that he might yet possess Sybilla. Madeleine had mentioned his intricate web of business connections stretching all across the Indies, and beyond. It would be easy enough to send out inquiries.

And if he found the girl, abandoned and desperate, he could afford to be generous. He'd have her brought back to Jamaica, and maybe he would set her up in a cottage of her own, in Montego Bay.

A virtuous bride to bear him the sons he wanted, and an enticing mistress, to pleasure him. He would be discreet about it, of course. Although even if such an arrangement became known, no one would think the less of a married man for keeping a beautiful young mistress on the side. Half the planters in Jamaica did the same, and their wives were sensible enough to look the other way.

Sybilla . . . He could see her now in his overheated imagination. Her supple young body was bared to him at last. Her golden eyes were shining up at him, filled with gratitude. Her auburn hair lay in loose, shining waves across her shoulders and the swell of her firm, pink-tipped breasts.

She wouldn't be able to hold him off any longer, or play the haughty young virgin. She would be willing, eager to submit to whatever demands he might make . . .

Aboard the *San Bartolomé*, in the captain's sleeping quarters, Sybilla stirred drowsily. She smiled at the memories of the night before. And then she reached across the wide, curtained bed, seeking for Gavin. But he no longer lay beside her.

She sat up and looked about the cabin. He wasn't anywhere in sight. Quickly, she rose and dressed, then hurried into the adjoining cabin. It, too, was deserted.

She tensed as she heard the slap of bare feet, the shouts of the men out on deck. For a moment she found herself remembering the first sounds of battle between the *Condor* and the Spanish galleon. Surely the *San Bartolomé* was not under attack?

Then she heard a seaman's lusty shout. "Over the side, mate—and into the boat. I'm goin' to get myself a dozen bottles of rum and a fine female to share them with me."

"Only one?" another male voice rang out. "I can handle two stout wenches all by myself."

"Remember that black-haired strumpet who used to

dance at the Laughing Dragon?"

Sybilla lifted her skirts and hurried to the cabin door, then hesitated briefly. She had been out on deck last night, but Gavin had accompanied her. No matter. She'd soon find him and he would take her ashore. Even on Tortuga, she was sure she'd have nothing to fear with Gavin beside her.

She opened the door and shaded her eyes against the blaze of sunlight that flooded the maindeck of the *San Bartolomé*. It was midmorning, and a cloudless, brilliant blue sky arched over the island.

She stepped back hastily to get out of the way of the sailors who stampeded along the deck. They came climbing out of the hatches or swinging down from the rigging, shoving one another to get a place in one of the small boats below, shouting like schoolboys on holiday. "I'll have me a fine boar, roasted over an open fire!" "It's a cask of rum for me— the best Demerara!"

Peering across the stretch of turquoise sea, she caught sight of the rockbound harbor of Tortuga. Even the name sent a faint, uneasy shiver coursing through her, but she reminded herself that she had nothing to fear. In this lair of pirates, Gavin's reputation would be known and respected. No doubt the taverns were already abuzz with the news of how he'd captured the *San Bartolomé* even though his own ship had been outgunned and outmanned.

She scanned the deck, searching for a glimpse of his tall, commanding presence among the milling men. But she could not see him anywhere. Perhaps he'd gone below deck to check on the Spanish prisoners confined in the hold. Or the galley slaves whose welfare concerned him so much.

"Good day to you, Mistress Thornton."

She turned to see Jeremy Randall beside her, a lean, elegant figure of a man in the silver-trimmed black suit he had worn when he'd come aboard the *Condor* masquerading as a Spaniard.

He swept off his plumed hat and bowed low before her. She returned his greeting, lifting the skirt of her green taffeta gown an inch or two above her high-heeled satin slippers and making a curtsey.

"*Buenas dias,* Don Diego," she teased him.

"Haven't you forgiven me for that little deception yet?" he asked, with a smile.

"I'm not sure," she said, as if she were considering the question most carefully. "You did look so ferocious."

"And all the while I was trying to play the chivalrous courtier, straight from Cadiz."

"Your accent was most convincing," she assured him with a smile.

"That is not remarkable," he said. "I grew up in Havana—my father was assistant to the British ambassador there."

"Indeed," she said politely. But already, she was looking past him. Still, she caught no glimpse of Gavin.

"Where is the captain?" she asked. "Has he gone below?"

"Captain Broderick went ashore," Jeremy told her. "He left in the first of the boats, right after we dropped anchor."

Gavin had not even bothered to wake her, and tell her his plans. He had gone off without a word to her. Perhaps she should not be surprised, considering how she had treated him the day before.

As soon as the *San Bartolomé* had weighed anchor yesterday at noon, Gavin had said that he had no intention of remaining in his quarters now that he had recovered from his wound. She made no attempt to talk him out of it, for she was still brooding over his cold, distant manner. She couldn't forget how he'd refused to speak to her of his plans of this new expedition. How he'd dismissed her as if she'd been no more than a trollop with whom he'd shared his bed for a night.

During the hours that followed she saw little of him, although she heard him out on deck giving sailing orders to the crew. But it was not until evening that he returned to the cabin to join her.

She kept up a casual conversation all through the elaborate dinner served by Don Alfonso's steward. Afterward, as they strolled on deck, she ran out of small talk and lapsed into silence. From time to time she stole a glance at him, but his eyes were fixed on the sea.

Perhaps if he had made the first move and drawn her into his arms she might not have been able to keep from responding. But he was still preoccupied, and he sent her off to bed, saying brusquely that he had work to do. Anger and humiliation raged within her, leaving no room for any other emotion.

Later, when he climbed into bed beside her, she pretended to be asleep. Although he brushed his lips over her cheek and stroked her shoulder, she forced herself to remain unmoving. It took every ounce of her willpower to keep from turning to him and pressing her body to his. Somehow, she managed to ignore the swift warmth that surged up inside her. Tomorrow perhaps she would relent. But it had not occurred to her that he would go ashore without her.

"Is anything wrong, Mistress Thornton?" Jeremy was looking at her with concern.

She shook her head, and forced a smile. "I fear my presence aboard ship is keeping you from visiting Tortuga."

"Why should you suppose that?"

"I thought Captain Broderick might have ordered you to stay here and keep guard over me."

He stared at her in surprise. "The captain gave me no such orders."

Two spots of color burned in her cheeks, and her voice shook with indignation. "I don't believe you. Gavin wouldn't go off and leave me unprotected, surrounded by these—these men—"

"No doubt we are a lawless lot, Mistress Thornton, but you've nothing to fear. You are the captain's lady, and there is not a man on this ship who'd dare to treat you with the slightest disrespect."

"Then why have you stayed behind?" she asked.

Jeremy looked a little embarrassed. "I was about to get into one of the boats when I saw you standing here, alone. I thought you looked troubled. If something's worrying you, perhaps I can be of service."

His voice, his expression of concern, reminded her of Lance, and for a moment she wished she might confide in him. But Jeremy was not her brother, she told herself firmly. He was only a well-bred young man who had instinctively offered his services to a lady.

Her pride saved her from making a fool of herself, by speaking of her distress. Instead, she raised her head and straightened her spine. "I confess I was curious about this island," she said, keeping her tone casual. "I'd hoped to go ashore for a few hours."

"No doubt the captain felt it was not a suitable place for a lady to visit." He offered her his arm, and led her aft. "At least you can get a better view from here." They stood side by side at the taffrail, and she looked out at the rocky harbor. "Tortuga—that means turtle in Spanish, doesn't it?"

"That's right," Jeremy said. "Columbus gave it the name, so they say. From a distance, it does look something like a sea turtle—speckled brown and humpbacked. But I didn't know you understood Spanish, Mistress Thornton."

"I learned a smattering of the language from Dolores de las Fuentes—a young Spanish lady who traveled with me aboard the *Bristol Belle*," she explained. But she could not take her eyes from the nearby island. Another boatload of rowdy, laughing sailors were rowing toward the shore, the sunlight glinting along their oars.

"The island is not nearly as large as Jamaica," she said.

"It's a good deal smaller," he agreed. "But the buccaneers had good reasons for choosing it as their headquarters. It belongs to the French West India Company, you see. The French governor, Bertrand d'Ogeron, welcomes our presence here, because otherwise he'd be forever fighting off the Spaniards. They're a greedy lot, who'd lay claim to all the New World, if they could."

He pointed across the glittering expanse of the sea. "There are other advantages to the island as well. It lies at the head of the Windward Passage."

"And why should that make it particularly desirable to—these buccaneers?" Only another word for pirates, she thought, and as distasteful for her to speak.

"The Passage stretches between Cuba and Hispanola," Jeremy explained. "At the southern end is the entrance to the heart of the Spanish Main. There the galleons ply their trade routes, laden with treasure like—like an orchard of golden fruit, ripe for picking."

"For looting—isn't that what you mean?" But as soon as she had spoken she felt a twinge of remorse. Although she was in low spirits over Gavin's unexpected departure, it wasn't fair to take out her bad temper on Jeremy.

He had arrayed himself in his fine apparel, and he must be as eager to go ashore as the rest of the crew. But he gave no hint of impatience. Instead, he was going out of his way to treat her with consideration.

"It's natural that a gently reared young lady should feel as you do," he said. "And I won't deny that you'll find no lack of degraded brutes among the men of Tortuga. Thieves and cutthroats who'd kill a man over a handful of coins and feel no remorse."

"And you and—Captain Broderick—have chosen to cast your lot with such creatures?"

"Men have joined the Brotherhood of the Coast for many reasons," he went on, his voice quiet and level. "Some out of sheer necessity. There are the Huguenots, for instance. They were forbidden to practice their religion back in France, and so they came to the West Indies, only to be hunted down and slaughtered by the Spanish. Here on Tortuga they found a refuge at last."

"And the others?"

"The English Cavaliers who fled from Cromwell's army, when the tide of war had turned against them, came out here. And so did Irishmen and Scots. Men from every part of Europe, heard of the freedom to be found on Tortuga, and they flocked to join the Brethren of the Coast. That's what we call ourselves." He gave her a wry smile. "The Spanish call us by several other names, none of them fit for a lady's ears."

Sybilla struggled to sort out her confused feelings. Suppose when Lance had escaped from England he'd had no relative to give him a home. Would he, too, have sought refuge here? It was a disturbing thought.

"And what of the women?" she asked. "I heard the sailors talking of the wenches of Tortuga."

"They're a mixed lot—like their men. Some are no different from those tavern wenches and common trollops back in Jamaica. But others came here seeking marriage—a whole shipload arrived from France some years ago."

Sybilla stared at him in disbelief. "What sort of woman would choose to come to such a place to find a husband?"

"Not the respectable kind, I grant you. Most were wards of the Convent of the Madelonettes, in Paris. The nuns who guarded them, called them 'debauched young girls who knew the truth about themselves.'" Jeremy's lips thinned. "They carried the marks of their sins on their bodies—one hundred lashes across the back."

Sybilla flinched at the thought of such fearful punishment. Surely no woman, however lacking in virtue, should be made to suffer such cruelty.

"But once they set foot on Tortuga and were wed, most were faithful to their husbands," he said.

"Then all the women here are either wives or—trollops."

Jeremy smiled. "It's not so simple as that. Some are independent by nature. They offer their favors freely, but only where they choose."

"And I suppose some are pretty," she said, with a frown.

"Why certainly—a few would be called beauties, in any society. I've known men who fought duels over them, and showered them with jewels a duchess might envy."

Sybilla struggled to hide the turmoil that gripped her. Even now, Gavin was roving about the island. No doubt he could have his choice among those free-and-easy females

Jeremy was talking about. He'd wanted to make love with her last night, and she had turned her back on him. Had she really convinced him that she was sound asleep?

"Captain Broderick's gone ashore on business." She turned to stare at Jeremy. He must have seen her anxiety reflected in her face. "He'll be returning to the ship, as soon as he completes his duties there on the island."

"What sort of business?"

"Why, he'll need a great many men for this new expedition—the most experienced and trustworthy."

"This expedition you speak of—" Sybilla began.

Before she could go on, a seaman hailed Jeremy from the bow. "There's room for one more in the boat—if you've a mind to go ashore."

Jeremy hesitated. "It's up to the captain to tell you about the expedition."

"Indeed, there's little he hasn't already told me." Under the circumstances, her lie was justified. It would be most unfair to try to coax information out of Jeremy. Or to keep the courteous young man from the pleasures of Tortuga any longer.

But after he had left she returned to the cabin. Soon she was pacing back and forth. Gavin might have gone ashore seeking additional crewmen for this mysterious new venture. But that didn't necessarily mean he would return as soon as he had taken care of business.

He might decide to spend the night on the island. Why not? The thought only added to Sybilla's growing torment.

He could take his choice among the beauties of Tortuga, and no doubt any one of them would be eager to share her bed with him. No doubt she'd be thoroughly skilled in all the ways of satisfying a man.

Perhaps there was even one particular woman Gavin had pleasured himself with before. A bold creature who would welcome him back with open arms. Sybilla was startled by the hot, primitive jealousy that came surging up within her.

But what right did she have to be jealous? She had no

claim on Gavin. He'd promised only to get her away from Hobart and send her off to Boston. Such a bleak, empty prospect, she thought.

Then she stopped her pacing and stood at the stern window, looking out toward the island. She was not on her way to Boston yet. Somehow, she would find a way to break through the barrier that separated her from the man she loved.

On the broad beach of Tortuga the bonfires glowed against the darkening sky. The wind rustled through the tall, coarse grass and tossed the fronds of the palms. Gavin seated himself on a fallen log, stared moodily into the flickering, leaping flames, and listened to the ceaseless rhythm of the waves. He caught the inviting smell of roast pig turning on the spits and heard the thump of a bung starter as a man broke out a cask of ale.

Although he had worked up a sharp appetite, he would wait until Abiathar arrived so that they might have their meal together and talk over the accomplishments of the day. No doubt his first mate had carried out his orders with characteristic energy and persistence.

And as for himself, he'd done well enough, rounding up new recruits for his expedition. The very mention of his name was enough to bring the buccaneers hurrying out of taverns and bawdy houses, flocking to him to volunteer their services. A few captains, whose vessels lay anchored in the harbor, offered to enlist, along with their entire crews.

Gavin had told them the terms of his articles of agreement, which he had already set down in detail. He would receive the largest share of the loot. The captains of the other vessel would be paid proportionately. And there would be additional recompense for those who were wounded in the coming battle. For the loss of both eyes or both hands, a man would receive eighteen hundred pieces of eight; if he lost both legs, fifteen hundred; for a right hand, six hundred; a left leg or either hand, six hundred. And there would be fifty to one hundred for any outstanding act of courage in the face of the enemy.

Like all such contracts, the document contained the final statement of, "No prey, no pay."

Gavin was sure that by the time the new ships were delivered and the expedition was ready to set sail he would have rounded up all the men he needed. Indeed, he might have completed his search today, but he had turned away more men than he had accepted. For an expedition such as this only the best would do. Sheer, raw courage would not be enough. He wanted men who could be relied upon to keep their heads no matter what unexpected turn the battle might take.

He moved from the fire and stared out over the harbor. He had no difficulty in picking out the distinctive shape of the broad-beamed *San Bartolomé*.

No doubt Sybilla had been startled when she had awakened that morning to find him gone. But it had been better this way. For she would have tried to persuade him to take her along, and her presence would have distracted him from his purpose.

The sooner he sent her off to Boston, the better it would be for both of them. Indeed, if his original plans had not gone awry because of the unforeseen attack by the *San Bartolomé*, Sybilla now would be settled in the far-off northern town of his birth.

He was distracted for a moment as he watched a girl go running by, her bare feet moving lightly across the sand. A booted buccaneer went charging close behind her. She laughed shrilly, enjoying the chase. Soon she would be coupling with her pursuer off in a nearby grove of trees, or behind an outcropping of rocks.

Gavin turned away, and fixed his gaze on the fire again, his gray eyes thoughtful. Sybilla . . . Probably it would have been better if he had resisted the temptation of that soft, white body, those golden eyes. He should not have taken her, even though she'd been willing. But he could not bring himself to regret the hours of loving he'd shared with her.

After he had carried out his expedition, he would return and find a way to get that brother of hers out of Hobart's sphere of influence. Lance would not welcome his interference at first. But once the young man found out that Hobart had known all along of his part in the rebellion and had tried to use his information to force Sybilla into marriage no doubt he would be anxious to get away from the islands and take her with him.

Gavin felt a pang of unwilling sympathy for Sybilla. It could never have been easy for her all these years, trying to live up to her self-appointed responsibility, to go on protecting Lance from the results of his reckless, impulsive behavior. A smile touched his lips as he found himself remembering her account of that childish adventure back in Somerset. She and Lance, tossed about in a rainstorm in a borrowed skiff.

He was Sir Francis Drake and I was the crew.

It must have taken courage for her to stand up to her hot-tempered father. And maybe it would have been better if she had not interfered, if she'd allowed Lance to take the thrashing he deserved. But her devotion to her brother had not allowed her to behave differently. That kind of gallantry, loving but misguided, was a part of her nature.

Then all at once, to his startled discomfiture, he found himself envying her. To be capable of feeling such tenderness, such a deep attachment to another human being—wasn't that better than living only for one's self?

"Jeremy said I might find you down here." He turned quickly, relieved at being interrupted by the sound of Abiathar's booming voice. The red-bearded mate was carrying a couple of wineskins. He dropped down on the log beside Gavin. "Enough of work for one day," he said. He looked over at the nearest fire, where a slab of meat was browning on a spit. "What we need now is a good meal and this wine to wash it down with."

187

A tall, statuesque girl with a thick mane of black hair came toward them. "Odette!" Abiathar called out with a grin. "You going to dance for us tonight?"

She gave him an answering smile, but her dark eyes were fixed on Gavin. "But of course," she said. "I can't disappoint such an audience." Her full skirt of crimson and purple brushed against Gavin's knee. Her voice was soft and husky, and she moved with sensuous grace as she leaned closer to him.

The firelight played over her smooth olive skin and touched the swell of her breasts, half-visible through the sheer silk of her blouse. No man could mistake the open invitation in her glance. "Later, perhaps, I shall dance for you alone, Captain."

When he did not answer, she gave him a look of surprise. On other visits to Tortuga, he would have responded quite differently. She waited for a moment, taken aback by this change in him, then shrugged slightly and drifted off to join a group of men gathered about one of the nearby fires.

Chapter Fifteen

By late afternoon Sybilla was too restless to remain in the seclusion of the captain's quarters a moment longer. She wrapped herself in a fringed silk shawl and went out on deck, hoping to catch a glimpse of Gavin's boat returning from Tortuga.

What a fool she'd been, to treat him with cool disdain last night, to turn away from him when he wanted to make love to her. She should have known better than to use such tactics on a man like Gavin.

But she promised herself that tonight, she'd make it up to him. If he arrived in time to join her for dinner, she would not sulk or say a word about her disappointment at being left behind while he went ashore.

She was already dressed for the evening, in a gown of honey-colored satin, with a low-cut, close-fitting bodice and a bell-shaped skirt. Her shawl concealed the rounded swell of her breasts from the eyes of the sailors who were milling about the deck. She would remove the shawl later tonight, in the privacy of the cabin, where only Gavin could see her.

They would dine together, and when he took her to bed she would respond to his caresses with all the warmth and passion she felt for him. She would give herself freely, holding nothing back. The anticipation of the night to come

189

sent a swift current of desire moving through her.

But when she reached the taffrail she could see only a single boat, bobbing up and down on the waves alongside the galleon. And this small craft had not returned from Tortuga, but was about to leave for the island.

Sybilla stifled a sigh of disappointment, then moved closer to the rail. She was puzzled by the unusual appearance of the boat's occupants. They were not part of Gavin's crew, she was sure of it.

They wore the same sort of clothing that Gavin's men had put on to go ashore: wide-legged canvas breeches, full-sleeved cotton shirts and brightly-colored silk sashes. But these men showed no anticipation, or even interest, about their destination. They did not laugh, or talk about the wenches, the gaming, the rum and ale that awaited them on the island. In fact, they scarcely spoke to one another at all. Their faces were haggard under their long, matted hair, and their garments hung loosely on their emaciated bodies. They squinted and shielded their eyes with their hands, as if the glare of the sunlight reflected on the water was painful to them. Some could scarcely sit upright, but lay slumped against the sides of the boat.

A barrel-chested sailor with a purple and yellow striped scarf tied around his head and a gold hoop in one ear paused beside Sybilla.

"Those men down there. Who are they?" she asked.

The sailor knuckled his forehead. "Them's some o' the galley slaves we freed from those Spanish whoresons—beggin' yer pardon, ma'm."

"They must have suffered terribly," she said. "And what's to become of them now?"

"Cap'n Broderick gave orders that they're to be taken ashore and lodged in *ajoupas*—palm thatch huts—on the beach. Belike the fresh air'll do 'em a power o' good, after bein' chained in that foul hell below decks."

No doubt they had committed serious offenses against the laws of Spain, to have suffered such punishment. But nevertheless, Sybilla felt her throat tighten with pity. "It must have been dreadful for them down there," she said. "How long were they held captive, do you know?"

The sailor shrugged. "Six months, a year, maybe. Though one said as how he might've been at the oars fer five years, but he didn't rightly remember. It's easy enough fer a man to lose his wits, chained like a beast and slavin' fer them Spaniards. I ain't no sweet-smellin' London fop, but when I went below to help unchain those poor devils, why the stink down in them bulwarks was enough to make a goat puke—"

He stopped speaking abruptly. "Yer pardon, Mistress Thornton. Guess I forgot myself. Such talk ain't fit fer a lady."

But Sybilla was too shaken by the man's words to feel offended. Would all those ex-slaves survive, even with the best of care? One gray-haired man, his cheeks hollow, his skin the color of parchment, stared straight ahead with sunken eyes that were empty of all feeling. Another was wracked with constant spasms of coughing.

"The cap'n is doin' all he can for 'em," the sailor told her. "He's payin' out of his own pocket to make sure the poor devils get plenty o' good food an' drink. An' if there's a barber-surgeon to be found on Tortuga, he'll hire the man's services as well."

"That's good of him," Sybilla said. She remembered the snatch of conversation she'd heard between Gavin and Abiathar, the day before. It had been plain even then that Gavin was deeply concerned over the welfare of the former slaves.

"They don't make 'em no finer than Cap'n Broderick. I'd follow him to hell, any time he gave the order." He grinned. "Belike I'll be gettin' my chance, an' soon."

The sailor touched his knuckles to his forehead again in a gesture of respect, swung himself over the side of the ship, then scampered down the rope ladder with the agility of a monkey; a few other crewmen followed, and then the small boat was pulling away. Sybilla watched it rising and falling with the motion of the waves as it headed for the rockbound harbor.

She was touched by Gavin's generosity toward the wretched men who had been set free from slavery and by the sailor's open admiration for his captain. But the man's words troubled him.

What had he meant when he had said he might soon be following Gavin to hell? Surely he was hardened to the usual risks of his lawless trade. Sybilla felt a cold knot of fear in the pit of her stomach.

She shaded her eyes and peered across the water, still hoping to catch sight of another small boat, the one that might be bringing Gavin back to the *San Bartolomé*; but once again she was disappointed. How long would it be before he returned?

She lingered at the taffrail, looking at the frigates and sloops that lay at anchor on every side. The setting sun gilded their masts, figureheads, and furled sails. It touched the small, low-lying clouds with cerise and gold. And gradually, the shadows veiled the towering, rock cliffs at either side of the entrance to the harbor.

A light breeze sprang up; it rustled the skirt of Sybilla's gown and tugged at her carefully arranged curls. With a reluctant sigh she turned away and went back to the cabin. She seated herself before the mirror in the sleeping quarters. Carefully she smoothed each wave and ringlet back in place, then fastened a small satin bow on either side of her head and arranged a few coquettish little curls at her temples. Tonight she wanted to look her most enticing, for Gavin.

From the adjoining cabin she could hear the clink of silver and the clatter of plates and goblets as the Spanish steward laid the table for dinner. Surely Gavin would be here any minute now.

But after putting off her meal until long after darkness had fallen she finally resigned herself to dining alone. She felt lonely and somewhat ostentatious, seated at one end of the long, candle-lit table. Although she had little appetite she

4 FREE BOOKS

TO GET YOUR 4 FREE BOOKS WORTH $18.00 —MAIL IN THE FREE BOOK CERTIFICATE T O D A Y

Fill in the Free Book Certificate below, and we'll send your FREE BOOKS to you as soon as we receive it.

If the certificate is missing below, write to: Zebra Home Subscription Service, Inc., P.O. Box 5214, 120 Brighton Road, Clifton, New Jersey 07015-5214.

GET
FOUR
FREE
BOOKS
(AN $18.00 VALUE)

forced herself to taste each carefully prepared dish.

Perhaps Gavin and Abiathar still were making the rounds of the waterfront taverns, seeking more crewmen. Jeremy had said that Gavin wanted only the most experienced and trustworthy sailors for his new expedition. But what sort of expedition would require so many extra men?

She mustn't allow herself to brood over the future, not tonight. And no matter how late he returned, she would not question or berate him.

She had to let Gavin know how deeply she cared about him, even if it meant swallowing her pride. And if her words did not serve to sweep aside the barriers between them, then later, when they lay together in the wide, velvet-curtained bed, she would find other ways to prove her love, without any words at all.

But the hours crawled by and still he did not return. The steward cleared the table, shaking his head when he saw how little she had eaten.

"Perhaps the meal was not to your liking, Señorita Thornton," he said. "If there is some particular dish you would prefer, the cook would be only too pleased to prepare it for you."

Sybilla forced a smile, assured him that the food had been excellent, and sent him away. Reluctantly, she retired to the sleeping chamber again.

She took off her honey-colored silk gown, hung it away carefully, and drew the gold-tipped bodkins from her elaborate coiffure. She brushed her hair until the loose waves shone like satin in the light of the overhead lantern. She bathed and afterward she touched the stopper of her perfume flask to her throat, her wrists, the cleft between her breasts.

She went through the contents of her trunk, and after a moment's hesitation she chose a nightdress of black Venetian lace. Madeleine had chosen this seductive garment for Sybilla's trousseau.

"It's not for you to wear on your wedding night," Madeleine

had said with a suggestive half-smile that had made Sybilla stiffen with revulsion. "You'll want to look sweet and virginal then. But a clever woman learns how to hold a man's interest by surprising him, from time to time. After you've been married for a while, you'll find that a gown like this will arouse your husband most powerfully."

She had hinted that she was prepared to explain a great deal more about the arts of satisfying a man. But Sybilla, revolted by the mere thought of lying with Nicholas Hobart, had discouraged Madeleine's confidences.

Now, as she studied her reflection in the armoire mirror, she smiled with anticipation of the coming night. The delicate lace, sheer as a gossamer web, barely concealed her pink-tipped breasts, her long, tapering thighs, and the russet triangle of her womanhood. She smoothed the clinging folds down over her hips and walked slowly to the bed.

She stretched out, resting her head against the pillows, Her smile lingered as she pictured Gavin's response when he saw her lying here, awaiting his pleasure.

The rest of the boats were returning to the *San Bartolomé*. She heard them scrap against the galleon's hull, and then the sailors were clambering over the side, talking loudly, sharing their experiences on the island.

They'd eaten and drunk their fill and had gambled away most of their loot from the capture of the galleon. Some had gone to see a cockfight, others had played at dice or cards, and a few were arguing about the relative merits of the two men who had taken part in an wrestling match in one of the waterfront taverns.

Her eyelids grew heavy and she smothered a yawn. She was drifting off to sleep when she heard one of the men saying, "What a sight she was—dancin' there on the beach. Naked as the day she was born, with the firelight shinin' on her hair—"

Sybilla sat bolt upright, wide awake and straining to catch every word.

"Odette's a rare one an' no mistake. With 'er butt swaying

an' finest pair o' tits a man'd want to see—"

"Me, I'd like t' do more'n just look at 'em."

"Quit talkin' about 'er. She ain't fer the likes of us! It'd cost a captain's share o'loot to pay fer a night with Odette."

She had no reason to be shocked by the sailors' talk. Hadn't Jeremy said much the same about the bold beauties of Tortuga? In more discreet words, of course, fit for a lady's ears.

She leaned forward, every muscle tense now, hoping against hope that she would hear Gavin's voice among those others. Surely he should be returning by now. Then slowly, reluctantly, she dropped back against the pillows. He hadn't come back aboard yet.

Tears stung her eyelids, but she blinked them back. When Gavin did return, no matter how late he might be, he would not walk in and find her red-eyed, her face puffy with weeping.

One by one, the men went below to their quarters, still talking of the pleasures they'd enjoyed ashore; but a few lingered on deck. From the bow, she heard the music of a guitar, and a deep baritone voice, singing a ballad of love. The plaintive melody that blended with thrumming of the wind in the rigging and the lapping of the waves against the side of the galleon moved her in spite of herself.

The joys of love, they last but for an hour,
The pain of love goes on, forevermore . . .

Surely that couldn't be true. The delights she had discovered in Gavin's embraces would grow and deepen with time. Every nerve came alive, at the thought of his body, joined with hers. For them, it was only the beginning . . .

The sailor was no longer singing, but she still heard the haunting notes of the guitar, borne on the soft air of the purple night. She closed her eyes and gradually, lulled by the music and the gentle, rocking motion of the ship, she drifted off into sleep.

*　　*　　*

When she awoke she saw the square of pale rosy light framed by the wide cabin window. And Gavin's tall shape was silhouetted against the glow of dawn. He had stayed on Tortuga all night. She shut her eyes again and forced herself to breath slowly, evenly, so that he would think she was still asleep.

"I'll have none of your silly play-acting tonight, my love." She felt Gavin's hand close on her shoulder "Look at me, Sybilla," he ordered her.

She obeyed, her thick, curving lashes shading her half-open eyes, but she could not bring herself to speak. In the growing light of the swift, tropic dawn, she saw his teasing smile. His glance raked over her.

"Surely you did not deck yourself out in that enticing nightdress because you were expecting to get a good night's sleep."

"It isn't night any longer—it's morning. And I *was* sound asleep, until you came lumbering in here—" Lumbering indeed. Gavin moved with the swift, easy tread of a jungle cat.

"In that case, you should be well-rested," he said. He sat down on the bed and took her in his arms. He began to stroke her back, his touch warm and caressing through the delicate film of lace, and her body responded swiftly, the first small flickers of desire racing through her veins.

He drew her head against his chest and for a moment she melted against him, soft and yielding. Then her nostrils flared, and her body tensed as she caught an unusual scent about him. Woodsmoke—that's what it was.

She remembered the sailors' talking about the woman called Odette.

"Dancin' there on the beach . . ." "Firelight shinin' on her . . ." "Not fer the likes of us . . ."

"Take your hands off me, Gavin Broderick!"

"Sybilla, stop this nonsense. You're behaving like a

196

spoiled child, and I'll have no more of it. I've been trekking from one side of the island to the other, trying to round up the men I need for my next voyage. A ship's captain has his duty to attend to."

"Duty—is that what you call it?" Her golden eyes narrowed. "Next you'll tell me you were trying to recruit that—that shameless creature—Odette—to serve on one of your ships!"

She could see that she'd caught him off balance—but only for the moment. To her chagrin, he smiled broadly, his white teeth gleaming against his tan skin, his gray eyes sparkling with amusement.

"No doubt she'd attract a great many volunteers," he said. "But I'm afraid such a voluptuous female would prove to be far more trouble than she was worth, aboard ship," he said. "The men would be fighting each other for her favors, instead of attacking the enemy."

Then he eyed her with curiosity, and his black brows drew together in a puzzled frown. "What do you know of Odette?"

"I've heard enough," she said. "And don't bother to deny you were near that fire on the beach." He laughed softly, and reached for her again, but she drew away. "You reek of woodsmoke."

"Do you find the odor distasteful?"

He slid her gown off one shoulder and began to stroke her soft white skin, but she pushed his hand away, and swung her long legs over the side of the bed. "You *did* stay to watch that brazen female doing her lewd dance, didn't you?"

"I saw her," he said, without a trace of guilt. "And I thoroughly enjoyed her performance. Odette's a fine-looking wench, and a most accomplished dancer. They say she used to perform for King Louis, himself, in the palace at Versailles."

"Dancing's not her only accomplishment, is it? No doubt she's had vast experience in pleasuring a man—far more than I—"

Gavin began stroking her again, then slipped his hand under the lace bodice and cupped her breast. His fingers flicked at her nipple. His touch made it harden and sent a tingling through her body. "I'll be only too willing to add to your store of experience." His voice was low and husky. "I want you, love. Now . . ."

She pulled away before he could feel her response. Hot resentment coursed through her. Was he arrogant enough to believe he only had to touch her, and she would forget her pride completely? Although she might not be able to control her instinctive physical responses, she would not allow herself to yield to them.

"You didn't even bother to wake me before you left this morning." But even as she reproached him, it wasn't easy for her to ignore the hardness of her nipple, where his fingers had touched her a moment ago. Or the ripples of warmth that spread outward from the pit of her stomach. And because she was angry at herself for her weakness, she spoke out more shrewishly than she meant to.

"You might have at least told me your plans for the day, instead of going off without a word."

"It seems you had no difficulty finding out all you wished to know."

"But I didn't!" Her nameless fears for him were stronger than her petty jealousy. She clutched at his arm, her face upturned to his. "You're preparing to go off again, that's all I know. And you'll be needing more ships this time—and a great many more men." Panic surged up in her, so that she could not retreat into silence again. She had to know what he was planning, even if it meant arousing his anger. "You're going to risk your neck in some sort of dangerous scheme—and you've told me nothing—" In spite of herself she pressed closer, burying her face against his shoulder, driven by her fear for him.

"There's nothing you need to know."

"You won't put me off so easily—not this time." Her eyes held his. She had to break through that stubborn facade, to make him see reason. "You're not meant for this lawless life, Gavin. You're a gentleman. You come of a decent, respectable family, you told me so yourself. Surely they must care what happens to you. How long has it been since they've had any word from you?"

"That's enough!" His voice was tight with anger. "I won't have you meddling in matters that don't concern you."

"Are you so afraid of your own feelings that you must pretend they don't exist?"

"What is it you want of me, Sybilla?"

She answered with equal directness. "When you put Lance and me aboard that ship for Boston, I want you to come with us."

His face hardened. "Suppose I don't choose to?"

"Sweet Jesú! Haven't you had enough of danger? Of looting and destroying Spanish ships?"

"I made an agreement with Hobart." His voice was firm and unyielding.

"Break it, then! Tell him he'll have to find another captain to take the risks while he sits safely back at Indigo and rakes in his profits."

"I've no intention of dissolving our partnership. Not for you—or any woman."

With one swift movement he freed himself from her clinging arms, and got to his feet. She watched as he took off his sash and his sword belt and placed them over a chair. He set his sword into a pair of iron hooks in the wall opposite the bed.

"As a matter of fact, I've already dispatched a messenger to Jamaica, to let Hobart know I survived the battle off Cuba and that I'm ready to go ahead with our enterprise as soon as I get my new ships."

Sybilla felt the muscles of her throat tighten. "That's why you're sending me off to Boston, isn't it? To get me out of the way?"

"I'm sending you to Boston because you'll be safe there."

"And suppose I refuse to go?"

He finished unbuttoning his shirt, and tossed it aside with an impatient gesture. "I'm offering you a haven, a place to start over. Why would you refuse?"

"To keep you from risking your life again. You say you need Hobart's backing for this new voyage. If Hobart finds out that—that you and I—that you took me away from him—he'd break the partnership fast enough."

"Don't flatter yourself, Sybilla. No doubt Hobart's still hot to bed you." His eyes raked her body with a cold stare. "What man wouldn't be?"

She stiffened, outraged by his brutal frankness, but before she could reply, he went on. "Right now, the man has other things on his mind. I've dangled such a rich prize before him that he'll not be satisfied until he gets his hands on his share. He needs my skills as a seaman, and I need those ships he's had built for me. Because this time, I'll need my own fleet to get what I'm after."

"And what is this—this prize?"

He towered over her, and she felt the growing tension in him. "When I sail again, I'll hunt down the plate fleet of Spain—and I'll smash it in two. With the *Condor*, the *San Bartolomé*, and six more ships, armed for battle and manned by the crews I've chosen, I'll trap the treasure galleons when they're bound for Porto Bello. I'll strip them of the wealth from all those Spanish colonies in South America. I'll strike a blow that'll help smash the power of Spain here in the New World."

He spoke with a fierce hatred, an obsessive determination that sent an icy current through Sybilla's body. Her lips parted and the color drained from her face. She stared up at him as though she were seeing him for the first time.

"I thought you were different from Hobart," she said slowly. "But I see that I was mistaken. You're two of a kind. Both of you are so filled with greed, so hungry for power, that nothing else matters."

Gavin's gray eyes darkened to ebony beneath the straight black bars of his brows. A ridge of muscle sprang out along his jaw, and a hard, deeply cut line appeared on either side of his mouth.

From somewhere far back in Sybilla's mind came the warning that she was going too far—risking too much. But now that she had found the strength to challenge him she could not hold herself back.

"You're ready to loot, to kill for your share of booty from this treasure fleet." Her voice shook but she went on. "You'll have no regrets about sending me away. You can scarcely wait to be rid of me—because I'm in your way."

"Sybilla, no. It's not like that. If only I could make you understand."

"I understand perfectly. Perhaps if I'd been more experienced, it would not have taken so long for me to understand the sort of man you are. You tried to tell me the first time we met that you had no room in your life for me, for any woman. You're not capable of lasting love. I doubt you ever could have been—"

"That's enough." The hard indifference in his voice shocked her into silence at last. "Believe whatever you choose about me."

He had taught her what it meant to be a woman and had awakened her senses, sharing with her an ecstasy more splendid, more overpowering, than she had ever dreamed of. But for her, there was more to love than the physical rapture between a man and woman joined in the act of passion. She needed to understand the dark forces that were about to drive him from her, perhaps forever.

"Gavin—don't shut me out!" she began, her voice shaking with anguish. She sprang from the bed and gripped his arms with all her strength, her eyes holding his, willing him not to look away.

"Don't you know that everything about you concerns me because you are part of me? You have been since that night back in Jamaica, when you took me for the first time. Nothing can ever be the same for me again."

She thrust herself against him, molding her body to his,

branding him with the heat of her flesh. For a moment he did not respond. Then his arms went around her, and he buried his face in her hair. Her voice was muffled against his bare chest. "Whatever you are, I must be, too. Maybe it's not the life I would have chosen—the one I was bred for. But I can't change now. I can't go back . . ."

He held her a moment longer, then slowly he unclasped her arms. He turned away, his movement slow and purposeful, and the light from the overhead lantern shone down on the crosshatched white lines that marked his tanned skin. "Sybilla, I lied when I said I'd gotten these scars in a shipboard accident."

"What does that matter now?"

He did not answer at once, but stood silent and immobile. She watched him warily, filled with a nameless fear. And even when he faced her again, she sensed that he wasn't seeing her; his eyes were fixed on a far-off vision, and he spoke with a depth of bitterness, of long-buried rage, that was frightening in its intensity.

"Those are the marks of a whip. For nearly two years I was a slave aboard a Spanish galleon. A magnificent vessel, the *Saragossa*, with her polished brass cannons, her giltwork gleaming in the sunlight, and the banner of Castile unfurled to catch the breeze."

Gavin's mouth twisted in a mirthless smile. "But the galleon didn't need even a puff of wind to keep her on course. Because the galley slaves were down below in the bulwarks, chained to the oars. Down in that foul hell, toiling to the beat of the overseer's drum. Sometimes we had to row at top speed for six hours at a stretch. Can you understand what that means?"

Unable to speak, Sybilla could only shake her head.

"Forward, up and then back, until your muscles knotted, and the pain made you dizzy, and then you were only one mass of pain, mindless except for the fear. Yes, Sybilla— even when you stop thinking like a rational man, you're still capable of the sort of fear an animal must feel. Because you knew that if you slowed down, if you lost the beat for even a moment, there was the lash to speed you up again."

She put a hand on his shoulder, but she wasn't sure he felt her touch. Even if she had wanted him to stop, she knew that, having loosed the dark flood of memories he'd kept dammed up inside him so long, there was no holding them back now.

"The galleon carried forty oars, with six men at each of them. There were four feet between one man and the next. We were chained to the bench, day and night. We slept at those oars, and we ate in our chains. Bread, crawling with maggots and foul water—and never enough of that."

Sybilla was sickened by the ugly images his words conjured up in her mind. "But surely they must have had to unchain you sometimes—"

"A slave might be unchained if he collapsed from exhaustion but the driver thought there might be some strength left in him. Then he was dragged up on deck and flogged. If he died under the lash, he was tossed overboard."

Sybilla gave a wordless cry of horrified disbelief and clutched his shoulder so fiercely that her nails drove into his flesh. He stared at her for a moment. A long shudder went through him, and then, for a time, he was silent. But when he spoke again, she realized, with overwhelming relief, that she had called him back from that terrible place in the past.

"Perhaps now you understand why I must go through with this expedition. Why I've got to do all one man can to strike back at the forces of Spain here in the Indies."

"But think of the risk! Even with all your skill as a seaman, and the loyalty of your crew, you were lucky to capture the *San Bartolomé*, against such odds." She forced herself to go on. "Your luck won't hold forever. What if you're captured again? Now that you know the punishment the Spanish mete out to pirates—"

"Pirates!" There was bitter fury in his voice. "I was no pirate when the Spaniards took me prisoner. I was master of one of my father's own merchant ships, bound for the Bahamas."

She stared at him in bewilderment.

"An unseasonable hurricane had driven our ship off course, and into Spanish waters. We had no more chance against the galleon that attacked us than a wren would have had against a hawk. Three quarters of my crew were killed. I was imprisoned in Havana, along with the other survivors."

"But when you were brought to trial, why didn't you explain about the hurricane?"

"The trial was a farce," he told her. "The Cuban court cared nothing about justice. The Spanish fleet is always in need of a fresh supply of slaves. Galley slaves don't live long, you see. Four or five years at most."

"Gavin," she said softly, "Those thing I said about you—comparing you with Hobart. How could I have known?" She put out a hand and touched his arm, as if to reassure herself that he was here beside her, that his unspeakable ordeal had not broken him. Then she kept silent, as he told her the rest.

During the first weeks of his captivity he'd seen other prisoners die around him. He'd watched as the guards had unchained each body and dragged it up on deck. He'd heard the splash of the sea as the corpse was heaved overboard. "Some members of my own crew—I'd grown up with them, back in Boston." His eyes went bleak. "After the first few weeks, I began to think that maybe they were better off than those of us who still lived. I stopped caring whether I survived or not."

Knowing Gavin as she did, Sybilla stared at him in disbelief, shocked that he should have given way to despair even in that hell. Perhaps he had been wracked with guilt, over the loss of his men. They had put their trust in him, had followed his orders, and he had failed them. No doubt, he blamed himself for their deaths.

She longed to comfort him, but she could find no words. And now he began to speak of Abiathar, who had been chained beside him on the bench. "He'd been a pirate—one of the Brotherhood of the Coast—and he made no secret of it. Lord knows why he gave a hang whether I lived or died—

but he did. And he managed to shake me out of my stupor. He got me to believe that as long as we could summon up the strength to go on, we still had a chance to escape from that living hell."

After that, Gavin willed himself to stay alive, moved by only a single purpose—to revenge himself on the Spaniards one day. It was a slim hope, but he would not let it go.

Then, toward the end of the second year of his captivity, the *Saragossa* was set upon and captured by a Dutch warship off the Leeward Islands.

"I was damned lucky to have Abiathar alongside me that day," he said. "When the Dutch grappling irons caught our hull, we were smashed up against them. Half the slaves were struck by their own oars. Some were killed outright, and the others were crippled for life—their backs were broken, their ribs crushed—"

Sybilla pressed her closed hand to her lips, to force back a sound of horror.

"Abiathar'd had experience in such disasters before. He shouted to me to do as he did. Together, we pushed our oar up and forward. Then he dropped to his knees and stretched out and I did the same. No time to ask him why." Gavin's face darkened as he went on. "The next minute, the oar cracked in two. The men around us were smashed to pieces—but it had passed over our heads."

The Dutch captain had ordered those few slaves who had survived to be set free. Although Abiathar had urged Gavin to accompany him to Tortuga, he had gone back to Boston, instead.

"My father had died during my absence," he said, "and my brother, Nathaniel, was running the family's shipping company. He tried to talk me into staying—said it was my responsibility to take my place in the company. But I couldn't. I sailed back to the Indies and hunted up Abiathar. I'd sold Nathaniel my shares in the shipping line, and I used the money to buy the *Condor*. Abiathar helped round up a crew, and we put to sea to hunt the Spaniards."

205

"And Hobart? Couldn't you have managed without such a partner?"

"Perhaps," Gavin conceded. "But he's been useful from the beginning. He's helped to dispose of our cargos through his many connections. He's provided the best victuals and supplies for the *Condor*. And now he is backing this expedition."

Sybilla looked at Gavin, seeing him with a new understanding. She moved closer to him, and rested her cheek against his arm. It could not have been easy for him to speak of the past. But if he had been able to let down his guard so far, he might yet be willing to make her a part of his life.

A renewed hope began to stir within her. Certainly, he had reason enough to hate his former captors; even she could not deny that. But somehow she must help him to rid himself of that corrosive hate. She had to find a way to make him give up his plans for taking the treasure fleet.

For if he were not killed by the Spaniards in the coming battle, he might be taken prisoner. She dared not allow herself to think of the frightful tortures that would be meted out to him if he should fall into their hands.

And even if he succeeded in capturing the treasure fleet, against all the odds, she knew that he still would not be satisfied. His search for revenge would go on and on until it destroyed all that she loved in him. She had to stop him now, or risk losing him forever.

Chapter Sixteen

Sybilla went to Gavin's side and put a hand on his arm; her touch was light and a little hesitant, for she could not be sure of his response. He turned and looked down at her. Then he brushed a lock of hair back from her face and ran his fingers along her cheek and over the line of her jaw, tracing the delicate contours.

She moved closer and tilted back her head, her lips parted to receive his kiss. Swiftly he drew her against him, and his mouth claimed hers with fierce hunger that sent a warm rush of sensation coursing through her.

She clung to him, her breath quickening, as she awaited the moment when he would lift her in his arms and carry her to the bed. But he freed himself and stood looking down at her intently, as if he were trying to impress every detail of her face upon his memory. When he spoke at last, his brusque tone made her insides tighten with apprehension. "Get dressed, Sybilla."

She drew her breath in sharply, bewildered by his words, and even more, by the harshness of his voice.

"I'm taking you ashore," he went on. "Pack your trunk, and don't waste any time about it."

Sybilla could scarcely believe that he was serious. She should have grown used to his abrupt changes of mood, but this was too much.

Somehow she mastered her quick flare of resentment. "Are we going to stay on Tortuga overnight?" she asked quietly.

"You're staying."

She looked up at him in shocked disbelief. "You can't mean to leave me alone there, among all those lawless men."

He smiled faintly. "That's not quite fair," he corrected her. "We buccaneers have a code of our own. Besides, I'm not going to abandon you on the waterfront, if that's what you're afraid of."

She felt a slight stir of hope and her lips parted in a tentative smile. Surely she had misunderstood him. He wasn't going to leave her and go sailing off.

"I'm placing you under the protection of Bertrand d'Ogeron, the governor of Tortuga," he went on. "He represents the French West India Company here." Although Gavin spoke in an impersonal tone, she sensed that he was holding his deeper emotions in check. "The governor and I have known each other for some time."

A corner of his mouth went up in a slight smile. "D'Ogeron was a privateer captain, himself, before he took to more peaceable ways. He still feels a certain kinship with the men of the Brotherhood of the Coast. You'll be perfectly safe and comfortable as a guest in his home."

"And it won't be for long, will it?" Her eyes pleaded for reassurance. "Only until you've finished enlisting seamen for your new ships."

Gavin's lips tightened and she could see that he was trying to repress his impatience. "Jeremy Randall will stay behind, to choose the rest of the recruits," he said.

"Then it's true—you are going to sail off and leave me." She could scarcely force the words out.

"I'll set sail on the *San Bartolomé,* on the evening tide. And Abiathar'll follow, aboard the *Condor.*"

Only an hour before, when he'd returned to the galleon,

he'd been eager to make love to her. Now he was going off without her. What had happened to change him so?

Unable to face such a prospect, she managed to clutch at a faint hope. Gavin wasn't himself, yet. He was still badly shaken, struggling to free himself from the private hell of his past, haunted by the memories of his years of suffering.

What a fearful experience it must have been for such a man, proud and arrogant as he was, to have been forced to submit to the brutality, the torment of slavery. No doubt he still bore the scars upon his spirit, even as he did upon his body.

But she would heal him, she told herself with quiet determination. In time her love would drive away the shadows that darkened his spirit. Even now she could make a beginning.

She took his hand and pressed it to her cheek. Her eyes moved toward the bed. "Come and lie beside me," she said softly. He wouldn't have to make love to her, not yet. She would only hold him, soothe him, until he fell asleep in her arms.

He understood, but he shook his head. "If I did that, Sybilla, I'd take you again. And afterward, nothing would be changed. I'd still have to leave you behind."

Although she could not bring herself to go on pleading with him, her eyes spoke for her; all the passion, all the tenderness of her ardent nature were reflected in their golden depths. But still, he held himself aloof.

"At least you can tell me where you mean to go."

"It's better if you don't know."

A growing fear engulfed her. "You're not sailing against the Spanish fleet—not so soon. You don't have your new ships yet, do you? Or enough men?"

"All that will take time. Meanwhile, I have certain other preparations to make. An expedition like this one requires careful planning. There's information that only I can get hold of."

209

She had to force herself to keep silent, to go on listening to his even and impersonal voice. "I don't know how long I'll be gone. But I'll come back as soon as I can. And before I set out to take the treasure fleet, I'll get passage for you and Lance on a merchant ship bound for Boston."

And he expected her to wait patiently here on Tortuga until he was ready to arrange her future—as if she were his chattel, without a will of her own. Outraged pride swept through her, and she could no longer remain silent.

"I won't go without you, Gavin Broderick—not to Boston—not anywhere! And I won't let you leave me in the governor's home, either—while you go sailing off, heaven knows where."

She reached out to grasp at his arm, but he stepped back. "You can't leave me. You mustn't." Her eyes glittered with unshed tears. "Why can't I make you understand? We belong together."

"No, Sybilla." His voice was not unkind, but it remained uncompromising. "There's no place for you in my life. There never can be. I made you no promises. I didn't try to deceive you."

He took her by the shoulders and held her at arm's length. "You're generous and warmhearted. I see now that I never should have told you about those hellish years I spent aboard the *Saragossa*. I saw the pity in your eyes, and heard the tenderness in your voice."

"If that's all you saw, then look again!" Her face was upturned to his, her eyes darkened to deep, burning amber. "I love you, Gavin! I'll love you all my life."

"And suppose you do? Do you really believe that's all that matters? You think you've only to say you love me, and that will blot out the past?" He looked down at her with a rueful smile.

"But what more have I to give you?"

"You've given me far too much already," he said. She heard the harsh regret in his voice, and she felt as if an iron

210

band were tightening around her throat. "You're generous, and passionate. You don't lack courage, either. And Lord knows, you're desirable. No man could see you as you are now, and not hunger to possess you."

He drew a long breath and made a visible effort to bring his feelings under control. "Listen, Sybilla. You've had a rough time of it, these past few years. It's not surprising that you've lost your bearings. But I'm offering you the chance to return to the sheltered, respectable way of life you were meant for. To find a man who will marry you, who'll cherish you and protect you. Who'll give you a life of security, a home where you can raise your children in safety."

"You're only saying all this because you want to be rid of me—and you want to feel noble and self-sacrificing while you're about it!"

"I'm saying it because it's true. Because you deserve so much and I've nothing to offer you."

"Haven't you? Not right now, perhaps—but I can wait."

She was caught up in a rising storm of outraged pride and fierce resentment. Wasn't it enough that he was preparing to leave her behind? Did he expect her to believe that he was doing it for her sake?

"Once you've captured the treasure ships," she went on, "you can provide me with a share of the loot—pieces of eight, bags of them—fine jewels and rich silks and—if that dancer—that Odette—can ask a captain's share for a single night of loving, then surely you owe me as much—"

His hands tightened on her shoulders, biting deep into her flesh. He shook her so violently that she thought her neck would snap. Her hair flew about her face in a blaze of russet fire.

"That's enough! You're not like Odette—or any of those others." Then he mastered his rage, and spoke more softly. "You weren't meant to be a pirate's woman."

"Maybe not. But I was meant to be *your* woman. And I have no choice unless—unless you're willing to give up this

211

plan of yours." She raised her chin and her eyes held his. "I can understand now why you felt you had to strike back at the Spaniards, after what you suffered at their hands. But that's all past. You mustn't throw away the rest of your life in seeking revenge."

"It's my life, to spend—or throw away—as I choose."

She flinched under his words and the hard, impersonal stare that accompanied them. But she refused to admit defeat. She cast about, seeking a way to get through to him.

"Then why not choose decency and honor? Your brother wanted you to take your place in your family's shipping company. You told me so yourself. You could sell the *San Bartolomé,* couldn't you? No doubt any captain on Tortuga would pay well for such a fine ship. And then you could buy back your shares in the business."

He looked at her and his brows went up in surprise. "I'd no idea you had such a practical turn of mind," he said. But he shook his head. "It wouldn't work."

"How can you be sure until you've tried?"

"You think I haven't? After that Dutch captain set us free from the *Saragossa,* I went home. I walked through the streets of the town where I'd grown up. I slept in my old room, with the samplers on the wall. I went down to the wharf, and watched the ships putting out to sea. I tried to feign interest when Nathaniel went over the ledgers with me and told me how the profits had increased while I'd been away.

"It was my duty to take my place in the business, that's what he said. To do my part to carry on the tradition my father had begun. Duty has always played a great part in my brother's view of life." Gavin shook his head slowly. His eyes were bleak. "And all the time, I knew it was no use. I couldn't be a part of that life, not any longer."

Sybilla drew a long, uneven breath, afraid to go on, yet unwilling to give up even now. "Perhaps it was too soon," she said. "You'd only just regained your freedom. And—"

She hesitated for a moment. "You went back alone. But you wouldn't be alone this time. I'd be with you."

She thought she saw a slight flicker of uncertainty in the depths of his eyes, and she went on speaking quickly. "You wouldn't have to stay ashore, like your brother. I know you were not meant for that kind of life. But surely you could find enough of a challenge, if you sailed as master of one of your family's merchant ships. And I'd go with you—"

"It's no good, Sybilla! I don't want to belong to you—to any woman, not that way."

She stiffened as if he'd struck her. She'd offered him her love, her whole future, and he'd refused it. And she couldn't even summon up the anger that might reconcile her to their coming separation.

"Get dressed. We're going ashore," he said, starting for the door. "I'll wait for you on deck." He started for the door.

What had become of her pride? Why couldn't she berate him, shout at him that she wanted him to put her ashore? And sail his ships against the Spanish fleet—or straight to hell for all she cared.

She drew in her breath, her body shaking with the force of her tumultuous feelings. But the words would not come. Instead she was running to him, across the length of the cabin. She flung herself against him and wrapped her arms around him.

"I won't let you go sailing off without me!" she cried. "If you have the right to choose your way of life, so have I. If I want to be a pirate's woman, that's what I'll be. And I won't look back, ever—or blame you for whatever may happen to me."

His eyes searched her face, but he made no response. Then, drawing away from her clinging arms, he strode out of the cabin.

A sense of loss, of utter desolation, swept through her. Somehow she managed to make her way to the velvet-padded seat beneath the window. She sank down, resting her head against the gilded sill.

She tried to find what consolation she could by reminding herself that Gavin would keep his promise about Lance, that he would find a way to get her brother out of Hobart's reach. Once in Boston, her brother would be safe from danger. He would make a new life for himself there, and provide for her.

She started as she heard Gavin calling out. "Lower the longboat."

Gavin was getting ready to leave her, and she dared not let herself think of a future without him. She told herself that she should have already put on a dress that would be suitable for going ashore, and packed her trunk. He would be furious when he returned to find her sitting here, still in her nightgown. She tried to will herself to rise, but it was useless. She was numb inside.

Then she heard him give another command. "Prepare to weigh anchor!"

Her head jerked up, and her lips parted. She sprang up from the window seat. Had she imagined those words? No, she had heard Gavin's voice, resonant and powerful, shouting the order to the crew.

Hope stirred inside her and grew swiftly, spreading through her whole body. From the deck came the slap of feet on the scoured planks, the volley of commands that sent the sailors scurrying up into the rigging. Then she heard the creak of the capstan and the slow rattle of the heavy iron links as the anchor chain was drawn up through the hawser. Her heart began to beat erratically, so that she could scarcely draw a deep breath.

A seaman called out, "Anchor's aweigh, sir!"

And Gavin's voice again. "Man the braces. Look lively there!"

The carpeted floor of the cabin canted sharply under Sybilla's feet, and she reached out to steady herself, clutching at the broad, carved sill.

"Loose tops'ls!"

The yards creaked and the *San Bartolomé* heeled away from the speckled mound that was Tortuga. The great galleon paid off into the wind. From now on, she would need a steady breeze to carry her across the seas, for no slaves would ever be chained to the oars of any vessel commanded by Gavin Broderick.

Sybilla heard the thunder of spreading canvas high overhead. The harsh grating of the spars, the thrum of the rigging. Peering out into the early morning light, she could see that the rocky walls surrounding the harbor were fading into the rosy mist.

But where was the *San Bartolomé* bound?

She would not question Gavin, not yet. Right now it didn't matter to her where they were heading. It was enough that she was with him. She remained standing at the window, her heart lifting as she watched the ship head for the jade green waters of the open sea.

A pirate's woman.

All at once the words echoed in her mind, blending with the sounds of wind and waves, becoming one with them. Only a few months ago, the mere thought of such a future would have been shocking to her. But she was no longer the same girl who had stood on the dock back in Montego Bay, who had bristled with outrage under the appraising glance from the tall, gray-eyed stranger in his plumed hat and scarlet sash.

She heard the cabin door swing open and she turned to face Gavin. What had made him change his mind? There was so much that needed to be said. But she could only ask, "What about Abiathar? The *Condor* was to set sail along with—"

"I've sent a message to him. He'll make my explanations to d'Ogeron and follow aboard the *Condor* on the evening tide."

His eyes moved over her, and he shook his head. "You chose to disregard my orders, I see." He spoke with mock

215

severity. "Perhaps you don't realize that on shipboard, a captain may mete out whatever punishment he chooses."

"Am I to scour the deck? Or climb up the rigging and stand watch?" He did not answer. He could not tear his gaze away from her. The glow of the morning sunlight, slanting in through the window, touched the white mounds of her breasts, the curve of her hips beneath the black lace web that sheathed her body.

But it wasn't enough. She wanted the reassurance of his embrace, the warmth of his fingers, caressing her, and the look she gave him, from under her lashes, told him of her need. She took a step toward him, her pulses quickening. She waited for him to lift her, to cradle her against his chest as he carried her to the bed.

Instead, he went past her to the small bedside table, filled the wash basin, and began to scrub himself vigorously.

"As I recall, you have a powerful dislike for the smell of woodsmoke." His mouth curved in a smile.

Her cheeks burned at the memory. "That was only because I thought you and Odette—"

His smile deepened. "You flatter me, my love. What made you so sure that, with all those hot-blooded lads who watched her dancing in the firelight out there on the beach, I'd be her choice for the night?"

He went on sloshing himself with water, until the drops glistened on the dark mat of hair on his chest and ran down his arms. "I wasn't the only captain ashore on Tortuga last night. There were a dozen others, who'd come back with enough loot to pay generously for her favors."

Sybilla glared at him. Why wouldn't he reassure her, by telling her that even if Odette had offered herself, he'd have refused? He began soaping the cloth again, slowly, deliberately, watching her all the while.

Unable to hold back any longer, she seized his arm. "That's enough washing for now!"

"You're quite sure? I wouldn't wish to offend your delicate sensibilities."

His familiar, teasing look sent her spirits soaring. Somehow he had succeeded in banishing his memories of the past. Perhaps the rise and fall of the deck beneath his feet, the white foam surging beneath the bow as the galleon ran before the wind, the billowing of the sails overhead, had been enough to restore him.

He moved closer, and she caught the clean, male scent of his body. A sensuous need moved deep inside her, warm and sweet as molten honey. She seized the cloth from his hand and tossed it into the basin. Then she was holding him to her.

"Your gown—it'll get wet."

"I don't care."

She moved her breasts against the hardness of his chest, stroked her nipples over the damp, curling hair, savoring the sensation. When she began tugging at his arm, he did not resist any longer. Together they landed on the wide, soft bed. And now he was kissing her, his lips brushing her cheek, the angle of her jaw, the line of her throat.

He raised himself only long enough to pull off his boots and breeches and toss them aside. She stroked his shoulders, then drew her fingers lightly down along his back.

"You are a shameless wench, aren't you?"

"And who made me so?" Her fingers moved lower, to caress the sensitive place at the base of his spine.

Her touch sent a hot rush of desire stabbing deep into his loins. Swiftly he eased her down on the wide bed. Lord, but she was beautiful, with the damp lace clinging to every enticing curve and hollow of her body.

His eyes lingered on the outline of a butterfly close to one of her rosy nipples. Then he bent his head and began tracing the intricate design with the tip of his tongue. He heard her cry of pleasure, and it stirred him to even greater urgency.

He drew the nipple into his mouth, and suckled at it. The

sensation of the hardening peak between his lips sent a surge of liquid fire coursing through him. He had to pause for a moment, to raise his head and take a deep, steadying breath.

Then his lips continued their eager journey, moving down to her belly, and lower still, to the russet triangle of her womanhood. He pressed his burning cheek against the curve of her thigh.

With a swift, impatient gesture, he pulled the skirt up around her waist. His tongue traced a line along the soft flesh. She made a sound of protest, and he paused.

"I've taught you much—but not all," he said, his voice soft and husky.

His fingers parted her and she caught her breath as his tongue flicked at the peak of her femininity. She gave a soft cry and he raised his head slightly. His fingers slid away and rested on the satin flatness of her belly. "There's more to learn—if you're willing."

She waited for him to go on, but he did not move. "Tell me," he whispered.

"Gavin—"

"Say it."

She caught the challenge. "Teach me," she said, her voice unsteady.

He was parting her again, to find the wellspring of her desire. Wave after wave of scalding sensation flooded her, moving through every nerve of her body. Scarcely aware of what she did, she raised her hips as if to deepen the intensity of her response.

Then, with one swift movement, he pulled himself up and looked into her face. Her head was flung back, and her eyes had darkened to blazing amber. She locked her legs around him, her thighs gripping his lean hips, drawing him deeper, and deeper still, to the core of her being.

She welcomed the fierce urgency that sent him thrusting into her, withdrawing, moving with long, lingering strokes. He slid his hands under her and gripped her buttocks, lifting her from the bed, supporting her with his steely strength, carrying her with him to the dizzying peak of fulfillment.

Later, as the midmorning light flooded the cabin, Sybilla lay with her body curved against his, her round bottom burrowing into his loins, his arm beneath her shoulders. He brushed the glowing auburn waves of her hair back from her cheek and kissed her lightly. She made a sound of drowsy contentment and moved against him.

"Keep on that way and I may never leave this bed." But even as he spoke he raised himself, resting his weight on one arm.

"The wind's shifted," he said. "I must give the order to shorten sail and change course a few points."

She sat up, resting against the pillows, her hair falling over her shoulders. "Are we bound for the Isle of Pines?"

"I'll see to that as soon as it's possible," he told her, with a slight edge of impatience to his voice. "Meanwhile, I'd suppose your brother's in no immediate danger."

"But—you were in such haste to set me ashore on Tortuga, and get under sail."

"And I am, still. Right now, we're bound for Cartegena, my love."

"Cartegena? But that's a Spanish port, isn't it?"

"It's one of the richest ports in all of South America," he told her. "Your childhood hero, Sir Francis Drake, captured it nearly a century ago, and brought back a treasure trove that awed Queen Bess herself."

Sybilla's lips parted and she steadied herself with an effort. "You don't mean to follow his example—not with only this ship and the *Condor,* surely."

"It's a tempting prospect, but I mean to take a far greater prize." Then, sensing her uneasiness, he added, "There'll be little danger in my visit to Cartegena, love. It'll only be—a kind of scouting expedition. To gather information I must

219

have for the attack on the treasure fleet."

Sybilla could no longer conceal her fear. "But you can't! You mustn't! How can you possibly hope to pass yourself off to the officials in Cartegena as Don Alfonso? Suppose he is known there?"

"I've no such plans," he said impatiently.

"Then how—"

"There are two entrances to the harbor," he explained. "Boca Grande and Boca Chica. And near Boca Chica, there's a small island, with a stretch of deep swamp. And an inlet deep enough to provide anchorage for both my ships. I'll meet Abiathar there, and leave the galleon moored well out of sight."

"And then?"

"Then I'll take command of the *Condor* again, and we'll sail her into Boca Grande. Those merchants in Cartegena will be only too pleased to do a bit of business with us."

Illegal business, she thought.

She tensed with apprehension, but she knew she must not interfere. She raised her lips for his kiss, then lay back and watched him dress. He gave her a brief smile as he left the cabin.

It was too late for second thoughts now, she told herself. She had joined her future with Gavin's of her own free will. Wherever he led she must follow without question or protest. Now she was starting to understand what it meant to be a pirate's woman.

Chapter Seventeen

The high-wheeled open carriage left the maze of narrow streets leading from Havana harbor to the outskirts of the city and drew up before a long, two-storied building on the Calle Colon. The moonlight gleamed on the smooth white facade, and on the intricate iron grillwork that shielded the deep-set windows.

Lance Thornton alighted and walked to the heavy teak door. The sound of the knocker echoed down the length of the street. After a brief wait, he found himself looking up at a tall, powerfully-built black manservant clad in green and gold livery and an intricately wrapped silk turban that made him appear even taller.

"How may I serve you, señor?" He spoke politely but his muscular body still blocked the half-open doorway.

"I was told that I should find Mr. Nicholas Hobart here," Lance said. "Thornton's my name."

The doorkeeper of the Casa de las Sirenas stood aside, and Lance entered the wide patio, which was lit by torches set in iron sconces. Their leaping flames illuminated a fountain of rose-colored marble, with the carved figures of three amply proportioned nude females twined about the base. Moon-silvered palms rustled in the evening breeze, and Lance breathed the heady fragrance of the bougainvillea blossoms

221

that cascaded over the high stone walls.

"El Señor Hobart has already arrived," the doorkeeper told Lance as he led the way across the patio. Lance followed him up an outside stairway to the broad gallery that ran along the second floor, and then into a large, candle-lit chamber, decorated in the Moorish fashion with silk-covered divans and small tables inlaid with ivory.

Nothing Lance had seen during his drive from the nearby waterfront had prepared him for such magnificence. Like most English visitors coming to Havana for the first time, he was unfamiliar with the custom of having shops, warehouses, private homes and establishments such as the Casa de las Sirenas mingled together in one district.

And after the weeks of living in a thatch hut on the Isle of Pines, eating scorched boar meat cooked over an open fire, and sleeping in a rope hammock, he needed time to adjust to these lavish surroundings. For a moment he wondered if this was all part of some vivid, erotic dream.

On one side of the candle-lit chamber, two girls were dancing to the primitive beat of drums and the wail of reed flutes. Lance felt a tingling in the pit of his stomach.

Some of the patrons—Cuban planters, wealthy merchants, and a few military officers—strolled about or took their ease on the divans while others chose the seclusion of the small alcoves at the sides of the chamber.

A few lingered to sample the delicacies spread on a long table; ornate silver trays and bowls held a rich and varied selection—doves in cream sauce, succulent meat pastries, baked crayfish, and brightly colored mounds of tropical fruit. Liveried servants kept the wine goblets filled to the brim.

A tall, slender woman in her forties, her lacquer-smooth black hair arranged in a high, elaborate coiffure fastened with jeweled combs, moved among the men, stopping from time to time to exchange a few words. Her body was sheathed in black silk, glittering with jet beads. From her air of quiet authority Lance decided that she must be the madam of the establishment.

Lance's mouth went dry and the blood beat at his temples. All these weeks he had lived a celibate life, avoiding the company of the two bedraggled sluts who were kept in a dirty, evil-smelling hut on the offshore island to serve the needs of Hobart's hired ruffians. He had not been tempted by the women, and he had thought it prudent to keep aloof from the men under his command, in order to maintain his control over them.

Now his senses were stirred at the sight of these lithe, seductive young girls swaying and whirling before him. Their skirts of gold mesh were slit to the waist; as they arched backward, their satin flesh drew taut over their flat bellies. The nipples of their firm, pointed breasts had been rouged to a deep crimson.

A stout, swarthy Cuban motioned to the tall, black-haired woman. "There's a fine specimen," Lance heard him say, and he pointed upward. "I've a mind to try her, Dona Caterina."

The woman tilted back her head, and looked up. "A discerning choice," she agreed, her painted mouth curving in a slight smile. "You'll find our lovely Graciela is most skilled and eager to please, señor."

Lance, his curiosity aroused, raised his eyes, then drew his breath in sharply. The Cuban gentleman was gesturing at a cage—one of several that hung suspended from the ceiling.

The candlelight flickered over the tall, olive-skinned young girl who peered out through the gilt bars. At a nod from the black-haired woman, the cage began to descend on its heavy chain. When it reached the marble floor, the girl stepped out; the Cuban gentleman led her through an archway and out into the darkness of the gallery.

Lance's gaze quickly went back to the cages. They had been carefully placed to catch the blazing light from the gilded chandeliers. As he looked more closely, he saw that the girls inside the cages were chosen not only for their lush, enticing beauty, but also for the variety of their coloring.

An onyx-eyed beauty, with coffee-colored skin, reclined in one of the cages. Her long slender neck was encircled with a gold collar. The curve of her hip and the flatness of her belly were outlined by a skirt of tangerine-colored silk. A sheaf of flame-colored feathers was fastened in her dark, close-cropped hair.

Close by, in another cage, a girl with a mass of light brown curls pursed her full red lips and ran her hands down along her thighs. She leaned forward so that the men below might get a better view of the large, firm breasts that swelled invitingly under her azure robe.

His gaze shifted to a pale, petite beauty, who might have come from his own native Somerset. She gazed through the bars of her cage with a dazed look in her violet eyes, and her honey-blonde hair fell about her like a silken cape. Her short tunic of cream-colored silk, fastened at the shoulder by a glittering amethyst, left one of her pink-tipped breasts bared.

"This way, señor, if you please." The doorkeeper's deep voice startled Lance out of his bemused state, and he followed the man across the spacious chamber toward one of the alcoves.

Nicholas Hobart, who had been watching Lance since he had come in, greeted him with a smile, but he did not rise from the low divan.

"A most charming aviary, isn't it?" he asked, nodding his head in the direction of the cages. "Doña Caterina tries to provide for every sort of taste."

"So I noticed."

"I wasn't speaking of appearances only," Hobart went on. "Those lovely creatures have been trained to please a man in any way he desires. Some of the patrons are rather jaded—they seek unusual diversions, if you take my meaning."

Lance cleared his throat and flushed slightly. Hobart glanced at him with amusement. No doubt the young man's experiences had been limited to a tumble under a hedge with the pretty daughter of one of his family's tenants, and more recently, in Montego Bay, an hour's release with one of the doxies who frequented the waterfront taverns.

Lance's hazel eyes hardened. "I assumed that you sent for me so that we might talk business, Mr. Hobart." His tanned skin drew tight over his cheekbones. "You led me to believe that I was to lead only a single expedition between the Isle of Pines and Santiago. And after that, I might return to Jamaica, but instead—"

Hobart held up a cautioning hand. "Shut the doors, if you please. There's no need to share our business with every passerby."

Lance obeyed, and Hobart motioned him to the divan across from his own. The low table between them held a large, silver bowl, with a ladle, and beside it a pair of tall goblets.

"This is a tasty concoction," said his host. "It's made of coconut milk, laced with brandy and rum and flavored with a few spices. I find it much to my liking, but if you'd prefer something else, Doña Caterina keeps her cellar stocked with an excellent selection."

"This'll do," Lance interrupted brusquely. Hobart was not disturbed by the curt response; he had been prepared for an outburst of indignation from the young man. He filled one of the goblets and handed it to Lance, who sipped the potent mixture, scarcely tasting it. But a warm glow spread through his veins, and he relaxed slightly.

"I see no need to conduct business in some dreary mercantile office—not when I come to Havana. And since you've been hard at work all this time, no doubt you'll welcome a night of relaxation in more civilized surroundings. And with an obliging young female for company. I'm sure those well-used sluts on the island have little appeal for a gentleman of your fastidious tastes."

But Lance brushed aside his employer's suggestive remarks. "How long am I to remain on the Isle of Pines?" he

225

demanded. "You said that I would earn a substantial sum for smuggling a single cargo into Santiago, but—"

"An unfortunate choice of words, Thornton. Here in Cuba, I prefer to think of myself as a trader. I make my profit by providing my customers with whatever commodities are in short supply. In this sort of enterprise, I can't be sure when my merchandise may arrive. Then there are the local officials, a greedy lot, to be paid to look the other way—and the uncertainties of wind and tide—"

"That's as may be," Lance interrupted. "What I want to know is how long you mean to keep me out there." He spoke with a touch of arrogance that set Hobart's teeth on edge.

"You will remain on the Isle of Pines as long as I consider it necessary."

Lance glared at his employer across the small table. "Perhaps you're forgetting that I have responsibilities of my own, back in Jamaica," he said. "I left my sister at Acacia Hall."

"In her aunt's care," Hobart reminded him. "There's no need to concern yourself about Mistress Sybilla."

"Have you brought a letter from her, at least?" Lance asked.

"I doubt your sister has much time for writing letters these days."

"Why not?" Lance drained his goblet and set it down.

"Mistress Sybilla is the most sought-after young lady back in Jamaica. Surely that shouldn't surprise you."

A troubled look crossed Lance's face. "Even so, it's not at all like Sybilla to neglect writing to me."

"The fact is, she had no idea I was coming here to meet you." Hobart managed to conceal his growing impatience. He had decided, before he'd sent for Lance, that it would be a mistake to tell him Sybilla had been carried off by the captain of the *San Bartolomé*. He'd keep that piece of information to himself for the present.

"Let us get our business out of the way," he said, refilling

226

Lance's goblet. Although the potent drink was gradually taking effect, Lance gave a detailed, accurate account of his trips between the Isle of Pines and the small port of Santiago. Here the illicit cargoes were loaded onto mules and carried off, to be sold to the local planters. Hobart nodded from time to time, but did not interrupt.

The young man had carried out his duties efficiently, Hobart thought. And he would go on doing so, as long as his services were needed. Not only had Hobart made an excellent profit from these last three smuggling expeditions, but Lance had proved himself to be scrupulously honest in his dealings with his employer.

Hobart already had checked with the Cuban merchants who handled his goods, and he had assured himself that Lance Thornton had held none of these valuable commodities back to sell on the side for his own profit. Over the years, Hobart had found few subordinates who had proved daring enough to handle this risky trade and had not tried to cheat him.

Now that Lance had been freed from the boredom of the warehouse in Montego Bay, he'd proved extremely useful. But if he were to learn that Sybilla had been ravished and abducted by the Spanish captain, the chivalrous young idiot would go running off in search of her.

"Mr. Hobart, I've carried out your orders—I've served you well. And not without placing myself in some danger, you'll admit."

Hobart's heavy lips twisted in a semblance of a smile. "You've made three trips between the Isle of Pines and Santiago. And you'll make another, within the fortnight. I'm expecting a valuable shipment of young coffee plants, all the way from Africa. I have a customer, a planter with an estate near Santiago, in the Sierra Maestra, who hopes to get such a crop to thrive in this climate. He's prepared to pay generously for the cargo."

Lance set down his goblet with such force that the table

shook. "See here, Mr. Hobart, we made an agreement. You gave me your word—"

"Surely you're not going to quibble over that," Hobart said. "Not when you stand to make a fortune by going on as you have."

"It'll be of little use to me, if I'm caught and thrown into a Cuban dungeon."

"There are risks in the trade, I won't deny it," Hobart interrupted. "But for a young man of your adventurous disposition—what do they amount to?" He shrugged, and his small eyes gleamed with anticipation. He paused and leaned forward, savoring the prospect of putting the arrogant young whelp in his place. "They are scarcely worth mentioning—compared with the reckless enterprise that sent you fleeing from England, a step ahead of the king's troopers."

Lance stared at Hobart in shocked disbelief. The color drained from his face, and his fingers tightened on the stem of his goblet.

"You're not likely to be arrested by the Cuban officials, for a little illegal trading, so long as I go on greasing the right palms." Hobart's voice was silky-smooth, but Lance heard the threat behind his words. "But as for treason—now that's far more serious. It could lead to the gallows—or to a term of slavery in the canefields."

"You have no proof—you can't have! I don't know where you heard this slanderous talk against me, but—"

"Spare me your indignation," Hobart said. "At least you escaped with a whole skin—which is more than can be said for the unfortunate young Monmouth. Just remember that you'll be a damn sight better off working for me than you'd be if the British authorities in Jamaica were to learn that you'd taken up arms against His Majesty." Hobart shook his head slowly. "You're young and strong, but I fear you wouldn't last long, swinging a machete out there under the blazing sun, or toiling in one of the mills. And think of the disgrace you'd bring on the Thornton name."

228

Lance turned away quickly but not before Hobart caught the look of desperation in his lean face. He started to get up, his eyes fixed on the door, as if seeking a means of immediate escape.

"There's no reason to panic. No one will ever hear of your youthful indiscretion—so long as you decide to be sensible."

"My uncle didn't betray me," Lance muttered. "I know he didn't."

That damned pride, again, Hobart thought. How he hated the English gentry and all they stood for. "I have many ways of gathering information about our fine Jamaica planters—and their ladies. One never knows when such knowledge may prove useful." He sipped his drink and patted his thick lips with his handkerchief. Then he chuckled softly.

"Take Madeleine, for instance. She's riding high now. Mistress of Acacia Hall, flaunting her French gowns and those fine jewels your uncle gave her."

"What has she to do with—what do you know of her?" Lance was momentarily distracted from his own plight, as Hobart had intended he should be.

"More than she imagines." Hobart gave a short bark of laughter. "No doubt your late uncle would have been dismayed to learn the truth about his bride. That blond charmer first arrived in the Indies with a down-at-the-heels troupe of strolling players who performed in shabby taverns from Barbados to Maracaibo. And she didn't hesitate to peddle her favors in the rooms upstairs, to earn a bit extra." He shrugged. "But that was long before she had the good luck to meet your uncle."

Lance's voice shook with anger. "And knowing that, you let me go off and leave my sister with her—"

"You must learn to master your hot temper." Hobart refilled Lance's goblet. "Mistress Sybilla has nothing to fear from Madeleine now." That was true enough, he added to himself. "As for you, so long as you go on in my service, you'll do well enough."

"How long do you mean to keep me on the Isle of Pines?"

"As long as I find it profitable. But don't forget that you stand to make a good profit for yourself."

"I've not seen a farthing, yet," Lance reminded him.

"You'd not sleep easy, if you had to guard your earnings from those jailbirds and gutter rats you live among, out there on the island. They'd cut your throat for a shilling. But as soon as you return to Jamaica, you'll find a handsome sum on deposit with Richard Dawkins. He's a goldsmith in Montego Bay, and my private banker. There'll be five hundred pounds for you, and maybe more. Enough to buy a decent parcel of land and get yourself established on your own plantation."

It was an impressive sum, indeed, enough to keep Lance Thornton reasonably satisfied, while he remained on the Isle of Pines. Not that Lance was likely to leave his present employment, knowing the risk he'd be taking. But the mention of the five hundred pounds would give the young man an added incentive to go on working with even greater zeal.

Hearing a knock on the louvered door of the alcove, Hobart swore softly. "Who the devil's that?" He opened the door and saw a small black boy in livery and turban looking up at him. "This gentleman says he must speak to you at once."

A tall, olive-skinned man stepped forward, and made a sweeping bow. "A thousand pardons for this intrusion," he said, not at all perturbed by Hobart's angry stare. "Permit me to introduce myself, Monsieur. I am Philippe Antoine Demarais at your service."

"I gave orders that I did not wish to be disturbed," said Hobart.

"My message will not wait," Demarais told him calmly. He was dressed like a fop, with a silk cravat, a long, embroidered vest, breeches of pearl gray satin, and a coat with deep cuffs, trimmed with silver lace. A light cloak fell gracefully about his shoulders. He might have been a courtier newly arrived from Versailles. But his lean, sharp-featured face, with its aquiline nose and alert black eyes belied Hobart's first impression.

"And who is this message from?" Hobart asked.

The Frenchman paused, resting a gauntleted hand lightly on the guard of his sheathed rapier. "The captain of the *Condor*."

Hobart felt a swift surge of triumph, as he realized that his luck had not failed him. Broderick had managed to escape and was champing at the bit, as eager as he was to get on their joint venture.

"Take a seat," Hobart said. But Demarais remained where he stood, his black eyes resting on Lance.

"The captain's message concerns a private matter."

"Mr. Thornton and I have completed our business," Hobart told him. And to Lance, "You must sample those pleasures we spoke of. You need not concern yourself with the cost—I'll settle your reckoning."

Lance got to his feet, but he did not respond at once to his employer's dismissal. "When you get back to Jamaica, I hope you will visit Acacia Hall and speak with—" He broke off, obviously reluctant to mention his sister's name in these surroundings.

Always the highborn gentleman, Hobart thought. But he, himself, was not burdened with any such scruples. "I shall tell Mistress Sybilla that you asked to be remembered to her. No doubt you'll hear from her soon."

Lance's mouth tightened and his hazel eyes narrowed with resentment. He and that sister of his—both filled with the devil's own pride, and quick to take offense. Lance turned on his heel and strode from the alcove, closing the doors with such force that they shook on their hinges.

"That young gentleman—Thornton," the Frenchman began.

"What about him?" Hobart was impatient to hear

231

Broderick's message.

Demarais seated himself on the divan, and crossed one booted leg over the other. "He is related, perhaps, to the fair Mistress Sybilla?"

Hobart gave him a hard, searching look. "You know the lady?"

"Alas, I've not had the pleasure."

"But you recognize her name."

"I heard talk of her, back in Tortuga. That's where I was, when Captain Broderick persuaded me to enlist in his service. He sent me to Jamaica, but as you'd already gone, I followed you here."

"But about Sybilla—Mistress Thornton. Do you know where she is now?"

Demarais looked at Hobart with some curiosity. "I heard some sailors from the *San Bartolomé* speaking about the lady. I was in a tavern on the waterfront in Tortuga. The men were in their cups, you understand."

Hobart forced himself to speak in an offhand way. "Did you hear anything of her whereabouts?"

"She was aboard the galleon, with Captain Broderick. He was born under a fortunate star. First he captures the *San Bartolomé,* against overwhelming odds. Then he takes possession of the cargo—and the young lady, as well." Scalding fury rose inside Hobart. He felt as if his lace-trimmed cravat were tightening—as if he might strangle.

"A beauty, from what I heard," Demarais went on, his eyes brightening with enthusiasm. "Hair like silken fire, and the golden eyes of a tigress. Though it would seem that Broderick had no need to tame her." He shrugged. *"Eh bien!* It's likely that many a lovely lady has been smitten by our dashing captain."

Beads of sweat sprang out on Hobart's forehead. He fumbled for his handkerchief with unsteady fingers, then wiped his forehead on his sleeve instead. "You bear an important message," he managed to say. "Let's hear it."

"I am to tell you that the captain is now in command of two ships, the galleon, and his own frigate, the *Condor*."

"His sailors told me as much, when they rescued me after the battle." But they had denied seeing Broderick, after they had recaptured the galleon. They had disclaimed all knowledge of his whereabouts. And those same sailors—Broderick's men—had said that Sybilla had been ravished and carried off by Don Alfonso. The lying bastards had been under orders from Broderick to mislead him deliberately. To throw him off the scent while their captain went off with Sybilla.

All at once, the pieces began to fall into place. Broderick had wanted Sybilla Thornton from that first day, when he'd seen her on the dock at Montego Bay. He'd insisted on driving her to Acacia Hall, leaving Hobart to talk business with Abiathar Pascoe.

And how many times had Broderick and Sybilla met after that? Was it possible that, even back there in Jamaica, while he was trying to persuade her to marry him, the little strumpet had already given herself to Broderick?

He realized that the Frenchman was eyeing him curiously. "As you say, Broderick's a lucky devil, indeed." His voice was hoarse, and he had to take a drink before he could go on. "As for me, I prefer to seek my pleasures with Doña Caterina's girls."

"I'll not keep you, then," the Frenchman said. "Captain Broderick says he's prepared to go ahead with the expedition as planned. You are to deliver the six new ships to the pre-arranged destination, by the date you both agreed upon—no later. They are to be fully victualed and armed for battle. It is of the greatest importance that there shall be no delay. Once the treasure fleet sets sail from Porto Bello, a few days can mean the difference between success and failure."

Hobart nodded. "Tell Captain Broderick I'll keep my side of the bargain. His ships will be delivered to him on time. And may fortune go with him."

The Frenchman rose, bowed, and took his leave. Hobart watched him stride through the salon and disappear through one of the arches leading to the gallery.

His thick fingers gripped the edge of the table as he struggled to control the hot flood of jealousy that threatened to drown all vestige of reason. Sybilla had played the gently reared young virgin—only to give herself to Broderick, like any dockside trollop.

She'd pay for that—she and her damned pirate. He'd have Broderick killed and he'd order Sybilla to be brought to him. There were plenty of men on Tortuga who'd do his bidding for a price. Or he might find a way to betray Broderick to the Spaniards, who would be only too willing to get their hands on the man who had wreaked such havoc with their ships.

But even as the incoherent thoughts went through his mind, a glimmer of reason remained. This was not the time to take revenge on Broderick. Later, after he had his share of the booty in his hands, he'd destroy the captain. And as for Sybilla . . .

He became aware of the pounding of the drums and the intricate, sensuous music of the flutes. He fixed his eyes on the dancing girls and saw that their gyrations were slower now. Each gesture, each movement stirred his senses. One of the girls bent her body backward until her ripe young breasts were pointed at the ceiling. The other dropped to the marble floor with one long, rippling movement; she lay stretched out on her back, her knees bent, her thighs parted. She arched her loins, then lowered them again.

His need for revenge, his long-thwarted hunger for Sybilla, seized at his vitals. If he had her here now, he'd throw her down on the floor and take her, in full view of every man in the room. But she was still out of reach.

He motioned to Doña Caterina. She came to him, and he gestured in the direction of the cage that held the violet-eyed blonde girl in the cream-colored tunic. "That one," he said, his voice thick and unsteady.

"Ah, yes. Lovely, is she not, señor?" Her painted lips curved slightly. "She has never known the touch of a man, however. She has much to learn. . . ."

"I'll have her."

The price would be high, but Hobart didn't care. He watched as the cage descended and the girl was led forth. The fear in her wide violet eyes acted on him as a stimulant.

He could scarcely wait until they were together in the dimly lit, private bedchamber. He threw her down on the bed, and she stared at him, stunned by the cold fury in his face. She tried to draw away, but he caught her and pinned her down with his weight. He began to knead her small, pointed breasts.

"You and your touch-me-not airs—this was what you wanted all along, wasn't it? You couldn't wait to lie with him, could you?"

He pushed the short skirt of her silk tunic up around her waist. Then he fumbled with his breeches. She cried out and his tongue stifled her wordless plea. He grasped her hips, his fingers digging into her soft flesh. He took her with swift violence.

And all the while, his hoarse voice went on, accusing her, reviling her—and calling her by another woman's name. . . .

Chapter Eighteen

"As soon as the sun comes up, you'll be able to catch a glimpse of the coastline of New Granada," Gavin told her. The deck of the *San Bartolomé* was nearly deserted in the predawn hours, except for the helmsman who stood at the wheel and a couple of seaman on watch in the rigging overhead.

"Won't you change your mind and take me with you when you go into Cartegena?" Sybilla's face was upturned to his, her eyes fixed on the strong jutting lines of his profile, highlighted by the dim glow of the lantern that swung overhead.

"Not a chance, my love," he said.

When the ship had lain at anchor in the harbor at Tortuga, Sybilla had told Gavin that she only wanted to remain with him, that she was ready to follow his orders without question or complaint. And back then she had been sure she meant every word. Then, after they had set sail, she had forgotten everything else. Caught up in the wonder of their loving, she had managed to shut out the past, the future, to lose herself in each moment of shared delight. For her, the brief voyage from Tortuga to the shores of New Granada had seemed an enchanted idyll.

But the idyll had ended only a few hours ago, when she

had awakened alone in the darkness. Even the steady rise and fall of the ship had not been enough to lull her back to sleep again.

She had dressed quickly and left the cabin in search of Gavin, and she had found him on the foredeck, clad in his full-sleeved white shirt and breeches. He stood leaning his folded arms on the broad rail, staring out into the blackness where sea and sky seemed to merge into one.

She had seen that he was lost in his own thoughts, and for a moment she had hesitated to speak. Then she put a hand on his shoulder, and he turned to look down at her. His lips curved in a faint smile, but it quickly faded at her mention of Cartegena.

When they had discussed the matter over dinner that evening, he had refused firmly. But she was determined to make him change his mind.

"You said there would be little danger in the city, for you and Abiathar," she reminded him. "Why should there be any greater risk, if I went along?" She saw the stubborn set of his jaw, but she chose to ignore it. "I haven't set foot on land since we left Jamaica."

"If that's all that's bothering you, I can put your mind at ease right now," he said briskly. "You'll be going ashore with the rest of us, as soon as we drop anchor farther up the coast. Costa Verde, that's what we call it, though I doubt you'd find the name on any chart.

"It's mostly jungle and swamp, deserted except for the goats and boar roaming about. Plenty of wood doves and pigeons, and the sea's so thick with fish you can practically catch them with your hands. You won't lack for food, that's certain."

Sybilla drew a quick, impatient breath, but he gave her no chance to interrupt.

"And I'll have the men build a hut for you on the beach, an *ajoupa*. It won't be much like one of the Great Houses back in Jamaica, but it'll keep out the rain and wind."

For him, the question was settled. He put his arm around her waist and drew her closer, but she sensed that his thoughts were already veering away.

"Abiathar should be joining us soon," he said. "We'll get the *San Bartolomé* anchored safely out of sight, and I'll see to it that you're comfortable before I start for Cartegena."

"Comfortable!" She stared at him, hard put to keep her temper. "On a deserted stretch of beach at the edge of a jungle. While you and Abiathar go off to one of the finest ports on the Spanish Main."

He laughed softly, and the sound infuriated her. "The beach at Costa Verde will scarcely be deserted, Sybilla, my love—not with the crews of both my ships camped there."

"But you said that Cartegena had shops, and great mansions. You told me about the ladies who dressed up to go driving about the plaza in their fine carriages every morning—and the fiestas—"

Gavin's smile faded and she saw his jaw tighten. "It's no pleasure trip I'm bent on," he reminded her. "I thought I'd made that plain enough before we left the harbor at Tortuga."

In the glow of the lantern, she saw the muscles of his shoulders and back go taut under his shirt, and she knew he was making an effort to keep his temper. "If we're to find out all we need to know, and quickly, it'll mean a trek into the hills, then a trip up the Magdelena River to the edge of the jungle."

"But why? What is up there?"

"A trading post where they deal in contraband. And information—at a price. If we took you along, you'd only slow us down."

Although she told herself she should have been prepared for his refusal, she had to look away, fearing that her eyes would betray the rebellious anger that smoldered inside her. He spoke as if he had forgotten the loving they'd shared during the voyage from Tortuga. As if it had only been a pleasurable interlude, to be forgotten now that he had more important matters to think about.

She tried to understand what the taking of the treasure fleet meant to him. How long had he been planning this venture, she wondered? Had the idea first taken shape in his mind during those endless, agonizing hours when he'd been chained to the oars of the galley? Or later, perhaps, when he had returned to his home in Boston, only to realize that he could not settle down there again?

Although she had tried to steel herself against the inevitable moment when he would leave her to lead his ships against the Spaniards, the thought of it filled her with terror. No matter how carefully he had planned the venture, he might not succeed. A few months from now, even if he were lucky enough to survive the battle, he could be lying in some Spanish dungeon.

But she must not let him see her fear. "I should think that a fleet carrying such treasure back to Spain would be heavily guarded."

"It will be. Except for one short stretch, when the galleons are making their way to the trade fair at Porto Bello."

She heard the rising excitement in his voice.

"A trade fair," she said. "That sounds lively." But she was careful to keep her tone casual. "Is it anything like the fairs back in Somerset, I wonder?"

Then, remembering that he had probably never seen an English country fair, she went on, "All the farmers come from miles around to sell their hogs and cows. Or to buy a new bull, or a pair of boots or a length of woolen cloth. There are cooking booths where they sell eel pasties, honey cakes and apple tarts—and ale. There's always plenty of home-brewed ale."

"Sounds pleasant," he said. "But the fair at Porto Bello's not like that. It's like nothing that could have existed in England—or anywhere else, for centuries. Except perhaps in Constantinople, back in the Middle Ages. Only those

239

caravans traveled by land, while these come by sea. Think of it, Sybilla. Gold and emeralds from New Granada. Pearls from Margarita and Rancharias. Silver and silks and indigo."

In the lantern light, Sybilla saw the hot glow in Gavin's eyes. Once she had accused him of being like Nicholas Hobart, greedy for riches. But now she knew that he was driven by a different obsession, equally powerful. And perhaps more dangerous. The need to capture the Spanish ships, to pay them back, in some measure, for his months of suffering aboard the galley.

"The wealth of the Spanish colonies, moving toward that sleepy little seaport town," he went on. "That's all Porto Bello is, most of the year. It lies on the west coast of Panama, and the climate's vile. There's either rain and mud, or scorching heat."

"Why should they choose such a place to hold their great fair?"

"Because of its location," he explained. "The harbor's large and easily defended. And the town lies at the Atlantic end of the mule track used by the Spaniards when they bring their goods across the isthmus. The Camino del Oro, they call it—the Gold Road. Besides, Porto Bello's guarded by the forts of San Lorenzo and San Felipe. They're two of the most heavily manned fortresses in the West Indies."

She looked up at him, her eyes darkening with fear. "And you hope to take the treasure fleet against such odds?"

He shook his head. "I'll have to launch my attack on those galleons before they reach Porto Bello. There's no other way. That's why I need to find out when they're due to set out from the western coast of South America. And exactly where and when they'll be joined by the convoy."

"But how can you be sure you'll get the information in time?"

"I must," he said quietly. He put his hands on her shoulders and looked down into her face. "My men trust me,

240

Sybilla. I don't intend to lead them to destruction. I promised them victory—and greater loot than they've ever dreamed of. I won't fail them."

"Maybe Mistress Sybilla would be better off going ashore with us at Cartegena, at that," said Abiathar.

He was seated with Gavin and Sybilla, beside a crackling bonfire on the beach at Costa Verde, down the coast from Cartegena. Two days had passed since he had arrived aboard the *Condor* to join Gavin and the crew of the *San Bartolomé*. During the interval Gavin's men had toiled night and day to establish their camp at the edge of a jungle of palms and pimentos, of vines and shrubs thick with brilliantly colored blossoms. They had already put up tents for themselves and built a hut for Sybilla.

Tonight they took a well-earned rest as they feasted around the fires that dotted the beach, and the breeze carried the smell of roasting boar, slathered with thick, spicy pimento sauce, of pigeon and wood dove, turtle meat and shellfish.

But although Sybilla tried to enjoy the festivities, she had not yet given up hope that she might persuade Gavin to take her along to Cartegena. And now, quite unexpectedly, here was Abiathar, lending his support.

"We could take her with us," he said.

"She stays here." Gavin glanced over at the thatch-roofed hut. "I admit she'll not have the luxuries she might have enjoyed in Governor d'Ogeron's home, back on Tortuga. But she's here of her own free will." His gray eyes challenged her, daring her to deny it.

Sybilla bit back an angry protest. Didn't Gavin understand that she was not complaining about the primitive dwelling his men had built for her? Couldn't she make him see that she only wanted to be with him in Cartegena—or any other port in the Indies, to make the most of the time

241

remaining to them? Once he sailed off to take the Spanish treasure fleet, who could tell how long it might be before they were together again?

"She'll be safe enough here," Gavin said.

Abiathar tossed aside a heavy bone, all that remained of a joint of boar meat, and wiped the pimento sauce from his mouth with a large red bandanna.

"Don't forget them Spanish prisoners," he said. "If they find out that they're so near one of their own ports, they might get the notion to try an escape."

Gavin's men had already towed the *San Bartolomé* into a deep inlet near the encampment, where it lay at anchor, concealed by the heavy foliage on either side.

"If the Spaniards should try any such tricks, they'll have cause to regret it," Gavin said. "At the first sign of an attempt to escape, the lads who are guarding them have my orders to cut them down with grapeshot and toss them into the swamps for the alligators to feast on."

His words sent an uneasy shiver coursing through Sybilla's body.

"If it was up to them lads, belike they'd have done that as soon as we landed here," Abiathar said. "And I'd have lent them a hand."

But Gavin shook his head. "The Spanish prisoners could prove useful. Particularly Don Alfonso."

"Maybe you're right at that." Abiathar chuckled. "Our fine nobleman put up a devil of a fuss when we lashed him to the mouth of the cannon."

Sybilla glanced from Abiathar to Gavin. This was the first she had heard of the treatment meted out to the former captain of the *San Bartolomé*. She sank her teeth into the fullness of her lower lip, half-afraid to hear anymore. But she had to know. "What do you mean to do with him?"

"Don't waste your time worrying over our noble guest," he told her. "I don't happen to share the Spaniards' taste for torturing their prisoners. Don Alfonso won't be overly comfortable, I'll warrant—not with the heat and stink from the swamp, and the stings of the insects that breed there. But the men will follow my orders. Neither he, nor any of the other Spanish prisoners will suffer any real harm."

"Unless we run into trouble in Cartegena," Abiathar said. "Then it'll be our lives in exchange for Don Alfonso's."

Seeing her startled look, he went on, "You see, Mistress Sybilla, that's one big mistake those Spaniards always make. They choose their ship captains according to their important connections. For all we know, Don Alfonso might've been telling the truth, when he kept yowling about how he was a near relation to that idiot king of his—Charles the Bewitched."

Sybilla was distracted, briefly, from her own concerns. "What a curious title for a king."

"Charles the Witless would suit him better," Abiathar said. "His people like to believe that he was bewitched in his cradle. But that ain't his trouble. Too much inbreeding, that's what does it. It's bad for dogs and horses, and I guess it don't do a man no good, neither."

He paused to refill his goblet. The firelight flashed on the rubies and emeralds set in the heavy gold rim. No doubt the goblet was part of his loot from the *San Bartolomé,* just as the too-tight green velvet coat had been. The heavy, humid air from the jungle had finally forced him to put aside the coat, however.

He leaned over and poured more rum into Gavin's goblet; he would have done the same for Sybilla, but she shook her head quickly. She was already a little dizzy from the Canary wine she'd drunk with her dinner. "But if the Spanish king's—not right in the head—how can he be allowed to rule so great an empire?" she asked. Although she had been tutored along with her brother and had learned something about the history of her own country, she knew little of the affairs of Spain.

"Charles—Bewitched or Witless, as you will—was only

243

four when his father died," Gavin explained, "and although they had to put him on the throne, it's his mother who's ruled as Regent ever since. With no end of conflicting advice from her council. And her lovers, as well. The Spanish court's been a hotbed of intrigue and dissension for years. That's why the colonies out here in the Indies are so badly governed."

"So much the better for us," Abiathar said. He helped himself to a custard apple and bit into it. Sybilla still had not ceased to wonder at the vast quantity of food the man could put away. "Take the governor of Cartegena," he went on. "He gives lip service to the laws of Spain. But he has to turn a blind eye to the goods we're bringing into the city. Otherwise, his citizens'd lack for every article from cheap cotton goods to clothe their slaves to needles and thread to sew up their own fine breeches. And as for machinery—parts for the sugar mills and such—Spain don't make 'em."

"But you're still taking some risk, going into Cartegena, aren't you?" Sybilla interrupted.

"I don't mean to set up a stall in the marketplace," Gavin told her with a grin. "The governor knows me. But only as the captain of a Boston trading ship. I'll get his permission—quite unofficially, of course—to hire a string of mules and native drivers and leave for the trading post as soon as possible."

"I could go upriver with you, couldn't I?" she began. "Abiathar said—"

"God's teeth!" Abiathar gave her a startled look. "I never meant we'd take you up the Magdalena. Even if Gavin was willin', which he ain't. That stretch of jungle beyond is hard going even for a man."

"Save your breath to cool your dinner, Abiathar," Gavin said. "I've already tried to explain the difficulties of such a journey. Sybilla's no more likely to pay any heed to you than she did to me. A more stubborn female I've yet to meet."

But there was a hint of amusement in his voice that

encouraged her to make another attempt. "Abiathar said I might be better off going on to Cartegena," she insisted.

"I was thinking you could stay in the city, maybe with Señor Mendez and his wife." She gave him a quick, grateful look. "He's a rich merchant, Mistress Sybilla," he went on. "He's built himself a fine, big house, with courtyards and gardens and fountains and such."

"And exactly how would it serve my purpose to take Sybilla to the city and leave her with Eduardo Mendez and his lady?" Gavin demanded.

She flinched inwardly at his blunt question, and looked away. His purpose. Was that all he could think about now? Of course it was. What reason had he given her to believe otherwise? She kept her eyes fixed on the towering wall of palm and pimento trees at the far end of the beach, hoping to hide the hot resentment that surged up inside her.

Ever since they had approached the shore of Costa Verde, Gavin was so taken up with his goal that he had not stopped to consider her feelings. Couldn't he understand how much she wanted to stay with him, if only for a little while longer?

She raised her chin and her golden eyes narrowed with determination. She could not hope to talk him out of his plan. All she could do was to try to help him carry it through. Then perhaps there was a chance he'd return to her. She must find a way to convince him that she could be of use to him. And quickly, before he and Abiathar went off to Cartegena, leaving her behind.

"Let me try to help you," she said.

He made an impatient gesture. "For the love of heaven, Sybilla. This is no game we're playing."

"I didn't suppose it was," she shot back. "I only meant that—maybe I can help to get some of the information you're seeking." Before he could interrupt again, she went on, "I'm not afraid to take risks."

She caught a gleam of admiration in his gray eyes. "I don't doubt your courage, Sybilla. I never have. A girl who'd risk her life to help her brother escape King James's troopers, after Sedgemoor." He put an arm around her shoulders and drew her close. "But courage isn't all you'd need. You've a straightforward nature—a sense of honor. What we're talking about here is spying. Not a very honorable pursuit, is it?"

"I don't care," she said stubbornly. "If it will help to bring you back safely."

"How can you hope to learn anything useful, unless you understand the conversation you may hear in Señor Mendez's home?"

"I can speak a little Spanish. And I understand it even better. I learned the language from Dolores de las Fuentes, who sailed along with me on the *Bristol Belle.*"

"Did you, now?" Abiathar said. He stroked his bushy red beard and nodded slowly. "You might be of some use after all. No telling what morsels of gossip you could pick up. Belike them Spanish ladies are no different from our own. Always clacking away like a flock of hens in a barnyard. Begging your pardon, Mistress Sybilla."

"I don't like it," Gavin said. "It could be risky for her." He lapsed into a thoughtful silence, and Sybilla felt her spirits rise. And least he had not dismissed the suggestion outright. With so little time remaining before he sailed off to fight the Spaniards, she had to make the most of every hour. And there was always a chance, however slim, that she might overhear something that might be of use to him.

"There'd be little enough danger for her, as a guest of Señor Mendez and his wife," said Abiathar. "As I recall, the señora does a good deal of entertaining—there's always plenty of visitors coming and going. If Mistress Sybilla was to keep her wits about her, no telling what she might find out."

"Maybe so," Gavin conceded. "But once we're up there in the savannah, Sybilla would need a way to get messages to us. Supposing she did overhear anything worth our knowing."

Gavin's arm was still around her, but she sensed that all his energies were focused on working out the details of the plan. "I suppose one of our men could act as go-between."

"There's something else," Abiathar said slowly. Sybilla was surprised to catch a trace of hesitation in his voice. It was not like the outspoken seaman to choose his words carefully. "You'd have to tell Mendez and his lady that Mistress Sybilla's your wife." He kept his eyes fixed on the leaping flames of the driftwood fire. "You know how stiff-necked these Spaniards can be when it comes to family matters."

Sybilla understood instantly. A respectable merchant of Cartegena might extend the hospitality of his home to a sea captain's wife, but not to the man's mistress, however well-bred she might be. She had learned something of the rigid social customs of Spain from Dolores de las Fuentes, along with the language.

Gavin remained silent for a moment, and she thought she saw a look of bitterness in the depths of his gray eyes, a tightness about his lips. Then he nodded. "That can be easily arranged, I suppose. There's no way Mendez would be likely to discover the truth."

Abiathar took a long swig of rum, set down his ornate goblet, then cleared his throat. "Come to that, there'd be no need to deceive our host," he said. "Not if you was to marry Mistress Sybilla before we get to Cartegena."

She felt Gavin's body go rigid. Then he dropped his arm from around her shoulders. He drew back silently.

"I'm captain of the *Condor* for now, ain't I?" Abiathar went on. "I could say the words, same as any minister, and set the whole thing down, right and proper, in the ship's log, with a couple of sailors for witnesses."

With one swift movement, Gavin was on his feet, his gray eyes smoldering. Sybilla was stunned by his response. It was plain that he drew on all his reserves of self-control to keep his anger in check. The firelight accented the tightness of his bronzed skin along the angular slashes of his cheekbones and the hard line of his jaw. For a moment he looked as if he might strike out at Abiathar.

But the red-bearded seaman stood up, taking his time about it, then hooked his thumbs into his broad belt. "Don't spend your rage on me, Captain," he said calmly. "Save it for when we lay our ships alongside the Spanish fleet."

Gavin drew a long, steadying breath, and when he spoke again, his voice was low and measured. "I've not forgotten what I owe you, Abiathar."

Those terrible months when the two men had been chained, side by side, on the rowers' bench aboard the *Saragossa,* Sybilla thought. If not for Abiathar's encouragement, Gavin might have succumbed to hopelessness. And later, during the attack by the Dutchman, the red-bearded pirate had saved him from death.

Gavin stepped back from the fire, keeping his eyes fixed on the other man's face. "But you are not to interfere in my personal affairs. Not ever again."

He turned on his heel and strode away over the sand, heading toward the edge of the sea. Sybilla stared after him, shaken by his violent response to Abiathar's suggestion.

Why had Gavin reacted that way? He had made it plain enough that the thought of marrying her was somehow unbearable to him. Her hands were clenched as she fought back the surge of pain and humiliation that threatened to overwhelm her.

Chapter Nineteen

Somehow she got to her feet and managed to take a few steps in the direction of her hut, willing her unsteady legs to support her. Her high-heeled slippers sank into the sand, slowing her down even more.

"Wait a bit, Mistress Sybilla." Abiathar was at her side with a few easy strides. "I shouldn't have spoken up like I did. Never thought he'd blow up like that."

"I suppose—you don't know Gavin as well as you thought—"

"Maybe he don't know himself all that well," Abiathar said. "He's had the choicest females from Tortuga to Vera Cruz. But he—"

"I don't doubt it." Although she tried to sound cool and indifferent, her voice betrayed her.

"But his feeling for you, that's special. I'd stake my life on it. He never cared a farthing about any of them—not since he lost his wife."

His wife. Gavin once had been married. Sybilla felt as though an icy wave had engulfed her, chilling her to the bone.

"I didn't know. He never said—"

"Come and sit down by the fire, Mistress Sybilla." He took her arm and led her back. "There, that's better." He dropped down beside her. "Never told you, did he?"

She shook her head.

"Belike it's not a tale fit for a lady to hear."

"He has told me how he was taken prisoner by the Spaniards. Was his wife—did she die back in Boston, before he could return?"

Abiathar shook his head. "That would've been bad enough. But what happened was a whole lot worse."

"Tell me."

"That voyage was his first as master of his own ship. His wife went with him. They'd only been wed a few weeks."

"And when their ship was captured? What happened to her then?"

Abiathar's weathered face hardened. "Those Spanish bastards threw them in the hold. Him and Verity—that was her name. They clapped Gavin in irons and chained him to the wall. Later that day, on the way back to Havana, they came for his wife. Dragged her up on deck. Drunk, they were, an' hot as a pack of rutting hounds on the scent of a bitch in—"

Abiathar stopped short. "Sorry," he muttered.

"And—then?" Sybilla could scarcely force the words past the strangling tightness in her throat. She dreaded what she knew would come next, but she must hear it all, if she were to understand the reason for Gavin's violent outburst only moments ago.

"That was the last he ever saw his wife. But he heard her for the next hour or so. Screaming for him to come and help her. And there was no way he could get to her, chained like he was. No way at all."

Abiathar kicked at a piece of charred wood with his booted foot, sending the sparks spinning and whirling upward. "She went on screaming, while the whoresons took their turn with her. Later on, right before the galleon dropped anchor in Havana, she managed to get free. She threw herself overboard."

Sybilla was too shaken to speak. She could only stare at him, her face drawn, her golden eyes dark with anguish.

"One of the guards told Gavin about it, afterward. From what I could figure, the guard didn't leave out none of the details, neither. And Gavin—he was no more'n twenty when it happened. I guess it left a terrible deep hurt in him.

"All that time, when we were prisoners aboard that damn galley, he never said anything about it. Not 'til one night, right after the Dutchman took the *Saragossa* and set us free. We'd been drinkin' in a tavern, Gavin and me. Makin' up for lost time, as you might say. Guess the wine'd hit him hard. That's when he told me about it. Never spoke of it again, though."

Abiathar sighed and shook his head, then sat with his elbows on his bent knees, staring into the fire.

Gavin had never spoke of it again, Sybilla thought, shivering slightly. But he had lived with the memories all this time.

Maybe he had blamed himself for what had happened to his bride. He'd told her that for a while after he had become a galley slave, he had lost all desire to survive—until Abiathar had made him see that if he stayed alive, and regained his freedom, he might get the chance to strike back at the Spaniards in his own way.

"I have a score to settle with them Spaniards, myself," Abiathar said. "And so have some of these others. They served aboard the *Saragossa*, too. Or one of those other galleons." He gestured to the groups of men gathered about the fires that dotted the beach. "But for Gavin, it's a different kind of feelin'—it goes deeper."

Sybilla nodded, her throat contracting with pity. She longed to go to Gavin, to stand beside him at the water's edge. To draw him close and tell him she understood. To try to comfort him. But she hesitated, fearing that he might turn away. Maybe he needed to be alone now.

Abiathar filled her goblet and this time she did not try to stop him. She drank a little of the potent rum. Although it burned her throat, she was grateful for the warmth that helped to relax her tense muscles.

After a few moments, she rose, bade Abiathar good night, and retired to the palm thatch hut. Gavin's crew had built a crude but sturdy frame from the mahogany wood that grew in abundance close by and had even hauled down the mattress from the galleon's sleeping quarters, along with most of the bed linen.

Sybilla got out of her gown and took her shoes off. Then, still clad in her petticoat and shift, she dropped down and pulled the sheet over her.

But when she closed her eyes, she found she could not sleep, for she was still haunted by Abiathar's revelation. A rush of pity swept through her as she thought of Gavin's bride.

Verity. What had she looked like? Had she been beautiful, perhaps? Had Gavin grown up with her back there in Boston, or had he met her by chance, in one of the seaports where his ship had dropped anchor? Verity Broderick, who had set forth on a honeymoon voyage, filled with joy, proud of her handsome young husband, master of his own ship at twenty.

No doubt she had spent many hours looking out to sea, dreaming of their future together, of the years that stretched before them. And the house he would build for her after she bore him their first child. The home where she would wait for him to come back from his voyages. But for Verity, there had been no such future.

Only a few weeks at sea. The hurricane that had struck without warning and driven their ship off course. Then the din of battle, the brief imprisonment. The unspeakable violation the Spaniards had inflicted on her. And the swift descent into the dark waters that had claimed her, and blotted out all memory . . .

But for Gavin, there had been no such escape. For him, there had been the long, grim months of slavery aboard the

Saragossa. The darkness and the filth and the lash of the slave driver's whip.

Sybilla shifted uneasily and wished that she had drained the whole goblet of rum. Through the chinks in the side of the hut, she could see the reddish glow of the fires scattered across the beach. She heard the voices of the men—talking, laughing, occasionally breaking into a few verses of a bawdy song. The cry of a wood dove. The clash of the wind-tossed palms and pimentoes, and the rustle of the coarse sea grass. And always, the steady rhythm of the waves.

Was Gavin still standing alone at the water's edge, looking out into the darkness?

Long after the seamen had gone off to sleep in their canvas tents or in hammocks slung between a pair of trees she could find no rest. She slapped at a mosquito, then another. Maybe she should have followed the example of some of the men, and rubbed herself with tallow before retiring.

She tensed briefly, as the rough sheet of canvas at the entrance to the hut was pushed aside. By the light of the fires that still glowed on the sand, she could make out Gavin's tall silhouette. He came inside, and she could hear him moving about, getting undressed. The mattress sagged under his weight as he stretched himself beside her.

Hesitantly she reached out and touched his hand. By the firelight that filtered into the hut, she saw him turn his head. "You'd better try to get some sleep," he told her. "If you're still set on sailing to Cartegena in the morning, you'll need your rest."

Although his voice was cool and expressionless, she felt reassured. He had decided to take her with him, after all.

"We'll leave the *Condor* anchored here in the lagoon," he went on. "Don Alfonso recognized her off the coast of Cuba. There might be a Spanish captain in the harbor at Cartegena who'd know her, too. We'll make the trip along the coast in one of the longboats, and take a few of the crew with us."

He bent his head and brushed a light kiss across Sybilla's

253

cheek, then turned away. She hadn't expected him to make love with her, not tonight. If only he would put his arms around her and hold her close, that would be enough to ease the turmoil inside her.

But a few moments later, she heard his even breathing, and knew that he had fallen asleep. Sighing, she closed her eyes and at last she too drifted off.

It was dawn when she woke with a violent start. Gavin had called out in his sleep, and the harsh, wordless sound still echoed in her dazed mind. He was thrashing about on the wide mattress, and when she raised herself on one arm and reached out to touch him his skin was damp with sweat. He went on mumbling incoherently.

She put a hand on his shoulder, wondering if she should try to wake him. A moment later he struck out at her, and she had to dodge swiftly to avoid the blow.

"Gavin—wake up!"

He sat up, and she could hear his hoarse breathing. She stroked his chest and felt the quick, unsteady rise and fall of the hard muscles beneath her palm.

"I'm here," she whispered, brushing his dark hair back from his face. He looked away quickly. She sensed his shame that she had seen him, shaken and vulnerable.

There was no way he could get to her, chained as he was. No way at all.

She could only guess what fearful visions had tormented him in his sleep, and she knew better than to speak her thoughts. Instead, she drew his head against her breasts and went on stroking his hair, her touch gentle and soothing.

She felt the shudder that passed through the length of his powerful body.

"Sorry I woke you." He tried to pull away. As he moved, his hand brushed across her shoulder, and her shift slipped down, baring the whiteness of her breast. Her arms went around him, and she held him closer. She felt the heat of his breath against the soft, pink-tipped globe.

Guided only by instinct, she cupped her breast in her hand and brought it to his mouth. She brushed her nipple over his lips. Still he did not respond. Had she been wrong to offer herself to him now? In spite of all those nights they had shared, there was still much she did not understand about a man's needs, his deepest feelings. Perhaps fear or grief—or an overwhelming sense of guilt—could drive all desire even from a man as passionate and virile as Gavin.

Then, before she could move away, his arms enfolded her, and all at once she knew that it did not matter whether or not he took her tonight. She did not care if he joined his body with hers, and fulfilled her needs. This time it would be enough for her if she could offer him a measure of comfort, if she could drive away the shadows that had engulfed him, possessed and tortured him as he slept.

She drew her breath in sharply, as his lips parted and he took her rosy peak between them, drawing it into the moist heat of his mouth. She felt the swift response that went surging through her body and stirred the hot need deep within the center of her being. But still she did not press herself against him. She willed her body to remain passive in his embrace.

Her hands moved, stroking his hair, his neck and shoulders, with a touch that was gentle and reassuring. Her nipple was hard now, bathed in liquid fire. He suckled harder, tugging, drawing her deeper inside, as if he could not get enough of her.

Driven by the aching fullness of her loins, she felt herself pressing against him, her thighs parting of their own volition. He released her nipple, letting it slide from between his lips. His mouth moved down, so that she could feel the heat through all those layers of silk and lace. He turned her on her side, pushed her petticoat up around her waist, and pressed his parted lips against the quivering skin of her belly.

He touched the tip of his tongue to the hollow of her navel, circling, flicking. The sweet torment grew until it became unbearable. She arched upward, her fingers thrusting into his thick, dark hair, holding him, guiding him to the source of her need.

Slowly, as if for the first time, he was parting her with his fingers, stroking the slick wetness of her. Taking the bud of her pleasure between his fingers, fondling, teasing. He cupped her bottom, drawing her closer still, lifting her, caressing her now with lips and tongue.

Then he raised himself. She felt his male hardness brush against her thigh, her belly. The touch of his arousal sent a white-hot current surging through every nerve of her body. And now his face was above hers. The first rays of the sun sent fiery fingers of light probing through the cracks in the walls, touching the planes of his face with a deep, radiant glow.

Even as he entered her, his eyes were locked with hers. He slid inside her moist satin sheath, and she felt herself closing around him. He moved slowly, in long, lingering strokes, stopping now and then to caress her back, the base of her spine, the rounds of her bottom.

He was moving faster now, and she moved with him, no longer held back by any lingering trace of uncertainty. Her body rose and fell to answer his quickening thrusts. She was consumed with a sweet-hot urgency that grew and grew until she felt she could not bear it a moment longer.

She threw back her head and cried out as he exploded deep within her. Caught in the surge of mounting rapture, she was carried away with him, higher and higher, to the crest of their shared fulfillment.

Now, as she lay locked in his arms, she sensed the coming of dawn. A bird in one of the trees near the hut gave a few tentative sounds. Even as she buried her face in Gavin's shoulder, to shut out the light that came through the tiny cracks in the sides of the hut, she knew that soon she must rise. He was taking her with him to Cartegena, and that was all that mattered, for now.

But would it always be enough to follow him and wait for him, never sure if she would see him again? She remembered how Abiathar had wanted to say the words that would make her Gavin's wife. And the cold fury in Gavin's eyes when he had refused.

In time, perhaps Gavin would learn to forget the past. No, not forget—that could never be. But perhaps one day he might set aside his grief, his gnawing guilt over what could not be changed. Only then would he feel free to take all she longed to give him—the joining, the melding not of flesh alone, but of spirit, too. In time, that day would come.

In time . . . but for her and Gavin, how much time was left? How many days before he went sailing off on a voyage from which he might never return?

Chapter Twenty

Sybilla walked to the carved ebony dressing table in her bedchamber at the home of the merchant, Eduardo Mendez in Cartegena. Gavin, who had already dressed for dinner and was adjusting the folds of his cravat, paused for a moment to look at her appreciatively. His eyes moved over the soft swell of her breasts and the curves of her hips, which were scarcely concealed beneath her clinging silk robe. Reluctantly, he turned his gaze away.

"You'd better ring for your maid," he said. "We don't want to keep Señor Mendez and his wife from their dinner."

"There's still a little time," Sybilla reminded him. The local custom of eating dinner at ten in the evening had taken some getting used to. Gavin would be leaving for the trading post tomorrow at dawn, and she needed a chance to ask his advice about a somewhat disturbing problem that had arisen only that afternoon.

She opened her lacquered jewel box and took out the heavy turquoise and gold necklace and earrings she would wear tonight with her aquamarine silk gown. Gavin had given them to her along with several other pieces of fine jewelry on their first night here in Cartegena.

Although she had not questioned him, she did not doubt that he had taken them from one of the chests on the *San*

Bartolomé. Pirate's treasure for a pirate's woman.

She felt a twinge of guilt, remembering how Eduardo Mendez had received her into his home with the gracious courtesy due the wife of his guest. And in the days that followed, his stout, dark-eyed spouse had done all she could to keep her pleasantly occupied while Gavin had gone about his business. He had left for the waterfront early each day, and had not returned before evening.

There was a great deal he had to do before he and Abiathar left for the journey up the Magdalena River to the trading post. He had to be down at the dock to oversee the storage of his cargo, which had been off-loaded from the *Condor,* and brought into the harbor in several small boats. He had to bargain for the pack mules; only the sturdiest, most sure-footed beasts would do, to carry the heavy crates and bales of goods over the jungle trails beyond the river.

"Mendez helped to choose Indian guides," Gavin had told her. "He swears they're the most reliable and experienced he could find—and I hope he's right. A couple of years ago, a party of Dutch traders were left to fend for themselves, after their guides stole their goods and took off into the jungle."

Sybilla did not question Gavin about the fate of the unfortunate Dutchmen. The grim expression on his face when he spoke of the incident told her all she cared to know.

Despite his reassurances, she was uneasy about his coming journey upriver and grateful to Angela Mendez, who had kept her so busy during this first week of her visit that there was little time for brooding. Señora Mendez had all the leisure she could wish for, a wealthy, generous husband, and a large staff of house servants to look after all six of her children.

Sybilla accompanied her on her morning carriage rides around the plaza, where the two of them stopped to linger in the shops dealing in fine silks, laces and brocades, jewelry of turquoise and silver from Vera Cruz, emeralds from the mines of New Granada, and pearls from the waters off

259

Cartegena. There were shops where one could find the finest leather goods: saddles embossed in gold, elegant boots and high-heeled slippers of cordovan leather.

On these shopping trips, Sybilla was accompanied by Tod, the copper-skinned, black-eyed Indian boy Gavin had chosen from the crew of the *Condor*. "The men call him Tod, because none of them can pronounce the lad's Indian name," Gavin explained. "And neither can I—it's Arawak, with at least six syllables. You'll find him thoroughly dependable, if you should need to get word to me up at the trading post."

Gavin had told Señor Mendez and his wife that Tod was Sybilla's slave. Since her arrival here, she had noticed that Indian or black boys, decked out in exotic costumes of satin and gold braid, and wearing Eastern turbans, were much in demand among the wealthier ladies. Although Sybilla understood Gavin's decision to say that Tod was one of these, she found the idea distasteful nonetheless.

No doubt young Tod, who had served as a powder monkey aboard the *Condor,* during the battle with the *San Bartolomé,* disliked the pretense, too; but he had accepted his new role without complaint, because of his unwavering loyalty to Gavin. Tod followed after Sybilla like a shadow, carrying her parcels from the shops, and riding on a perch at the back of the Mendez carriage.

Late in the afternoon, when Sybilla rose from her daily siesta, she joined her hostess in the large, airy courtyard, with its high walls covered with trailing crimson and purple bougainvillea, and its marble fountain. Here Angela Mendez and her guests—the wives of other prosperous merchants—sat sipping their foaming chocolate, flavored with vanilla, from small silver cups, nibbling on frosted cakes or candied rose leaves, and exchanging the latest gossip.

But so far, although Sybilla had listened carefully, she had not managed to pick up even one piece of information that might be of use to Gavin. Although the ladies mentioned the coming trade fair, none of them said exactly when it was to begin.

At last, Sybilla had decided she must do what she could to find out what he wanted to know, without showing undue curiosity. "Forgive my ignorance of your customs," she had said. "I would have thought that the fair might begin on the same day each year."

Luz Ojeda, the wife of a silk merchant, smiled and shook her head. "Would that it were so!" she exclaimed. "But you see, Señora Broderick, it takes much time to gather the fleet back in Cádiz, and to choose its officers from among the highest ranking noblemen. The sailing date may be postponed several times before the fleet sets out at last."

Sybilla longed to question her more closely, but she did not dare, for fear of arousing suspicion. Gavin had warned her to be discreet, to listen closely and say as little as possible.

"And when the ships do arrive from Cádiz and unload their wares in Porto Bello," said Teresa Gonzales, "the prices for the most ordinary articles will be outrageous, as always. A set of iron stays for a corset will sell for ten times their rightful value. *Dios mio!* It's no wonder that our governor is obliged to admit outsiders to keep us supplied with such necessities."

"Teresa, *por favor!*" Angela Mendez interrupted. The other woman went crimson with embarrassment, as she realized her lapse of courtesy.

"A thousand pardons, Señora Broderick. I meant no offense. Indeed, if it were not for men like your husband, we ladies might leave off wearing corsets altogether—" Then, realizing that she had verged upon yet another indelicacy, Señora Gonzales fell silent.

The conversation quickly shifted to domestic matters: the difficulties of finding suitable slaves, whether Indian or black, to train as house servants; the complications of keeping up with fashion, here in this colonial outpost; the endless problems of pregnancy and child-rearing. Sybilla

261

had to make an effort to concentrate on the monotonous conversation. Her lids began to droop, for the heavy, flower-scented air and the steady ripple of the fountain were lulling her into a drowsy state.

Then she started, as she realized that Placida Ramirez, a sallow-faced lady was speaking to her. "Tell me, Señora Broderick, do your physicians in the town of Boston favor swaddling for infants?"

The question caught Sybilla completely off guard, since she had never even set foot in Boston and knew nothing of the care of infants. She lowered her eyes to hide her confusion. "I'm not sure," she managed to say.

"You have no children of your own, then?" the woman persisted. Sybilla shook her head, fervently wishing that she could find a way to divert Señora Ramirez to another topic.

Angela Mendez came to her rescue. "Señora Broderick has been married only a few months," she said. "No doubt, in another year or two, she will present her handsome *capitán* with a fine, strong son."

Sybilla's breath caught in her throat. She looked away, shielding her face with her fan.

A fine strong son. Gavin's son.

Until now, the thought of pregnancy had rarely crossed her mind. Perhaps she had refused to allow herself to consider it, under the circumstances. So far her monthly courses had always come at their regular time. She raised a silent prayer. *Sweet Jesú, don't let me be with child!*

She would never forget how violently Gavin had dismissed the mere suggestion that he might marry her. She was sure that the last thing he wanted was a pregnant mistress, clinging to him and impeding his plans.

Then, all at once, she felt an ache of emptiness, followed by an instinctive longing, such as she had never known before. And she realized that, against all reason, she wanted to bear Gavin's child one day. A sturdy, gray-eyed son, or a small, dark-haired little girl.

"—and you have chosen a most opportune time to visit our city," Señora Broderick."

Sybilla was roused from her thoughts in time to catch a few words of Luz Ojeda's chatter. "I do not exaggerate, when I say that here in Cartegena, we have the greatest carnival in all the Indies. Music and fireworks, bullfights—and every night, a dozen balls, with dancing and feasting until dawn."

"Is the carnival to be held soon?" Sybilla asked politely, trying to feign enthusiasm, even as she repressed a sigh of disappointment. She would have nothing useful to report to Gavin on his last night here in the city. Perhaps he was already sorry he had brought her along, instead of leaving her in the camp at Costa Verde.

"The Torrealtas will make an even greater display than usual," Luz went on.

"And why not?" said Angela. "With such an important guest, they will surely wish to make a splendid impression."

"I wonder why the lady's husband did not choose to accompany her." There was a flicker of malicious curiosity in Placida Ramirez's eyes. "After all, the Torrealtas are his relations."

"I caught a glimpse of la Condesa, Dolores Torrealta y de las Fuentes, herself—she was riding in her carriage. Young and pretty, she was," said Luz.

"Dolores de las Fuentes?" Sybilla interrupted. She knew it was the Spanish custom for a wife to keep her own name, using it after that of her husband.

"You have also seen the wife of the governor of Panama?" Luz asked.

"No—not here in the city—but I do know her. We traveled together aboard the ship that brought me to Jamaica. Dolores—la Condesa—taught me to speak your language." Sybilla frowned slightly. "I'm sure she said it was the lieutenant governor she was to marry."

"The former governor was recalled to Spain—no doubt the change took place while your friend was en route to

Panama City," said Teresa. "There was some sort of scandal. . . . The women are told so little of these political matters. But whatever the circumstances, your friend is now the wife of the governor of the Isthmus—el Conde Ramón Torrealta—a nobleman of one of the greatest families of Spain."

Fans stopped their slow waving, and every pair of eyes was fixed on Sybilla with deep interest. To think that the young wife of a colonial sea captain should be acquainted with so august a personage as la Condesa de Torrealta y de las Fuentes!

"How fortunate for you!" Angela exclaimed, her dark eyes round with excitement.

"Fortunate? But why?" Sybilla began to wish she had not mentioned her acquaintance with Dolores. Gavin had cautioned her to remain as inconspicuous as possible.

"Ah, but you are too modest!" Angela went on. "As a friend of la Condesa, no doubt you will receive an invitation to the Torrealtas' home."

"Perhaps you will attend the ball!" Luz exclaimed. "If so, you must be sure to notice everything—the gowns, the jewels, the decorations—so that you may describe them to us afterward."

"And the table," said another. "No doubt they will prepare a marvelous banquet."

Sybilla had put off sending for her maid that evening, so that she might describe the incident and get Gavin's advice on what she should do next. Quickly she gave him an account of her conversation with Angela and her friends.

"I did not mean to create such a stir," she finished. "Angela Mendez and her friends were positively overcome with envy when I said that I knew Dolores." Sybilla gave him a faintly apologetic look. "And now Angela insists that I must send a message to her—to la Condesa—telling her that

I'm here in the city."

Gavin was silent for a moment, his dark brows drawn together in a thoughtful frown, as if he were weighing her words carefully. What could be so important about an invitation to a carnival ball, Sybilla wondered?

"Do as she wishes." It was not a suggestion, but an order.

"I wouldn't enjoy the ball, not without you. If only you could put off this journey to the trading post for a few weeks."

He threw her an impatient look. "I've told you that at this stage of the game, every day counts. Señor Mendez will be only too happy to escort you to the Torrealta mansion, along with his wife. Your friend, the Condesa, will invite them both, since you are staying here as their guest."

"But why should you care if I go to this ball or not?"

Gavin's eyes hardened.

"Because the most important officials in Cartegena, in all of New Granada, are likely to be there."

His hand closed on her arm, and she felt his urgency in the pressure of his grip. "Eduardo Mendez may be one of the richest merchants in Cartegena," he went on quickly. "But he would not be invited to the Torrealta home. And neither could you, if it were not for your friendship with Dolores Torrealta y de las Fuentes. Once inside the house, you might overhear something that will be of use."

He led her to the small writing desk beside one of the tall windows, set paper, quill and inkstand before her, then pulled out the chair for her. But Sybilla, moved by a sudden reluctance, remained standing.

"You're taking it for granted that Dolores will wish to renew a shipboard acquaintance," she said. "Now that she is so important—a condesa, and the wife of the governor of Panama—maybe she won't care to see me again."

"It's worth a try," Gavin insisted.

But still she could not bring herself to do as he wished.

"Surely, you can let her know you're here in the city—

265

that's perfectly proper." She caught the impatience in his voice.

Perfectly proper, she thought, with a touch of bitterness. To deceive their host and hostess, and now, Dolores—to return treachery for friendship.

Gavin released his grip on her arm; then he cupped her chin in his hand and tilted her head upward. He searched her face intently. "You're having second thoughts, aren't you? Maybe you're even wishing you'd stayed behind at Costa Verde."

"No—truly! I want to help you all I can. Surely you know that. But Señora Mendez has been so kind to me, welcoming me into her home, keeping me occupied while you were gone each day, introducing me to her friends. She trusts me, Gavin. And Dolores will, too."

Sybilla turned her eyes away. No doubt he thought her a sentimental fool. She braced herself for his angry outburst.

But his arms went around her and he held her against him. "Sybilla, my love." His voice was deep and reassuring. She inhaled the smell of castile soap, of freshly starched linen, and his own warm, familiar male scent. He stroked the loose waves of her auburn hair. "I should never have involved you in all this. You're forthright and honorable. There's no deceit in your nature."

"That doesn't matter. If I can save you from even a small part of the danger you'll be facing, when you have to sail out to meet the galleons . . . If I can help to keep you from harm, that's all I ask."

He drew her closer, his lips warm against her cheek, as he kissed her lightly. She turned her head and his mouth found hers. Her lips parted to receive his tongue and meet it with her own. He was a part of her now. She could not imagine a life without him. And there was nothing she would not do to try to bring him back safely after the battle.

For a moment they stood locked together in a timeless kiss of infinite tenderness. Then slowly, reluctantly, he raised his mouth from hers and held her away. He smiled down at her, his gray eyes warm and caressing.

"Don't torment yourself, love," he said. "Stay here and enjoy the carnival while I'm away. You needn't try to get an invitation from the Condesa. You don't have to write to her at all." She looked at him in surprise. He meant every word he was saying.

"No doubt Mendez will have a lavish carnival ball of his own. And the gentlemen will fight for the privilege of dancing with you, my love." She caught a brief flicker of regret in his eyes. "I've never danced with you, Sybilla. I wish I'd had the chance."

"There will be time, later." But even as she spoke, she felt a stab of fear. What if he went out to do battle with the Spaniards and never returned?

She had wavered for a moment, wanting to accept the escape he had offered her. But now she felt a new and over-powering determination.

Resting her head against his chest for a moment, she rubbed her cheek against him. She savored his closeness. How much she loved him. There was no way she could talk him out of his plan—that she knew. And the assault on the treasure fleet would be dangerous enough, no matter how well-prepared he might be. She had to do what little she could to bring him back safely.

Slowly she drew away from him, and seated herself before the desk. Then she picked up the quill, dipped it into the silver inkstand, and began to write the note.

Eduardo Mendez's carriage swung into line behind the procession of glittering vehicles moving slowly up the road leading to the mansion of the Torrealtas. The coachman and footman were decked out in their glittering, gold-braided livery, and the four black horses, the finest in the Mendez stable, stepped out jauntily, the plumes atop their heads swaying in the night breeze.

Sybilla peered out through the window at the other carriages, some of them even more splendid, with gilded crests on their doors to announce the rank of the occupants. And beside a few of these vehicles she caught an occasional glimpse of a gentleman who had chosen to make the trip from the city, mounted on a prancing steed with a gold-embossed saddle and bits of jingling gold fastened to the bridle.

Torrealta slaves, clad in midnight blue slashed with silver, lined the road, holding their torches aloft to light the way for the guests. The mansion, a huge structure built in the fanciful baroque style, was set on a rise overlooking the rest of the city.

From the streets below the breeze carried the boisterous shouts and the singing of the revelers: the beating of drums and the thrumming of guitars. All of Cartegena had turned out to celebrate the carnival that marked the end of the pre-Lenten season.

Angela Mendez smoothed the billowing skirt of her purple taffeta gown and gave a sigh of pure ecstasy. Through the slits in her black silk mask her brown eyes glowed with anticipation.

"The carnival ball of the Torrealtas," she said, and she gave a heartfelt sigh of satisfaction. "I have longed to be here, since I was a little girl." She reached over and pressed Sybilla's hand. "And now, here I am at last—thanks to you, *Sybilla mía.*"

Even as she smiled at the other woman, Sybilla cringed inside. Then she reminded herself of her promise to Gavin, before his departure. She would do whatever was necessary to be of use to him.

"If only your husband were not away on business," Angela was saying. *"Que lástima!"*

Although Angela knew perfectly well that Gavin's business had to do with the selling of contraband, the merchant's wife had never mentioned it to Sybilla. After all, *Capitán* Broderick was not the only foreign ship master who kept the citizens of Cartegena supplied with trade goods, in defiance of the laws of Spain. So long as her Eduardo had seen fit to invite him into his home and even the authorities in Cartegena had given permission for the *capitán* to go up the Magdalena, why should she concern herself over the matter?

As for Sybilla Broderick, she had proved to be a most agreeable guest, charming and well-bred, for *una inglesa*. But at times Angela had thought she saw a troubled look in the young woman's face. What possible cause could Sybilla have to be unhappy?

She was young and beautiful, with that splendid auburn hair of hers, like silken fire, and those striking golden eyes. And her husband must be deeply in love with her to have brought her all this way with him, instead of leaving her at home in Boston, to wait for his return. When Sybilla and her husband had been together, Angela had sensed the deep passion they shared; it seemed to vibrate like an invisible force between them.

Now, as the carriage moved through the great iron gates and into the torchlit courtyard of the Torrealta mansion, Angela gave Sybilla a sidelong glance, at once admiring and envious. Who would have thought that a sea captain from the British colonies up north would have found himself such a lovely young wife?

And her gowns! She had brought along a trunk filled with the most fashionable garments of fine silks, taffetas, brocades and laces. And a collection of jewels fit for an *infanta*.

Tonight Sybilla had chosen a gown of tawny russet silk, with an overskirt of gold Venetian lace. About her slender, white throat, she wore a necklace of fire opals set in heavy gold, and she wore matching opal earrings. Her hair had been arranged in an elaborate coiffure, parted in the center, with long curls falling across her shoulders, delicate tendrils at her temples, and an intricate chignon at the back of her head.

Sybilla kept her eyes fixed on the carriage window, thankful for the silk mask that helped to conceal the upper half of her face. For as the carriage drew nearer the mansion she was seized with a growing panic. She reminded herself that she did not have to go through with her plans even now. Gavin had told her so.

She could be free to dance, if she chose, to make polite conversation and enjoy the feasting and the fireworks. If Dolores found a few moments to speak with her privately, no doubt la Condesa would have much to tell of her magnificent wedding, of her lofty new position and her many social obligations as the wife of the governor of Panama.

But perhaps Dolores would want to know something of Sybilla's experiences, since she had left the *Bristol Belle* in Montego Bay. And if so, what was there to tell her friend?

Lies—nothing but lies!

She would have to create a suitable description of her meeting with Gavin—one fit for the ears of the Condesa Torrealta y de las Fuentes. She would have to weave a tissue of falsehoods. Her first meeting with Gavin at the home of friends; his swift, impassioned courtship; and then their marriage ceremony. She would have to speak affectionately of her devoted aunt, who had arranged a splendid wedding reception for the couple at Acacia Hall. . . .

But Gavin wasn't her husband, and he was not a respectable Boston sea captain, either. As for her Aunt Madeleine, Gavin had said the woman was no better than the madam of a bawdy house, and he'd been right. She stiffened at the mere thought of that scheming creature who had tried to force her into marriage with Hobart.

I can't go through with this. I can't. Sybilla's teeth caught at her lower lip, and her fingers gripped the sticks of her fan too tightly.

"You must not be shy, *querida,*" Angela was saying. "No doubt your friend, la Condesa, will be pleased to see you again."

The carriage came to a halt and one of the footmen sprang down from the back to assist the occupants to descend. Close up, the Torrealta mansion was even more impressive; with its stone cupolas and turrets, its huge iron-hinged doors, and its deeply recessed windows covered by iron grillwork, it looked like a cross between a palace and a fortress. A fortress she was about to enter under false colors.

Even as she walked slowly toward the doors, her head high, the torchlight striking red and gold sparks from the fire opals at her throat and ears, she wished with all her heart that she could be with Gavin, out there in the jungle country above Cartegena. Though it might be as bad as he had said— infested with snakes and alligators, with prowling jaguars and ocelots—she would not be afraid with him beside her.

Raising her chin higher, she took the arm Señor Mendez offered her, and went through the arched doorway into the huge reception hall beyond. Sybilla scarcely had a chance to admire her surroundings. She caught a vague impression of a black and white marble floor, of marble columns and great tapestries, and silver everywhere—silver mirrors, silver braziers, and candles set in silver holders.

A young woman in a gown of black taffeta detached herself from the guests with whom she had been speaking and came forward to greet Sybilla. It took her a moment to recognize Dolores, for the girl had changed during these past months. Diamonds blazed about her throat and in her dark hair, which she wore coiled high upon her head.

She appeared older and more dignified than she had during the weeks of the voyage aboard the *Bristol Belle,* but perhaps that was only natural, considering that she was no longer merely Dolores de las Fuentes, but also the Condesa Torrealta, wife of the governor of Panama. But Sybilla sensed that the change went far deeper. There was a worldly look about her and a touch of disillusionment in her eyes.

She took Sybilla's hand in hers, then acknowledged the presence of Eduardo and Angela Mendez with a gracious but distant smile, as if she could not quite recall having invited them here.

As another couple approached, Dolores said softly, "We will talk, later, Sybilla *mía*." And then she moved on to join her husband's relations in welcoming the other guests.

With Sybilla on one side and his wife on the other, Eduardo Mendez followed the throng into the ballroom, with its crystal chandeliers and polished floor. As soon as the musicians in the gallery struck up the first dance, a stately pavane, Sybilla was besieged by admiring males. A saraband followed, then a gavotte.

But during the next two hours, although she never lacked for partners who showered her with elaborate compliments, even while they devoured her with their smoldering glances, she heard nothing that would be of the slightest interest to Gavin.

She had soon discovered that it was not easy to flirt delicately with a Creole gentleman while fending off his none-too-suble hints about the possibility of an assignation later on. Although he knew she was *Señora* Broderick, this did nothing to cool his ardor. Sybilla had already discovered from Angela and her friends, that while the virginity of the Cartegenian maidens was closely guarded, it was common enough for a lady to take a lover after she was married.

Sybilla had no chance to speak with Dolores again until midnight, when dinner was served. The dining room had been transformed into a bower, where the scents of the pink oleanders, crimson roses and ferns mingled with the heavy perfumes of the ladies. White cockatoos preened themselves in their wicker cages. The long tables were spread with a

272

lavish array of delicacies, but Dolores scarcely touched her food.

"I said your family would arrange a match for you, Sybilla—and so they did. I was hoping to meet your dashing *capitán*. What a pity he could not be here with you."

"It would seem we have both been left to our own devices tonight," Sybilla remarked with forced lightness.

Dolores flushed slightly. "Ramón is busy—always so busy with important affairs of state. And then, too—"

She broke off, as a liveried servant approached and held out a silver tray with an envelope on it. Dolores picked up the letter, then went pale when she saw the seal that fastened it. Without waiting, she tore it open, and her eyes moved quickly over the contents.

A moment later, the color left her face, and she went rigid. Her dark eyes remained fixed on the sheet in her hand. "I trust you have not received bad news?" Sybilla reached out and took her arm. Dolores forced a smile that looked more like a grimace of pain. Sybilla realized that her friend was trembling slightly.

"Shall we go outside for a breath of air?" Sybilla asked.

Dolores shook her head. "I mustn't draw attention to myself. There already has been enough gossip about me, since I arrived here without my husband." She stopped short, and allowed one of the servants to refill her plate: then looked down with revulsion at the elaborately prepared delicacies.

"After supper there'll be the fireworks," she told Sybilla, her voice scarcely more than a whisper. "When the guests go out into the courtyard to watch the display, you must come upstairs with me—there is a balcony outside my chamber. No one will overhear us there."

Chapter Twenty-One

The fireworks began an hour after midnight, and the guests hurried out to the walled courtyard to watch the brilliant display that was to climax the evening's festivities. Dolores had been dining with a handsome, dark-haired young army officer in one of the deeply recessed alcoves. Rising from the divan, she caught Sybilla's eye, and motioned to her to leave the room.

Although she was puzzled by her friend's almost furtive air, Sybilla followed her back into the ballroom, up a wide staircase, and along a hall with a high, coffered ceiling and heavy tapestries. When they reached the bedchamber, Dolores entered first, dismissed her maid with a gesture, and drew Sybilla inside the room. Through the tall windows Sybilla caught a glimpse of the brilliant flashes of light from the fireworks, and heard the guests' exclamations of pleasure.

Dolores shut the heavy, carved door leading to the hall. Sybilla looked about her, impressed by the luxurious chamber, which was dominated by the great, canopied bed, with its brocade hangings. The rest of the furnishings— intricately carved ebony cabinets and tables, inlayed with engraved silver or mother-of-pearl; a marble clock set with jewels—looked equally costly and imposing.

But Sybilla was unable to give much thought to her surroundings, for she was troubled by her friend's agitated manner.

"That letter you received at supper—" she began.

"Wait a moment," Dolores cautioned her. She walked to the door with a quick, light step, then flung it open. She paused, and looked up and down the shadowy hallway before closing it again.

"It's all right," she told Sybilla. "The maid's nowhere in sight." But she appeared reluctant to speak, even here in the privacy of her own bedchamber. Taking Sybilla's hand, she led the way out to the covered balcony with a marble bench and majolica flower pots filled with masses of fragrant mimosa plants.

"There's no room for anyone to hide out here, thank heaven."

Sybilla looked at her with concern. Why on earth should Dolores feel it necessary to take such extreme precautions here in the home of the Torrealtas? This was not like her. During their voyage across the Atlantic, the Spanish girl had been such a lighthearted companion, filled with anticipation over her coming marriage, open and cheerful in her conversation.

But now Sybilla sensed a certain watchful air about the young Condesa, as if she were forever on guard against some hidden danger. In spite of the warmth of the sweet-scented night air, Sybilla felt a small, cold prickling sensation move over her skin. Was it possible that Dolores was suffering from some sort of nervous malady, the aftermath of a tropical fever, perhaps?

A rocket boomed out, and a fountain of silvery fire came showering down from overhead. By its brilliant glare, Sybilla studied her friend's face closely.

Dolores gave a brittle laugh. "Have no fear," she said. "I've not become *una loca*. My wits are perfectly sound."

275

Sybilla flushed with embarrassment as she realized that Dolores had guessed what she had been thinking. "These precautions are necessary, I assure you. Here in this house, I am spied upon, as I was in the governor's palace in Panama City. Only there it was even worse, with an army of slaves and flunkies to watch my every action, and report back to my husband."

She drew Sybilla down beside her on the marble bench, which was heaped with silken pillows. Then she shrugged slightly, her smooth white shoulders set off by the closely fitting black taffeta bodice of her gown. "One becomes used to taking measures to assure one's privacy."

Although Dolores could not quite conceal her annoyance, there was a kind of resignation, a matter-of-fact acceptance of her situation. Sybilla was convinced that, whatever experiences had changed her disposition, Dolores was not suffering from some sort of hysterical malady.

"Forgive me," Sybilla said. "But when I spoke with you at supper you seemed different from the way I remembered you."

"No doubt I've changed. I suppose I've adapted to the circumstances in which I find myself now. How else was I to survive?" But even as she tried to speak with cynical detachment she leaned forward, and her dark eyes shone with the warmth Sybilla remembered.

"You can't imagine how pleased I was to discover that you were right here in Cartegena!" She pressed Sybilla's arm with spontaneous affection. "To realize there was a friend nearby for me to confide in."

"But surely there's at least one woman among all your relations here in this house—"

"They are my husband's relations, not mine," Dolores interrupted. "Ramon's mother, old she-devil—his sisters and maiden aunts." She took her hand away, and, reaching into a pocket in her full skirt, she drew out a sheet of folded paper.

"Ramón, el Conde de Torrealta—Governor of Panama."
She spoke her husband's name and titles with a loathing that
Sybilla found deeply disturbing. "This letter I was given at
supper—it is from him. He has ordered me to return home to
Panama at once."

"He has ordered you? I don't understand. Was there a
quarrel? Have you run away from him?"

Dolores shook her head. "Nothing so dramatic, nor so
final, *Sybilla mía*. It was only that I needed to have this short
time apart from him. A last taste of freedom, if you will." She
sighed. "I knew it couldn't last—that I would have to return
to him. To that prison they call a palace. But I did hope I
would be able to be with Pedro through the carnival."

"Pedro?" Sybilla recalled the darkly handsome young
man in the scarlet and gold of a high-ranking Spanish army
officer. Dolores had danced with him most of the evening
and had dined with him in that secluded alcove.

There has already been enough gossip about me.

Her words came back to Sybilla now, with a new meaning.

"Your marriage is not quite—all that you had hoped for?"
Sybilla asked.

Dolores threw back her head, and her heavy diamond earrings caught the blaze from the shower of fireworks that
flared against the purple sky. Her shrill laugh filled Sybilla
with growing uneasiness.

"Marriage! What did I know of marriage—or of the man
my parents had chosen for me when I was still a child?"
Dolores spoke in hard, clipped tones. "Do you remember
how I told you of my betrothed—how pleased I was that my
parents had arranged such an excellent match? How I teased
you, when you assured me that you would never marry a
man you did not love—much less one you'd never met?
Perhaps now it is your turn to laugh at me."

"Dolores! How can you possibly think I'd make a
mockery of your unhappiness?"

"Forgive me," the other girl said quietly. "That was most

277

unjust of me. It's only that I can no longer be sure who is my friend, who is to be trusted."

She slipped the letter back into her pocket. Then she reached out, plucked a sprig of mimosa from the plant nearby, and began to shred it to bits. And all the while, her dark eyes searched Sybilla's face. "Tell me, *amiga mía,*" she asked abruptly, "are you in love with your husband? Has your marriage been a happy one?"

Sybilla flinched inwardly at the mention of her "marriage," and she searched for an answer that would not be an out-and-out lie.

"I love Gavin," she said. But the words could not begin to convey the depth of her feelings. "How can I tell you what I feel for him," she went on. "When he's away from me, he's never out of my thoughts. I wake up at night in the bed we shared, and reach for him, and when I remember he's gone, even for a little while, there's this—it's a kind of aching emptiness. But when we're together again and he holds me close—and I feel the warmth, the strength of him and I breath in the scent of his skin . . ." Sybilla stopped short, thankful for the darkness that hid her burning cheeks.

"There is no need for you to be ashamed," Dolores said quickly. "I've felt that way sometimes, with my Pedro. If only we could have had a few more nights together before Ramón forced me to return. I wanted to stay until the end of the carnival—only until then."

"You won't be seeing Pedro, once you've gone back to Panama?"

Dolores shook her head. "His regiment has been ordered to Lima. He is to sail right after the carnival. I was resigned to that. But now I find I am to be robbed even of the little time we might have had left." Her voice faltered slightly, but she made an effort to keep control of herself.

"*Sybilla, mía*—how I envy you. How wonderful to be married to the man you love. To know that you will be together, always. That you have no need to count the hours.

278

You miss him when you are apart—but you know he'll come back. Have you any idea how lucky you are?"

Although Dolores's words struck her like so many blows, she managed to conceal her feelings. "But we were speaking of your marriage."

"My marriage was a mockery from the beginning." Now, she fixed her eyes on Sybilla's face with disturbing intensity, and her words came rushing forth, as if she had kept them bottled up far too long, for want of someone to confide in.

"I left the *Bristol Belle* at Colón—that's the largest port on the east coast of the Isthmus. It's not far from Porto Bello."

In spite of her deep concern for her friend, Sybilla could not help but be distracted for a moment at the mere mention of Porto Bello. But she had given up hope of learning anything tonight that Gavin did not already know.

Sybilla sighed and turned her attention back to her friend's account of her arrival in Colón. If it eased Dolores's burden to share these confidences, then at least this evening at the Torrealta ball would not have been completely useless.

"Ramón was there at the dock to meet me," Dolores went on. "He was attended by a great retinue of soldiers and local dignitaries. And dozens of slaves. *Dios mío!* How he preened himself, when he told me of his promotion to the post of governor. How he gloated over the disgrace of his predecessor. Knowing him as I do now, I suspect he had a hand in the former governor's dismissal.

"Then he told me of his plans for our wedding in the great cathedral in Panama City—" Dolores made a small sound: she might have been choking back a sob. "And all the time I was praying that it was a nightmare. That I would awaken in my own bedchamber in my parents' home, back in Seville."

She clutched at Sybilla's hand tightly. "Tell me about your husband. Your *Capitán* Broderick. He is young and strong? And handsome?"

Sybilla nodded. "Gavin is—" She smiled. "I've never asked his age, but he's not yet thirty. And he's tall and his

279

eyes are gray, but sometimes they look almost black, like the waves when there's a storm brewing. And his body is deep bronze, tanned all over by the sun. Handsome?" She considered the word thoughtfully. "To me, he is beautiful. I never knew a man could be beautiful, in quite that way."

Even as she was speaking it was as if she could see Gavin again as she had seen him that night in Jamaica, when she had lain beside the waterfall and looked up from the bed of velvety moss to find him towering over her in the moonlight. Her heart speeded up, as she relived the moment: her gaze moving over the splendid breadth of his shoulders to the flatness of his belly, his hard, lean flanks, and long, muscular legs.

But Dolores's next words brought her back to the present with a start. "Ramón Torrealta is old enough to be my father. Only my father is a fine-looking man for his years. He still can ride and hunt with the best of them. But as for Ramón—there he stood, with that stooped, bony, spindle-shanked carcass of his decked out in purple satin and silver braid. His skin was yellow, and it hung in wattles—like a vulture's. And the whites of his eyes were yellowish, too."

Her full red lips twisted in a grimace of distaste. "He leaned on a beribboned cane, but even so, he needed one of his soldiers to help support him. He'd just recovered from a fever, he said."

"He can't be blamed for that," Sybilla pointed out, casting about for some small consolation. "Perhaps when he has regained his health completely—"

"As if he ever will! Swamp fever—that's what he has. It's caused by the evil vapors that rise from the river valley. Once a man is stricken, the fever returns again and again, with aches and chills and all manner of disgusting ailments." She shuddered. "I could scarcely bear the touch of his hand on mine."

Sybilla felt a stirring of pity for Dolores. She was remembering the deep revulsion she had felt at the prospect of marrying Nicholas Hobart, even though he'd been in robust health. Perhaps it wasn't fair of Dolores to criticize Ramón so bitterly, but Sybilla could understand her friend's shock at seeing, for the first time, the man who was to be her husband.

"It took almost a week before we crossed the Isthmus and arrived in Panama City," Dolores went on. "We traveled in sedan chairs, engraved with the Torrealta coat of arms, and trimmed with coral and gold; they were so heavy that the slaves had all they could do to carry them. And the company of soldiers marched on either side, to guard us."

"To guard you—from what?"

"From *los Cimarrones*—the Untamed." Even now, her eyes were shadowed by remembered fear. "Ramón told me about *los Cimarrones*. He said they were some of the black slaves who'd been brought from Africa to help build the road. They had overpowered their guards and escaped into the jungle. They only came out at night to attack unwary travelers.

"We traveled through the jungle, and the air was so hot and damp every stitch of my underclothing clung to my skin. And I thought I should suffocate inside my sedan chair. A horrid wilderness it is, with screeching monkeys swinging through the trees overhead and crocodiles, sunning themselves on the banks of the Changres. And the snakes! I have always loathed even the smallest, most harmless snake. But these . . . the bushmaster. The fer-de-lance. Their bite is poisonous, and one can scarcely see them among the branches and the vines. There were lizards, too. One of them was crawling up the side of my chair, when I screamed and a soldier killed it with his saber—the creature was five feet long."

Dolores laughed again, that same short, mirthless laugh Sybilla was coming to recognize. "We made the journey over *el Camino de Oro*. The Road of Gold. The slaves have another name for it—*Via Maldita*."

"The—Accursed Way?" Sybilla asked.

Dolores nodded. "Those black slaves I was speaking of—most did not escape. Many died, while they were building the road. That's why their descendants believe it is haunted. They swear that they can hear the groans of the slaves who carried the heavy stones until they collapsed and died under the lash. But I heard only the chattering of the monkeys and the cries of the jaguars and the pumas that stalk the jungle at night.

"The inns we stopped at were dirty, and even the best quarters were crude and uncomfortable. But at least Ramón gave me a room of my own."

Sybilla saw that Dolores's hands were tightly clenched in her lap. "It wasn't until after our wedding reception at the palace—when the guests led us to our quarters, and left us there, wishing us joy of one another. When I had to lie with Ramón for the first time—"

"I think I understand," Sybilla said quickly, not wanting to hear any more.

"Do you, indeed! You, with your handsome young husband, your gray-eyed *capitán?*"

Another rocket exploded in the air, sending down a shower of light against the night sky. "But forgive me, Sybilla. I have no right to begrudge you your happiness."

Dolores was silent for a brief time, and when she began to speak again, her voice was bleak and filled with despair. "It would have been awful enough if Ramón had taken me, that night."

"He didn't?" Sybilla could not restrain her surprise.

"He couldn't. Not that he didn't try. He pawed me, he clutched at me with those bony fingers, until I was sore and bruised all over. He tried to force me to do all sorts of—revolting things. . . . And then he berated me. He said it was my fault he wasn't able to—perform as a man should." She made a sound of wordless disgust. "And it went on like that for the first few weeks of our marriage. Until he started guzzling wine each night. To give him the confidence to approach me again. He'd come stumbling into our bed, maul me about, and fall into a stupor." She turned and stared out over the balcony railing.

"And then you met—Pedro."

Dolores nodded. "He was stationed at the garrison next to the governor's palace. It was his duty to ride beside my carriage, when I went out each day. We began to talk to one another. He, too, is from Seville." She turned back to face Sybilla. "I'm not ashamed of what happened between us. Only—now I think—I'm sure I am with child."

Sybilla gave a violent start, her eyes widening with shocked dismay. No wonder her friend had reacted as she had to the letter from her husband, ordering her to return to Panama City.

"But if you are increasing, you won't be able to conceal your condition for long. And since your husband has never—since he can't—" Sybilla lapsed into embarrassed silence.

"Ramón probably suspects that there is another man, though he has said nothing so far. But if he found out that I am carrying my lover's child, there's no telling what he might do. He's too much of a coward to kill me, but maybe he'd find someone else to get rid of me. Does that shock you, Sybilla? Such things have happened before."

"What if you don't go back? Maybe Pedro would take you with him, when he has to leave here."

"It would create a scandal that would ruin his career." She shook her head. "I couldn't allow that to happen."

"Then perhaps you could make some excuse to stay in Cartegena until after the baby is born. Not here with your husband's family, but—" Sybilla searched her mind for some solution to her friend's dilemma. "Maybe if I were to speak to Señora Mendez, she might know of someplace—"

"No! You will tell no one." Dolores's voice was hard and disillusioned, drained of all hope. "I will return, as Ramón

283

ordered, within the fortnight."

"But why is your husband suddenly so anxious to have you come back to him?"

"Not because he misses my company. He needs me with him at this—this Porto Bello fair. It is a most important event, here in this corner of the empire. He writes that the first ships from Spain have started arriving earlier than expected. And he must be leaving for Porto Bello before the end of the month."

Sybilla's heart jerked, then began to pound against her ribs with an erratic beat. She froze, all the muscles in her body so tense that they began to ache. Her golden eyes were fixed on Dolores's face with a look of such intensity that the other girl was somewhat taken aback.

"Ah, Sybilla, you must not be afraid for me. I'll give my husband no excuse to have me poisoned for bearing another man's bastard and giving it the noble Torrealta name. Don't look so shocked, *querida*. I will do what I must."

"But I don't understand. How can you—"

Then she remembered overhearing talk about a pregnant young girl back in Somerset, who had swallowed a brew of tansy and ergot, given her by a midwife. The girl had died in agony, a few days later.

"Dolores, you must not take some dangerous potion to try to rid yourself of the child. Promise me you won't be so foolish."

"Never fear," Dolores reassured her. "I've no intention of risking my life. Or destroying Pedro's child. I'll find a way to get Ramón to consummate the marriage—or I'll get him too drunk to remember what happened. By the time I have to stand beside him at Porto Bello, through all those endless ceremonies—the greeting of the admiral from the Spanish flagship, the banquet in his honor, the opening of the fair— Ramón can take pride in showing me off. I will be the living proof of his manhood—his ability to get a woman with child. . . ."

*   *   *

It was nearly dawn when Sybilla rode home in the carriage with Eduardo Mendez and his wife. Somehow, she was able to offer a polite comment, from time to time, while Angela chattered breathlessly, her round face aglow with triumph, as she relived every moment of the Torrealtas' ball.

"Wait until I tell Placida and Luz and the rest of the magnificent gowns, and the jewels the ladies wore. And that supper—and the fireworks!"

She turned a curious glance on Sybilla. "I looked for you in the courtyard, but I could not see you anywhere."

"I watched the display from the balcony above, with Dolores. We had a fine view from there."

Angela clasped her plump hands together. "La Condesa invited you to her own chamber—only think of it. Such an honor, *Sybilla mía!* Now, aren't you pleased that you took my advice and wrote your friend that you were here in Cartegena? Think of all you will have to tell your husband when he returns."

Sybilla managed a smile, as she longed for the moment when she would be alone, to force her confused thoughts into some semblance of order. She did, indeed, have much to tell Gavin; but it would not wait until he came back from the trading post.

After she had said good night to her host and hostess, after her maid had helped her out of her ball gown and into her nightdress, after the girl had brushed her hair and departed, Sybilla's mind was still in turmoil.

The light had changed from pale blue to crimson outside her windows, but she remained sitting up in bed, propped up against the pillows, her body tense, her nerves stretched to the breaking point. At last she sighed, pushed back the light coverlet, and swung her legs over the side of the bed. She put on a silk robe and high-heeled slippers and walked to the window.

Pushing aside one of the drapes, she stared to the south, where the mists were starting to lift over the distant hills. Somewhere on the savannah, beyond the hills, stood the trading post where Gavin had gone to gather the vital intelligence he needed. But only a few hours ago she had discovered the one piece of information he needed most and could not possibly have ferreted out yet.

The first ships from Spain had arrived at the Isthmus far earlier than expected, and news of their unexpected appearance off Porto Bello could make all the difference between the success or failure of Gavin's expedition.

Sybilla knew she must get word to him as quickly as possible. She only had to write a brief letter, and send for Tod, who would take it up to the trading post. Gavin had assured her that no one could move through the jungle and up the Magdalena faster, or with greater safety, than the copper-skinned young Indian lad.

Why, then, was she still standing here at the window, unable to do what must be done? The answer came, and with it, a growing apprehension that held her immobile. Her heart began to thud against her ribs, and she felt that she could scarcely breath. Until this moment, she had forced herself not to look ahead, but now she had to consider what must happen as soon as she sent word to Gavin.

He would return to Cartegena at once. They would leave the city for Costa Verde, where he would gather the men who waited there, and then they would go on to Tortuga. If the new ships provided by Nicholas Hobart were already riding at anchor in the harbor, he would give orders to set sail at once.

Gavin would have to launch his attack on the treasure galleons without delay, while they were still strung out along the coast of New Granada, and before they were joined by their convoy of warships. But even if he did so, he could not be sure of victory.

A shift in the wind, a musket ball fired by a Spanish sharp-shooter from the rigging of a galleon, a mainmast crashing down under the impact of a Spanish cannon—any of these, or a dozen other disasters, would be enough to bring defeat.

Suppose Gavin should be taken prisoner. She knew well enough what brutal treatment he might expect from the enemy. And if he fell in battle—but even now, she could not bring herself to face the thought of a future without him.

He would return to her safely. He must. And what then? She tried not to think that far ahead, but the question hammered at her brain and would not go away. She knew Gavin. She understood the forces that drove him. And she was certain that a victory over the Spanish fleet would not satisfy him.

Such a triumph would only make him bolder, more reck-less. He would sail out across the Caribbean again and yet again, and with each successful voyage more buccaneers would flock to join him. They would fight one another for the chance to sail under the battle flag of Captain Gavin Broderick.

Sybilla went numb with despair at the prospect. She rested her head against the carved window frame, and closed her eyes for a moment, as if to shut out her vision of the future.

How could she go on loving a man who lived only for vengeance? Yet, she knew she could not bring herself to leave him. And if she stayed, she would have to accept him—not as he was now—but as he might one day be. Completely ruth-less, devoid of all trace of humanity.

She remembered Dolores's envious words, when she'd told her how lucky she was to be married to the man she loved. But Gavin was not her husband. And now, with time running out, she faced the loss of all hope of marrying him and building the kind of future she longed to share with him. She would never be his wife, never know the joy of bearing his children, of raising them in safety, of teaching them the meaning of honor and decency.

Unless . . . She raised her head. A vague plan began to take shape, filling her with renewed courage. She wasn't beaten yet. And she wasn't going to be, if she could help it. Her golden eyes narrowed as her thoughts moved quickly.

What if Gavin did not learn of the arrival of the Spanish warships until it was too late, until the fair was underway and the assembled convoy lay at anchor in the harbor at Porto Bello, heavily armed and waiting to escort the treasure fleet back to Cádiz?

In the light of the tropical dawn, Sybilla struggled to make a decision that would shape her whole future—and Gavin's too. She had given him her promise to try to help him in any way she could. Even if it meant deceiving Eduardo Mendez and his wife, and Dolores. She had given her word to the man she loved. Could she break it, for his sake, as well as her own?

If she could, she might be able to convince him that he could not go on living for revenge, that it was time to put his dangerous, roving existence behind him and return with her to Boston. To his home and family and the way of life for which he had been bred.

But now a new fear stirred inside her. What would he do if he discovered that she had deliberately deceived him? She knew the capacity for violence that was a part of him, and she dreaded the thought of facing his cold fury.

She told herself that she was allowing her imagination to take control over her common sense. Gavin need never find out that she had prevented him from carrying out his plans. He had no way of knowing what Dolores had told her at the Torrealtas' mansion last night.

But suppose he returned to Cartegena within the next few days? In this seaport, such news would travel fast. Perhaps he would arrive in time to see the cargoes of silver and gold, of precious gems and fine silks, piled on the docks, or being carried onto ships bound for Porto Bello?

If that happened he would not give up his plan. Even though the odds would be greater, that would not stop him. She knew Gavin well enough to realize that, under the circumstances, he would leave for Tortuga all the sooner, to gather his forces for the attack.

At this stage of the game, every day can make a difference.

That was what he had told her, the night before he had left for the trading post. If there was even the slightest chance that he might intercept part of the treasure fleet before it reached the safety of Porto Bello, he would take the risk. And his men would follow him with unwavering loyalty.

Sybilla turned from the window, and began to pace the floor. All at once her fears fell away, and she felt only an unshakeable determination. She had to make certain that by the time Gavin returned there would be no chance at all.

She must word her letter carefully, in such a way as to convince him that the fair would not begin for two months, or perhaps more. Then, afterwards, he would think only that she had been misinformed. He would have no cause to suspect that she had told him a deliberate lie.

He must not come back until the narrow streets of Porto Bello were already swarming with the merchants from Panama, Mexico, Peru, the Argentine, and the distant Philippine islands. Until the assembled might of the Spanish warships lay waiting at Porto Bello, like a pack of fierce hounds, guarding their flock from the prowling wolves.

Only then would he be forced to abandon all hope of taking the treasure fleet. He would be badly shaken at the collapse of all his plans. But she would be there at his side. She would comfort him. And somehow, she would find a way to convince him that the time for revenge was past.

Chapter Twenty-Two

Gavin studied the chart spread out before him; other charts and maps lay to one side, tightly rolled and tied with heavy cord. A cool breeze, blowing across the broad savannah, rattled the half-open shutters and lifted the edges of the parchment he was examining. He smoothed it with an impatient gesture and scrawled a notation on one side.

He glanced up to see Abiathar emerging from the adjoining room in the small wooden house they shared here at the straggling settlement that had sprung up in the shadow of the Andes, not far from Bogotá.

Gavin repressed a grin at the sight of his friend, for the huge, red-bearded mate had donned the resplendent, gold-braided bottle green velvet coat he had taken from the *San Bartolomé,* and a wide-brimmed hat heaped with ostrich plumes. The cooler, drier climate here on the savannah made the wearing of such finery more bearable.

"Thought I'd be takin' a ride into Bogotá." He grinned. "Some of the men were tellin' me about a fine tavern in the city. They say there's plenty of good food and drink to be had and the wenches are prime."

He gestured at the sheet of parchment on the table. "You been working since morning. Why not leave this stuff and come along?"

Gavin did not answer at once. During the past weeks, he

had managed to get hold of most of the information he had come for; some of it he had bought, and the rest he had acquired in exchange for the contraband goods he had carried through the jungle and up the Magdalena to the high plateau above.

The charts before him covered the most frequently traveled trade routes between Vera Cruz, Peru, the Argentine, and the distant colonies in the Philippine islands. The routes the Spanish galleons would be likely to follow, when they headed for Porto Bello.

Since early morning, Gavin had been busy making careful notations, concerning the number of brass cannons, the quantities of ammunition each ship would be carrying; how many sharpshooters; how many experienced gunners would be aboard. Such facts must be taken into account, in preparing for the coming expedition. He had even grudged stopping an hour ago for a meal of piquete—a spicy pork and chicken stew—and wine.

"Now, if they was British merchantmen, it would be easier to be sure of the facts," Abiathar was saying. "Them Spanish merchants are a slippery, two-faced lot."

Gavin shrugged. "I've allowed for all their usual subterfuges," he said.

Both he and Abiathar had long been familiar with the elaborate system of deceptions used by the Spanish colonial shipowners to evade government trade regulations and enrich themselves. They hired extra cannons and ammunition for their galleons and kept them on board until the government inspection had been completed and the manifests signed. A horde of "sailors" were lined up on deck—dockside idlers who had been brought aboard for the purpose.

It was necessary for these Spanish colonists to make a pretense of following the strict rules laid down by the *Casa de Contratacion* back in Seville; for that all-powerful government agency ruled colonial commerce. It served as a clearinghouse for foreign trade and also controlled all cargoes, customs posts, permits, papers, and personnel associated with ships sailing for, or coming from, the colonies of Spain's far-flung empire.

Before the treasure galleons set sail, however, the additional arms and men were put ashore to make more room for the unlisted cargo.

It proved to be a most profitable form of double-dealing, so long as a heavily laden galleon did not have the misfortune to run afoul of pirates before she reached the safety of Porto Bello. Few merchant galleons, overloaded with cargo, could hope to outsail the buccaneer vessel, with its greater speed and mobility.

Gavin, determined to make the best use of his captured galleon, had already left orders with his men at Costa Verde to strip the decks of the *San Bartolomé* of any obstructions that might interfere with their moving swiftly from side to side. Her bulwarks were to be raised to waist height to hide the crew from sight until the moment when they were given the order to attack.

"Them Spanish customs men know right enough, what the merchants and shipowners are up to, overloading their ships like that," Abiathar said with a grimace of contempt. "But as long as they get their palms greased, they don't mind lookin' the other way."

Gavin nodded. *"Lo que el Rey manda se obedece, no se cumple*—that's the motto they live by out here in the Indies. What the King commands is obeyed—but not carried out."

"A scurvy lot, they are. Any one of them'd sell his own sister at auction in Tortuga, if the price was right."

"It's the common folk back in Spain who suffer most from this monopoly," Gavin said. "What with the enormous taxes on their daily necessities, they can barely survive, much less prosper."

"And with all them trade laws, that addlepated Spanish king won't be master of the Indies much longer," Abiathar observed.

Gavin's face hardened. "No doubt. But I mean to do all I

can to speed that day." He bent his head over the chart again, dipped his quill in the inkstand, and started making more notations.

"You plan to go on workin' all night?" Abiathar asked, shifting impatiently as he glanced toward the door. "Put them charts aside and ride down to Bogotá with me. The change'll do you good. And we'll still have time to spare, before the first treasure galleons start out for Porto Bello. Mistress Sybilla said so in her letter."

His weatherbeaten face split in a wide, approving grin. "I told you the lass would make herself useful if we brought her with us to Cartegena, didn't I? You got to admit she's done even better than we expected."

"It was sheer luck that she managed to get herself invited to the Torrealtas' ball," Gavin reminded him. "She'd never have been asked to set foot in that house, if the Condesa hadn't been visiting there."

A corner of his mouth turned down in a grimace of distaste. "I'm still not sure I should have allowed Sybilla to get involved in all this."

Abiathar's bushy red brows shot up. "And why not?" he demanded. "The lass can be trusted. Feelin' like she does about you, there's nothing she wouldn't do to help."

Gavin shot him a warning glance, but the mate chose to ignore it. "She's that fond of you, I wager she'd stand at your side on deck when we steered into battle if you was to say the word."

Gavin released his breath with a sound of exasperation. But Abiathar went on. "I never was one to put my trust in any female. But Mistress Sybilla—she's different. She's a real fine lady."

Abiathar hooked his thumbs in his belt, set his booted feet apart, and gave Gavin a long, challenging stare.

"I don't question her honesty," Gavin said. "Nor her good breeding. That's what troubles me. This sort of treachery and double-dealing she had to use goes against all she was brought up to believe in."

"But she's cast her lot with you." Abiathar reminded him. "She made the choice, and she'll stick by it."

"She chose foolishly. She acted on impulse, without realizing what she was doing," Gavin interrupted. "A girl like Sybilla—how could she be expected to understand the code we live by?" He was speaking to himself now, rather than to Abiathar. "I should have left her behind in Tortuga, under the protection of Governor d'Ogeron."

"Maybe so. She'll be goin' to stay in the governor's house soon enough. There's no place else you can leave her, when it's time for us to go after the treasure fleet." He paused, and an uneasy look crossed his broad face. "But after we come back, what then?" Abiathar, with his unimaginative courage, refused to consider the possibility that they might not return to Tortuga, their ships laden with the booty from the defeated Spanish galleons.

"As soon as we've brought our loot back to Tortuga and divided the spoils I'll put her on the first merchantman, British, Dutch or French, that's bound for Boston. She'll be safe there."

"Suppose she don't want to be safe? Not if it means leavin' you?" Abiathar looked faintly embarrassed by his own words, for they smacked of the sort of sentimental foolishness he'd always scorned.

"She'll go—if I have to tie her hand and foot, and carry her aboard." Gavin said brusquely. "Besides, her brother'll be along to keep guard over her until the ship's out to sea."

"Guess it's the only way," Abiathar agreed.

Gavin rolled up the wide sleeves of his linen shirt, and glanced down at the chart. "If you mean to get into Bogotá by nightfall, you'd best get started."

"Sure you won't change your mind an' ride along?"

He shook his head. "It's true, we have more time than I'd expected, and I mean to make good use of it. We'll leave as little as possible to chance."

"Please yourself. But if you should change your mind later on, that tavern I'm heading for is called el Burro Blanco. I mean to eat and drink my fill. Then I'll find me a fat young wench with black hair, tits like casava melons, and a big round arse on 'er.

"What female in all Bogotá could resist you, decked out as you are in that fine velvet coat and those plumes? I warrant they'll be clawing each other's eyes out for the chance to bed down with you."

But in spite of Gavin's determination to remain behind and go on working, he felt a sudden stir of restlessness. He wasn't used to being confined to a desk, that was it. He rose, stretched his tall, muscular frame, then went as far as the porch with Abiathar, who was already heading for his horse.

Gavin lingered outside to fill his lungs with the clean, dry air that blew across the savannah. His eyes glinted with amusement as he watched Abiathar mount and take hold of the reins. Although the bearded giant had lost no time in mastering the powerful stallion by sheer physical strength and determination, he rode like a man who was more at ease on the deck of a pitching frigate in a gale then in the saddle.

Gavin turned away, and headed for the door. Then a brilliant splash of color caught his eye. The back country of New Granada was thick with flowering vines and shrubs of every kind, and he had seen countless orchids of purple, mauve, amethyst and cream.

Yet now he found himself staring at a spray of yellow blooms that grew close beside the porch railing: golden orchids, with delicate flecks of brown amber. Moved by an impulse he did not quite understand, he broke off the spray and turned it between his fingers. He stood on the porch, watching the fading crimson glow of late afternoon sunlight, reflected from the snowcapped peaks of the Guadalupe and Monserrate. It was an impressive sight, but his eyes were drawn away by the spray of orchids in his hand.

Golden orchids. The same rare, unforgettable color as Sybilla's eyes.

What the devil had come over him, that he should be standing here, staring at the flowers, like some moonstruck school boy? Yet, he could not bring himself to toss the spray of orchids away. Instead he carried it back inside the shack and placed it on one side of the table, atop a pile of rolled-up charts.

The sound of the stallion's hooves had already died away along the trail, but although Gavin bent over his charts again, he found it increasingly difficult to concentrate. Belike it would not have mattered if he had put off this night's work to ride with Abiathar, for a few hours of drinking and wenching at el Burro Blanco. He, too, had heard the men here at the trading post praising the ripe sensuality of Bogotá's wenches. And after nearly a fortnight here at the trading post he felt a need for a tumble with a willing girl.

But all at once he realized that he didn't want a tavern girl, who would smile and swing her hips with a voluptuous motion. Who would bend over when she served his drink, to give him a good look at her breasts. A girl who would smile at him, as she would any man who came through the door with a full pouch of coins. He was in no mood to settle for a night of skillful but meaningless lovemaking, the sort that had satisfied him all these years.

He wanted Sybilla. Wanted her with an overpowering need that stunned him by its very force.

The hot flood of feeling caught him off guard, and he drew in his breath. He wanted her here, looking up at him, her eyes wide and golden, her long, dark lashes tracing shadowy crescents on her cheeks. Her face upturned to his, her red lips parted to receive his kiss.

He could hear her saying his name, her soft voice muffled against his chest, her long, shapely thighs pressing urgently against his. A swift heat stirred inside him, searing his loins, filling him with an aching hunger. His hands gripped the edge of the table, the carved wood cutting into his palms.

Sybilla.

He clamped his lips together and tried not to think about her white body, the clean scent of her auburn hair, the silken-smooth feel of her breasts. Her pink nipples hardening as he took them between his lips. Her hands, swift to touch him, to caress him in all the ways that stirred him to unbearable heights of wanting.

Her body arching beneath him, her thighs parting. The moist satin sheath closing around him, drawing him up inside her, higher, deeper, until he could no longer hold back from the shattering moment of climax.

He released his breath, and now he was remembering that night in the thatch hut on the beach at Costa Verde, when he'd awakened, still caught in the grasp of his nightmare. He had been assailed by the same dream many times before, and he had opened his eyes, his breath rasping in his throat, his body clammy with sweat, his muscles rigid.

But that particular night had been different, because Sybilla had been there beside him. Her arms had comforted him, her body had warmed him, her soft, reassuring voice had led him back to reality.

She would have had every right to draw away from him, in anger or contempt, after the way he had treated her earlier that night. Why the hell had he turned on Abiathar with such violence when his friend had offered to perform a marriage ceremony aboard the *Condor?*

He damn well knew why.

Gavin picked up his quill, dipped it into the inkstand, then pressed it against the chart with such force that the tip split apart and a few drops of ink spattered on the parchment. He pulled out his knife and started to sharpen the point once more.

He knew why he had lashed out at Abiathar. And why he had turned away from the sight of Sybilla's white, stricken face, the naked pain in her eyes, and gone striding away from the campfire—why he had stood down there by the water's edge alone, staring out to sea. The answer lay spread before him, as if written on the chart that covered the table.

Within a few months, the expedition would be more than a set of lines and maps, drawn on parchment. His men, his ships, would be heading into battle against the full strength of the Spanish treasure fleet. And Sybilla would be left behind on Tortuga, to get through the nights of waiting.

Suppose he had listened to Abiathar and gone through with the marriage ceremony. If Sybilla was not meant to be a pirate's woman then she would be no less vulnerable if he had made her his wife.

But there was another reason, buried so deeply that even now, he could scarcely bring himself to face it. Yet he knew that he must.

He'd had a wife who had loved him and trusted him to protect her.

He went on staring at the chart, with unseeing eyes. And his lips shaped the name, Verity. But when he tried to call up the image of her face he realized with a pang that it had faded over the years.

"Verity." He said her name aloud, there the deserted shack high on the savannah in this alien outpost. And now he saw the shy, gentle girl with her wide blue eyes, her light brown hair drawn back smoothly under her prim gray bonnet. A cloak of the same drab color had concealed her small, slender body, and the wind from Boston harbor had tugged at the heavy homespun fabric.

Verity had grown up in the care of her aunt and uncle, stern Puritans, both of them. Even when she had promised to marry him, on that long-ago afternoon, she had not felt free to part her lips for his eager kiss. He had felt a little disappointed by her reluctance, but scarcely surprised.

On their wedding night, he had tried to be patient, to deal with her gently, for no doubt she'd been taught that such sensual pleasures were a part of the male prerogative. A decent wife gave herself dutifully and looked forward to bearing children as a reward for her submission.

There had been no time for her to learn anything different. Gavin's mouth tightened, two deep lines bracketing his lips, as he remembered their brief marriage and the way it had ended. Guilt twisted his insides and his hands closed into hard fists.

He should never have taken her on the voyage at all. She could have remained behind, safe and secure, in his parents' house. But he had wanted her with him on his first voyage as master of his own ship, and she had gone along willingly, trusting him to care for her and protect her. She sailed with him on a voyage straight to hell. . . .

The sunlight had faded, and Gavin paused to light the lantern that hung from a beam over the table. He sharpened the quill and went back to his work. No sea venture was without its hazards. But he would do all in his power to make sure that he struck the Spanish with such speed and force that his own ships would return victorious and laden with spoils greater than any brought back to Tortuga before. And with the lowest possible casualty rate among his own men.

Gradually, he lost himself in his work, and soon he was only dimly aware of the sounds around him: the rattling of the shutters, the rustle of the tall grass bending in the night wind.

But all at once he froze and set down his pen, his brows drawing together in a frown, his gray eyes alert and wary. He caught the creak of the rickety porch steps outside. This wasn't Abiathar's heavy, booted tread, but the scrape of bare feet, moving slowly, uncertainly, stumbling across the porch now. And another sound: the clank of metal dragging against the wooden planks. Gavin rose, his eyes fixed on the door, his hand closing around the handle of his knife.

The door swung open and in the light of the overhead lantern. Tod, his copper-colored face drawn with exhaustion, stood clutching at the doorframe. The Indian boy swayed for a moment and would have pitched forward, but Gavin was beside him. He lifted the boy and carried him to the cane bench near the window. Tod had left the trading post four days ago; he should have been approaching Cartegena by now. He'd had his orders. What the devil was he doing back here?

Gavin's face hardened, his high, angular cheekbones jutting out sharply, as he caught sight of the livid bruises on the boy's wrists. Around one ankle, he saw a metal band and a short length of broken chain. And those cuts across the smooth copper-colored skin—only a whip could have made them.

Gavin felt a killing rage, but he forced it back. He had to see to the boy's needs at once. He poured a cup of wine, then he supported the boy's shoulders and forced the liquid between his lips.

Tod choked, then swallowed.

"Who did this to you?" Gavin spoke quietly, but his voice shook with barely suppressed fury. He had always felt responsible for the welfare of every man who served under his flag. Tod had sailed aboard the *Condor* and carried out his duties as powder monkey with a grown man's courage. After that, he had taken on the distasteful task of posing as Sybilla's slave. He had made his way up the Magdalena and through the jungle swiftly, carrying his message.

He drained the cup, then managed to speak. "The guards—they caught me the day after I left, Captain." His onyx eyes were fixed on Gavin's face. "I tried to hide. But in broad daylight . . . If I could have reached the jungle, I'd have had a chance. Out on the open plain, without a rock or tree . . ." He shook his head.

"Who were these guards?"

"They protected the mule train. Never have I seen so many men and beasts, Captain. All moving at great speed. Mules so heavily laden that they could scarcely keep up the pace. And the slaves, too—driven with whips, like the beasts."

Gavin leaned forward. A sudden warning sounded in his mind. He refilled the cup and held it to Tod's lips again, but after the first sip, the boy pushed it away.

"I must not fall asleep. Not before I finish telling you—"

"Go on, then."

"The mule drivers needed new slaves—to take the place of

those who had died, crossing the mountains."

Gavin nodded, as he weighed the boy's words. Mules and slaves, laden with crates, crossing the mountains.

"Where were they coming from?"

"I could not find out—not at once. They chained me with the other slaves. But the second night after they caught me— That was when I heard the drivers talking. They were traveling from Peru, Captain." He paused only long enough to draw his breath. "They carry ingots of silver—from the mines at Potosí."

The words struck him with the force of a blow. But although he had to know more, he was able to restrain himself briefly.

"Are you badly hurt, boy?"

Tod's eyes glowing with fierce pride. "Those pigs—they could not hurt me. A few cuts with the whip. They are nearly healed."

Gavin took the boy at his word. He must find out the rest, and quickly. "Their destination?" he demanded.

"Cartegena, first. To load the silver on the ships—"

"What ships?"

"The treasure ships. Bound for Porto Bello."

"You're mistaken, damn it!" An icy current poured through his body. "You didn't understand—you got it all wrong!"

The boy shook his head. His eyes did not waver. "I understood, sir. They were traveling from Peru, with silver for the fair at Porto Bello."

"That's not possible."

The boy spoke respectfully, but there was no mistaking the stubborn certainty in his voice. "I saw the crest on the doublets of the guards. The Potosí crest, Captain Broderick. The great crown and the—the columns. I saw the words, though I could not read them."

Gavin repeated the motto, in a low, expressionless tone. "I am the rich Potosí; of the world I am the treasure; I am the king of mountains, and I am the envy of kings."

Damned arrogant bastards. Their own nation was in chaos, their people starving, and still those who ruled Spain ignored the needs of the common folk there while they fought to keep their monopoly here in the New World. They drained the treasures of these colonies, destroying or enslaving the Indians who had owned the land for centuries.

"I kept waiting for a chance to get away. To get back and warn you, Captain."

Gavin nodded, but even as he listened, he was remembering Sybilla's message. She had been certain that the ships had not yet arrived from Spain, that the trade fair would not begin for at least another two months. And she had assured him in the letter that her information had come directly from la Condesa Dolores Torrealta y de las Fuentes, the wife of the governor of Panama.

"They drove us hard—with a handful of meal, and a little water, to keep us going." Gavin forced all other thoughts from his mind, as he listened to the boy's words. "They were under orders to reach Cartegena as soon as possible."

The boy spoke quickly, his voice filled with urgency, for he knew the vital importance of the news he carried. "Even the guards grew weary. The next night, they slept. And those who'd been appointed to watch us—they drank too much, and finally, they, too, began to doze.

"Then one of the slaves who was chained in the same squad with me—he gave the signal. We held our chains tight so as not to make a sound, until we got across the clearing and into the jungle. As soon as we were far enough away, we broke our chains. Pounded them with stones. The others—wanted me to go with them, back to their village."

"But you came here instead, to warn me." Gavin was moved by the boy's unwavering devotion to duty. He would see that Tod received an extra share of the loot, after they had taken the galleons. Then he stiffened, as he realized that, unless he moved fast, there would be no loot—no expedition at all. "Go on, boy," he urged.

"The warships from Cadiz were sighted off Porto Bello,

nearly three weeks ago. That's all I know, Captain."

And it was enough. Gavin could fill in the rest for himself. Even now, runners were carrying the word to the far-flung settlements from Vera Cruz to Lima. Trading ships laden with indigo, cochineal, dyewoods, and hides were sailing for the Isthmus. And at the plaza in Porto Bello, merchants were setting up booths made of logs and sailcloth.

"I traveled only by night and hid by day. I didn't want to be caught again and—"

"All right, lad. That's enough for now."

It was time to see to the boy's immediate needs. Gavin found part of a loaf of bread and the remains of the stew left from his own meal. He dipped a chunk of bread in wine and handed it to the boy, who munched avidly. "Finish it, and drink the rest of the wine. Then go to sleep," Gavin told him. After Tod had regained his strength, there would be time to file off the fetter on his ankle; to bandage his cuts and bruises. Tod was tough and resilient, and a good thing, too. He and Abiathar would have to get back to Cartegena as quickly as possible, and he would not leave the boy behind.

Gavin's eyes hardened as he thought over Tod's words. In the light of what the boy had told him, Sybilla's message made no sense. Unless the Condesa had given her false information. That must be the answer. He could think of no other plausible explanation.

Tod drained the cup, and Gavin rose to leave; but the boy clutched at his sleeve. "Captain—there is something more—"

"Tell me."

"When we were escaping, one of the guards stirred. So I— I got my chain around his neck." The boy's voice faltered. "I took his life—before he could awake." His eyes searched Gavin's as if asking absolution.

"If he'd caught you, he'd have killed you without a second's hesitation," Gavin said firmly. "Don't think about it again. Try to sleep. I'll go find Abiathar, but I'll be back by morning."

"Yes, sir." Tod's eyelids had already begun to droop. He

was exhausted, and the wine had done its work. Moments later, he was lying on his side and breathing evenly. Gavin found a coarse blanket and covered him. The boy was wiry as a young sapling. He would mend quickly.

Then, leaving a jug of water, the stew pot, and the rest of the loaf on the floor, Gavin thrust a pair of loaded pistols into his belt, put on his riding cloak, and left the house.

Abiathar might decide to linger in Bogotá until tomorrow night, if he found the pleasures at el Burro Blanco to his liking. Gavin could not afford to wait that long.

Half an hour later, he had left the trading post far behind. He was galloping through a wooded stretch, then on to the bank of a wide, rushing stream. His stallion's hooves thundered over a wooden bridge. The moon flooded the countryside with light, so that he could make out the unfamiliar trail without too much difficulty. He bent low over the horse's neck, and the wind whipped his cloak out behind him.

But even now, as he went moving on at a gallop, he could not put Sybilla out of his thoughts. He'd been right about her. He cursed himself for a fool. She had tried to help him, but somehow, she had given herself away. Had she been trusting enough to have confided in the Condesa? That would have been like Sybilla; straightforward, impulsive—unable to hide the purpose of her visit to the Torrealtas' mansion.

He eased his horse to a trot, to give the beast a brief respite. His eyes rested on the snowcapped mountain peaks, gleaming against the purple sky.

He should have left Sybilla in Tortuga. What had possessed him to bring her along, not only as far as Costa Verde, but into Cartegena, itself? His lips curved in a wry smile. She had not been to blame. He had taken her with him because he could not bring himself to leave her.

Because he wanted her with him until it was time to sail

against the Spanish fleet.

As if to escape his own thoughts, he spurred the horse to a gallop once more. They moved through the darkness, toward Bogotá, and el Burro Blanco.

He left the savannah behind and now he caught sight of the rooftops of Bogotá silhouetted against the moonlit sky; but even as he turned the stallion into one of the narrow, slanting streets, he could not stop thinking about Sybilla.

He had set her a task to which she was not suited either by nature or experience. If Tod had not been captured by the guards of the Potosí silver train, if he had not escaped and returned to the trading post so swiftly, there would not be the slightest chance of undertaking the expedition with any hope of success. And even now, the risks had increased drastically.

If he sailed his ships against the treasure fleet once they had been joined by the convoy, he would be leading his men into certain disaster. Perhaps, even now, the odds were too great. Maybe the crews he had enlisted would back down, in the face of such odds. And how could he blame them?

He slowed his horse to a trot once more, for the streets of Bogotá were crowded; the city, built in the shadow of the Andes, was the seat of the viceroy of New Granada. Couriers and traders went about their business at all hours. Carriages and sedan chairs carried pleasure seekers to social gatherings in the mansions of the wealthy and to the taverns and brothels in the less savory quarter of the city.

Abiathar sat at a round wooden table, in one of the back rooms of el Burro Blanco. A plump, half-clad girl, her tangled hair falling down over her bare shoulders, sat beside him, while another was sprawled across his knees. The remains of his dinner littered the table, and he was drinking from a half-empty bottle, when Gavin swung open the door. The mate looked up with a grin. "I figured you might change your mind and take the night off," he said, waving him to a seat. "Take your choice, Captain—either one of these beauties'll give you a fine ride—"

The hard, set look on Gavin's face made him break off. He shook his head, as if to clear it. "Get them out of here," Gavin said tersely. Abiathar gave a slight shove to the girl who lay in his lap. "Be off—both of you," he said. They stared at him in surprise, but when he tossed them a few coins they smiled and sauntered out in search of other company.

"What's amiss?" Abiathar asked. He pushed aside the platter, heaped with the remains of a roast pig, and set his elbows on the littered table.

"The fleet from Cádiz has dropped anchor in Porto Bello harbor," Gavin said. Ignoring his friend's look of stunned disbelief, he gave him a brief account of Tod's unexpected arrival at the trading post earlier that evening.

"If the convoy's spread out along the Isthmus to keep guard over the treasure ships we haven't a chance," Abiathar began.

Gavin did not answer. His bronzed skin was drawn tightly over the sharply defined angles of his face.

"But the message said—"

"Sybilla was mistaken—or deliberately deceived by the Condesa." He gestured impatiently toward the door.

Abiathar thrust his huge arms into the sleeves of his velvet coat, clapped his plumed hat on his head, and followed Gavin out of the tavern. "How could the lass have let herself be tricked that way?" he muttered.

"That's what I mean to find out, as soon as we reach Cartegena," Gavin told him.

Chapter Twenty-Three

"I could not leave Cartegena without seeing you once more, Sybilla."

Although Dolores had put off her departure as long as possible, she could delay no longer; she had received a second letter from her husband, informing her that, unless she returned immediately, he would be obligated to come and escort her back to Panama City.

Even now that Señora Mendez had tactfully withdrawn from the courtyard of her own home so that Sybilla and Dolores might say their farewells in privacy, the young Condesa still maintained her facade of quiet dignity. There was a calm resignation in her dark eyes, but Sybilla, remembering their conversation on the night of the ball, knew that her friend was still grieving over her separation from her lover.

"I shall miss you," Sybilla said.

Dolores hesitated, then said impulsively, "Why not come along with me for a visit? You've told me your husband's business will keep him away from Cartegena for a month, or even longer. Surely it can't be very lively for you here, with Señora Mendez and her friends for company."

In spite of her outward composure, it was obvious that Dolores was eager to have Sybilla with her for moral support, now that she could no longer avoid her inevitable return to Panama City.

"I'm sorry, my dear," Sybilla said. "I promised Gavin that I would wait for him here in Cartegena."

"And no doubt I frightened you, when I told you of my journey across the Isthmus. But I am sure once we reached the fair at Porto Bello, you would be amply rewarded. It's a marvelous spectacle—one you would never forget. According to all I've been hearing from my husband's family, there's nothing like it anywhere in the New World—or back in Spain, either.

"You could not buy anything for yourself, because of those ridiculous trade regulations!" She hesitated for a moment, and gave Sybilla a faintly embarrassed look. "But you would only have to choose whatever caught your fancy, and I would make the purchases for you. And at the most reasonable prices. As the governor's wife, I do enjoy certain privileges."

"That's most thoughtful, but I—"

"You could return home to Boston laden with splendid gifts for all your relations."

Sybilla flinched and looked away, at the sparkling waters of the fountain in the center of the courtyard. One falsehood had led to the next, and she already had told Dolores that when she and Gavin returned to his home port they would go to stay with his family.

"I'm sorry, Dolores," she said. "But when Gavin returns to Cartegena, I must be here. He'll want to set sail at once."

"You'll be going straight back to Boston?"

"I'm—not sure." Sybilla searched her memory, trying to recall the names of some of the ports Gavin had told her about. "We may drop anchor off Charles Town—that's in the Carolinas. And perhaps in New York harbor—my husband's business ventures take him to so many places."

Places like Tortuga—the lair of pirates and outcasts from every corner of the Spanish Main.

Sybilla found herself wishing that Angela Mendez had remained out here in the courtyard; her lively chatter would have smoothed over awkward moments like this one. But the merchant's wife lingered inside the house, still dazzled by the honor done her by Dolores's unexpected visit.

To think of having La Condesa Dolores Torrealta y de las Fuentes as a guest in her home! And the Torrealtas' gilded carriage standing outside the front door, for all to see. The sides of the vehicle were emblazoned with the family crest, and the footmen, bewigged and clad in their liveries of midnight blue satin, surely would draw the attention of every passerby. Angela could scarcely wait to preen herself before her envious friends, when next they came to visit her.

"Then you don't really know how long it will be before you set sail for home," Dolores said. "You do lead a most adventurous life," she added, with a wistful smile. "And with the man you love beside you. How fortunate you are, *Sybilla mía.*"

Sybilla put a hand on her friend's arm. She was filled with pity as she thought of the future that lay in store for the pretty young Condesa.

"You must not be concerned for me," Dolores said. "I have made the only possible choice. I know what must be done, and I will get through it somehow." A look of contempt and dislike shadowed her dark brown eyes. "Maybe after I have presented Ramón with the proof that he is still a man—when he is convinced that he has fathered an heir to the illustrious Torrealta line—he will be satisfied to leave me alone."

"And perhaps one day, you and Pedro will find a way to be together again," Sybilla said.

"Perhaps." But there was little hope in her voice. "Think of me, sometimes, when you are sailing to those far-off ports and—"

"Dios mío! Such a day!" Angela's voice, shrill with excitement, could be heard from within the house. "First a visit from la Condesa, and now . . . Your wife did not think you would be returning for some time yet, *Capitán* Broderick," she went on. "How pleased she will be to see you! She is

outside in the courtyard—"

Sybilla sprang to her feet. Her heart began to thud against her chest. But the happiness she felt at Gavin's return was shadowed by a sense of foreboding. Why had he returned so soon? Surely, after he had received her message, there had been no reason for him to return.

Now that he was back here in Cartegena, he would find out soon enough—if he had not done so already—that the Spanish galleons had already arrived from Cádiz, that they were anchored off the Isthmus. He would have to come to terms with the truth: his own ships no longer had a chance of capturing the treasure fleet.

Sybilla's throat tightened with fear, but she tried to find reassurance. Gavin had warned her that she would be unlikely to succeed in gaining any useful information, that she lacked the temperament necessary for acting as a spy. True, he might blame her for having made the attempt and failed, but surely he would have no reason to suspect that she had deceived him intentionally.

The weeks that lay ahead would not be easy, she told herself. But she could cope with Gavin's silent brooding, his outbursts of temper, and she could be there to comfort him until gradually he had resigned himself to the unforeseen circumstances that had forced him to abandon his plans. If words were not enough, she would offer him solace in the warmth of her embraces. Somehow she would see him through the difficult days ahead.

Why, then, was she gripped with this mounting tension? Even as she heard him coming down the hallway that led to the courtyard, she felt darts of fear flicking at her nerves. She breathed as deeply as her tightly laced stays would allow, as she tried to steady herself.

And now he was here, emerging from the shadows of the archway that opened onto the courtyard. She saw at a glance that he must have come directly to the Mendez house without stopping along the way to refresh himself after his long journey. His boots were covered with the thick dust of the trail; and his steel gray coat and breeches were creased and travel-stained. He wore no lace-trimmed cravat, and his linen shirt was open at the throat. A lock of his dark hair fell across his mahogany-tanned forehead.

She longed to run to him at once and throw herself into his arms; but something about his rigid stance, and the lines of tension in his face, made her hold back. "Sybilla, my dear. Señora Mendez said you had company." He took her arm, and all at once she remembered the need to observe the proprieties. She introduced him to Dolores.

In spite of the fact that he was under stress, he made the Condesa a courtly bow and thanked her for having offered Sybilla her companionship during his absence.

Dolores acknowledged his words with a smile and a graceful inclination of her head. "I am sorry you did not return in time to accompany Sybilla to our carnival ball," she said.

Then, with a sorrowful look in her dark eyes, she took Sybilla's hand. "I must be leaving now." She turned to Gavin. "I am to embark for Panama early tomorrow, *Capitán* Broderick, and there are still many preparations to be made."

She touched her lips to Sybilla's cheek in a formal gesture of farewell. But Sybilla drew her close and embraced her warmly; she tried to convey her sympathy and understanding in the gesture.

As they drew apart, Dolores said, "I don't wonder that you insisted on remaining here to await your husband's return." She smiled, her eyes sparkling, so that for the moment she looked like the carefree young girl Sybilla had known during the voyage aboard the *Bristol Belle*.

"Your *capitán* is as you described him, *Sybilla mía.* Indeed, you scarcely did him justice."

Then, catching the puzzled look in Gavin's eyes, she added, "I tried to persuade Sybilla to come along for a visit to the fair at Porto Bello. But no! She said she must be here in Cartegena to welcome you when you returned."

"Did she, indeed?" Sybilla moved uneasily, under his

steady, searching look.

"But no matter," Dolores went on. "I shall find a gift for her there. And if I send it to your family's residence in Boston, *Capitán* Broderick, perhaps it will have arrived before you drop anchor in your home port."

The color drained from Sybilla's face, and she could only stare at her friend in shocked dismay. A suffocating fear caught at her throat. She tried to speak, to silence Dolores somehow, but she sensed that even now it was too late.

"That is most generous of you, madam," he said, with a slight inclination of his head. "As for Sybilla's refusal to attend the fair, you must understand that she is still unfamiliar with some of the customs of New Granada. I have not yet had the opportunity to tell her of the wonders of the fair at Porto Bello."

Although Gavin spoke casually, Sybilla caught the swift, cold suspicion in the look he gave her.

"Ah, but she knows all about it," Dolores informed him. "I told her on the night of the ball. Although, from what my Torrealta relations have said, one cannot appreciate its many wonders without having seen them at first hand. The splendid ornaments of gold and silver—pearls from the Great South Sea, as large as Malaga grapes—the fine silks from the Orient."

"To think you could have resisted such delights, my dear," Gavin said, his voice deceptively quiet.

"And who knows how long it will be before another such fair is held?" Dolores went on. "True, the fair is supposed to be held each year, but my father-in-law has told me that it is not always possible to assemble enough men and ships for a convoy powerful enough to guard these valuable cargoes from the pirates who infest these waters."

Then Dolores broke off as she became aware of a certain tension in Sybilla and her tall, gray-eyed husband, a charged stillness of the sort that preceded fierce tropical storms. Was she to blame, with her talk of pirates, she wondered?

Although the buccaneers were recruited from among the

Dutch and the French, it was well-known that many of the most daring were English. Even now, the citizens of Cartegena had not forgotten the attack on their city by *El Draque*—Sir Francis Drake, more than a century ago.

Perhaps, Dolores thought, she might have offended Sybilla's husband. As for Sybilla, her face had taken on a chalk-white pallor.

But Sybilla was scarcely conscious of her friend's troubled gaze. For one sickening moment, the glittering spray from the fountain, the crimson bougainvillea, the blue sky overhead, all blended in a whirling blur. The flagstones of the courtyard seemed to shift beneath her feet.

Gavin knew the truth now. He knew, beyond the slightest doubt, that she had betrayed his trust. She had deceived him intentionally. The message she had given Tod to carry to the trading post had been filled with lies.

Her legs went weak and she was sure that she would faint. But she dug her nails into her palms, and somehow she managed to regain a measure of control over her emotions.

"It has been so good to see you again, Dolores," she managed to say. "But truly, there is no need for you to send me a gift."

"It is my pleasure," Dolores assured her. "There will be so many rare treasures to choose from at Porto Bello." She turned to Gavin. "Even you would be impressed, *Capitán Broderick.*"

"No doubt I would, madam." He spoke with quiet courtesy, his tone even and controlled. But Sybilla saw that his eyes had gone dark, so that the iris and pupil seemed to be of one color. For an instant the muscle at the corner of his jaw twitched slightly.

"And now I really must take my leave," Dolores was saying.

He offered the Condesa his arm and escorted her into the cool dimness of the hallway. "I trust you will have a safe journey home to Panama," he was saying. But as Sybilla followed, it seemed to her that her own movements were as stiff and jerky as those of a jointed doll.

In the hallway, Angela Mendez joined them, her round face still aglow with pride at having entertained a member of the nobility under her roof. Even after Dolores had entered her gilded carriage, assisted by one of the footmen, after the splendid vehicle had disappeared from sight, the merchant's wife lingered in the doorway.

"La Condesa is so young and pretty! Charming and gracious, and with such an air of dignity, too. But it is only to be expected—her own family is one of the oldest in Seville, and as for the Torrealtas—"

"You must excuse us," Sybilla managed to say, when Angela Mendez was forced to pause for breath. "My husband is fatigued from his journey."

"But certainly," Angela said. "I shall not detain you, *Capitán*. I shall give orders to my cook to prepare a special feast for your return. The food served at our country inns leaves much to be desired."

Gavin turned to her with a slight bow. "I'm afraid it won't be possible for us to join you at dinner, Señora Mendez. There's been an unexpected change in my plans. I must sail with the evening tide."

Sybilla stiffened and drew in her breath sharply, but he was still speaking to Señora Mendez. "If your husband has not yet returned before I must take my leave, no doubt you will be good enough to convey my respects to him. And my thanks for his hospitality to me—and to my wife."

Before his startled hostess could answer, he held out his arm to Sybilla, and the look on his face warned her not to hesitate. They mounted the stairs side by side. His forearm felt iron-hard beneath her fingers, and he moved so quickly that it was all she could do to keep up with him.

As soon as they were inside the bed chamber and he had closed the door, he drew away from Sybilla as if her touch burned through his sleeve. Her immediate impulse was to escape, to run back down the stairway and out of the house, to get as far away from him as possible.

Instead, she forced herself to remain standing before him. This was Gavin—the man who had held her in his arms in the darkness, who had taught her all she knew of loving.

But when she raised her eyes to his and saw the look in their cold gray depths, fear surged up inside her. Her hand went to her throat, as if she half-expected he might spring at her and choke the life out of her. The powerful muscles of his chest and shoulders strained against the dusty fabric of his coat, and his booted feet were planted apart. She braced herself for his furious tirade.

But he stood there, looking down at her, and the silence stretched between them until she could bear it no longer.

"Tod hasn't returned here yet," she began. "I know he can take care of himself, but I wish I knew where he—"

"The lad is down at the waterfront right now, with Abiathar." His mouth curved in a sardonic smile. "Sorry to disappoint you, my sweet."

"Disappoint me?" She stared at him in bewilderment.

"No doubt you were hoping he'd never made it as far as the trading post. That he drowned in the Magdalena. Or torn to pieces by a jaguar, perhaps. But he got through safely with that letter of yours."

She clenched her jaw tightly, to keep it from trembling. And although she longed to sink down on the edge of the wide, curtained bed, she forced herself to keep on her feet.

"That letter," he went on. "A few sentences scrawled on a bit of paper, but they were enough to destroy months of planning. Six ships built—hundreds of men gathered together, waiting for the order to set sail. And you—with those innocent eyes, and the brain of a scheming, lying trull!"

"Gavin, if you'll only listen for a moment. If you'll let me tell you why I—"

But he went on, as if he had not heard her. "I've ordered Abiathar to hire the fastest sloop he can find. We will sail for Tortuga at sunset."

"You aren't going back to Costa Verde first—to get your men aboard the *Condor* and the *San Bartolomé?*"

315

His cold stare silenced her. "You don't care a brass farthing about my ships, or my crew." He gave a short, brutal laugh. "But you are very much concerned about what I mean to do with you. Concerned? You're scared out of your wits, aren't you?"

She longed to deny his harsh, mocking words, but she knew that her face would give her away.

"There are all sorts of interesting possibilities, aren't there? I could offer you to the keeper of one of the local bawdy houses. You'd fetch a good price with that lovely body of yours. Or I could ship you down to Costa Verde, and turn you over to my men."

This wasn't Gavin. It couldn't be. This was a hard-eyed stranger. Her insides twisted into a hard knot of fear.

"Never fear, Sybilla. I'm not about to leave you on the waterfront here in Cartegena, or on the beach at Costa Verde. You're coming as far as Tortuga with me."

He paused for a moment, and she felt her terror begin to ebb away. "I made you a promise, and I'll keep it," he told her. "Even a pirate like me has a few shreds of honor left from better days. That's more than can be said for you, isn't it, Mistress Thornton?"

She flinched under the lash of his words and the contempt in his eyes. How could she possibly get through to him now?

"I know you must hate me," she began. "But that's because you don't understand. That night at the ball—Dolores told me that the Spanish ships had arrived sooner than expected. I knew that I had to keep the truth from you."

"You disappoint me, Sybilla. Aren't you at least going to try to invent a new set of lies—or haven't you had time yet?" He gave a short, hard laugh that chilled her to the bone.

"I deceived you purposely, when I wrote that letter," she said. "And I would do it again."

She saw his look of surprise—and something more. A trace of admiration, perhaps.

"You've never lacked courage, Sybilla," he said. "I think

316

I've always known that. Too bad I also gave you credit for a sense of honor. What a fool you must have thought me, when I said that you would find it difficult to stoop to deceit, if it suited your purposes."

His eyes hardened. "You hadn't any qualms about sending me that message."

"You're wrong, Gavin—I did! You can't possibly know what it cost me to make such a choice."

He flexed his fingers and although she felt a pang of primitive animal terror, she fought it down. Instead of retreating, as all her instincts urged her to do, she made herself move closer, until she stood directly in front of him, her face upturned to his.

"I will explain, if you give me a chance," she said. Somehow she kept her voice steady. "But if you expect me to grovel, to plead for your forgiveness, you are mistaken. I did what I had to do, to keep you out of harm's way. And I would do it again."

"You meant for me to stay up there at the trading post until it was too late to lead my ships into battle—and you did it for my sake?" He expelled his breath with a harsh, impatient sound.

"Is that so difficult for you to understand?" She reached out and gripped his arms. "I love you, Gavin. I shouldn't think there'd be any need for me to say so, not now. I couldn't bear the thought of losing you. And when I saw a way to keep you from this venture, I took it.

"I lied to you—because I couldn't face the thought of your being wounded—or taken prisoner by the Spaniards, tortured by them. Sweet *Jesú*, do you think I ever could forget what you told me about the horrors you'd suffered, chained to the oars of that galley?"

She thought that she saw a flicker of understanding in his eyes. Emboldened, she moved closer and grasped his arms tighter. "Only this time you might not even have survived to to be taken prisoner. Even the Spanish merchant ships are armed. One well-placed shot from their cannons might have

317

blown the *Condor* to pieces. I haven't forgotten the battle with the *San Bartolomé*. You weren't badly wounded, it's true. You recovered quickly. But the next time—" She raised her chin and spoke with a firmness that surprised her. "I had to see to it that there would be no next time."

"You had to see to it—" He stared at her as if he doubted what he was hearing. "And what gave you the right to make such a decision for me?"

"I wasn't thinking about my rights. Only that I love you, and that I could not bear the thought of losing you."

He looked down at her and some of the cold anger faded from his eyes. She felt a brief surge of hope. Surely, she could make him understand.

Abruptly he pulled himself free of her grasp. Caught off balance, she staggered backward and before she could steady herself, her legs struck the side of the bed. She fell across the smooth silken coverlet.

Gavin advanced on her with a measured tread, like that of a jungle cat stalking its prey. She lay looking up at him, unable to move a muscle, or make a sound.

He leaned over her, placing an arm on either side of her body. For one terrible moment, she thought he might tear off her clothes and take her by force, moved not by tenderness or passion, but by a brutal desire to humiliate and punish her.

She gave a wordless cry of protest, and turned her face away. But he caught her jaw in a steely grip. "Look at me, damn you."

He moved closer, bracing his knee on the edge of the bed to steady himself. "You're proud of yourself, aren't you, my sweet?"

She gave a small, wordless sound of protest, but he gave her no time to answer. "Brave, noble Sybilla—using whatever means you could find to keep me out of danger." She winced at the cold mockery in his voice. "But that's not quite true, is it?"

"I—don't know what you mean—"

"Don't you? Surely you've not forgotten the night I stayed on Tortuga. Those things you said when I returned to the ship. Such a gallant speech. You wanted to sail with me. To be a pirate's woman, and share my future, wherever it might lead."

"I meant it—every word—"

"Did you?" His eyes moved over her body, searing her with cold fire. "You certainly managed to convince me, I'll credit you with that. You offered yourself to me, hot and willing, like any dockside wench on the island."

She glared up at him, her eyes flashing with topaz fire, at his words.

"But you put a high price on that soft, white body of yours, didn't you?" he went on. "You weren't willing to settle for a purse of gold coins or a jeweled bauble. Not the highborn Mistress Thornton. You wanted what any respectable young lady wants. Security. Respectability. And a wedding ring to seal the bargain."

Outraged pride freed her from the fear that had kept her immobilized. She raised herself slightly, her hair falling about her shoulders. "And is that so unforgivable?"

He had loosened his grip on her jaw, but her flesh still ached from the pressure of his strong fingers.

"Perhaps not," he conceded. "But you should have chosen more wisely. I told you as much, the first day we met back in Jamaica."

But that was before he had made love to her. Before she had surrendered herself to him, body and soul. Didn't he know that there could be no other man for her?

"I have to give you credit for your quick wit and your determination, Sybilla. A few more weeks up there at the trading post, and I might have lost all hope of capturing the treasure fleet." She stared at him, uncomprehending. A sudden dart of panic shot through her.

"You thought you had it all figured out, didn't you? But I had a small stroke of luck, one that even you, with all your scheming, could not have anticipated. I found out about the arrival of the ships from Cádiz, while I was still up on the savannah."

"But—that's not possible!"

"I learned the truth from Tod. Never mind how. And on the journey back here to the city, I used the time to alter my plans."

"But you have no chance of taking the galleons—not now. Surely you must see that."

He grasped her wrist and jerked her from the bed. Then he set her on her feet. "Pack your trunk, Sybilla. Get one of the maids to help you. I want you ready to leave this house within the hour."

"And when we get to Tortuga?"

"You'll be safe enough at Governor d'Ogeron's home there, until I return."

Her panic grew until it took possession of her. "Gavin, for the love of heaven! You aren't going to try to take those ships. It's not possible any longer."

"It will be more dangerous than it would have been without your lying schemes," he said grimly. "But if my men are willing to follow me, I'll take the treasure fleet yet."

"No—you can't! It's too late—you'll never come back—"

"That's a possibility. But if I do, I'll find your brother and bring him to you. I'll get you both safely aboard a ship for Boston."

He turned and started for the door. Then he paused and turned his head.

"And after that, I hope I never set eyes on you again."

Chapter Twenty-Four

The night breeze blew in across Montego Bay, ruffling the waters and tugging at the edges of the tattered playbill nailed beside the door of the Blue Dolphin. Nicholas Hobart paused briefly to scan the lettering, which was illuminated by wavering light from the lantern over the tavern door.

LIONEL FROBISHER, ESQ.
Presents
THE FROBISHER PLAYERS
in
THE DUCHESS OF MALFI
by
John Webster

A mirthless smile touched Hobart's lips, as he pushed open the tavern door, and made his way across the noisy taproom. The landlord, catching sight of his guest, came bustling forward.

"Master Frobisher's waiting for you in the private parlor, sir," the man said with an obsequious bow. "The rest of his troupe's out in the stable, bedding down for the night. There wasn't much of an audience tonight. The yard was half-empty."

The low-ceilinged taproom was crowded enough, however. Sailors, dockhands and overseers from the nearby plantations took their ease, drinking, laughing raucously, bawling out a snatch of a ballad, and grabbing at the barmaids who came to serve them.

Hobart brushed past the landlord, who called after him. "Shall I have a bottle sent in, sir? We have an especially fine brandy that might suit your taste."

"Your ordinary port'll do," Hobart said. He shouldered his way between the tables and moved on to the private parlor at the end of the hallway. Once inside, he shut the door behind him and paused to look over the tall, dark-haired man who had risen from his seat.

Lionel Frobisher might once have been handsome, Hobart thought, but now there was a gaunt, hollow-eyed look about the manager of the theatrical troupe. His black velvet doublet was frayed and his lace shirt cuffs were grayish.

"Have I the pleasure of addressing Mr. Nicholas Hobart?"

Hobart nodded. The other man smoothed his doubtlet and made a sweeping bow. "Lionel Frobisher, at your service, sir. I trust you enjoyed tonight's performance."

"Didn't see it," Hobart told him brusquely. He waved Frobisher back to his seat, and took the one opposite, at the round oak table.

"I had planned to leave the island with my players, after we completed our engagement," the manager went on. "But I assure you, Mr. Hobart, that should you care to have us come out to your plantation and give a private performance, for the entertainment of you and your guests, I should be only too happy to prolong our stay.

"We have an extensive repetoire, sir," he went on in a deep, resonant voice. "There is *The White Devil*—one of Webster's most moving tragedies, I've always thought." When Hobart did not reply, the manager's face fell slightly. "Perhaps you would prefer something of a lighter sort. We could perform *The Knight of the Burning Pestle*—that's sure to amuse—"

322

"I'm not here to hire you and your ragtag mummers," Hobart interrupted. "I've never cared for such tomfoolery."

Two spots of red appeared on Lionel Frobisher's haggard cheeks, and his deep-set eyes burned with indignation. But before he could protest the insult to his troupe, one of the serving maids came bustling in. She took her time as she set down her pewter tray; then she opened the bottle and filled both glasses, leaning over the table, to offer the men a better view of the ample breasts bulging over the top of her tightly laced bodice. She smiled invitingly at Hobart, awaiting his further pleasure.

But he waved her off. "That's all. We don't wish to be interrupted again."

She tossed her mane of thick, flaxen hair, and left the parlor, her broad rump swaying under her skirt.

Frobisher hesitated, as if undecided about sharing the hospitality of a man who had just spoken of the theatrical profession with such undisguised contempt. But after all, the boorish Mr. Hobart was paying for the bottle. The manager shrugged and raised his glass.

"Your health, sir," he muttered, taking a long swallow. "Since you do not choose to engage my troupe, may I ask why you wished to speak to me in private?"

"You had a visitor here last night. Mistress Madeleine Thornton of Acacia Hall."

Frobisher looked disconcerted: but he recovered himself quickly. "Perhaps the lady you mention was in last night's audience. I really could not say."

"Mistress Thornton didn't come to see the play. She arrived after the performance and went upstairs with you."

"Mr. Hobart! I cannot permit you to impugn the moral character of a respectable lady."

"I see you do remember her now." Hobart gave a brief, ironic laugh. "The lady's morals aren't in question," he went on. "No doubt you wished only to talk with her. But as you usually sleep in the stables, along with the rest of your troupe, you were obliged to part with half a crown, to hire

323

the room so that you and Mistress Thornton might converse in private."

The manager gave him a startled look. "How the devil do you know all that?"

"I know a good deal more," Hobart said. He flicked a speck of dust from the lace cuff that fell halfway over his thick hand.

"What gives you the right to pry into my affairs?"

"I was a friend of Oliver Thornton, the lady's late husband. And now she has been left a widow, living alone out there at Acacia Hall, with no male relatives to protect her. Let us say I choose to take a neighborly interest in the lady's welfare."

Hobart took a sip of his wine, grimaced, then set down the glass. "I heard of her visit to you last night. Never mind how. It struck me as most peculiar that she should come down to the waterfront, and at such a late hour. Scarcely what one would expect of a lady of quality, is it?"

"Madeleine wasn't always a—" Frobisher shifted uneasily in his chair, drained his glass, then refilled it.

"Perhaps you were going to say that she wasn't always a lady of quality."

"I don't believe I take your meaning, sir."

"Yes, you do. Don't waste my time, Frobisher. I already know she was once a member of your troupe."

Frobisher's eyes were wary now. "All right, then. Suppose she was? That was years ago."

"I know that, too. She did not care to remain with your troupe, though. Perhaps she was seeking greater scope for her—talents."

"Talents! She had no natural gift for acting. But she was young and pretty—with a certain sprightly charm about her."

"Shouldn't think she'd have needed more than a fine pair of tits and that sprightly charm, as you call it, to be a success in your troupe. But maybe she made herself useful in other ways. Maybe if business was slow, you found her a man or two, who'd pay you for her services."

Frobisher pushed back his chair. "I'm damned if I'll remain here and listen to more of your insults."

"You'll stay where you are, until I tell you to go." There was an edge to Hobart's voice. The manager froze, then dropped back into his seat.

"Did you know when you brought your troupe here to Jamaica that Madeleine was living on the island? That she was now the owner of Acacia Hall?"

"Certainly not. The players had already been here for a few days, when I chanced to catch sight of her in Montego Bay. She was riding by in an open carriage. It was a moment before I recognized her, all decked out in her elegant finery. And then, too, after so many years—"

"Still a good-looking woman, but changed." Hobart grinned. "No doubt she was overjoyed to meet you again, after such a long separation."

Frobisher stared down at the table. His eyes were narrow, his thin face sullen. "She stared right past me, as if she'd never seen me before."

"It's possible that she really did not recognize you."

"The hell she didn't—ungrateful slut! And after all I did for her."

Hobart knew better than to interrupt. He nodded with a show of sympathy and waited for Forbisher to go on. The manager, moved by anger, had thrown caution aside.

"A common little vagrant, that's what she was, when I first saw her in London. A runaway kitchen maid, hanging about the streets in Billingsgate, stealing salt fish from the open stalls. One of the fishwives saw her, and was belaboring her with a stick when I happened to be passing. I got her away from there, and made her part of my troupe."

And you bedded her soon enough, Hobart thought. But he remained silent.

"But now that she's made her way up in the world, she goes riding by in her fine carriage. Pretending not to know me! Me, her own husband!"

Hobart managed to conceal his stunned surprise. He picked up his glass and drank again, disregarding the indifferent quality of the wine.

"You lived together as husband and wife, when she toured with your troupe?"

"She *was* my wife, I tell you. Madeleine cozened me into marrying her, all legal and proper. Conniving little trollop."

"Your lawful wife," Hobart said. "That does put a different light on the matter." He shrugged his heavy shoulders slightly. "But even so, you should not blame her too harshly. No doubt she was startled at seeing you after all these years. She came to see you here last night. Women are such unpredictable creatures, aren't they?"

Then, all at once, his broad face hardened. "How much did she pay you to keep your mouth shut about that marriage of yours?"

"Pay me?" He glared indignantly at Hobart. "Sir, you are quite mistaken if you believe I would stoop to taking money from her, in exchange for—"

"Blackmail's a serious offense, Frobisher."

"You have no proof, and you'll get none! You surely don't expect Madeleine to accuse me of trying to blackmail her. How could she—without destroying her own reputation." Frobisher spoke with growing confidence. "The law takes a hard view of bigamy, Mr. Hobart. I'm sure my dear wife knows that, as well as you do."

Hobart managed to assume a crestfallen air.

"It would seem we have nothing more to discuss." Frobisher glanced regretfully at the half-empty bottle on the table. "I'll take leave of you now." He spoke with a touch of his former bravado.

"You'll leave when I say so. Not before." Hobart leaned forward, skewering the other man with his pitiless stare. "There are other offenses I can charge you with."

"Other offenses?"

"You've only just come to Jamaica. Perhaps you don't know who I am."

"I know you own a great plantation called Indigo. And warehouses as well. The landlord told me—"

"Maybe he didn't tell you that I also serve as a magistrate. It's a burdensome duty, at times. But we men of property must fulfill our civic responsibilities." He paused, to let his words sink in. "I could see to it that you and your troupe were thrown into jail on a charge of offending public morals."

"That's a damned lie! Our repertoire contains nothing that mightn't be performed in London's finest playhouses." But there was the tremor in his voice, and he looked fearfully at Hobart.

"A lewd and indecent performance," Hobart went on. "I'd have no difficulty in finding a dozen spectators to support the accusation."

"Surely you wouldn't do that, sir. Why should you wish to persecute a man in my circumstances?" The manager's air of bravado had dropped away completely. "I—the fact is, my troupe's been having a hard time of it lately. Vulgar spectacles, that's what they want here in these islands. Bull-baitings, ropedancers, jugglers. I've been forced to cast my pearls before swine!"

"Sorry to hear it. But maybe you'll find a more appreciative audience elsewhere. Let's hope so, for your sake, Frobisher. Because if you're not out of Jamaica before sunrise tomorrow, you and your friends'll find yourselves in jail. Or standing in the pillory, being pelted with rotten fruit and dead cats by the waterfront loafers."

"How can I leave now? I haven't yet earned my passage money, Mr. Hobart."

"Surely you were able to cadge a loan from your dear wife when you saw her last night."

"Only a pittance. The lying slut said she'd bring more tonight. In exchange for the marriage document—"

"But she never came back, did she?" Hobart snorted. "Doesn't surprise me. You're lucky she didn't give her plantation manager the word. Otherwise, you'd have been lying in an alley right now, with your skull split in two. Or rotting at the bottom of Mo' Bay harbor."

Frobisher gave him a terrified glance. "What am I to do?"

"Don't give way, man. I'm inclined to be more generous than your wife," he said with a touch of irony in his voice. "The marriage document—you still have it?"

"Yes, Mr. Hobart—I can bring it to you at once, sir."

"Do so, and be quick about it. I'll give you ten pounds in exchange. And free passage aboard one of my ships. She'll be weighing anchor in a few hours, bound for Charles Town. A thriving settlement, I'm told. Your players may find greater favor there."

The pale, milky light of dawn touched the sky above the Blue Mountains. Hobart leaned back against the seat of his carriage, his thick lips curved in a smile. He patted the pocket of his coat, where a creased but legible document reposed. As soon as he reached Indigo he would lock the parchment away in his strongbox.

Madeleine Thornton, a runaway servant girl, a former actress and sometime whore. And a bigamist. Her marriage to poor old Oliver had not even been legal. And that criminal offense, should it become known, would deprive her of all her property and land her in jail.

Hobart saw no purpose in taking action against the mistress of Acacia Hall—not yet. She had made a substantial payment on her debt to him, and she would go on paying.

It was enough that he had come into possession of this new piece of information about the lady. Who could tell when it might prove useful to him?

Chapter Twenty-Five

"Look there, Captain." Abiathar raised his muscular arm, and pointed across the glittering blue-green water toward the fleet of eight ships riding at anchor in the secluded cove on the coast of Tortuga. "There's your fleet, ready and waiting. And a rare fine sight it is." The two men stood together on the foredeck of the sloop that had carried them back from Cartegena.

"Hobart came through with his part of the bargain," Gavin said.

Sybilla, who was seated in the stern sheets, tensed as she heard the grim satisfaction in Gavin's voice and saw the hard set of his jaw. He lifted his telescope to his eye to examine the ships more closely.

She had no doubt that Gavin was prepared to go ahead with his plans despite the odds. There was no longer any way she could stop him. She dared not even try. Not now.

During the voyage from Cartegena, he had provided her with sufficient food and a cot in the small cabin. He had bedded down on deck along with Abiathar and Tod. But he had scarcely spoken a word to her.

Now Sybilla got to her feet and smoothed the skirt of her apple green muslin gown. Shading her eyes, she looked across the water at the fleet that now lay a cable's length from the sloop. She recognized the lines of Gavin's flagship, the *Condor,* newly painted, its brasswork glittering—sleek and menacing as the bird of prey for which it had been named. Close beside it lay the *San Bartolomé,* the sun glinting off the gilded carvings of her wide, square stern, her decks stripped for action.

And beyond these two, she saw Hobart's six vessels, brand-new and straight from the dockyards, each armed with forty guns. She could only make out the name of one of them: the *Invincible.* In spite of the heat from the blazing tropical sun, an icy chill moved through her. How could any vessel—how could Gavin's whole fleet—prove invincible, against the might of the Spanish convoy that lay in wait off Porto Bello?

Less than an hour later, Tod was driving a hired cart down a wide, unpaved street that bore the grandiose name of Rue du Roi de France. It was lined with taverns and gaming houses and crowded with buccaneers, vendors of fruit or trinkets, and hard-eyed trollops.

When they reached the end of the street, Gavin called out to the Indian boy to stop before a small house of sun-dried white bricks, topped by a sloping red tile roof. He and Abiathar swung themselves down. Sybilla stood looking down hesitantly. When Gavin made no move toward her, Abiathar lifted her to the ground, then shouldered her trunk and led the way to the house.

"I thought we would be staying at one of those taverns back there," she said to the red-bearded seaman.

"You'll have more privacy here, Mistress Sybilla," Abiathar told her.

Gavin led the way inside, and she hurried after him with Tod and Abiathar bringing up the rear. After coming out of the glaring sunlight, Sybilla blinked and waited for her eyes to adjust to the semidarkness within.

"What now, Captain?" Abiathar asked.

"Take the trunk upstairs," Gavin said. "We've no time to lose, rounding up the men."

He turned to Sybilla. "You go upstairs, too. And don't bother to unpack. You won't be staying here long." His voice was cool and remote, as it had been whenever he'd had need to speak to her during the past few days.

Her spirits went plummeting lower, for she realized that he meant to set sail as quickly as possible. She searched her mind desperately, trying to think of some way to delay him. But she knew that any such attempt would be useless and would only increase his resentment against her.

As she followed Abiathar up the short flight of steps she heard Tod asking, "Shall I come with you, too, sir?"

"Not this time, lad. You're to stay here with Mistress Thornton."

Sybilla tried to draw what small comfort she could from Gavin's words; at least he felt some responsibility for her safety.

But when she was left alone in the small, sparsely furnished bedchamber upstairs she felt a rising despair. She stood at the narrow window, watching Gavin and Abiathar emerge from the house. She gazed after them until they disappeared into the crowd.

Even now, with no one to see her, she refused to give way to tears. Instead, she forced herself to look over the tops of the dusty palm trees, over the red roofs of the small settlement and out to the glittering turquoise sea beyond the cove. By leaning forward, resting her hands on the sill, and standing on tiptoe, she could catch a glimpse of the tall masts of Gavin's ships.

The sails were tightly furled, the gunports closed. But it would not be long before the crews went aboard. When Gavin gave the order they would go racing up the rigging, and the great canvas squares would be spread wide, to catch the wind.

The pirate fleet would head for the waters off the Isthmus, and when their enemy was in sight Gavin would take his place on the *Condor*'s quarterdeck. At a signal from him, the men would take up their battle stations. His crimson flag would rise to the masthead, a challenge to the might of Spain.

It was early evening when Abiathar came back. He knocked, then came inside and stood staring at the food spread on the table before her: a chicken baked to a golden brown, a pork pie, a pile of fruit and a bottle of wine.

"The captain had all that sent over from the tavern where we ate our dinner, more'n an hour ago," he said reproachfully. "And you haven't even touched it yet."

She forgot her pride as she asked, "Did Gavin come back with you?"

"He's gone out into the harbor to look over the ships. He'll be wanting to inspect every plank and beam with his own eyes."

He gave her a worried look. "You ain't had a bite since before we docked. You ain't comin' down with a fever, are you?"

She shook her head. "But if I were, why should you care? I'm sure you despise me—as Gavin does." Her throat tightened, as she raised her eyes to his. "He won't ever forgive me, will he?"

"How would I know?" Abiathar muttered, obviously embarrassed. "He's got other matters on his mind, right now. He wants to be sure they followed his orders to the letter, when they built and provisioned those new ships. He'll be lookin' over the rigging, the canvas. We'll be needin' plenty of ammunition this voyage. Cannon balls and muskets. Cutlasses and boarding axes, too."

"Abiathar—for the love of God! Won't you try to stop him?" She sprang up out of her chair and clutched at his sleeve, her eyes wide and beseeching.

"If you're set on lettin' that good food go to waste, you'd best drink your wine," he said impassively. "It'll steady you."

At another time, she might have been amused by the bearded mate's preoccupation with food and drink, but not now. "You're Gavin's friend. You saved his life once before—when you were prisoners together aboard that galleon. He told me about it. Are you going to stand by now, and let him go to his death?"

"I'll not be standing by," he said. "He's made me master of the *San Bartolomé.* I'll be ready to set sail when he gives the word. Young Jeremy Randall's to be in command of the *Invincible,* and that Frenchman, Demarais, will be captain of the *Faucon.*"

"How can you and the others go on with this—this mad venture now? Surely you know you've no chance to take the treasure fleet!"

"Gavin says we have. That's good enough for me—and it'll be good enough for the rest of 'em. You'll see."

"But if only you would refuse to sail with him, if you'd try to convince Jeremy and the others that the expedition is doomed from the start, Gavin would have to abandon this impossible plan."

Abiathar's face reddened and he glared down at her from under his bushy red brows. "You know what that'd mean?" he demanded. "If the captain were to back down now, every buccaneer on Tortuga'd lose all respect for him. Not one of them would ever sail under his flag again."

"And would that be so terrible?" An uncontrollable surge of anger went coursing through her. "Suppose Gavin never led these pirates on another expedition? Suppose he were to turn his back on the Brotherhood of the Coast?

"What would he have left, after that?" Abiathar demanded.

She tilted back her head, and her eyes held his. "Gavin has a home. And a place in his family's shipping business. And he could have far more."

"He could have you for his wife. That's what you're sayin'." He shook his head. "He won't marry you, Mistress Sybilla. Not now." He spoke with calm certainty.

"You can't know that," she protested.

"I know Gavin. He'd never let himself be tied to a female who wants to chart his course for him. One who'd stoop to trickery to get her way."

"All right, then!" Sybilla's voice held an edge of hysteria now. "He needn't marry me. He can send me away and never see me again. I don't care—if only I can leave, knowing he's given up this senseless folly."

"He won't give it up. He's sailing against the Spanish fleet."

"He can't! You must stop him!"

And when he did not reply, she lost control. Throwing herself against him, she pounded her fists on his huge shoulders, his massive chest.

She might have been attacking a granite cliff. He stood immobile while she vented her fury on him. Sobs wrenched her body until she could scarcely breath. Glimmering sparks of light began to swim before her eyes, and Abiathar's huge body blurred before her. Her knees buckled, and she would have fallen, but he seized her about the waist, and lifted her into his arms.

Then, somehow, she was back in the chair, and he was standing beside her, leaning over her. His eyes searched her face. "Easy there," he said. He pulled the cork from the bottle and pushed it toward her. But her hands were trembling so violently that she could not grasp the bottle. He held it to her lips. "Drink up."

She swallowed and felt a soothing warmth move through her. But her breathing was unsteady. "Again," he said. Once more, she drank. Her muscles loosened, and her hands were steadier.

Abiathar set the bottle down on the table. "Now, I'll have no more of your bellow-weatherin'. You're goin' to sit quiet an' hear me out. Understand?"

Unable to speak, she could only nod in assent.

"This plan of Gavin's was a risky one, right from the first. Now, what with your harebrained meddling, it'll be a deal more dangerous. But Gavin Broderick's not a fool or a madman. He'd not be leadin' his men into battle, unless he believed there was a chance of victory. That's why they'll follow him."

"But he planned to take the treasure fleet before the convoy arrived. I don't understand how he—"

"No more do I," Abiathar interrupted. "Nor his other captains, neither. The rest of us are sailin' under sealed orders." Seeing her uncomprehending look, he explained. "We won't know his new battle plan until after we've put to sea."

Sybilla stared at him, and as she grasped the full import of his words, she felt a deep pride in Gavin. He was like no other man she had ever known: strong and daring, surely. But he was so much more. He lived by his own code of honor, a sense of responsibility toward those who trusted him. That was why he could inspire such unswerving loyalty, even in these tough, lawless buccaneers.

And she had seen yet another side of him. She remembered his tenderness, his understanding, during those first nights of loving they had shared. He had restrained his own powerful needs until she, too, could touch the heights of ecstacy.

Love welled up in her, a sweet, hot aching that possessed her. And she knew that she could not let him go without seeing him once more.

Abiathar got to his feet. "You'd better have a bite to eat, before we leave," he said.

"You're meeting Gavin?"

"That's right."

"Take me with you."

"I'll do no such thing. I already hired a driver. He's waitin' outside for you, with his mule and carriage—a sorry-lookin' rig, but I couldn't find no better. He's to take you to Governor d'Ogeron's house."

Sybilla, playing for time, forced herself to break off a piece of the pork pie. She swallowed without tasting, then took another sip of wine.

"That's better," Abiathar said, with an approving nod. "Finish up now, and we'll get moving."

He gave her an encouraging pat on the shoulder. "The governor's got a handsome place. It's high up on a hill on the eastern end of the island, away from the waterfront."

"I'll go to Monsieur d'Ogeron's home," she said. "But first I've got to see Gavin."

"Sink me, if you ain't the stubbornest female I ever knew!" he shouted. He took an audible breath and forced himself to speak more quietly. "It won't do no good, Mistress Sybilla. The captain don't want you there."

"Where is he? Down at the cove?"

"That's right. But you're heading straight for the governor's house, and so I tell you!"

She got to her feet, her head tilted back, her shoulders squared beneath the bodice of her muslin gown. "If you don't take me I'll find my way alone."

"Of all the daft notions! Tortuga's no place for a young lass like you to be wanderin' around. An' it's gettin' dark now, in case you ain't noticed."

"No doubt I'd be quite safe if you were to take me with you to the cove," she said. "But since you refuse, I have no choice."

He glared at her, but she did not take her eyes from his.

"I suppose if I were to tie your hand an' foot and toss you into the cart, you'd cozen the driver into turnin' you loose. Or chew your way through the ropes, like a bull terrier bi—" He broke off and hooked his thumbs into his belt.

"You win. I'll take you along. But you're to stay out of sight. And don't make a sound, neither. No cryin' or carryin' on. If Gavin were to know I'd gone against his orders, there'd be hell to pay."

"Yes, Abiathar," she said.

Torches flared against the night sky. A freshening wind blew across the cove. It tossed the fronds of the palms at the far end of the beach. The tall stand of trees and the heavy tropical undergrowth of ferns and broad-leaved vines served to shield the rickety open carriage from sight.

Sybilla pulled her light cloak more closely around her. The driver, who was seated up on the box, hunched his shoulders under his coarse cotton shirt. From the back he looked as bony and decrepit as the mule that was hitched to the shabby conveyance.

Abiathar, accompanied by Tod, had already made his way out of the grove and onto the beach below. Sybilla drew in her breath sharply as she saw close to a thousand men gathered about a high rocky ledge.

A tall, commanding figure, bathed in the ruddy glow of the torches, Gavin stood atop the ledge. He wore black breeches and a white shirt with full sleeves. A baldric of crimson leather trimmed with gold was fastened across his broad, powerful chest. His hand rested on the jeweled hilt of his sheathed sword.

Sybilla caught sight of Jeremy Randall among the small knot of men gathered at the base of the ledge. She leaned forward and watched as Abiathar shouldered his way through the crowd to take his place with those who had been chosen to command the pirate fleet.

Then, as she heard Gavin's voice, she forgot everything else. It rang out, strong and resonant, above wind and tide and sent a shiver racing along her spine.

"When you first signed on to sail with me you knew the risks. They were formidible, even then. Now, with the Spanish convoy anchored off Porto Bello, the odds against us are far greater."

337

"Bugger the odds!" a rough voice shouted. "Think o' the prize to be gained!"

Gavin held up his hand for silence. "The spoils are enormous. As great as any man among you could wish." He looked over the faces upturned to his. "But such riches will not be ours for the taking. Make no mistake about that. We'll be battling against a far more powerful force than we've ever faced before." He paused, to allow his words to sink in.

"Some of you have not yet signed the articles. And as for those who have, they are free to withdraw here and now. You still have time to reconsider. All of you. But once we've weighed anchor, there'll be no turning back."

In the brief silence that followed, Sybilla saw the men turning their heads to look at one another. These were tough, seasoned buccaneers, who knew well enough what dangers now awaited them. Some in the crowd bore the scars of sword and cutlass across their tanned, weatherbeaten faces. Others had known the horrors of a Spanish dungeon or had toiled at the oars of a galleon, driven like beasts under the lash.

Surely, Sybilla thought, there must be those who would heed Gavin's warning, and turn away. But even as she tried to convince herself, she heard a man shout from somewhere in the crowd.

"Withdraw, is it? Not me, Captain Broderick!"

Then others were calling out from all sides, their voices echoing along the windswept beach.

"We'll singe the beard o' the Spanish king!"

"An' we'll send his captains slinkin' home, like a pack o' mangy curs."

"The dons'll get no gold from Porto Bello this time!"

And now they were moving forward, shoving, jostling one another in their eagerness to get closer to the ledge where Gavin stood.

Sybilla recognized Jeremy Randall's voice. "I'm with you, Captain!" He drew his sword from its scabbard and raised it high, like a young knight pledging fealty to his leige lord.

"And I, Demarais! My men and I will follow where you lead!" The torchlight ran gleaming along the tempered steel of the French captain's sword.

"Them dons'll have no chance against us—not with Captain Broderick in command!"

"We'll loot their galleons, an' smash their convoy into a heap o' kindlin'."

Sybilla was scarcely aware of the shiver that ran through her. Until this moment, she had gone on clinging to the frail hope that perhaps, if enough men were to turn away, Gavin would have no choice but to give up the venture. But now she saw those men who had not yet signed the articles jostling forward to do so. And those who had already put their names, or made their marks, on the sheets of parchment, raised a shout that echoed through the night.

"Broderick! We'll follow Captain Broderick!"

Her gaze was fixed on Gavin. But now she saw not the leader whose men were prepared to storm the gates of hell at his command, she saw the only man she had ever loved, or ever would. She watched the light move over his cheekbones and the line of his jaw. And she knew that she might be seeing him for the last time.

The next moment, he sprang down from the ledge and turned his face toward the sea. He raised his arm in a gesture of command and pointed toward the ships that rode at anchor.

And he called out his command. "Come on, then!"

"Gavin!" A voice cried out, high and filled with urgency. Her voice.

Driven by her uncontrollable need, scarcely aware of what she did, she was climbing out of the carriage. A thorn-covered vine caught at her billowing skirt, but she freed herself, and then she was forcing her way out of the thick, heavy undergrowth. And now she was running across the moon-washed sand.

"Gavin—wait!"

Her hair shone red-gold in the torchlight. Her cloak was blown back by the wind, and her muslin gown was pressed against her body, revealing the rounded thrust of her breasts, the curve of her long thighs. Some of the men caught sight of her. A few paused to turn an appreciative glance in her direction.

But if Gavin had heard her call out to him, he gave no sign. He went striding on toward the edge of the cove. Sybilla struggled to get through the tightly-packed bodies that surrounded her.

"Make way there," one of the seamen shouted hoarsely. "Make way for Cap'n Broderick's lady." Others took up the cry and stood aside, clearing a path for her.

Gavin stopped, then turned around.

Heedless of all else, she lifted her full skirt and hurried forward. Although her high-heeled slippers slowed her down, as they sank into the sand with every step, she reached his side at last. She stood, her face upturned to his.

She could not hold him back. She only wanted him to draw her close, so that she might feel the hard strength of his body against her own, and breathe in the warm scent of him.

"Gavin . . ." She put her hand on his arm.

He loosened her grasp, as a man might shake off the clutching hands of an overeager dockside trollop. "You should not have come here."

His eyes searched the crowd. "Abiathar," he called.

"You mustn't blame him. He tried to make me go directly to the governor's house. But when I said I'd come here alone he agreed to take me with him. He was only trying to protect me."

"I'll get someone to take you to d'Ogeron's house now."

"There's no need. I have a carriage waiting. It's back there, behind those trees."

He nodded brusquely. "Then you'd better go now."

She longed to throw herself into his arms. She wanted him to hold her, to promise he'd come back to her. But his look, his tone, kept her at arm's length.

She forced herself to step away from him. Her pride would not allow her to give way to tears, as long as he stood watching her. After he had gone, there would be time enough for weeping.

But she could not go without some word of farewell. And all at once, she remembered the sailors' wives, calling out to their men from the dock, that day she had sailed from England.

She raised her head, and her voice was steady. "May you have fair winds—and a safe return."

A stocky seaman heard her and he grinned. "Well said, lass. Now, give the captain a kiss for luck."

She glanced at Gavin, and hesitated. With his men looking on, he reached out and drew her to him. But his lips only brushed hers lightly. It was no more than a gesture, and she knew it. She felt a stab of despair.

Then, all at once, his arms tightened about her so fiercely that her breath caught in her throat. She felt the hard muscles of his thighs against hers. His mouth urged her lips apart, and she yielded to the swift invasion of his tongue. His kiss deepened until the blood began to pound in her temples. She reached out and caressed his hair, his neck and shoulders.

For one timeless instant, it was as if they stood alone on the beach, under the night sky.

Then he lifted his mouth from hers. He cupped her face between his palms and his gray eyes held hers, in a long, searching look. "Sybilla," he said softly.

He turned away. And she was aware, once again, of the jostling crowd of men. Gavin motioned them forward, leading the way to the shore. Small boats bobbed up and down at the water's edge, ready to carry the men out to their ships.

Sybilla could not remain here on the beach any longer. If she did not see the *Condor* set sail, maybe she could pretend that none of this was really happening. That Gavin was not leaving her. She could hold on to the memory of his embrace and shut out all thought of the future, if only for a little while.

She turned and made her way back, the seamen standing aside once more to let her through. She kept her eyes fixed on the palm grove where the carriage waited.

The tall trees and heavy undergrowth of shrubs blocked out the light of the receding torches. The driver got down and lifted her onto her seat, then mounted to his perch in front, without speaking. He cracked his whip over the back of the mule. The rickety vehicle lurched forward along a path so narrow that the foliage brushed against Sybilla's face and shoulders from time to time.

But she was scarcely aware of her surroundings. She sat huddled on the seat, her face buried in her hands. Even now she could not weep. A frozen numbness enveloped her, and she allowed herself to be carried along in a kind of daze.

But slowly, gradually, her feelings began to stir. Her fingers went to her lips, still warm and tingling with Gavin's kiss. Would she ever know the touch of his mouth again, the hard strength of his arms, drawing her against him?

She remembered all those men who had stood there in the torchlight, shouting their defiance of the Spanish fleet. They trusted Gavin to lead them into battle, to challenge the might of Spain, and to emerge victorious from combat, no matter how great the odds might be.

But even as she sought to draw strength from what she had seen and heard down there in the cove, another memory stirred in some shadowy corner of her mind.

It had been a warm summer morning, then, and the air had been heavy with the scent of apple blossoms. A defiant band of men, some mounted and carrying swords and muskets, others on foot, armed only with scythes and cudgels, had gone out to fight. Her throat tightened as the memories took shape.

She could see Lance and his comrades once more. They, too, had been sure of victory; convinced that, although outnumbered, they could win the battle at Sedgemoor. That they could defeat the trained, heavily armed troops of the King.

And she remembered, with mounting anguish, how the young Duke's army had been routed before the sun had gone down on that summer afternoon.

Her hands closed into fists and she pressed her lips together tightly. She would not allow herself to remember the straggling procession of survivors, many of them wounded, who had fled their pursuers only to be hunted down like animals and slaughtered, or dragged off to be sentenced at the Bloody Assizes.

She cast about swiftly, seeking for some way—any way at all—to distract her thoughts. Looking about her, she tried to concentrate on her surroundings.

But something was wrong. The carriage was no longer following the road through the wooded stretch of palms, pimento trees, and vines. Instead it jolted along over a deserted stretch of sand not far from the shore. She caught the crash of waves breaking against a line of high, jagged rocks.

She forced herself to try to remember what was it Abiathar had told her, back in the small house on the Rue du Roi de France? He had said that the governor's house stood far from the waterfront; high above the shore, on the east end of the island?

She did not know in which direction the carriage was moving, but it certainly wasn't climbing upward. A nagging uneasiness stirred within her. The man who had driven her down to the beach, along with Abiathar and Tod, had been stooped and bony, and he'd worn a coarse shirt.

She leaned forward and tried to get a closer look at the silent figure seated up on the box in front of her. His shoulders looked wider under his dark, shapeless coat.

Had he been wearing a coat, when he had helped her to get back into the carriage? She had been too shaken, after her parting from Gavin to notice such details.

"Are you sure this is the way to the governor's house?" she called out. Her voice sounded a trifle breathless.

The man did not answer, or even turn to look at her. He only cracked his whip again, urging the mule forward. Fighting back her mounting fear, Sybilla forced herself to speak out again. "You do know how to get to Governor d'Ogeron's home, don't you?"

"I'll get ye where yer goin'."

Sybilla got to her feet, and held onto the side of the swaying carriage for support. The driver turned his head at last. He had a wide, flattish face, and a thick neck.

"You're not the man Captain Pascoe hired—the one who drove us to the cove. Where is he?"

"Where he won't be makin' no trouble to nobody." He stared at her, with a mirthless grin. "Now sit yerself down and stay quiet, if ye know what's good fer ye."

But Sybilla remained standing, her hands still clinging to the side of the carriage to keep from being thrown off balance. "Let me down at once!"

He jerked on the reins and brought the mule to a halt. She wrenched open the carriage door and started to climb down. But she was hampered by her full skirts, and by the time she reached the ground he already had swung down from his high seat. He stood directly in front of her, blocking her way.

"Where are you taking me?"

He seized her by the shoulder with one meaty hand. "You'll find out soon enough. Now get back inside and keep your mouth shut."

"I won't! Not until you explain—"

344

Before Sybilla could finish, his free hand shot out, and he struck her across the face. Her ears rang with the force of the blow. She slumped forward, falling against him, and she gagged at the rank odor of his body. He lifted her up and tossed her into the back of the carriage. Then he climbed in after her and leaned over her.

"Cap'n Broderick's woman, ain't ye? But he ain't here to help you, now."

"When he gets back—"

"If he gets back. Which he might not."

Anger blazed up within her, giving her renewed strength. "Gavin Broderick will capture the fleet. And he'll come back. If you dare to harm me, you will answer to him."

For a moment, the driver hesitated. She kept her eyes fixed on his face, sustained by a force of will she had not known she possessed.

"You stay put, then. An' keep yer mouth shut. Understand?"

She held her head high, but she remained silent. It would not be wise to push this man too far.

He climbed back up on his high box, and the carriage lurched forward again on its creaking wheels. Sybilla held herself erect on the seat, staring into the darkness, as she was carried on toward her unknown destination.

Chapter Twenty-Six

"Here's yer pigeon, Varner. I snared 'er, neat as you please."

The driver drew to a halt in a wide clearing, surrounded by a tropical forest, thick and dark. Sybilla glanced about her at the fires and the men who clustered around them; she caught a glimpse of a few women, too. From somewhere close by, she heard the pounding of the surf against the rocky shore.

Varner, a big, shaggy-haired man, fixed his pale, cold eyes on Sybilla, who drew back against the seat. He wore knee-length breeches of tanned animal hide, a loose cotton shirt, and a long knife thrust into his belt.

"Did you have any trouble gettin' hold of her?"

The driver shook his head. "She lit out runnin' down the cove. Wanted to bid her man good-bye. When she got back, it was me lifted her into the seat."

"And the man who drove her to the cove?"

"Slit 'is throat, I did. Tossed him into the brush. Neat bit o' work, if I say so. Well worth the ten shillings ye promised me."

"Not so fast," said Varner. He jerked his shaggy head in Sybilla's direction. "Did she raise a fuss when you carried her off?"

"Didn't even notice I wasn't the same one who'd brought her from town. She was still shook up bad, after takin' leave

346

of 'er captain. Not that anybody would've heard 'er, what with all that cheerin' an' shouting about how they was goin' to sink the dons, and bring back the gold." He held out his hand. "Speakin' o' which—" He paused, grinning expectantly.

Varner pulled out a pouch and counted a handful of coins into the driver's outstretched palm. "Not a word about this," he warned. "Else it'll be you layin' in the swamp with a slit gullet."

"Ye can trust me, Varner. The wench is yours, now."

Before Sybilla could make a sound of protest, Varner pulled open the carriage door, reached up, caught her around the waist, and dragged her down. He set her trunk on the ground beside her. The driver slashed at the mule's bony back, and the carriage went swaying across the firelit clearing and into the darkness of the forest.

Varner shifted his grip to Sybilla's wrist. When she tried to pull away, his fingers tightened with cruel force. The ragged, hard-bitten lot gathered around the fires rose now and began to crowd around to get a closer look at her.

"Good-lookin' trull," one of the men remarked, raking her body with lust-filled eyes.

"Trull, my arse! This one's a fine lady—sink me if she ain't."

"Trull or lady—they're all the same in the dark, ain't they?"

Sybilla fought down her revulsion at their crude appraisal. A stout woman with a mop of greasy hair, whose torn blouse scarcely concealed her huge breasts, stretched out a hand and clutched at her wide muslin skirt. "Lor, what a fine gown, with all that lace trimmin'." The woman gave a drunken cackle. "Bet she's got lace on 'er drawers, too."

She started pulling up Sybilla's gown, but Varner struck out and landed her a blow that sent her sprawling in the dirt. "Keep off, all of you."

They shrank back like a pack of savage hounds confronted by a brutal master. Varner must be in command here, but the thought offered Sybilla no reassurance at all. What could she expect from a man who had ordered the murder of another and then had made sure he'd gotten his money's worth before paying?

The shaggy-haired leader of this band of ruffians had planned her kidnapping with some care. But what did he want with her? There were plenty of women for the taking, here on the island.

Before she had time to consider the question further, he lifted her off her feet and carried her across the clearing to a long low house built of logs and topped with a thatched roof. He kicked open the door. Too dazed to struggle, she remained limp while he bore her across a dark room and into an adjoining cubicle.

Here a single lantern glowed dimly. It hung from an iron hook over the narrow bed in one corner. He tossed her down on the thin mattress and stood staring at her.

A sickening suspicion began to take shape in her mind. Was it possible that Varner held a grudge against Gavin, for some real or imagined wrong? Had he only waited for Gavin to set sail, before taking her prisoner, so that he might use her as a means of revenge?

And if so, what more likely way would such a brute choose, than to possess his enemy's woman?

"Don't you touch me!" Driven by fear and disgust, the words came unbidden.

She lowered her eyes, before his hard stare. But her gaze came to rest on his large hands with the coarse tufts of hair on his knuckles. She began to inch backward across the bed. "Don't come any closer!"

"I give the orders around here."

She kept moving away until she felt the rough logs of the wall pressing against her back. He gave a short, contemptuous laugh. Then he turned away. Striding to the outer door, he flung it open.

"Kitty!" he shouted. "Get in here, and be quick about it."

Too shaken to try to understand what was happening,

348

Sybilla remained where she was, her legs drawn up under her full skirt. When he returned, a dark-haired girl was following at his heels.

"Kitty'll keep watch on you," he said. "You're not to stir from the house. The shutter on that window's barred from the outside. And so's the one in the other room. There're men on guard in the clearing, day and night."

"What do you want with me?"

He ignored the question. "Just you do like I say. Otherwise, I'll have to teach you who's master here."

His eyes bored into hers. "I can do it without leavin' a mark on that smooth skin o' yours. I got my own special ways."

He turned his head. "You know all about that, don't you, Kitty?"

The color drained from the girl's face and she moistened her lips.

"Don't you?"

"Yes, Varner. I know." Her words sent darts of cold terror shooting through Sybilla's body. What sort of monster was this man who held her captive?

Even after he had left the house and slammed the door behind him, she remained huddled in the corner, too frightened to speak.

"He means what he says," Kitty told her in a dull, expressionless tone.

Sybilla studied the girl by the light of the lantern overhead. Kitty was probably no more than twenty, with thick, curly black hair and dark blue eyes. Her body was trim and shapely under her worn blouse and tattered skirt. But she had an air of hopeless resignation about her that robbed her of any trace of beauty.

"There's a jug of water, there on the window sill," she said. "And you'll find a chamber pot under the bed. Varner'll have one of the men bring in your trunk, when he gets around to it."

"What does he want with me? How long does he mean to

349

keep me here?"

"He doesn't tell me his plans." The dark-haired girl turned and started for the other room.

"Don't go, not yet."

"I won't be far off," Kitty told her. She disappeared into the darkness beyond.

Sybilla heard her rummaging about the larger room. She returned with a tattered blanket. "I'm going to sleep right here."

She spread the blanket on the threshold, outside Sybilla's door, and stretched herself out. "You might as well get some rest, too," she said, before turning her back and settling down.

But although Sybilla was exhausted, her fear kept her awake, and staring into the darkness, as she tried to make some sense out of her situation. If Varner had meant to rape her, he could have done so when he had carried her in here. None of his followers would have tried to stop him.

She remembered his threat: he would teach her who was master, without leaving a mark on her. At the time, she had been too terrified to consider the full import of his words. But now, she forced herself to try to figure out what he meant to do with her.

He knew that Gavin had sailed out to capture the treasure fleet. There were probably few here in Tortuga who had not heard all about the expedition by now.

Varner was holding her for ransom.

What other possible reason could he have for planning her kidnapping, then leaving her unmolested? He had never intended to possess her; he meant to keep her here, and exchange her for whatever he could get from Gavin.

The tension inside her began to slacken a little. If she had guessed aright, then he would see to it that she was alive and unharmed, when Gavin returned.

No! She would not allow herself to think about the possibility that he might not come back. Such thoughts would crush her spirit completely. And it would take every ounce of courage and strength she possessed, just to keep her going through the days to come.

Quickly, she made a plan of her own. She would try to appear docile before her captor. She would obey his orders without the slightest protest. That would not be difficult, so long as he made no attempt to molest her, and kept the other men from doing so.

She sat up and reached around behind her, to open the top buttons on her bodice. It wasn't easy, for her fingers were trembling, but somehow she managed. Now, if only she could get out of her tight stays. But she decided to let that go. It would be better not to disturb Kitty, now that the girl had gone to sleep.

She lay back on the thin, straw-filled mattress. It felt rough and scratchy. And the small room was hot and stuffy with the shutters closed. But finally, oblivious to such minor discomforts, she closed her eyes and drifted off into the heavy sleep of sheer exhaustion.

When Sybilla awoke, the sunlight slanted in through the louvered shutters. She sat up and glanced around, trying to get her bearings. There was no table or chair, no cupboard for her clothes. But someone had carried her trunk inside, and set it at the foot of the bed. She must have been sleeping deeply indeed, for she had not heard a sound.

"Awake, are you?" Kitty came in, balancing a rough-hewn wooden slab against her hip. It served as a tray, to hold a bowl, a wooden spoon and a chunk of bread.

She set her burden down on top of the trunk. "You'd better eat while it's hot."

The bowl was filled with a stew of shellfish, rice and beans. It smelled surprisingly good, and Sybilla realized that she was ravenous. She remembered how Abiathar had urged her to eat yesterday. But then, she had been able to think of nothing except getting down to the cove to see Gavin before he left.

Had his fleet already reached the Isthmus? Was he preparing for battle, even now?

She must not allow herself to think about Gavin, not yet. She moved to the foot of the bed, so that she could use the trunk as a table, and looked doubtfully at the spoon, which was none too clean.

"If you're looking for a silver spoon, my lady, you won't find any. Use that one, or sop up the stew with your bread, like the rest of us do."

Sybilla hesitated for a moment, then, seeing she had no choice, she obeyed. But she was puzzled by the resentment in Kitty's voice and the open hostility in her eyes.

After she had satisfied her hunger, she realized how hot and sticky she was, having slept in her clothes.

"Please, may I have some water?"

"Your jug's still half-full," the dark-haired girl said.

"I meant, water to wash with."

"It's enough I have to keep watch on you and bring you your food. I'm not about to carry a bucket all the way from the spring, so you can have your bath, my fine lady."

"I'd gladly carry my own water bucket, but I've been forbidden to leave the house."

"Then you'll have to do without," Kitty told her. "You got a room all to yourself, and a bed. That's more than the rest of us get."

Was Kitty resentful of the special privileges Sybilla had been given? Or was there some deeper reason for her dislike? Even in the brief time they had been together, Sybilla had sensed that Kitty was different from the other women who lived with these ruffians.

"You come from England, don't you?" Sybilla asked.

"Devon. What about it?"

"I came out to the West Indies from Somerset."

"Better for you, if you'd stayed there."

Sybilla considered the other girl's words. If she had not

come to Jamaica, she might never have met Gavin. She looked past Kitty, and her thoughts went back to that brief moment down at the cove last night.

Give the lass a kiss for luck, one of the sailors had said. And at first, his embrace had been no more than a gesture. But once his arms went around her, she had felt his ardent response. There had been no mistaking the deep feeling that had taken possession of him in spite of himself.

Had he forgiven her, then, for having deceived him? She would not know that until he returned. But right now it was not important. It was enough that she had the memory of his parting kiss, to hold onto. Her lips curved in a smile, and her golden eyes went misty.

"You're thinking about Captain Broderick, aren't you? Hoping he'll come and get you away from here." Kitty's words brought her back to the present with a jolt.

"He will. He must."

"I wouldn't count on it."

Sybilla stared at her indignantly. "I know him. You don't. When he finds out where I am, he'll come for me."

"When your gallant captain returns to Tortuga—if he does—you may be far away."

"But you're wrong! Varner went to a great deal of trouble to have me brought here. He left me unmolested, and he's keeping me under guard until—"

"Until Old Nick comes to fetch you."

Kitty broke off, and her hand flew to her lips. Her blue eyes filled with fear.

"Old Nick?" Sybilla remembered that the tenants on the Thornton estate back in Somerset had used that name when speaking of the devil. Her father had explained that they were afraid to call the evil one by his right name.

"Surely you don't believe that your leader can conjure up the devil," Sybilla began.

"I never said that. I only . . . For the love of heaven, stop chattering and leave me in peace." Plainly shaken, Kitty started from the room.

Sybilla sprang up and seized her arm. "Wait! Tell me what you meant about Old Nick—"

Kitty pulled free. "I'll get you that water you asked for," she said quickly. "Clean and fresh, from the spring. You can have a bath, if it'll make you feel better." She glanced at the trunk. "I guess you have lots of fresh clothes in there."

Sybilla did not know what to make of this complete change in Kitty's attitude. The girl sounded frightened half out of her wits, and anxious to placate Sybilla in any way she could.

Sybilla stared at her with mounting uneasiness. As long as she had believed that she was being held for ransom, she had been confident that she was reasonably safe. Now she had no idea what to expect.

"Please tell me, Kitty. I must know what Varner means to do with me."

"He isn't about to talk over his plans with the likes of me— or of these other sluts in the settlement. He keeps us here to pleasure his men. Or himself—when he feels the need." Her voice trembled slightly, and Sybilla saw the self-loathing in her blue eyes.

"I'm sorry."

"I don't want your pity." There was defiance in her bearing now; and perhaps a trace of half-forgotten pride. "I'll carry your bath water, and help you change your clothes. Only don't ask me any more of your questions. It'll be safer for both of us that way."

Sybilla knew she would get no more information out of Kitty, not now.

When Kitty returned with the water, she found Sybilla going through the contents of her trunk. She set down the bucket and drew closer, to stare wistfully at a blue gown with a full skirt, trimmed with ecru lace.

"I had a dress like that once. The lace wasn't so fine, but it was pretty." Her voice softened. "I wore a blue ribbon tied around my hair."

She glanced down at her blouse, so badly worn that it was nearly transparent, and her skirt with its torn ruffle drooping over her bare ankles. "Guess you think I'm lying, don't you?"

"Why should I think that? I can't know how or why you came here. But I do know you're not like those women I saw out there in the clearing last night."

"I'm a lot worse off. Most of them were born and raised in the gutters and alleys, back in London, or Marseilles. But I . . ." She turned her face away.

Sybilla looked at her helplessly. "Take the dress," she said. "It should fit you, and the color matches your eyes."

"Thank you, my lady." There was no mistaking the hard mockery in Kitty's voice. "I'll be needing such a dress to wear, when some fine gentleman comes calling on me."

Sybilla, her nerves already stretched taut, could not restrain herself. "You hate this place, and who can blame you for that? But you're not closely guarded, as I am. There must be some way for you to slip out of the settlement."

Kitty shrugged. "I'm free to go across the island to the harbor at Manzanilla, when we need supplies. What good does that do me?"

"There are ships in the harbor. It would mean a risk, but if you were to stow away aboard a merchant ship bound for home—"

"Home? I have no home. My family'd never take me back, after I brought such disgrace on them."

Knowing nothing of Kitty's past, Sybilla was at a loss for an answer. "The dress is yours, if you want it," she said simply. Then she stripped and began to wash with the water from the bucket.

But her thoughts lingered on what Kitty had just said; that she was free to go to Manzanilla. She dried herself and put on a fresh shift. "How often do you go for supplies?"

"Depends on when we start getting low on rum or flour." She gave Sybilla a searching glance. "If you have any notion of getting me to help you escape, you can forget it

355

right now. Varner'd catch both of us. He'd skin me alive, and as for you . . . Have you forgotten what he said he'd do to you, if you tried to get away?"

"I haven't forgotten." Sybilla could not repress a shiver, as she thought of the shaggy-haired brute. "But if you went down to the waterfront, you could stand about in the market stalls. Maybe you know some sailor who would speak freely to you."

"More than one." But this time, there was no mockery in her smile—only understanding, and perhaps a touch of sympathy.

"You want to know what's happening to your captain, don't you?"

Sybilla put a hand on her arm. "If only you could bring me some word, I'd be so grateful."

"The way they guzzle up the rum, I could always say we were running low. I'm not making any promises, mind. Varner said I was to stay here and keep watch over you."

"One of the other women could take your place for a few hours, couldn't she?"

Kitty hesitated. "Suppose the news I bring back isn't what you're hoping for."

"It would be better than waiting. And not knowing."

Kitty had said she would try to help, but as the days went by Sybilla felt herself sinking into despair. The girl had made no more mention of going down to the harbor, and Sybilla dared not risk arousing her companion's uncertain temper.

Once, when it suddenly occurred to her that Governor d'Ogeron might have started a search for her, she had confided in Kitty. "I'm sure Gavin must have sent word to the governor to expect me. Since I haven't arrived at his home by now, he may be wondering what's become of me."

"Varner's too clever to leave anything to chance. He's likely to have thought of that, too. And figured out some way to put the governor off the scent, you can bet on that. He

356

means to keep you hidden here until—"

"Until Old Nick comes to fetch me away," Sybilla said, trying to restrain her impatience at such a fantastic notion. "That's nonsense and you know it."

"Maybe so. But it wouldn't surprise me if the devil came and fetched *him* away some day."

The following morning, a slatternly woman came shuffling into Sybilla's room, carrying her breakfast.

"Where's Kitty?"

"Gone off in the wagon at daybreak, with a couple o' the men," the woman said.

Sybilla had to look away so that she would not betray her feelings. Somehow she forced herself to start eating with an appearance of appetite. Kitty had kept her promise, after all. But in spite of her excitement, she felt a pang of concern for the other girl. "Did Varner give her permission to go?"

The woman laughed shrilly. "Ain't likely she'd go off otherwise. But don't go gettin' any wrong notions. I mean to watch you real careful-like, 'til she gets back."

It had been over a week since Gavin had set sail from Tortuga. He should have sighted the Spanish convoy the following day. Perhaps Gavin had captured the fleet, against all the odds. Maybe his ships were already on the way back to Tortuga. If so, Kitty would hear about it.

Never had the hours crawled by so slowly. Sybilla sat on the bed, her muscles aching with pent-up tension, her eyes fixed on the shuttered window. She had learned to measure the time by studying the angle of the sun's rays as they slanted through the wooden slats.

In spite of her boast that she would watch Sybilla carefully, the slatternly female had plopped herself down on the floor in the outer room, taken a bottle of rum from under her skirt, and was slowly lapsing into a drunken stupor. But nothing on earth would have persuaded Sybilla to try risk an escape. Not today. If only Kitty would get back.

*   *   *

It was sundown before she saw Kitty coming through the door.

Springing to her feet, she raced out to meet her. "Did you . . ." But Kitty silenced her with a warning look.

Sybilla could scarcely hold back her questions, while Kitty roused the drunken slattern and sent her away. Then she motioned to Sybilla to come into the bedchamber.

"Were you able to find out about Gavin? Did he attack the Spaniards? Is he safe?"

"Captain Broderick's ships captured the treasure fleet."

"You're sure?" Only now could she allow herself to admit her doubts as to the outcome of the battle.

"You heard what I said."

Considering the wonderful tidings she had brought back, she spoke without any particular elation. She sounded much the same as she had on the night of Sybilla's arrival here. But Sybilla reminded herself that she could scarcely expect the other girl to share her own overwhelming relief, her soaring joy over Gavin's victory.

"Tell me all you were able to find out." Her legs had begun to tremble, so that she could not remain standing. She drew Kitty down beside her on the edge of the bed. When Kitty did not reply at once, Sybilla clutched at her arm. "How long since the battle? How soon before he's expected back?"

Then, stopping only to catch her breath, she went on. "His ships—were any lost in battle?"

"At least one of them was. Captain Broderick ordered it to be used for a fire ship. I talked to a sailor, in front of one of the taverns. He told me—"

"A fire ship?" The word had an ominous sound. "What's that, Kitty?"

"The crew fills a space between decks with anything that will burn fast. Resin, tallow, tar. And gunpowder, in iron pots. They lay trains of powder and bundles of brushwood in a kind of trail. And then the crew—all picked men who're willing to take such a risk—they steer the ship straight into the midst of the enemy fleet and set her afire."

"But surely the men on the fire ship haven't a chance of surviving."

"Some might—with luck. If they can get over the side fast enough, and into the boat they're towing astern. One fireship can destroy four or five of the enemy, if she's got the wind with her. But this sailor I was talking to, he said he wouldn't serve on a fire ship. Not if they were to offer him a chest of gold."

But Gavin's men would not hesitate to carry out his orders, no matter what the danger. Sweet Jesú! Had Abiathar been aboard the fire ship, she wondered? Or Jeremy Randall? She would have to wait until Gavin came back to find out about the others.

"I'll never forget what you've done for me today, Kitty. When Gavin comes for me, I'll see to it that he helps you get away. I promise."

Kitty looked at her, without a flicker of emotion in her dark blue eyes. The other girl's complete lack of response was beginning to unnerve Sybilla.

"You've nothing to fear from Varner now," she said. "When Gavin gets here he'll deal with him as he deserves."

"Gavin Broderick won't be coming back."

For a moment, Sybilla stared at her blankly, unable to take in the meaning of her words.

"But you said—"

"I said his ships took the treasure fleet and were on their way back to Tortuga. But not the captain."

An icy hand closed around Sybilla's throat, and grew tighter. She tried to speak but the words would not come.

"It was his own ship Captain Broderick set afire. He didn't make it over the side before she blew up."

A swift, rushing sound filled Sybilla's head. It went on and on, growing louder all the time. But not loud enough to drown out the other girl's voice. "I couldn't let you go on waiting, hoping he'd come for you. Because he won't—not ever."

Sybilla stared at Kitty in frozen silence until the other girl got to her feet, her voice shaking with anger. "Don't keep looking at me like that. Like you're blaming me."

"No, you're not to blame. I am."

"You're daft," Kitty cried. She seized Sybilla by the shoulders. "Your man knew the risk he was taking."

Sybilla shook her head slowly. If she had not deceived Gavin, the risk would not have been nearly so great. And if she had understood him better, she might have realized that he would not abandon his plans, no matter what the odds.

"Gavin's dead. Because of me."

"Stop talking that way!" Kitty tightened her grip on Sybilla's shoulders and shook her fiercely. "You've had a bad shock. But you got to keep your wits about you."

"Why?" Sybilla's voice rose shrill and out of control. "What difference does it make? Maybe if I were to take leave of my wits I'd be better off."

Kitty put one hand over Sybilla's lips, while keeping a tight grip on her shoulder. "Stop that before somebody hears you and tells Varner." She leaned over Sybilla. "If you go daft, you're done for. You won't be worth anything to him."

Although her words were meaningless, Sybilla caught the desperate urgency behind them.

"You going to keep still?"

Sybilla managed to nod.

Kitty released her. She let herself fall back against the bed, and she stayed there, looking at the thatched ceiling overhead. She never noticed when the other girl left her alone.

After awhile she saw the sunlight had disappeared. Varner's followers gathered about their fires. The clearing echoed with their loud talk, their harsh laughter. One of them roared out the words of a bawdy song, and the others joined in.

But Sybilla scarcely heard them. Although she hadn't lost her grip on reality, as Kitty had feared, her thoughts were far away. She was back with Gavin, reliving their time together. Brief images, remembered sensations, moved across her mind.

Her face, against the hardness of his chest. And the mat of dark hair, crisp and curling beneath her cheek. The shape of his cheekbones, high and angular. The curve of his lips. The male scent of him, when they lay close in each other's arms, after making love. His strong, vibrant body, only ashes now. Ashes caught in the wind . . . borne across the sea . . .

The next day, Sybilla rose and took up the motions of living. She bathed, changed her dress, even ate her breakfast. Kitty seemed deeply relived by her quiet demeanor, but she spoke no consoling words; in fact, she scarcely spoke at all.

Sybilla remembered Kitty's cryptic warning. Varner would have no use for a woman who'd lost her wits. She tried to figure out what the other girl had meant, then abandoned the effort.

Better to let herself drift along, numbed, indifferent. Even when Kitty came and led her outside, she asked no questions.

She paused, blinking in the unaccustomed glare of the noon sunlight. Then her eyes flew open, and she cried out in stunned surprise. She was not looking at Varner. Her unbelieving gaze was fastened on Lance. And the man who stood beside him. Nicholas Hobart. *Old Nick.*

Chapter Twenty-Seven

Sybilla stood quite still for a moment, and then she ran straight to her brother. She reached up and placed a hand on either side of his face, as if to reassure herself that he was really here.

"How did you find me?"

"It was Mr. Hobart who discovered that you were in Tortuga," Lance told her. He put his arm around her and drew her closer.

Hobart came strutting up to them with a self-satisfied smile. He made an incongruous figure in this primitive setting, for he wore a green satin coat, trimmed with gold braid, and a carefully curled black periwig.

"I gave your description to the officers of all my trading vessels, and I ordered them to make inquiries about you, at every port of call," he said. "As soon as I got word that you had been brought here to this nest of pirates by Captain Broderick, I sent instructions to Varner to search the island, and rescue you."

"Lance, he's lying!" Sybilla interrupted. "Varner had me kidnapped. He's been holding me prisoner ever since he had me brought here. If it had not been for Kitty, I don't know what might have happened to me. She gave me what little help she could."

Sybilla glanced about, but Kitty was nowhere in sight. "Where's Kitty?" she demanded of Varner. With Lance at her side, she no longer feared her captor. "What have you done with her?"

"Your sister seems somewhat confused," Hobart said.

"And no wonder." Lance's arm tightened protectively about Sybilla's shoulders. "When I think what she must have had to endure, as Broderick's captive!"

At the mention of Gavin's name, Sybilla started violently. "Forgive me," Lance said gently. "No doubt it will take time for you to get over the memory of your ordeal. But you're safe now. He looked down at her with a reassuring smile. "As soon as Mr. Hobart's rewarded Varner for his assistance, we'll be on our way."

"Lance, for the love of heaven—you've got to listen to me. Varner's been holding me prisoner, and now Old Nick—Hobart I mean—doesn't even try to deny that he hired this monster—"

"Old Nick," Hobart repeated, shaking his head. "The poor girl's in a far worse condition than I'd feared. Lance. But once we're back in Jamaica, we'll all go straight to Indigo. She'll be able to rest there, in comfort, until she has recovered from her experiences." Before Sybilla could protest, he went on with an air of authority. "Right now, you'd better help her inside, Thornton. Do what you can to calm her."

But when Lance tried to lead her back to the cabin she resisted with all her strength.

"No! Don't make me go back in there. Varner kept me prisoner in that place. The first night I came here, he threatened me with—he didn't say how he meant to torture me, if I tried to escape."

"You're confused, Sybilla," Lance said gently. "If not for Mr. Hobart, I shouldn't want to think what might have become of you, after that damned pirate abandoned you."

"But that's not true. It wasn't the way he says. You've got

363

to listen to me."

"Hush, dear. We'll speak of it later."

"We'll speak of it now!" Sybilla cried in desperation. "After you left Jamaica, Hobart tried to force me into marrying him. And Madeleine threatened me. She said she'd have me driven from Acacia Hall. You were far away—I couldn't think how to get word to you. And so I turned to Gavin for help."

She felt a searing anguish, even as she spoke his name. But she had to convince her brother that she was telling the truth, and quickly.

"Gavin Broderick saved me from a forced marriage to Hobart—and after the battle between his ship and the *San Bartolomé,* I went with him willingly. I loved him, Lance." Her voice faltered.

"I'm afraid you're right, Hobart," Lance said. "She's beside herself."

She freed herself from her brother's comforting embrace and turned on Hobart. "You greedy hypocrite. You've been posing as a pillar of society in Jamaica. You've grown rich on the profits from Gavin's expeditions. He and his men risked their lives, while you stayed safe in Indigo."

She ran her eyes over him with a look of boundless contempt. "Except for your finery—that satin coat and periwig—you're no better than Varner."

"Varner is a rough sort," Hobart admitted to Lance. "Perhaps when he realized that your sister was in this unfortunate condition, he may have been more forceful than one would have wished. But you can understand. He had to restrain her, to keep her from running off, until we were able to get here."

"He's twisting everything—you mustn't let him deceive you this way," she pleaded to her brother. "Where's Kitty? If only you can find Kitty, she'll tell you the sort of man Varner is—the terrible things he's done. Lance, you've got to listen to me."

"Certainly, dear," Lance soothed her. "Why don't we go inside the cabin right now, and see if we can find her."

Sybilla stared up at her brother, her eyes filled with dismay. He might have been speaking to a helpless little girl who was in need of his protection.

"What have you done with Kitty?" she screamed at Varner. "I promised I'd help her, as soon as Gavin got back—" A sob caught in her throat. "But he's not coming back, is he? I'll never see him again."

Lance lifted her in his arms and cradled her against his chest. "Hush now, Sybilla. I'm here. I won't let any harm come to you."

She felt her strength ebbing away, and she let herself go limp in his arms. He was carrying her toward the cabin, using his shoulder to open the door wider.

"Varner kept me locked in a little chamber—no larger than a cell—at the back of the cabin." She started to struggle, pushing against him, trying to get free. "Don't take me in there again."

Lance set her down just inside the door. "We'll stay right here and wait for Hobart," he said. "I won't leave you."

"Don't talk to me as if I were an idiot child." Somehow, she was regaining her self-control. "Whatever I've said about Hobart is true. Surely you know by now that he's not the respectable gentleman he claims to be. I don't know how he persuaded you to join his band of smugglers on the Isle of Pines but—"

"Plenty of perfectly respectable merchants here in the Indies are engaged in the smuggling trade. I knew what I was getting involved in, before I sailed from Jamaica. But I had to find a way to get enough money to take you away from Acacia Hall, and provide you with a proper home. And I'll be able to do that now."

In spite of her inner turmoil, Sybilla was gradually becoming aware of a change in her brother, a new maturity about him. She heard it in his voice and she saw it in his face.

365

"I know Hobart's not what he pretends to be," Lance was saying. "But without his help, I never would have found you here. Even so, once he gets us back to Jamaica, we won't stay on the island any longer than we have to. There are plenty of thriving Dutch settlements we can go to."

"He said I was to come with him to Indigo."

"And so you shall." Hobart stood in the doorway. "It will be your home from now on, Sybilla."

Lance gave him a startled look, but he ignored it, and went on. "I offered your sister an honorable proposal of marriage, before that pirate carried her off," he told Lance calmly.

"We celebrated our coming marriage at a ball, and invited all the gentry of Jamaica. She accepted my betrothal gift, a topaz necklace."

"Sybilla, is all this true?"

"There was a ball—and I had to take his gift—but you don't know the reason why I had to—"

Hobart ignored her. "I am still willing to make Sybilla my wife," he went on. "I shall try to overlook all that's happened to her."

"I'm not sure I understand you, Hobart." All at once, she heard a hard edge to her brother's voice.

"We'll talk it over at a more suitable time," Hobart said quickly.

"You will explain yourself here and now."

"As you wish, Thornton. Though I should think you'd want to spare your sister from being reminded of her disgrace."

"Go on." Her brother spoke with deceptive calm now, but she recognized the threat beneath his words, even if Hobart did not.

"Good Lord! How much plainer do you want me to be? You know well enough that few men in my position would keep a promise of marriage to a girl who—"

Lance took a step forward, his eyes fixed on Hobart's broad face. His lean body was rigid with outraged pride. She wanted to assure him that she would never marry Hobart, but that could come later.

"Speak out, and have done with it," Lance challenged the man.

"All right, then. When I offered to make her my wife, she was innocent, untouched. Now that she's the cast-off mistress of a pirate—"

Before he could finish, Lance sprang on him with such force that he swayed and staggered backward. He would have fallen to the ground, outside the open door, but her brother seized him by his gold-braided lapels and held him upright.

"Have you gone as crazed as your sister?" Hobart spluttered, his face turning brick red below his heavy periwig. "How many men in my position would keep their promise and go through with a marriage to a female who'd been used and left on the beach in Tortuga?" He looked her over as if she were a slave on the auction block, and a suggestive note crept into his voice. "Who knows how many other men have shared her favors, since Broderick deserted her?"

Lance let go of Hobart, drew back his arm and lashed out with his open hand. Sybilla scarcely realized what had happened until she heard the sound of the blow, like the crack of a whip, and saw the white print of her brother's fingers against Hobart's ruddy cheek.

"Since you are the injured party, you have the choice of weapons."

Sybilla, who was still standing in the doorway, saw Varner and his men begin to move in closer, drawn by the threat of imminent bloodshed.

"I should not choose swords, if I were you," Lance went on, as he removed his coat and tossed it aside. "You're not a young man. You're getting thick about the middle. And you're probably short-winded, as well. Better make it pistols. That way, you'll have an even chance."

"No, Lance!" Sybilla cried out. "Don't say anymore!"

But he did not take his eyes from Hobart's face. "Which is it to be?" he asked.

"Get back, you addle-brained fool," Hobart warned. "I'm willing to forget you struck me. But from now on, you'd do well to keep that hot temper of yours under control. "I've said I would marry your sister, and so I shall. If she behaves decently and shows me the gratitude I deserve, I might even try to forget what she's been."

He turned and started to walk away, but Lance grabbed his shoulder and spun him around. He smashed his fist into Hobart's face, splitting his lip. A few drops of blood appeared on the foaming lace of his cravat.

"Get this madman off me," Hobart shouted.

Sybilla called out a warning but she was too late. Varner slipped around and seized Lance from behind, wrapping a muscular arm around his throat.

Lance fought to free himself, but Varner's grip tightened. Sybilla heard her brother make a strangled sound that was cut off abruptly. He sagged forward, unconscious.

"Want us to kill 'im?" Varner asked.

"That won't be necessary," Hobart said. "Just tie him up securely."

Varner released Lance, and let him fall to the ground. The men bound him with strips of rawhide, dragged him to the nearest palm, and fastened him to its trunk.

Sybilla started to go to him, but Hobart held her back. "He's safe enough. For now."

Knowing Hobart as she did, she understood his unspoken threat. "When your gallant brother comes around, it'll be up to you to make him see reason. Since you are so devoted to him, you'd do well to use all your powers of persuasion."

"I'll do anything you ask—only don't let Varner near him again." She could not conceal the fear that was coursing through her.

"I see you've come back to your senses. Now, if you're willing to do as I say, he won't be harmed."

She looked anxiously at Lance, then turned back to face Hobart. "What is it you want of me?"

"As to that, I've not quite made up my mind yet," he said. "I could keep you for my mistress. Though even that's more than you deserve." His eyes moved over her slowly, lingering on the curves of her body. "You've lost your virtue. But I can't deny that I find you as enticing as ever. And far more experienced in pleasing a man, no doubt. I may marry you after all. It's no easy decision—"

"Don't trouble yourself, Hobart. I've decided for you!"

That voice, strong and touched with hard irony.

Gavin's voice.

Sybilla whirled around and stood motionless. She felt as if her heart had stopped its beating. Gavin stood on the rise, where the path led out of the wall of trees and vines, and down to the clearing below.

She stared up at him, as he stood silhouetted against the deep green of the forest. He wasn't real. He couldn't be. Had she taken leave of her senses?

But he descended swiftly, sword in hand, his face dark with rage. And she knew that he was no illusion. Certainly there was nothing otherworldly about Abiathar.

The bearded giant came charging down behind Gavin, brandishing his cutlass. "Let me at that whoreson! I'll split 'im from gullet to gizzard and string his guts to a palm tree!"

And other buccaneers crowded into the clearing, some of them stripped to the waist, with bright silk scarves tied around their heads. They were armed with muskets, cutlasses, pikes and boarding axes, and they yelled like fiends as they kept coming on.

Varner's gang of cutthroats, taken by surprise, looked to their leader. "Fight for your lives!" As he gave the order, he drew a knife from his belt and led them to meet the attack.

Hobart made a grab for Sybilla and tried to force her in front of him as a shield, but she twisted free. She started to fight her way through the mob of struggling men, to get to Gavin.

But a small, hard hand closed on her arm. "You can't—not yet." Kitty was dragging her into the nearest thicket, pulling her along. Low-hanging vines and branches whipped against Sybilla's face as she stumbled on. A shot rang out, then another.

"Get down," Kitty cried, tugging desperately at her arm.

When Sybilla, dazed and breathless, could not respond quickly enough, Kitty shoved her to the ground and dropped down beside her in the tall grass.

"Broderick wouldn't wait for the rest of his crew to join him. They're still out searching the island. Let's hope the men he's brought with him will be enough—" The rest of her words were lost in the din as the forces met head-on.

The clearing was a cacophany of sound: the crack of musket fire, the clash of steel, the cries and oaths of the wounded. Sybilla raised her head and peered through the tall grass, trying to make sense out of the bits and pieces she could glimpse from her hiding place: Abiathar, pausing for an instant to stare down at Varner's prostrate body writhing in the dirt, while blood poured from a wound in his chest; Demarais, the lean French captain, his wide shirt sleeves billowing out, his blade moving with dazzling speed, and practiced skill; Jeremy Randall, fighting his way to Lance, using his sword to cut the rawhide strips that held her brother bound to the tree.

Watching anxiously from her hiding place, Sybilla could see that Lance was not only conscious again, but alert and tensed for combat. He seized a sword from the grip of a fallen man, and whirled about to confront the nearest of Varner's followers.

The man moved in, swinging a machete. But Lance shifted with lithe speed, got under the man's guard, and ran him through. Then he placed his booted foot on the man's prostrate body and pulled the blade free. He slashed another man across the face and kept going, moving toward Hobart.

But Gavin had already fought his way through to the cabin, where he stood facing Hobart. "This one's mine," he called out to Lance.

Sybilla raised herself higher and began to inch forward through the underbrush. Now she was close enough to hear Hobart crying out above the surrounding din.

"Broderick—I'm unarmed!" He put out his open hand.

But Demarais smiled, and placed the jeweled hilt of his own sword into Hobart's meaty palm. "Allow me, monsieur," he said. "It's a fine weapon, I assure you."

Hobart looked about as if hoping for help from Varner, or one of his men. But Varner was scarcely moving after the slash from Abiathar's swinging cutlass, and his hard-pressed followers had all they could do to hold ground against the onslaught of Gavin's buccaneers.

"Defend yourself, Hobart." Gavin raised his blade and took a step forward. Hobart veered to the side. Then, as if realizing that there was no escape, he lunged at Gavin, who parried the clumsy thrust.

"Who's the fop in the wig?" Sybilla heard Kitty whisper.

"Old Nick—Nicholas Hobart."

"Your captain'll cut him down in no time."

Sybilla had no reason to doubt it. But as the duel went on, under the blazing afternoon sky, she began to feel bewildered, and uneasy. Although the sweat streamed down his face, and he was panting for breath, Hobart still stood his ground.

Gavin kept his own blade circling closely around Hobart's. Sybilla realized that so far, Gavin had chosen to ignore every opportunity to strike the final blow.

"What's he waiting for?" Kitty asked.

Gavin moved in with a skillful riposte. Hobart disengaged, and Gavin shifted position. Now he was maneuvering Hobart backward, against the wall of the cabin.

Hobart drew a long, whistling breath. His periwig hung

askew, and his satin coat clung to his thick body.

With one swift movement of his arm, Gavin struck the sword from Hobart's hand. And an instant later, the point of his own blade was pressing against Hobart's throat.

"Abiathar!" Gavin raised his left arm, in a gesture Sybilla did not immediately understand.

But Abiathar did and he made his instant response. He let out a quarterdeck roar that echoed from one end of the clearing to the other. "Throw down yer weapons, ye filthy scum. Else ye'll be joining yer leader in hell!"

Varner lay on his back, his unseeing eyes still open. His men hastened to obey. A few tried to escape into the forest, but Abiathar and the buccaneers stood blocking their way.

"Broderick—don't kill me—" Hobart begged.

"Give me one reason why I shouldn't."

"I'm a rich man—" Hobart fought for breath to go on. "I'll pay anything—everything I own—"

"My men and I took the treasure fleet." Now he deliberately raised his voice, and spoke so that every man in the clearing was bound to hear him. "We've already divided up the shares."

A low growl came from one of Varner's men and spread through the ranks of those who were still on their feet.

But Hobart seemed oblivious to the sound. His eyes were fixed on Gavin with a look of frantic desperation.

"You've nothing left to bargain with," Gavin told him.

"You're wrong—there's still—Acacia Hall. Sybilla—"

Lance stepped forward, gripping his sword. "If I hear my sister's name from your lips once more, I'll silence you for good."

Although he could not move, with Gavin's blade still pressed to his throat, his small eyes shifted in Lance's direction. "Your uncle's plantation—it's not Madeleine's—never was—it belongs to you—"

Gavin's brows went up. "What sort of trick is this?"

"No trick—I swear it. Madeleine's marriage to Thornton's

uncle—bigamous—a fraud. She was still married . . ."

"Go on," said Gavin. He lowered his sword a few inches.

"Married to a shiftless wretch—a player . . . I have papers—in the strongbox . . ." He was running out of breath, his chest heaving. "Indigo—my study . . ."

With a shaking hand, he reached into his coat, fumbled, then tossed a bunch of keys at Lance's feet.

But Lance did not even look down. His eyes were fixed on Hobart's face.

"He may be telling the truth, for once," Gavin observed quietly.

"I am," Hobart pleaded. "I swear it, Thornton. Your uncle's plantation—it's yours . . ."

"Pick up the keys," Gavin told Lance. He hesitated a moment, then complied.

"You won't let Broderick kill me now—"

Gavin said, "I never had any intention of killing you."

Hobart stared at him doubtfully. Then his shoulders sagged with relief. "You won't regret it—I promise—"

"It's you who'll have cause for regret," Gavin told him. "We're leaving. But you'll stay behind, with Varner's men. I don't think you'll find them particularly merciful, now they know they're not getting any part of the Spanish loot you promised them." He gave a brief, mirthless smile as he turned away from Hobart.

"Captain—she's safe—right here—" But Sybilla scarcely heard Kitty's shrill cry.

As Gavin came toward her hiding place, she was already on her feet. She ran to him, and her heart soared as she felt his arms around her.

Chapter Twenty-Eight

Sybilla sat close beside Gavin, in the garden of Governor d'Ogeron's home. She kept her face pressed against his shoulder. The breeze was fragrant with the scent of jasmine and pimento trees.

The last rays of the setting sun lingered over the hibiscus blooms, the sago palms and bamboos. But for the moment she was oblivious of her surroundings. She was only aware of Gavin's closeness, the hard strength of his arm around her, his cheek resting against her hair.

"I thought I'd never see you again," she said softly. "Kitty told me you'd been killed when the fire ship exploded." She reached up and stroked his hair. "It wasn't true, any of it. You're here."

"Kitty's tale wasn't all lies," Gavin told her. She drew back slightly and searched his face. "I made it over the side of the *Condor* with little time to spare. That was moments before she rammed the powder magazine of the Spanish admiral's own flagship."

"But Kitty made me believe you'd been killed in the battle." Even now, she could scarcely bear the memory of those terrible hours, when she was certain she had lost Gavin forever. "She told me—"

"You can't blame the girl," he said. "She was too afraid of

Varner to go against his orders. Hobart's orders, really. Varner was only his tool."

"Hobart wanted me to go away with him quietly. Perhaps to marry him. I suppose he believed he could control me more easily, once I'd been convinced that you were dead." She spoke slowly, with growing comprehension.

"Don't think about it," Gavin said. "He won't trouble you or anyone else, ever again."

He broke off, and she saw that Lance was coming along the flagstone path. Her brother stopped and stood before them.

His hazel eyes rested on Gavin with a long, speculative look.

"I think perhaps you'd better go inside the house, Sybilla," Lance said. "I want to speak to Gavin."

Her fingers closed tightly around Gavin's hand. "I'm staying."

Lance sighed and shook his head. "No doubt it would be useless to try to persuade you to leave."

Gavin's mouth curved in a faint smile. "Your sister's a most determined lady. But I suppose you've known that for some time now."

But there was no hint of amusement in Lance's face. And it came to Sybilla once more, that her brother was different now; with a certain self-assurance she had not seen in him before.

"You protected my sister from Nicholas Hobart, when I wasn't back there in Jamaica to take care of her. And again today, you rescued her. I owe you a debt of gratitude."

"You owe me nothing," Gavin said quietly. "Sybilla and I—"

"Hobart gave me his own account of what happened after you captured my sister. I believed him, then. But now, I'm damned if I know what to believe."

"You may believe that I went with Gavin willingly," Sybilla told her brother. Her fingers tightened around

Gavin's hand and she moved closer to him. "I'll go with him again. If he still wants me."

"I never stopped wanting you," Gavin told her. "I never will." He raised her hand to his lips and pressed his mouth to her palm, ignoring Lance's indignant stare.

"I've said I'm grateful to you for preventing Sybilla from marrying that swine, Hobart," Lance went on. "But I am her brother. And if you think I'm about to give her my permission to go following you across the West Indies, you are mistaken."

"Lance, please," Sybilla said. "There's so much you don't understand."

But Gavin got to his feet and faced Lance squarely. "In your place, I'd probably feel the same," Gavin told Lance, without a trace of irony.

Sybilla gave Gavin a startled look.

"But I have no intention of remaining here in the Caribbean." He paused, and although his eyes were still fixed on Lance, she knew that his words were meant for her, as well.

"Suppose I were to ask your consent to marry her tomorrow, and then take her home to Boston with me. What would you say to that?"

Until this moment, Sybilla had not spoken to Gavin about their future. It was enough—more than enough—to have him alive and safely beside her.

Lance looked from Gavin to Sybilla, and he could not mistake the joy that came into her eyes. Her face, her whole being, seemed filled with a radiant glow he had never seen there before.

"You have the right to question me about my future prospects," Gavin went on. "Boston may be lacking in some of the amenities you both knew back in Somerset. But I promise to give your sister the home she should have. She will be respected by my family and our neighbors up there."

"I don't question your ability to provide for Sybilla," Lance said dryly. "There's no one in Tortuga who hasn't heard of your conquests. I've already spoken with Governor d'Ogeron. And he tells me that he holds you in high esteem. But when you offer my sister a fortune in pirate gold—"

"It's not so different from smugglers' gold, I should say. But that's not important. My share of the Spanish loot will be put to honest use. I mean to invest in my family's shipping company."

"Gavin, wait!" Sybilla heard herself speaking the words she thought she would never say. "I'm yours. And I think I know myself a little better now. I want to marry you. But Abiathar said you could never be content with a wife who tried to—" She searched her memory. "To chart your course for you."

"Abiathar was right about that. He understands me well enough." Gavin looked directly at Sybilla, his gray eyes holding hers and now he was speaking only to her. "I've done what I set out to do," he told her. "I've struck my blow against the might of Spain, back there at Porto Bello. Now I want to return home, to take my place in my—in our family. I want my wife along with me."

He turned to Lance and held out his hand. "It would mean a great deal to Sybilla, and to me, if we might have your consent." He spoke with the same respect he might have shown her father, under different circumstances.

She glanced anxiously from Gavin's face to her brother's. Her ties with Lance could not be broken easily. She felt a surge of relief as she saw him take Gavin's outstretched hand. "You may have Sybilla as your wife," he said.

Then he added, thoughtfully, "It won't be easy losing her, though. We've scarcely had a chance to be together again."

"But there'll be plenty of time now," Sybilla told her brother eagerly. "You're coming back to Boston with us. Gavin has said so, all along. He will make a place for you in the shipping company, and you'll have a home of your own."

"Aren't you forgetting something?" Once more, she heard the new firmness in his voice and saw it in the lines of his tanned face. "Acacia Hall is Thornton property. If Madeleine had not deceived Oliver Thornton, the plantation would have passed directly to me."

Sybilla got to her feet, stunned by what he was saying. She turned to Gavin, her eyes pleading for his support. "Do you think Hobart was telling the truth? Is it possible that Madeleine was already married when she went through that ceremony with Uncle Oliver?"

"Hobart never hesitated to twist the truth to suit himself," said Gavin. "But in this case, I believe him. He was always seeking to find out all about his neighbors in Jamaica. He pried into their personal affairs, so that he could use his knowledge to gain power over them."

"Perhaps, but—"

"Let me finish, Sybilla. He managed to find out that Lance had fought for Monmouth's cause at Sedgemoor."

"I know," Lance said slowly. "He told me as much, back in Havana. He wanted to keep me out on the Isle of Pines as long as it suited his purpose. But what made him share that information with you?"

"Sybilla told me."

"And Madeleine knows, too," Sybilla said quickly. "You see, you can't go back to Jamaica. You've got to come to Boston with us—"

"So now you're about to try to chart Lance's course for him." Gavin interrupted. "Don't do it, Sybilla. He's capable of making his own decisions."

"But if Madeleine decides to fight for Acacia Hall, she might charge him with treason."

"That's most unlikely," Lance reminded her. "I hold the key to Hobart's strongbox, remember? Once I take possession of those papers he spoke of and can prove that Madeleine was never Uncle Oliver's lawful wife, she's likely to gather up whatever money and jewelry she can lay her greedy hands on, and disappear." He gave Sybilla a reassuring smile. "All I want is Acacia Hall. And I'm prepared to take whatever risk is necessary, to claim what is rightfully mine."

"Maybe the risk won't be so great, by now," Gavin said. Sybilla gave him a puzzled look.

"Your brother fought against the King, that's true," he said. "But the state of affairs back in England's changed, since then. King James was never beloved by his subjects. I don't believe he ever really understood them.

"And since the battle at Sedgemoor the King's made a great many serious errors in judgment. Even out here in the Indies, there's been talk that he may not be able to hold his throne much longer."

Lance nodded. "I hope that may be so," he said. "But whatever the odds, I'm going back to Jamaica, and lay claim to my uncle's plantation. I think he would have wanted it that way."

He kissed Sybilla affectionately. "Now I'd best leave the two of you to make your own plans for the future."

He turned and walked away, in the direction of the governor's house.

Chapter Twenty-Nine

Sybilla watched Lance disappear into the lengthening shadows of the tall palms that lined the sides of the path leading to the house. Her throat tightened. After he set sail for Jamaica, how long would it be before she saw him again?

Sensing her mood, Gavin put his arm around her and drew her head against his shoulder.

"Lance doesn't need you to protect him any longer," he said quietly. "He's capable of managing his own affairs now."

"But to think of his leaving so soon . . ."

"He'll be here tomorrow, to give me your hand in marriage," Gavin reminded her.

She caught her breath, and her pulse speeded up. A swift, warm current began moving through her. "You meant it—about our being married tomorrow?"

"I've already discussed the plans for the ceremony with Governor d'Ogeron," he told her. "He's ordered his servants to get the preparations underway."

"You were so sure of me?" She tried to sound reproachful, but she could not keep the soaring joy out of her voice, not now, with Gavin close beside her.

"I knew I'd forgotten something," he said. "If it's a formal proposal you want, Mistress Sybilla, I'll be happy to oblige you at once." He released her and started to rise, but she caught his hand in hers and drew him down on the bench again.

She laughed softly. "I can see you've decided to become a thoroughly respectable gentleman, Captain Broderick." For a moment, her golden eyes glinted with a teasing light. But it quickly faded, and when she spoke again, her voice was serious.

"The sea's been your home for so long, Gavin. How can you ever hope to be content, living all your days ashore?"

"I never intended to. We'll have our house in Boston, but I'll keep on sailing. Only now, I'll be master of one of our family's merchant ships."

"You'll take me with you?"

"You don't think I'd leave you behind?" He cupped her face in his hands, and bent his head, so that his mouth covered hers. She parted her lips to receive the slow, searching movement of his tongue and met it with her own. The warmth deep inside her flared into a soaring flame.

She felt the hard strength of his body, the muscles of his arms tightening about her. Her breasts began to tingle as they were pressed against his chest. He lifted his mouth from hers to trace the moist heat of his tongue along the curve of her throat. She clung to him as he eased her backward against the marble bench.

She wanted him to take her, to possess her completely. But she fought back her aching need. "Not here . . ."

He raised himself and searched her face. Then he stood up and drew her to her feet beside him.

"Come along, love." Her eyes met his with a questioning look. "There's a flight of steps leading from the edge of the garden down to the beach."

The rock steps, set into a steep ledge, were already half-hidden by the growing darkness, but Gavin led the way, keeping a firm hold on her hand. The descent was a long one, and they paused for a moment, part of the way down. She reached out and stroked his cheek; her fingers traced the line of his jaw.

"Gavin." She spoke his name softly, wonderingly.

"What is it, love?" he asked.

"I was thinking how lucky we've been," she told him. "If you hadn't come upon the settlement when you did—" She could not bear to think what might have happened, if Gavin had arrived even an hour too late.

"That wasn't pure chance," he said, taking her hand again and leading her on down the remaining steps. "When I came ashore and found you had never arrived at the governor's house, my men and I split up into search parties right away. We began scouring the island. In one of the taverns, I came across that sailor, the one Kitty had questioned a few days before. She had spoken to him of a girl who was being held captive in Varner's camp. A girl who was desperate to find out what had happened to me during the battle with the Spaniards."

Sybilla heard the tension in his voice. She could only imagine what he'd felt, when he had realized she was in such danger.

"And then?" She urged him on.

"The sailor didn't know exactly where the camp was hidden. I got together all of my crew who were down at the waterfront, and we set out to find the place. Even so, we might've been too late, if it hadn't been for Kitty."

"How did she know you'd already dropped anchor off Tortuga?"

"She didn't. She was heading here, to the governor's house, but she'd only gone a short way when she ran into our search party."

"And she led you back to the camp." Sybilla was deeply moved by the thought of Kitty's loyalty. "She was terrified of Varner—but somehow she found the strength to try to help me." Her hand tightened around his. "Gavin, we must do what we can for her."

382

They had reached the foot of the steps now. The beach lay before them, broad and empty under the rising moon. Palm fronds rustled and the tall sea grass made a sighing sound, as the wind swept in from the sea.

"If she wants to sail to Boston with us, I'll make sure she finds honest work there."

Sybilla smiled up at him gratefully. "It wasn't easy to persuade her to stay overnight at the governor's house, but I managed to. She'll wear the blue dress after all. At our wedding."

Gavin drew her against him, lifted her face between his hands, and silenced her with a long, lingering kiss. Her arms went around his neck, and she stroked his hair. Slowly, enticingly she began to move her body against his.

He groaned, deep in his throat. Then he drew away long enough to take off his coat, and drop it down on the sand. "Let me," she said. She unbuttoned his shirt, then began to unfasten the buckle of his belt. "I'll do the rest," he said.

When he had finished, he turned to her and began stripping off her garments, one by one. She stood for a moment, her long hair wind-tossed about her face, her slender body bathed in the silver glow of the rising moon. Gavin caught his breath, then reached out for her.

"The night before our wedding," she said, moving back a step. "Do you think this is quite proper?"

He tried again to catch hold of her, but she darted past him, running lightly down along the sand. Her laughter came to him, carried on the night breeze. He took off after her in swift pursuit, and caught up with her at the edge of the sea.

"You mean to be a model of propriety from now on, Sybilla?"

Even as he spoke, he drew her against him. She gave a shiver of excitement as his hands began moving lightly over her shoulders, and down along her spine. Her skin was damp with the spray from the waves.

"Do you?" He cupped the rounds of her buttocks and drew her against his pulsating hardness. "Do you?"

"Not now," she said, her voice trembling with her need for him. "Not ever."

Together they dropped down on the sand. Her arms went around him and she held him against her. Unable to delay any longer, she opened herself to him.

But even before she felt the swift thrust of his entry, before he had joined his body with hers, she knew that they were already one. And they always would be, through all the years that lay ahead.